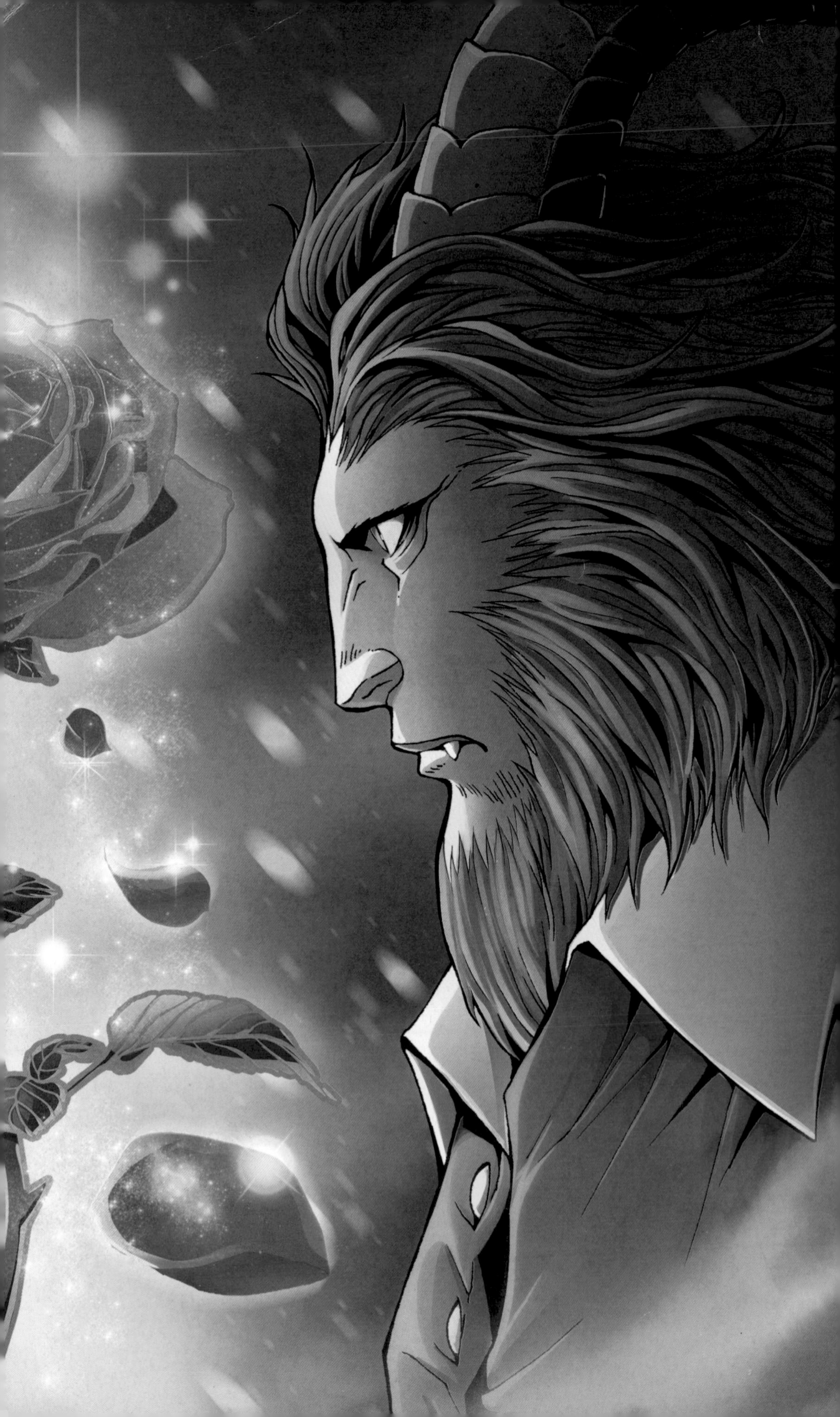

Contents

Bonjour and hello!

We welcome you to take a journey to the hidden heart of France as we reintroduce *The Beast's Tale*. This two-volume manga series was first released in 2017, shortly after the live-action movie release. Five years later, we are thrilled to present you with this new full-color edition of this manga! This volume of the series has been one of our favorite projects, so we wanted to create something unique that was just as inspired as the original version!

This book follows a selfish and unkind prince who's cursed to live his life as a hideous beast until he finds love, and we wanted to introduce a coloring style that evolves just as much as the Beast does. This creative interpretation starts with a dark and muted color palette representing the Beast's fall to despair. As his temperament changes, he learns to love Belle and becomes kinder to his staff. We see the colors subtly begin to change to reflect his new view of the world.

To see Belle's more vibrant and colorful view of the world, we invite you to read *Belle's Tale*, also available now. We hope you enjoy this tale as old as time!

--- The TOKYOPOP Team!

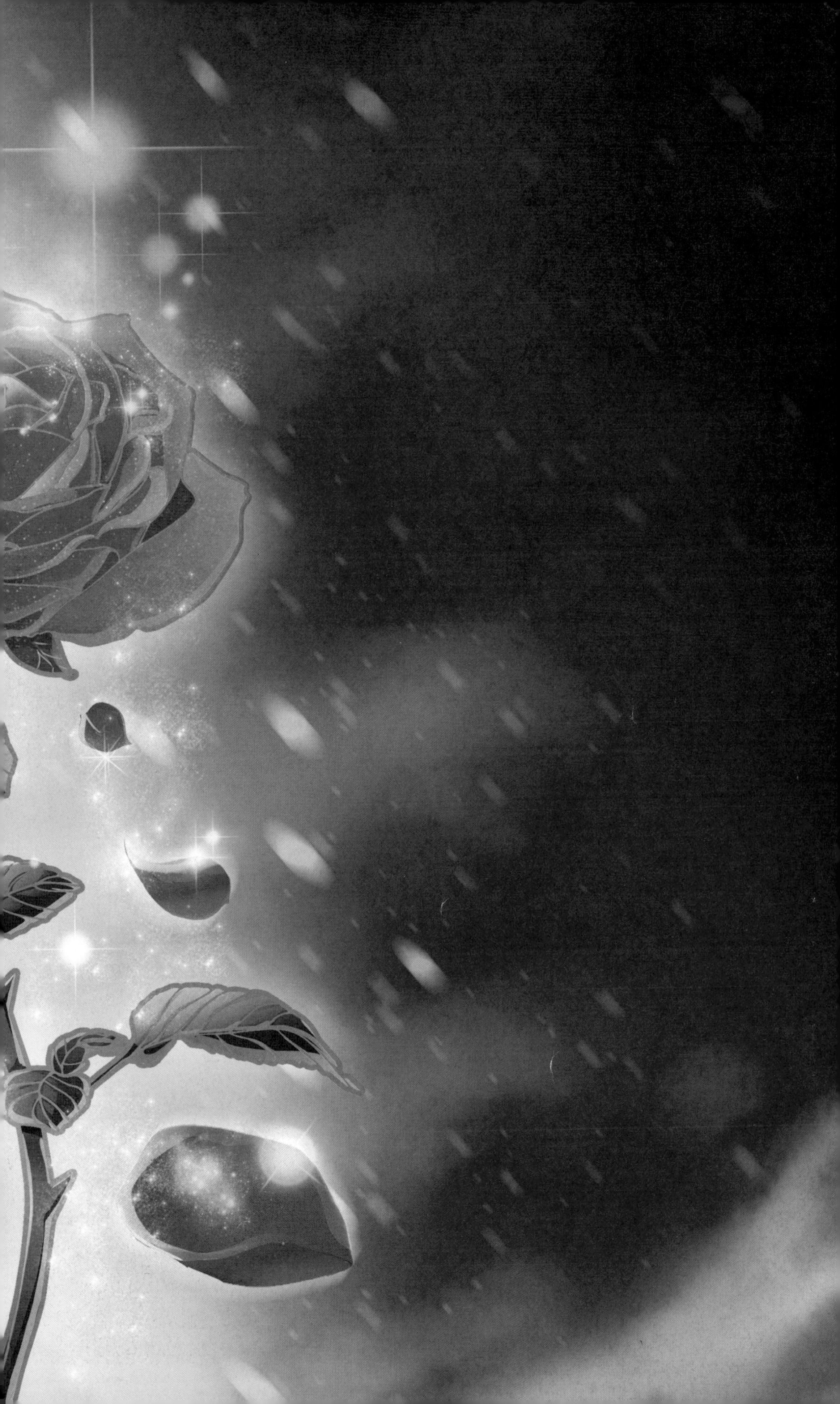

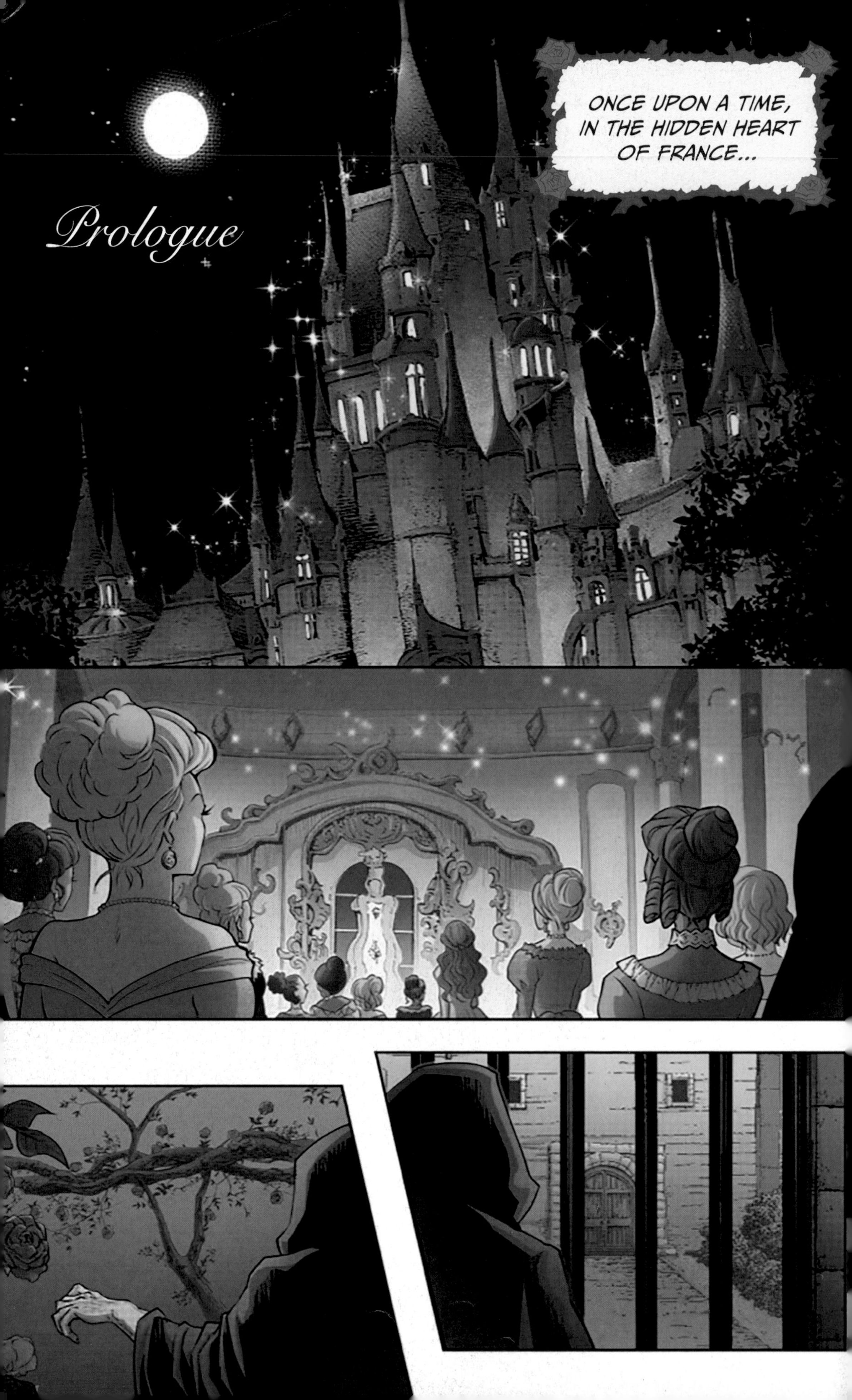
ONCE UPON A TIME, IN THE HIDDEN HEART OF FRANCE...
Prologue

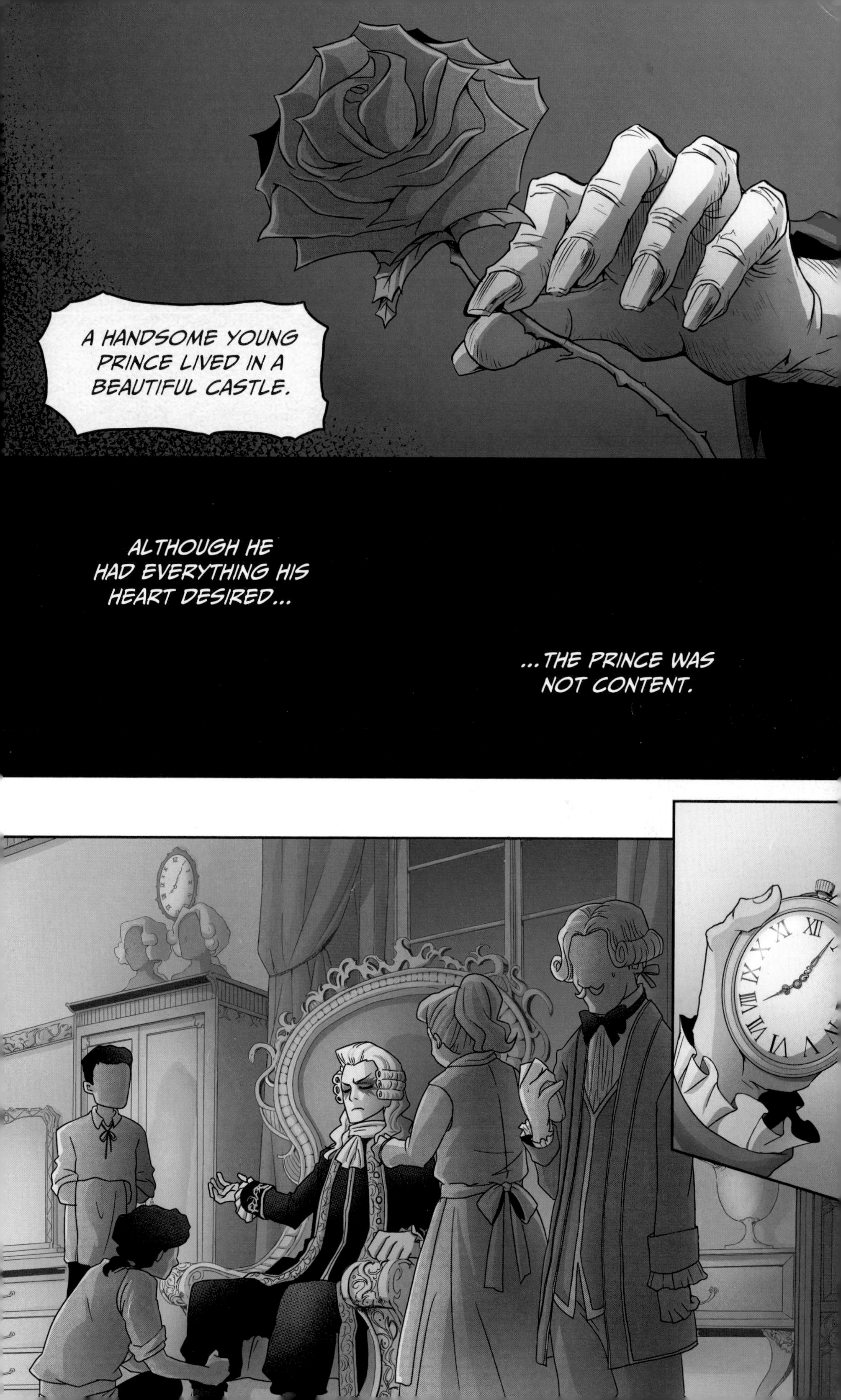
A HANDSOME YOUNG PRINCE LIVED IN A BEAUTIFUL CASTLE.
ALTHOUGH HE HAD EVERYTHING HIS HEART DESIRED...
...THE PRINCE WAS NOT CONTENT.

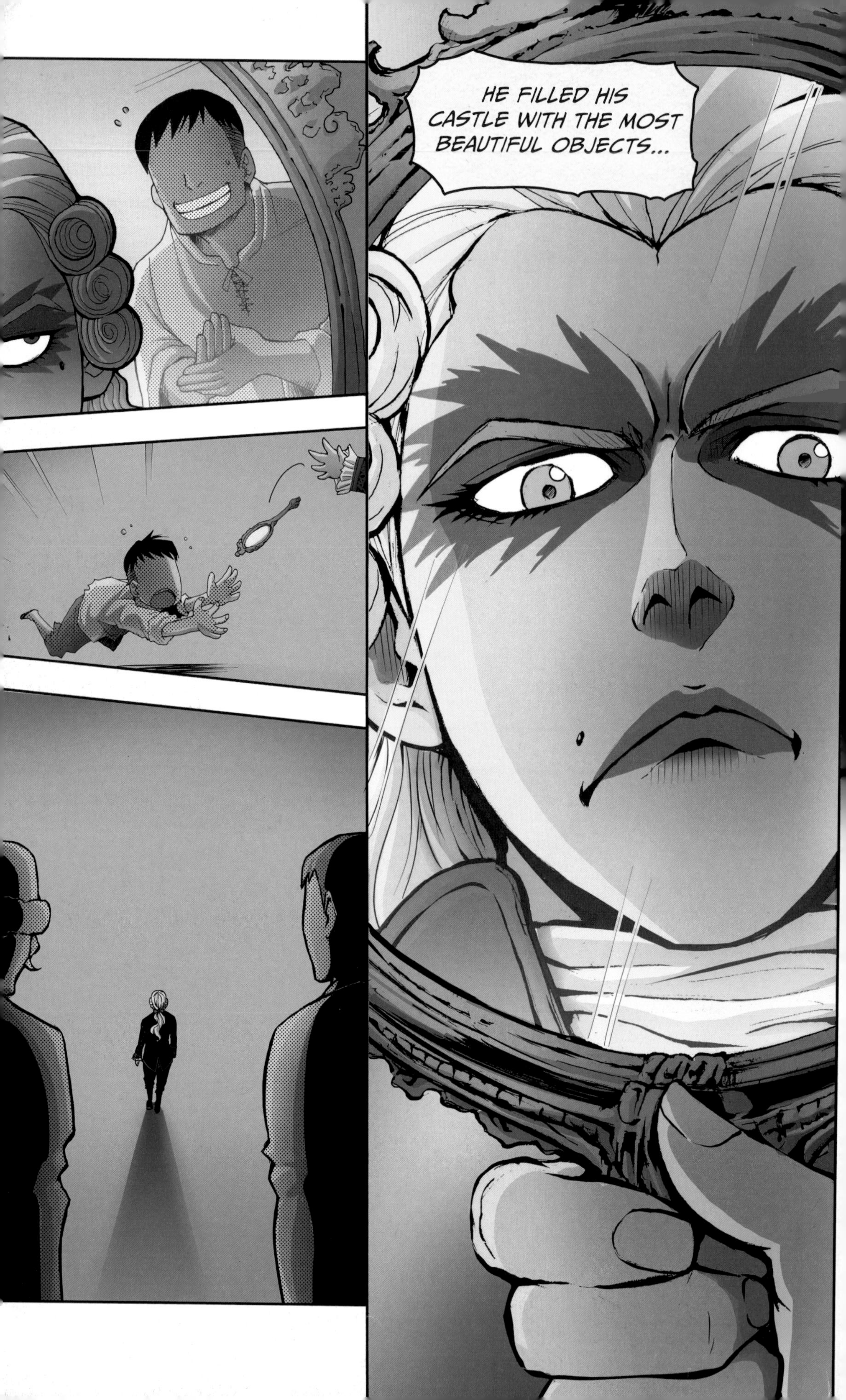
HE FILLED HIS CASTLE WITH THE MOST BEAUTIFUL OBJECTS...

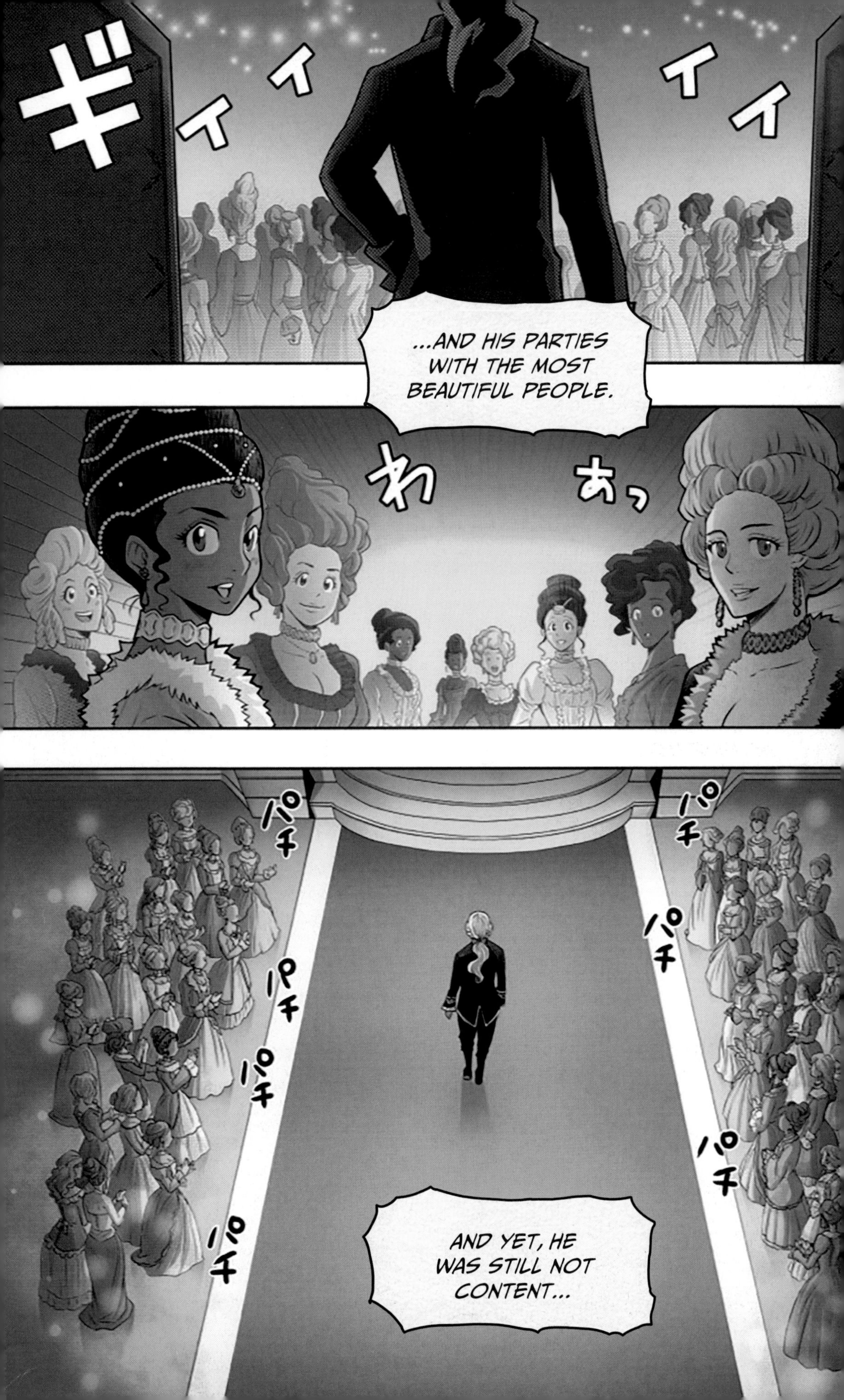

ギィィ
ィィ
...AND HIS PARTIES WITH THE MOST BEAUTIFUL PEOPLE.
あっ
わ
パチ
パチ
パチ
パチ
パチ
パチ
AND YET, HE WAS STILL NOT CONTENT...

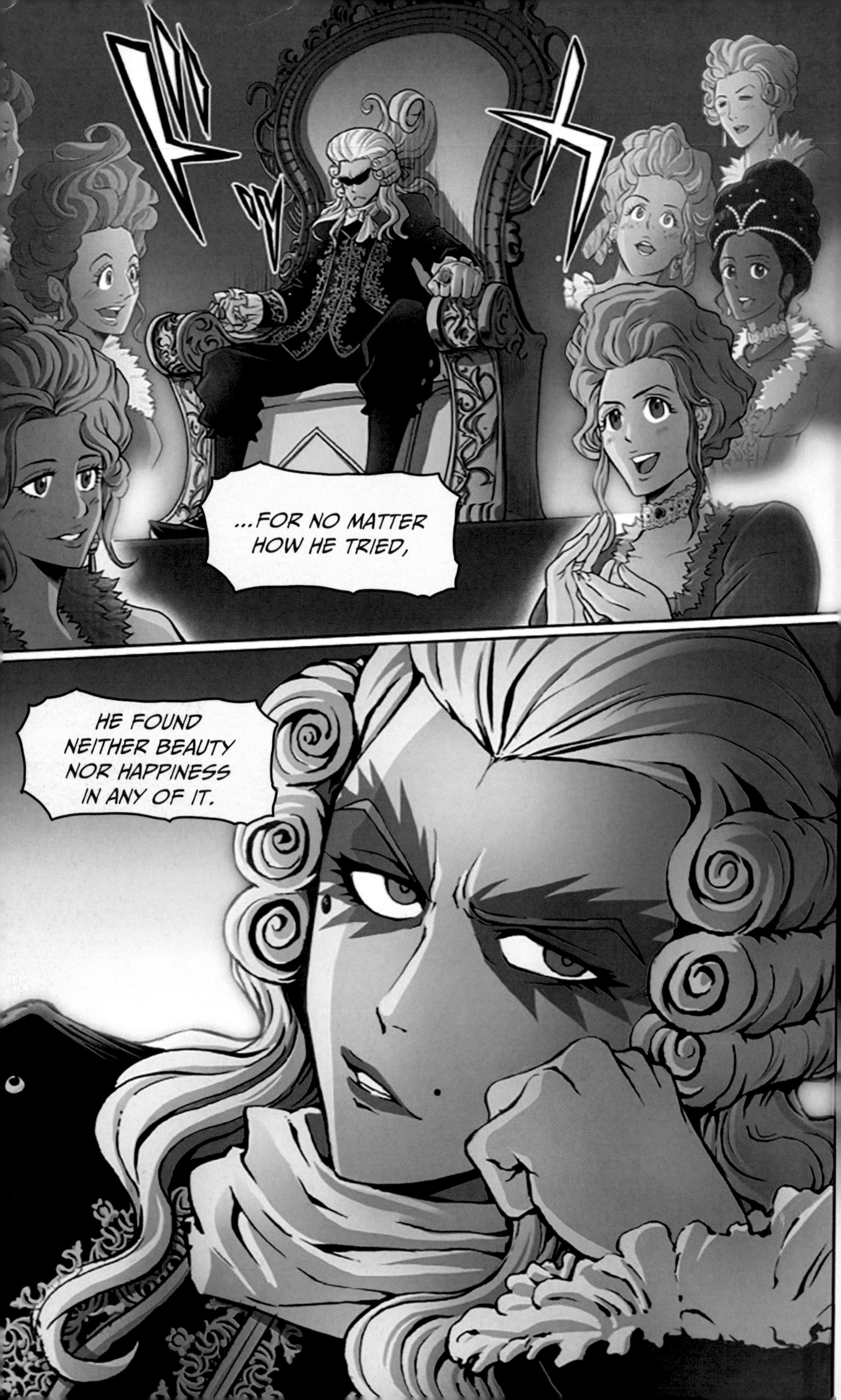
...FOR NO MATTER HOW HE TRIED,
HE FOUND NEITHER BEAUTY NOR HAPPINESS IN ANY OF IT.

THAT IS NOT HOW THE STORY ENDS...

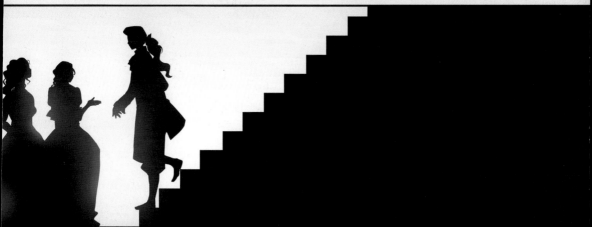

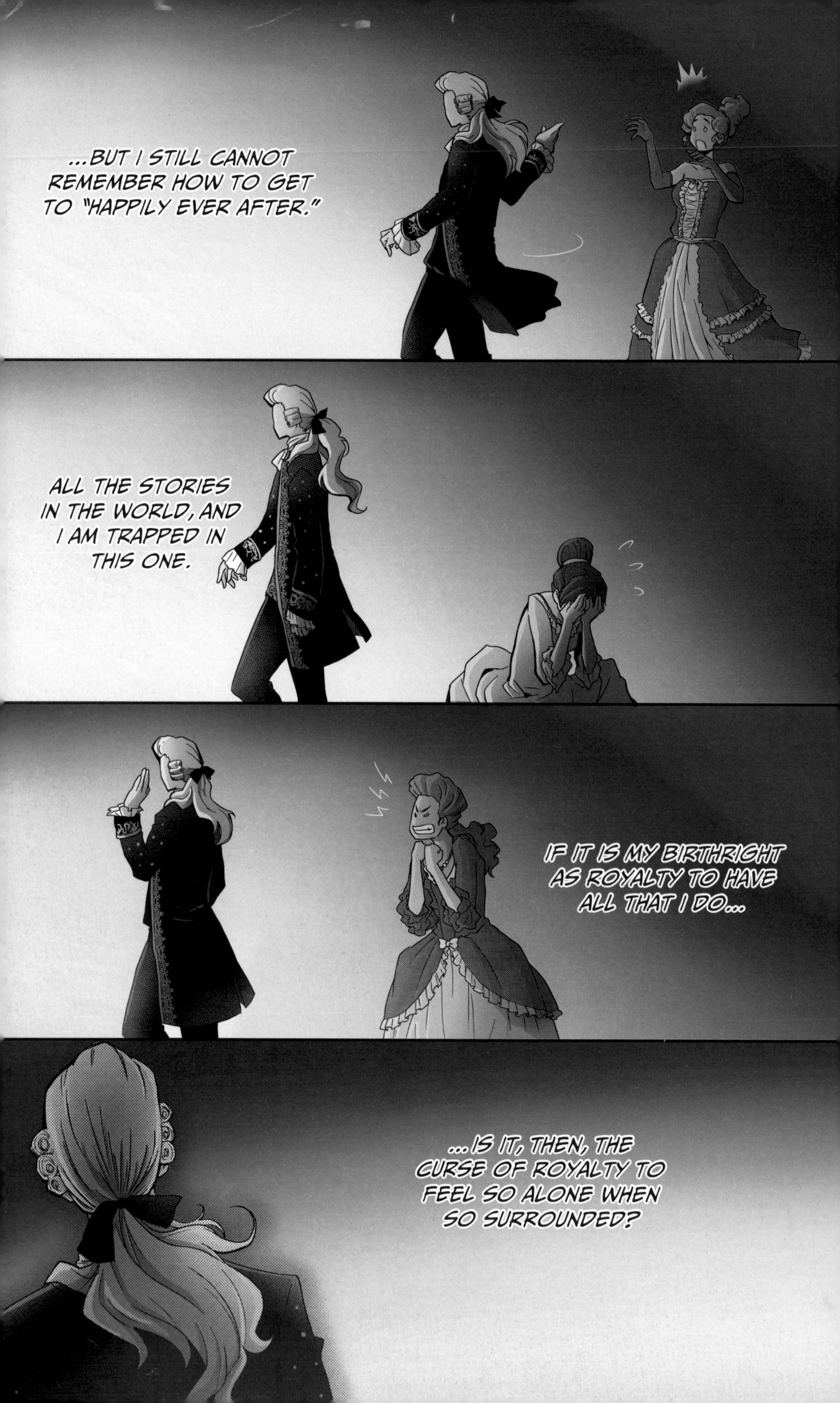
...BUT I STILL CANNOT REMEMBER HOW TO GET TO "HAPPILY EVER AFTER."
ALL THE STORIES IN THE WORLD, AND I AM TRAPPED IN THIS ONE.
IF IT IS MY BIRTHRIGHT AS ROYALTY TO HAVE ALL THAT I DO...
...IS IT, THEN, THE CURSE OF ROYALTY TO FEEL SO ALONE WHEN SO SURROUNDED?

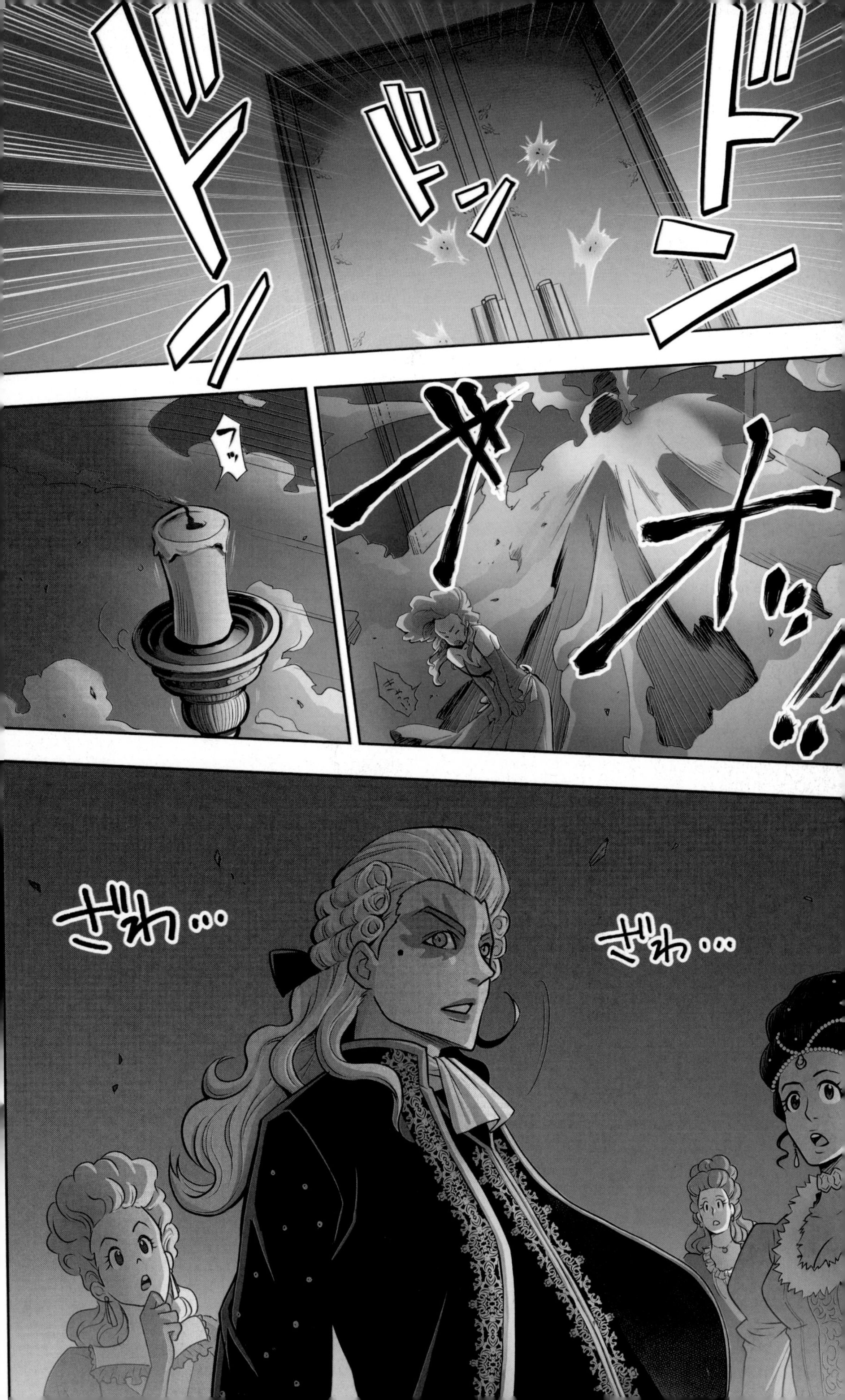
ドドン
ドドッン
ドドン
ギオッ!!
キャッ!?
フッ
ざわ…
ざわ…

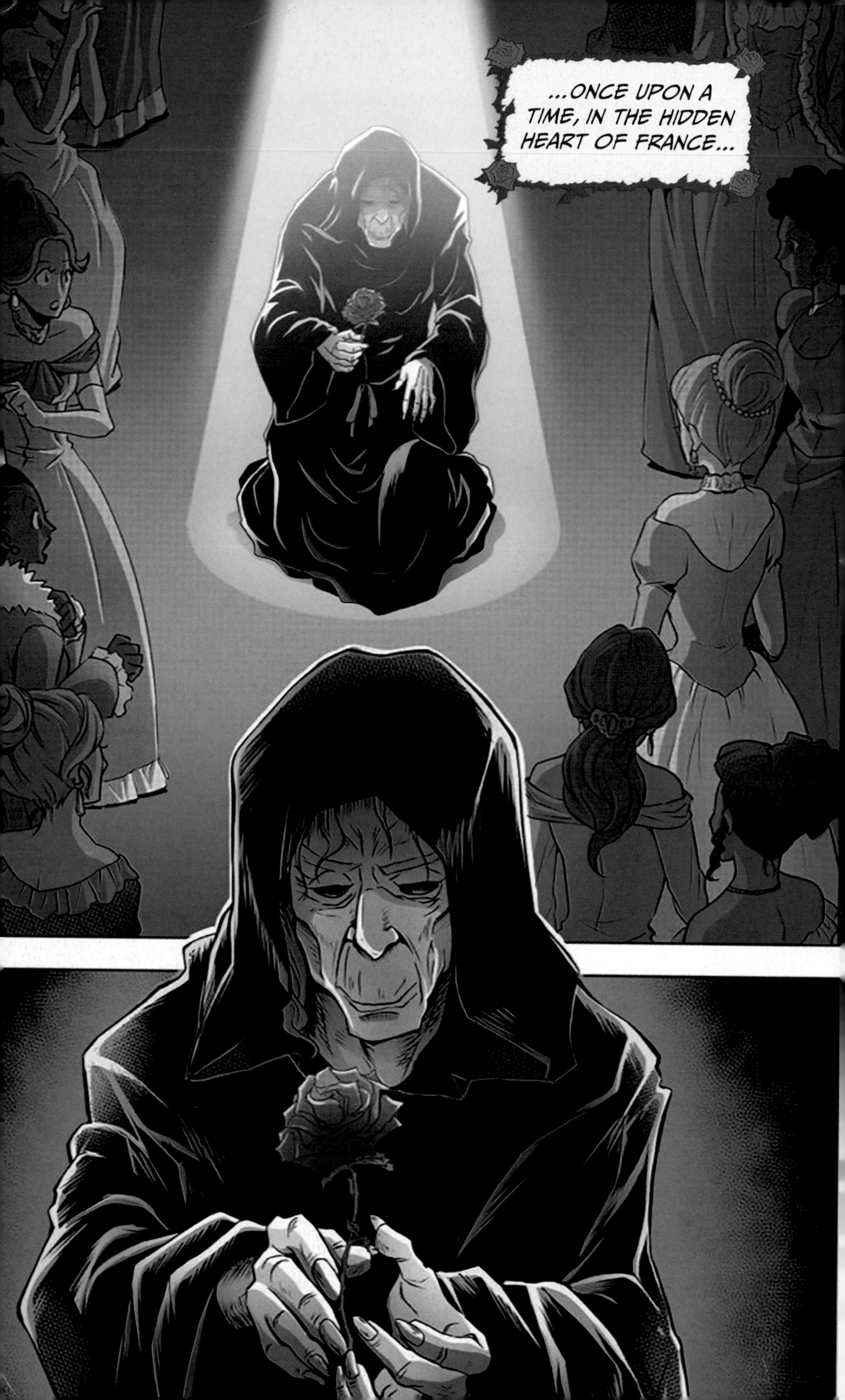
...ONCE UPON A TIME, IN THE HIDDEN HEART OF FRANCE...

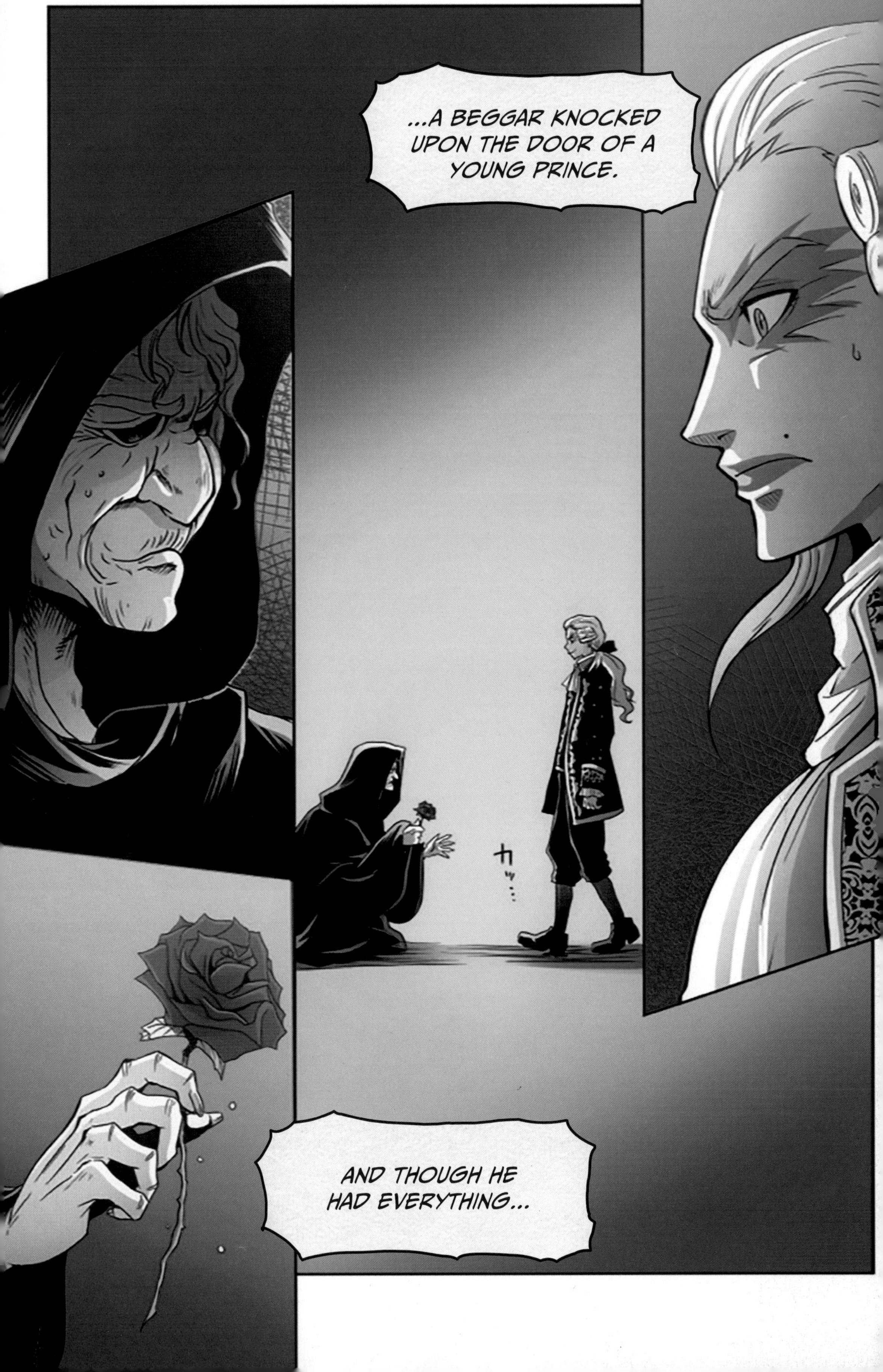
...A BEGGAR KNOCKED UPON THE DOOR OF A YOUNG PRINCE.
カッ…
AND THOUGH HE HAD EVERYTHING...

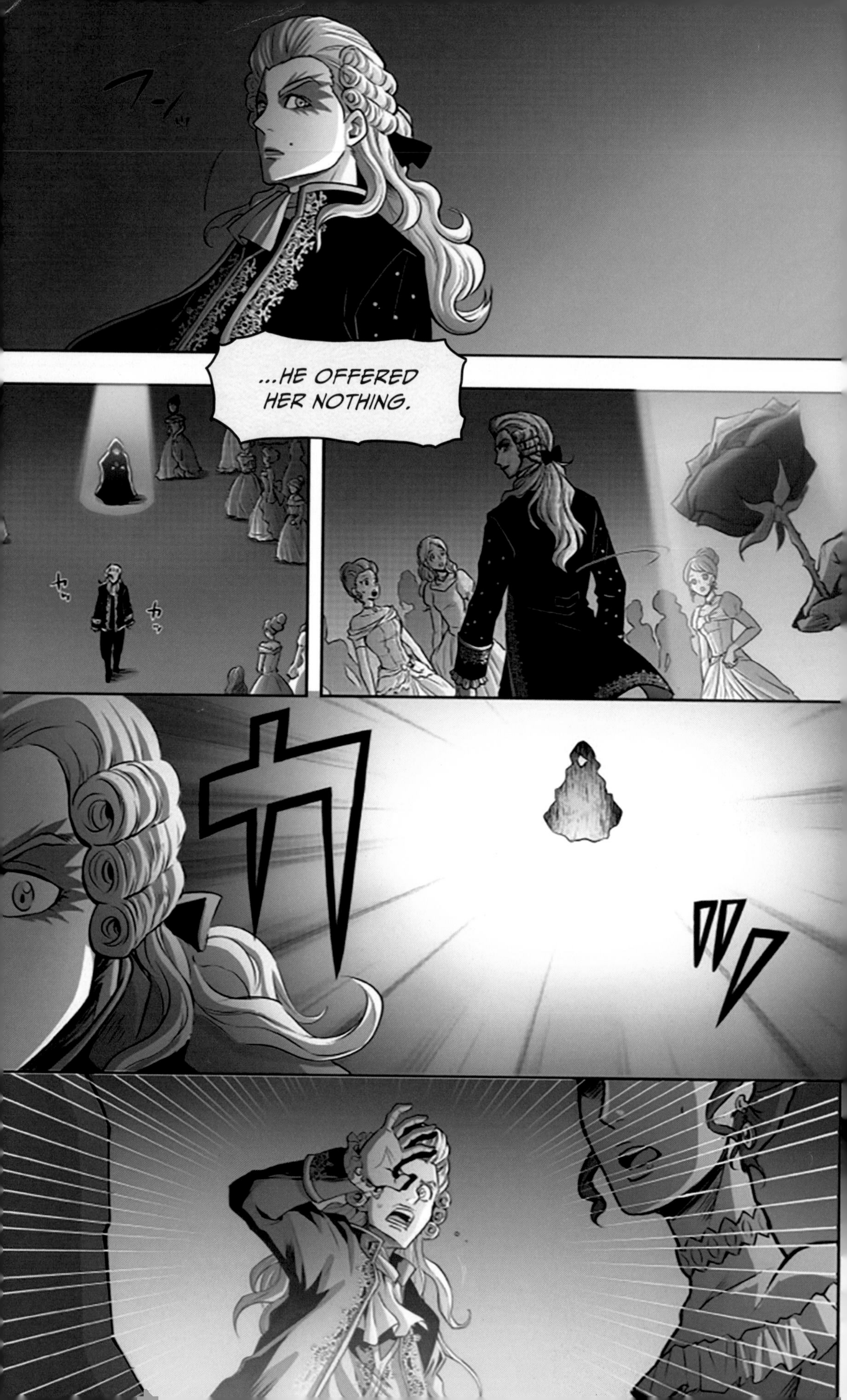
...HE OFFERED HER NOTHING.

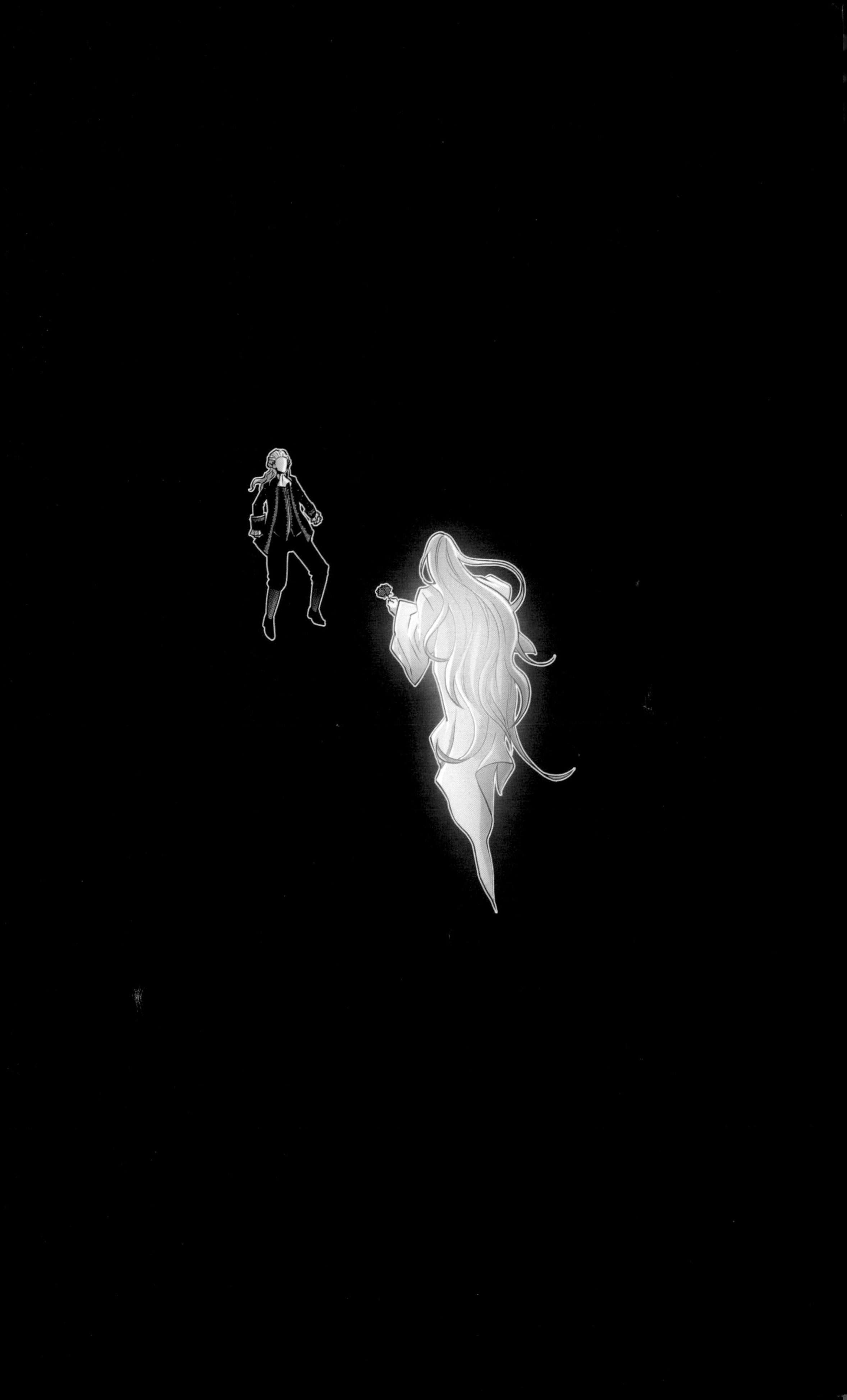

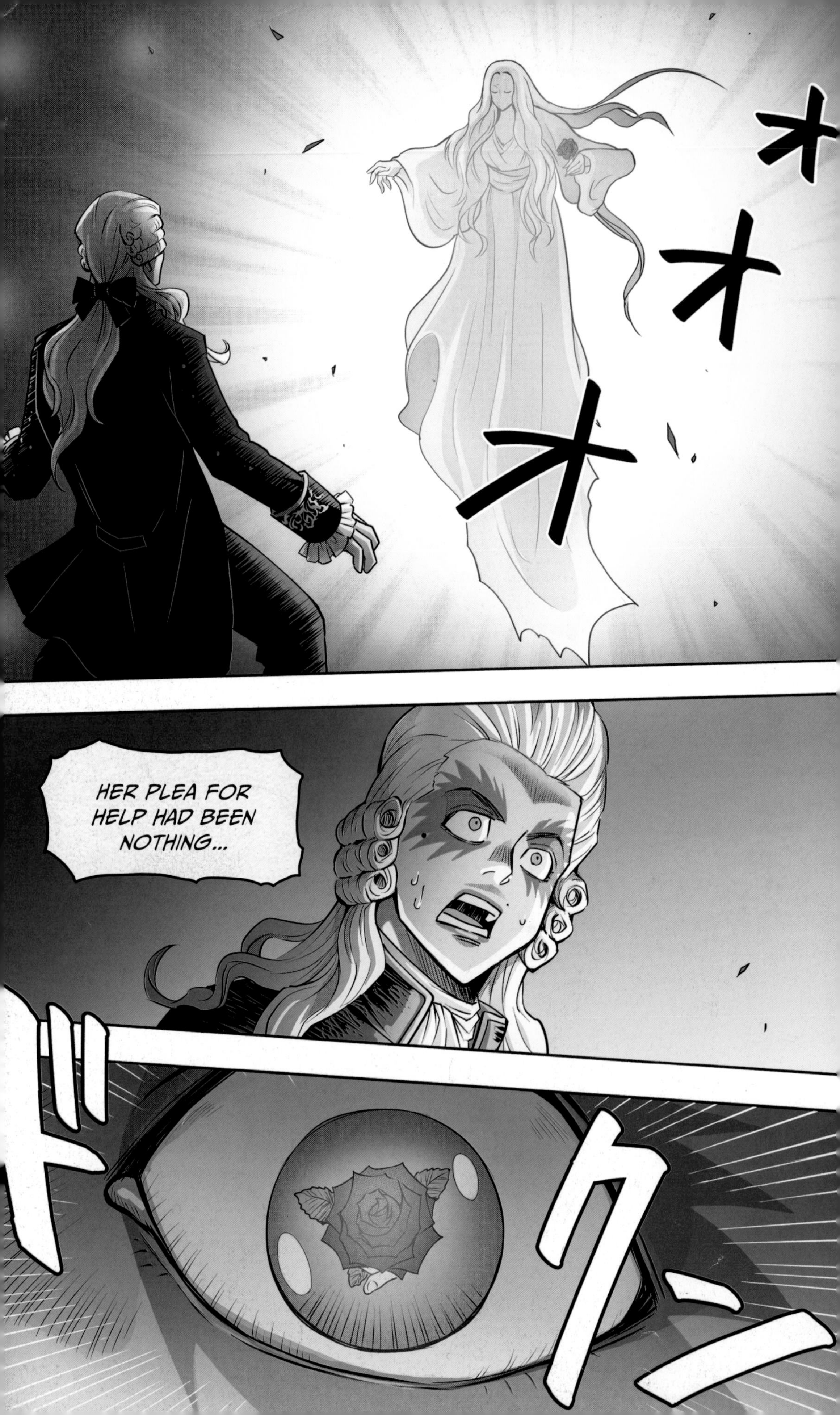
オオオ
HER PLEA FOR HELP HAD BEEN NOTHING...
ドクン

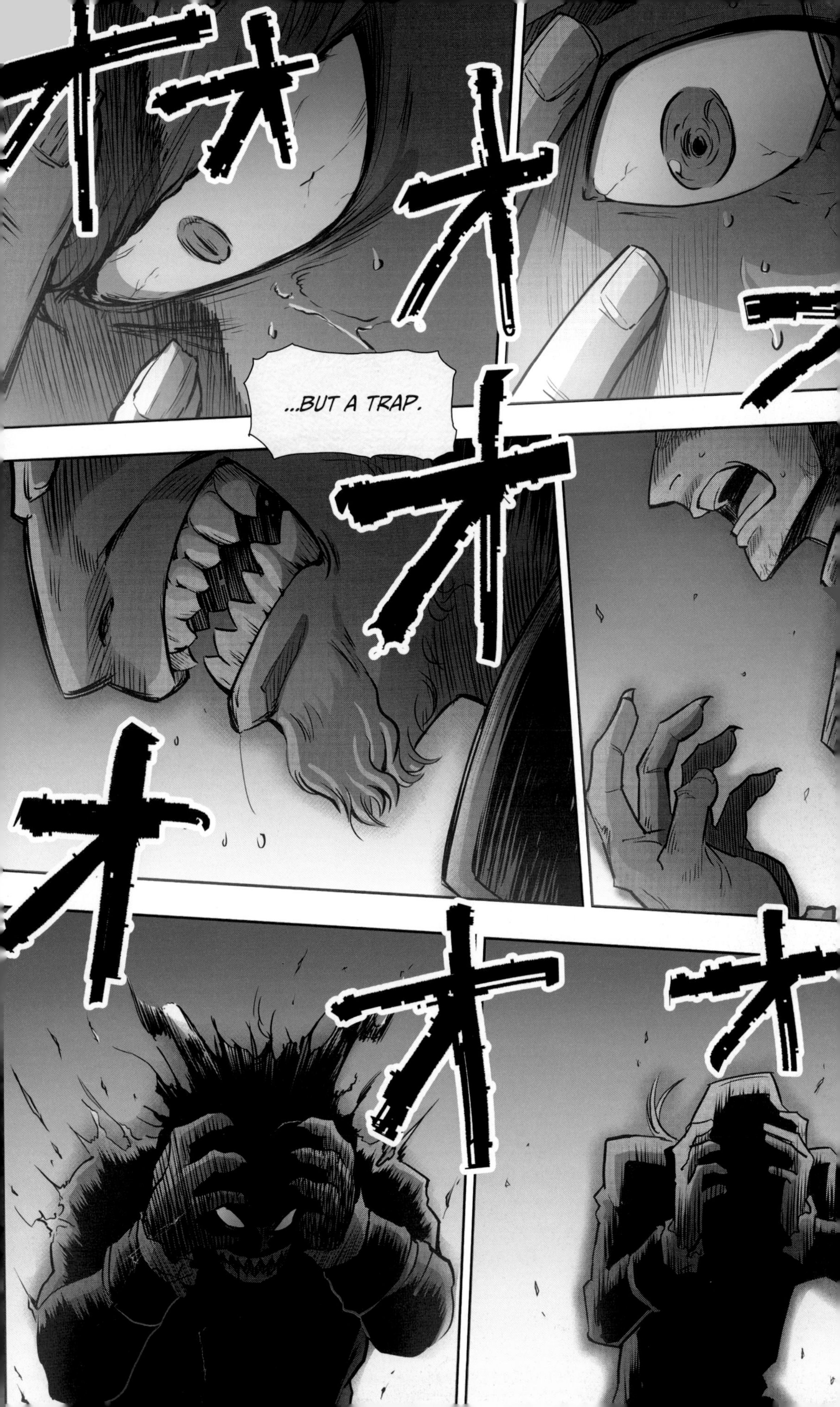

ア
オオオオオオオ
...BUT A TRAP.

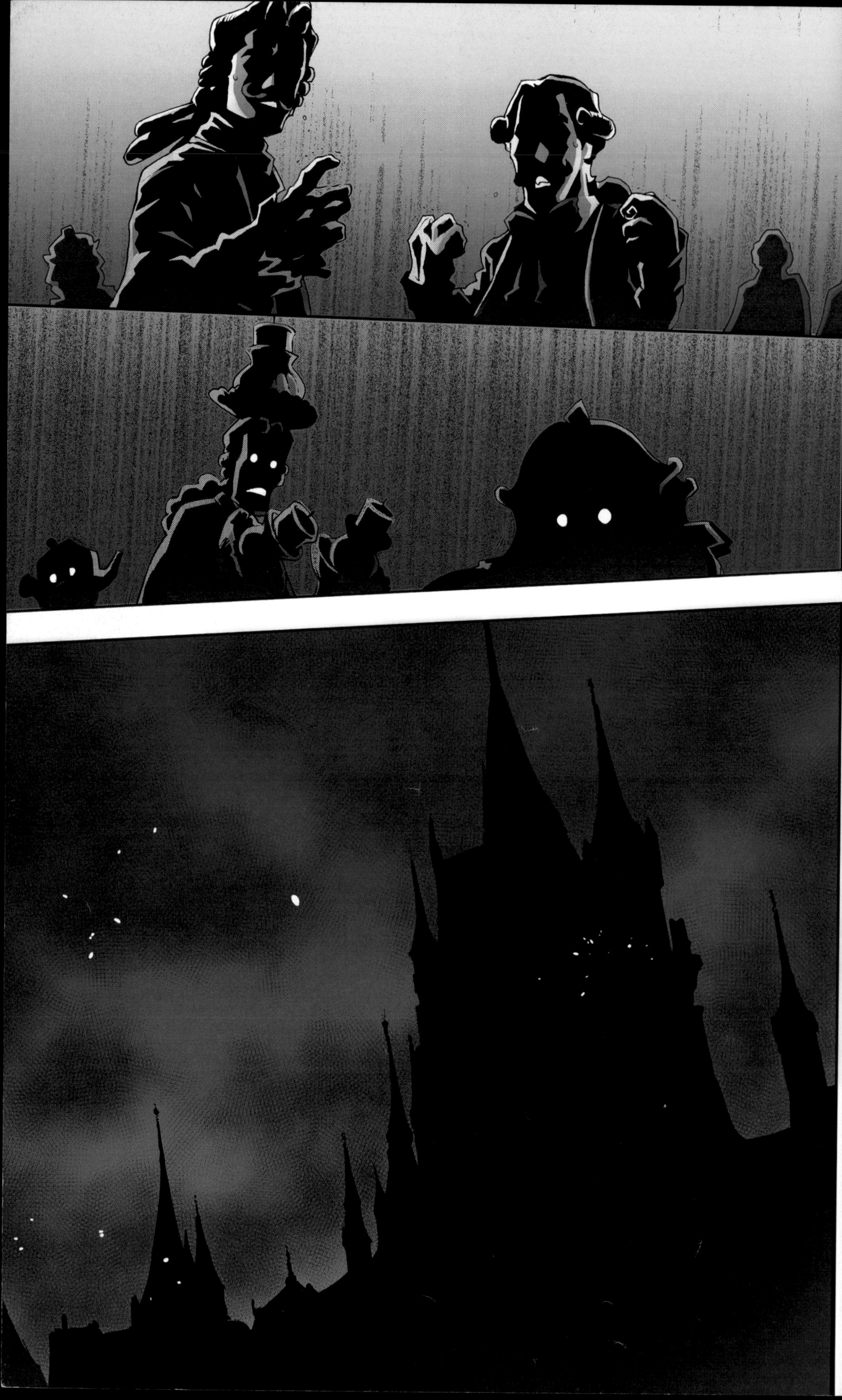

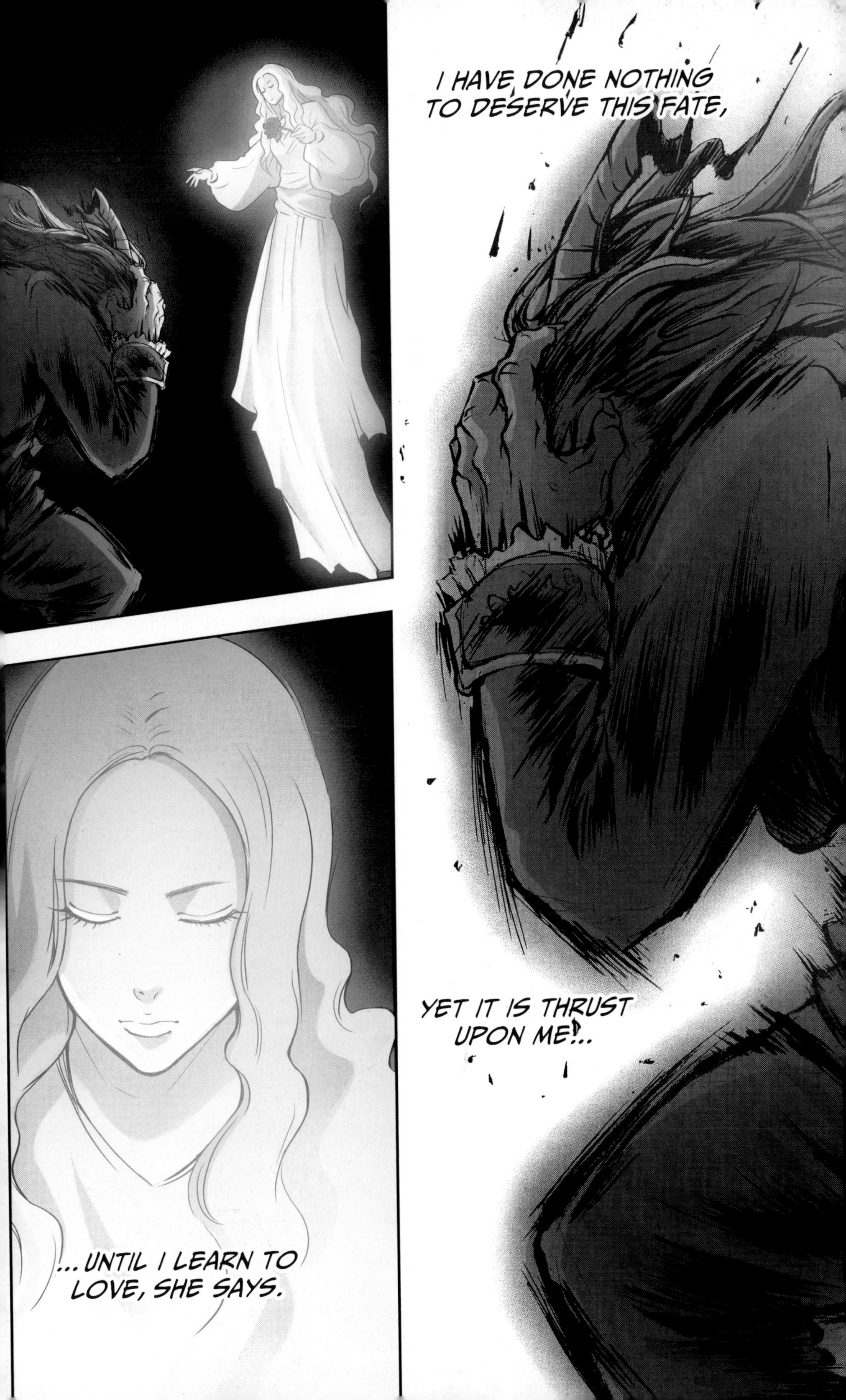
I HAVE DONE NOTHING TO DESERVE THIS FATE,
YET IT IS THRUST UPON ME!...
...UNTIL I LEARN TO LOVE, SHE SAYS.

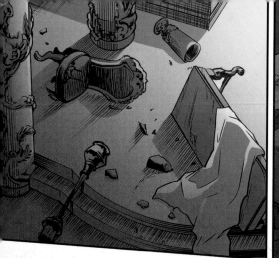

AND THE ROSE SHE OFFERED WAS JUST ANOTHER CURSE...

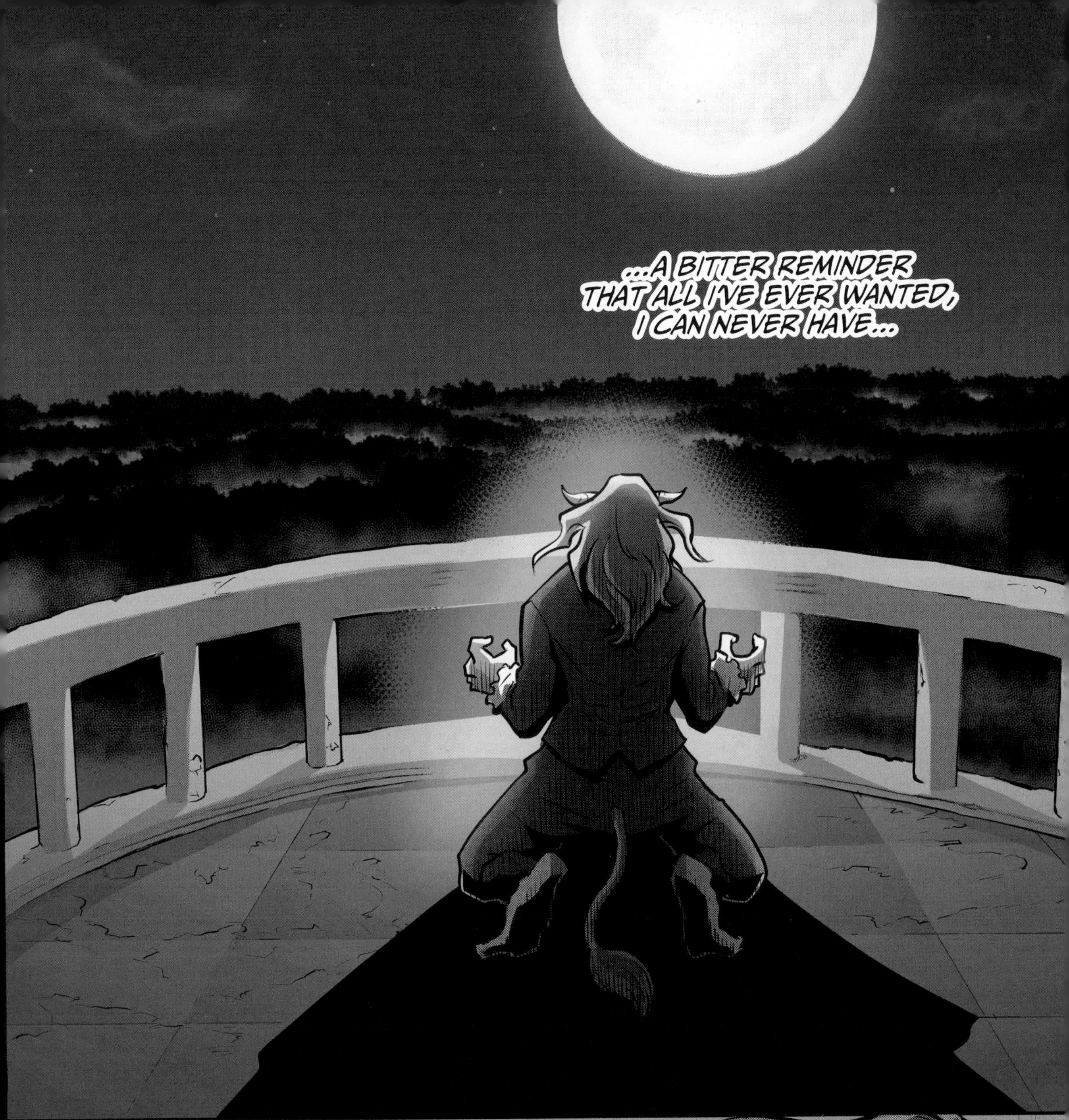
...A BITTER REMINDER
THAT ALL I'VE EVER WANTED,
I CAN NEVER HAVE...
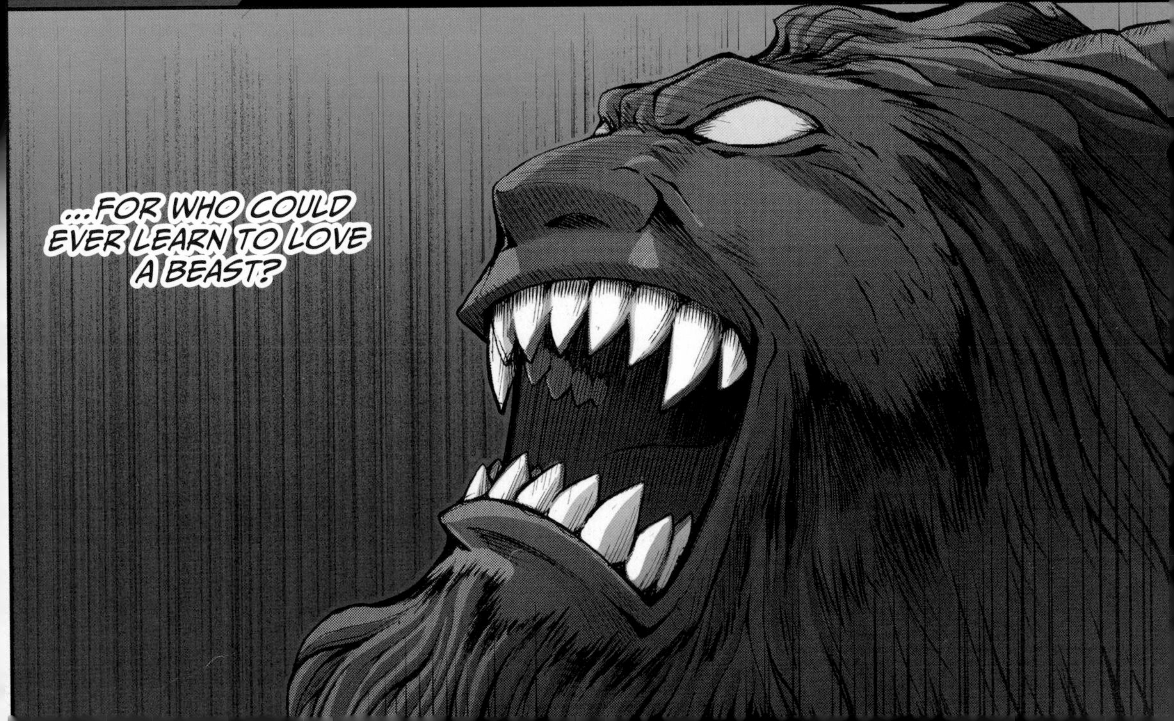
...FOR WHO COULD
EVER LEARN TO LOVE
A BEAST?

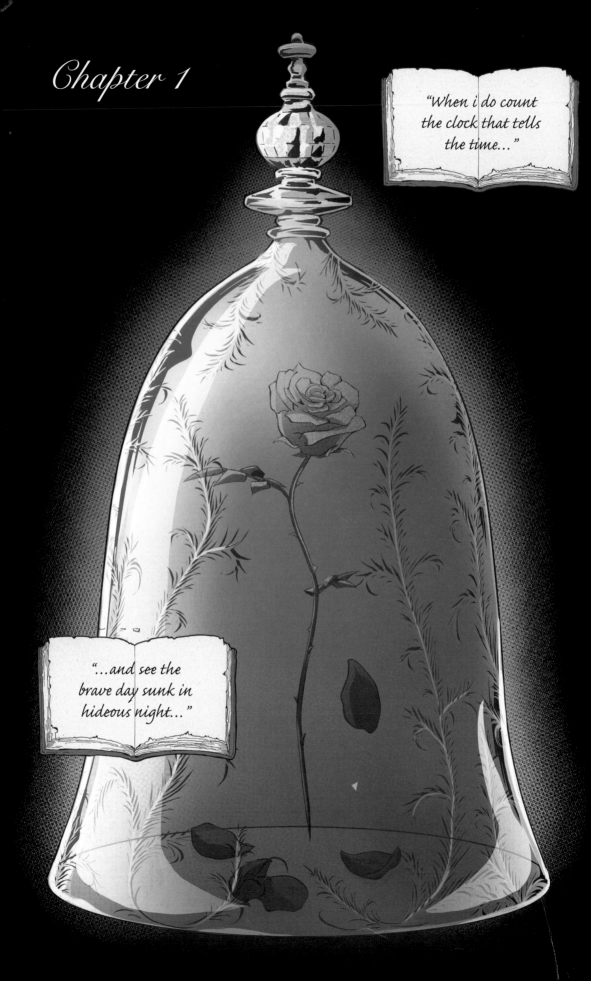

Chapter 1

"When i do count
the clock that tells
the time…"

"…and see the
brave day sunk in
hideous night…"

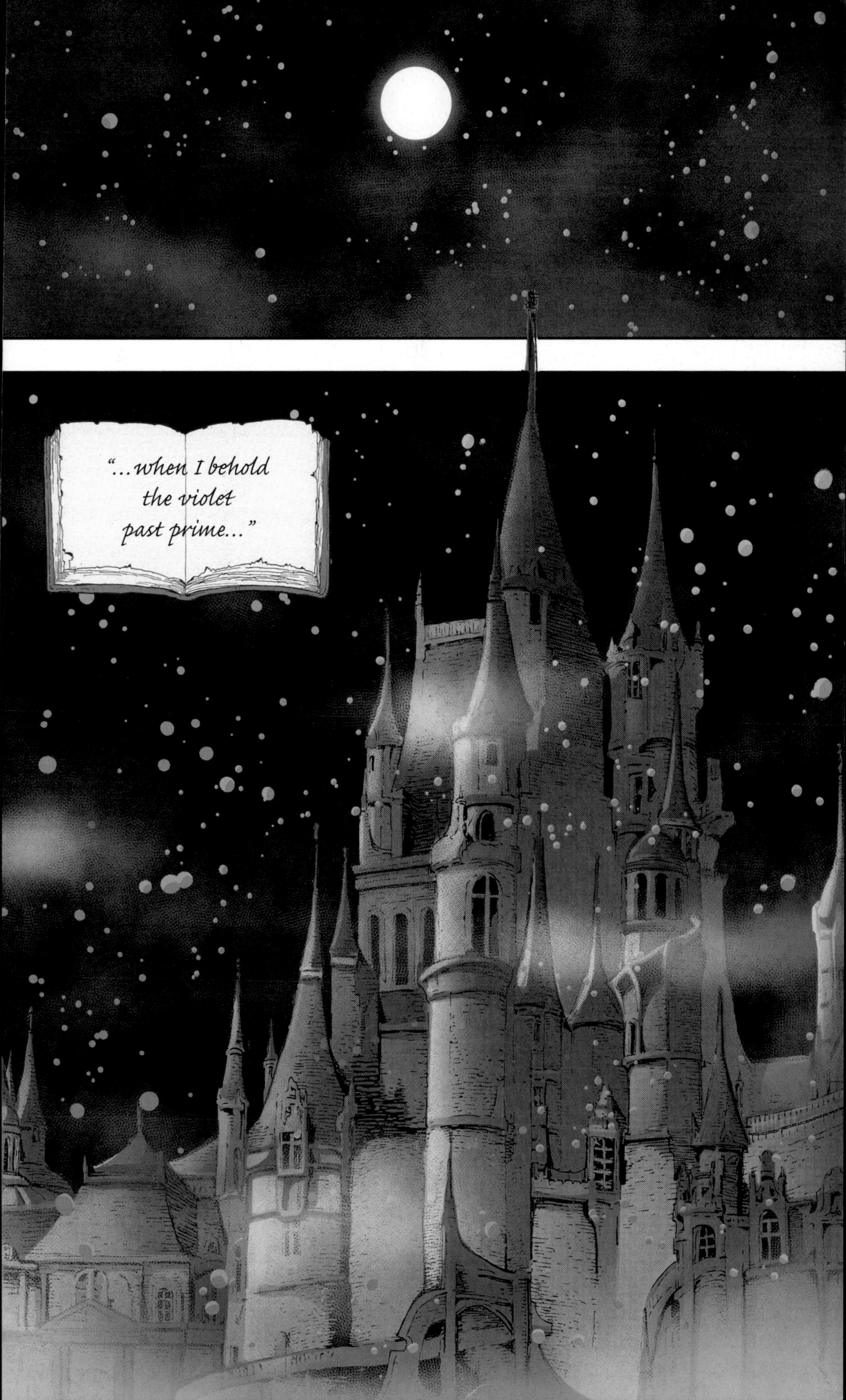
"...when I behold the violet past prime..."

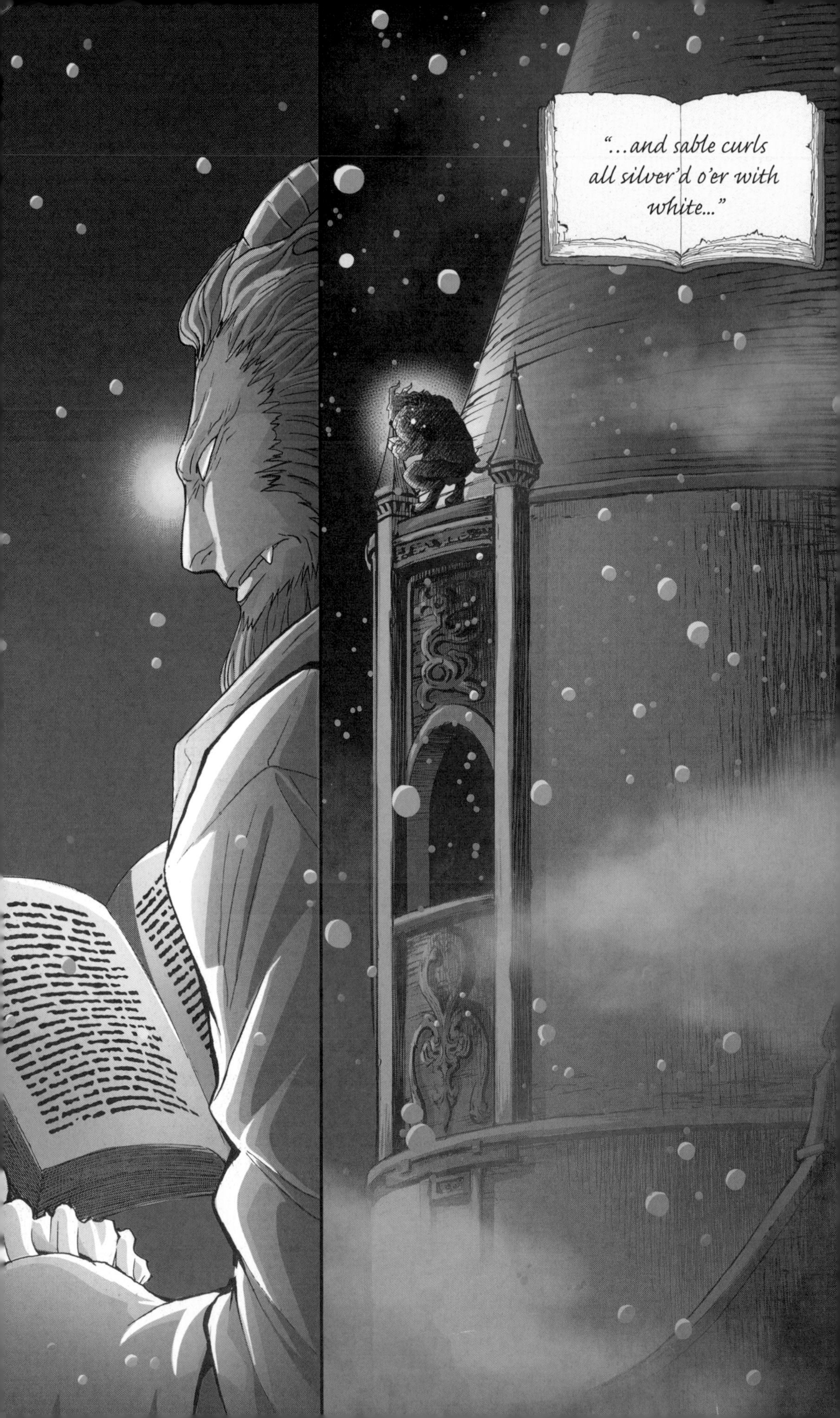
"...and sable curls all silver'd o'er with white..."

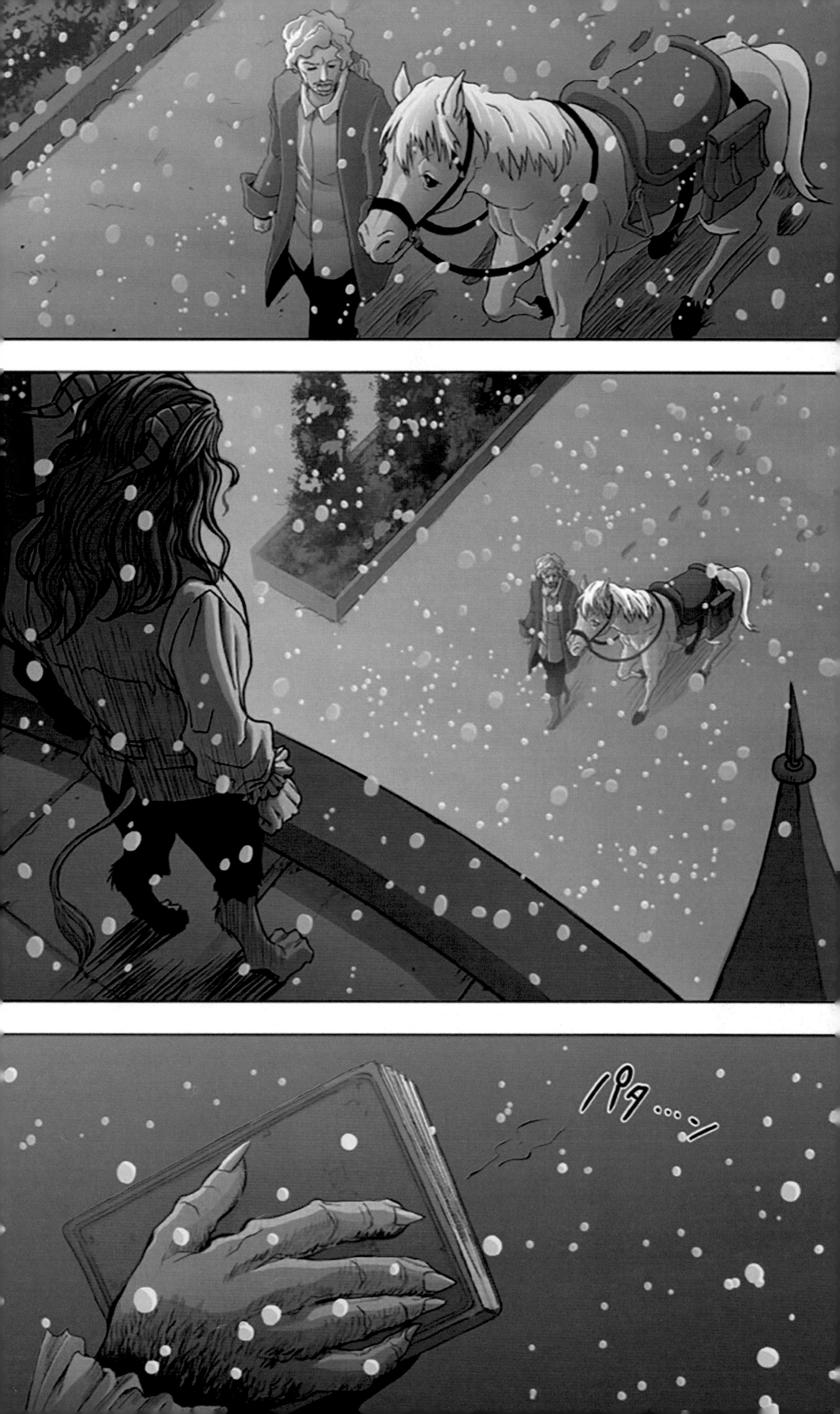
パタ…ン

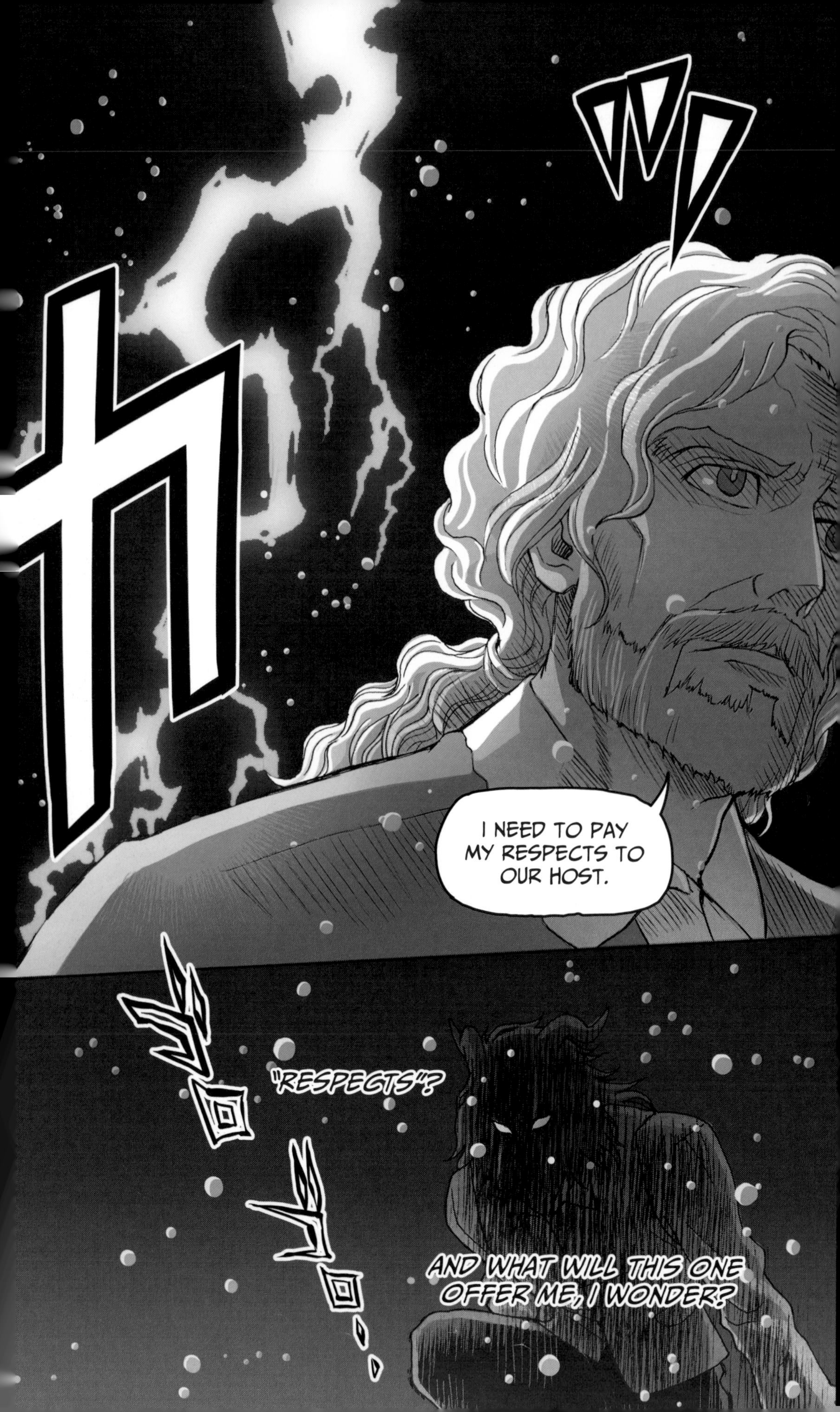
I NEED TO PAY MY RESPECTS TO OUR HOST.
"RESPECTS"?
AND WHAT WILL THIS ONE OFFER ME, I WONDER?

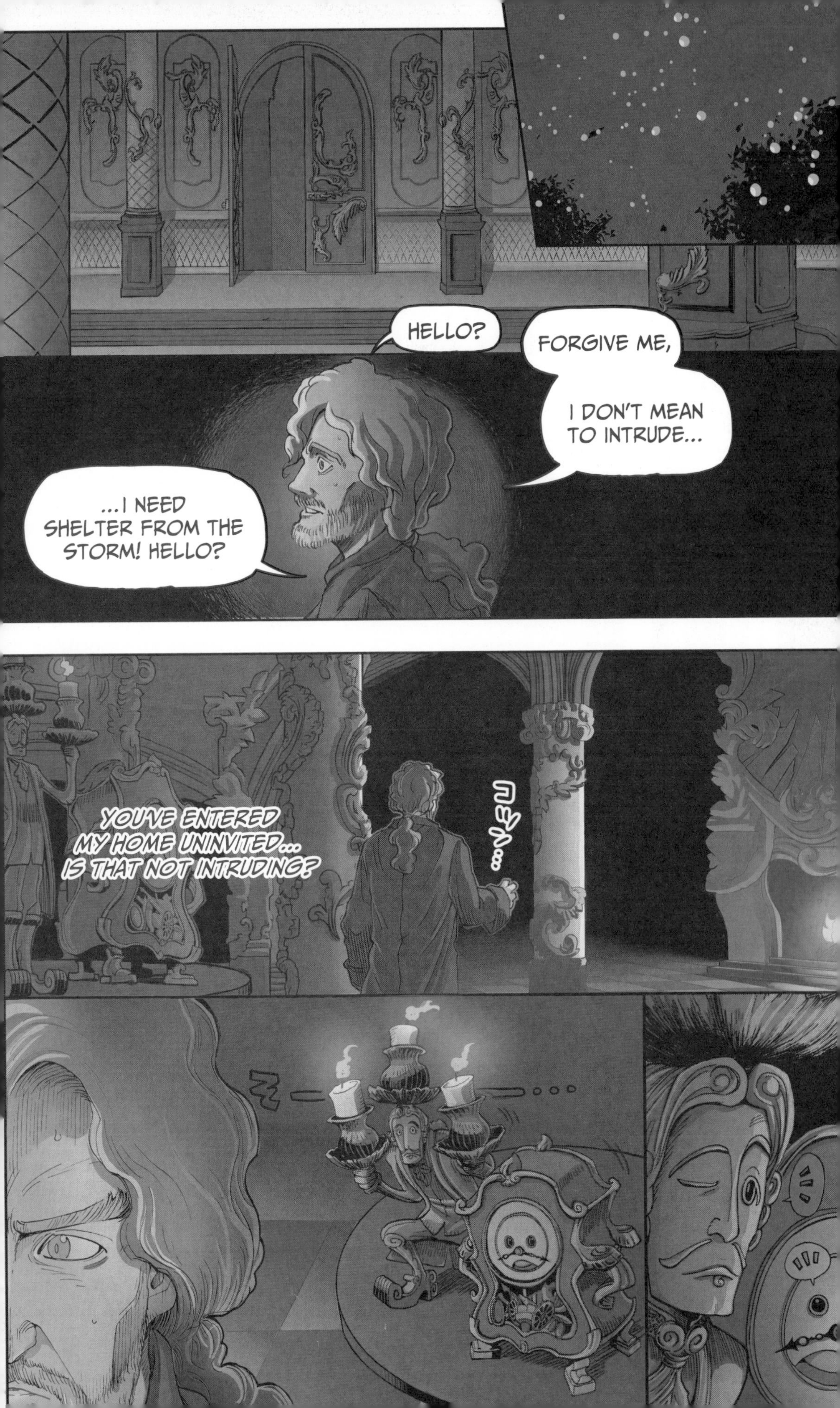
HELLO?
FORGIVE ME,
I DON'T MEAN TO INTRUDE...
...I NEED SHELTER FROM THE STORM! HELLO?
YOU'VE ENTERED MY HOME UNINVITED... IS THAT NOT INTRUDING?

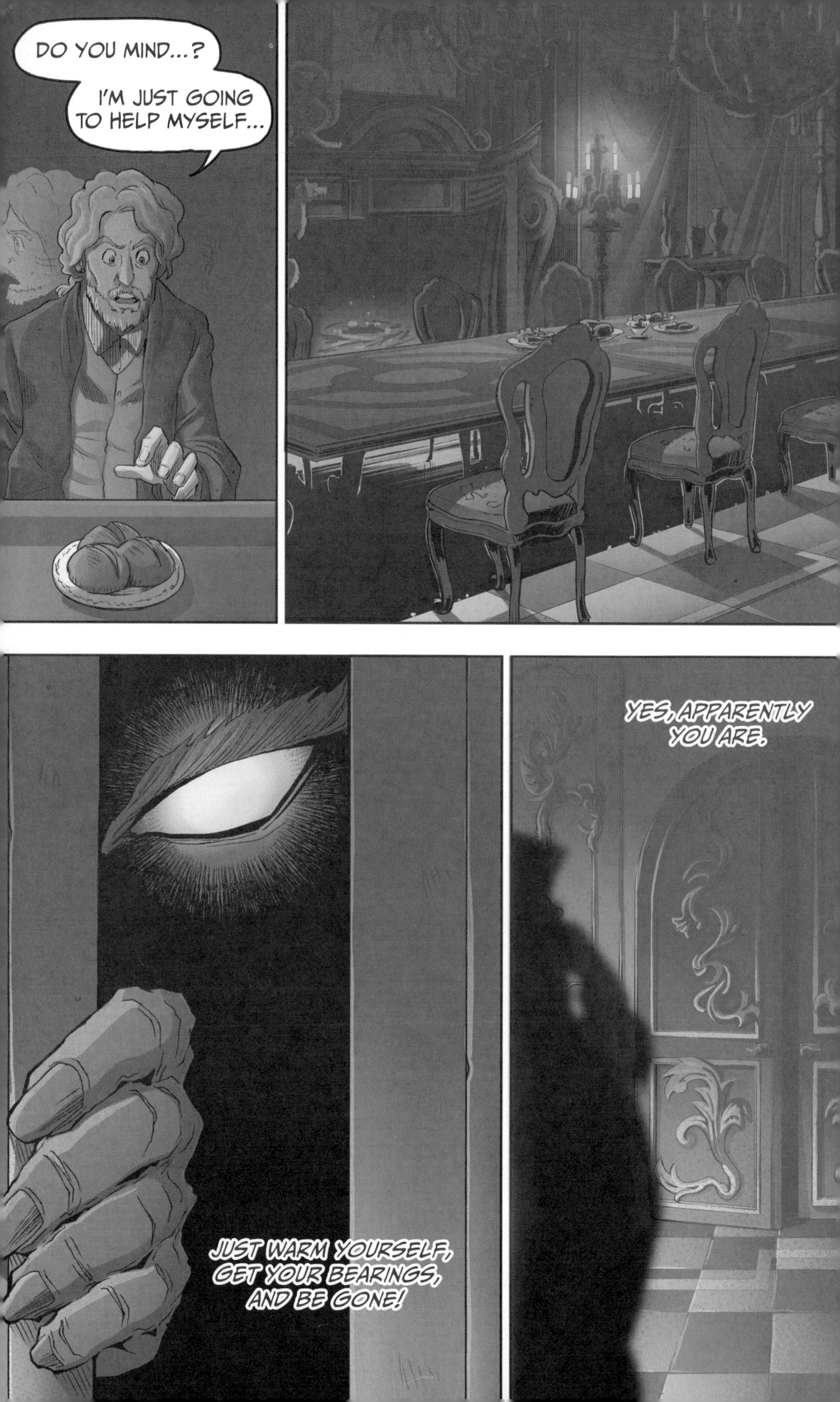
DO YOU MIND...?
I'M JUST GOING TO HELP MYSELF...
YES, APPARENTLY YOU ARE.
JUST WARM YOURSELF, GET YOUR BEARINGS, AND BE GONE!

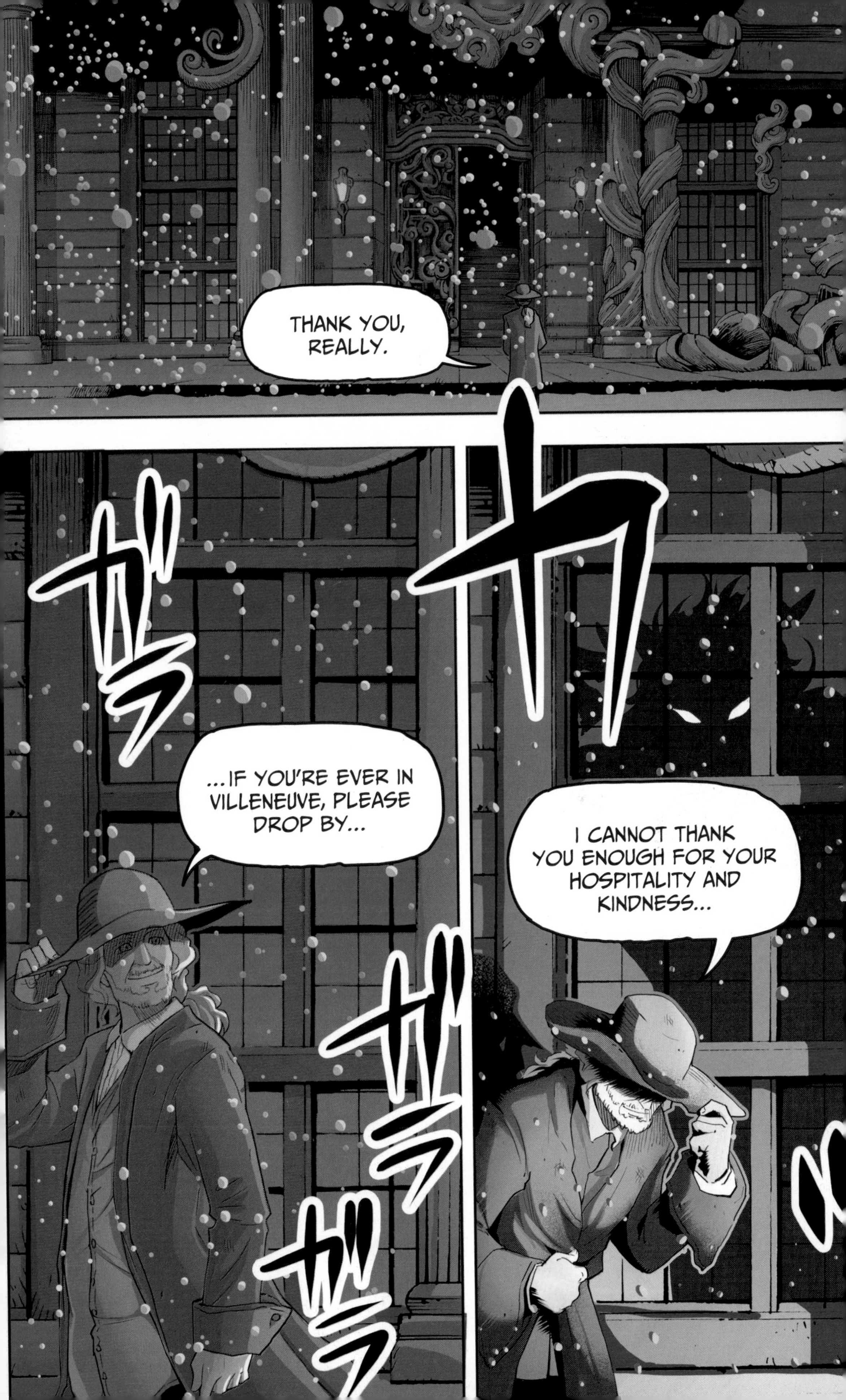
THANK YOU, REALLY.
I CANNOT THANK YOU ENOUGH FOR YOUR HOSPITALITY AND KINDNESS...
ガラ
ガラ
...IF YOU'RE EVER IN VILLENEUVE, PLEASE DROP BY...
ガラ

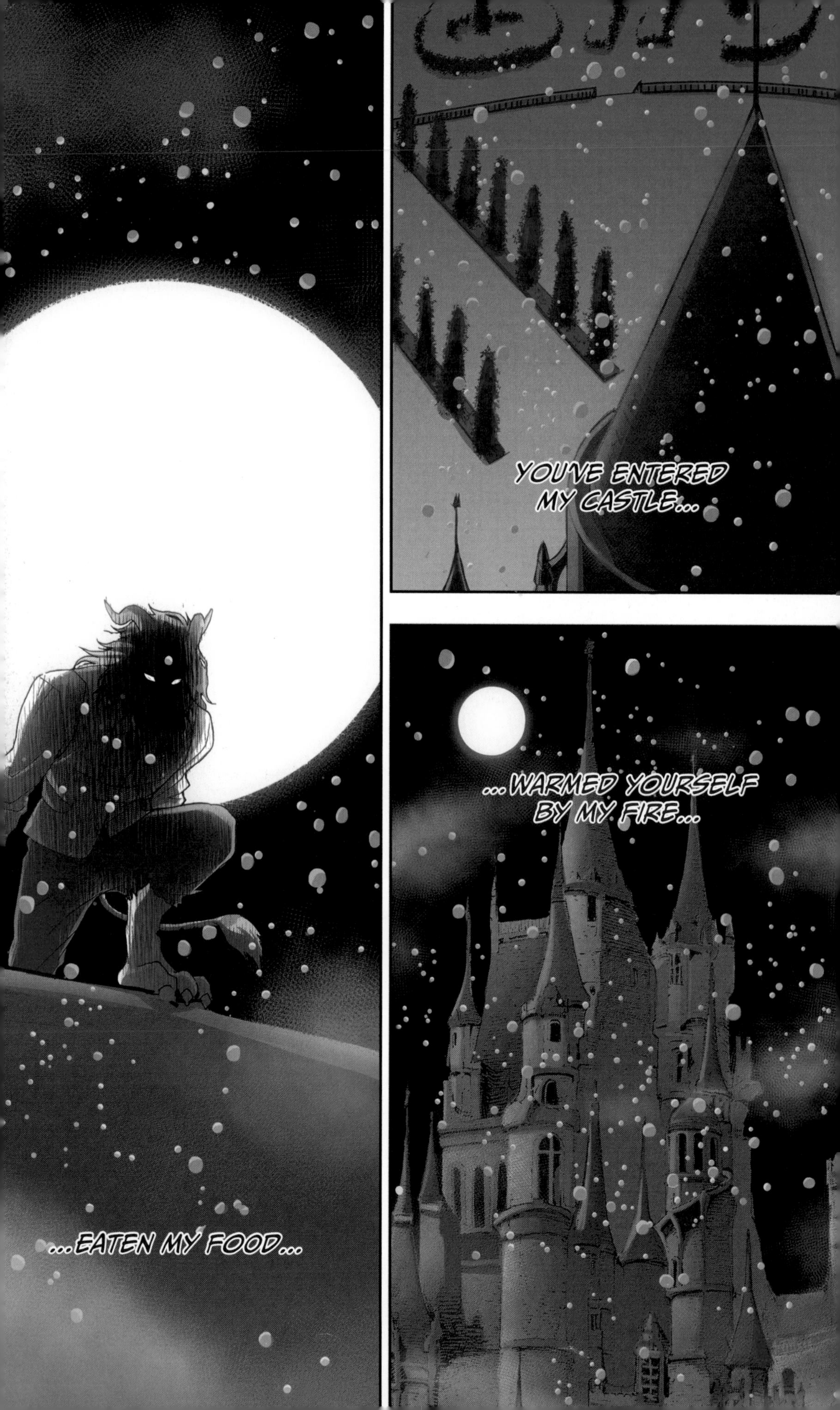
YOU'VE ENTERED MY CASTLE...
...WARMED YOURSELF BY MY FIRE...
...EATEN MY FOOD...

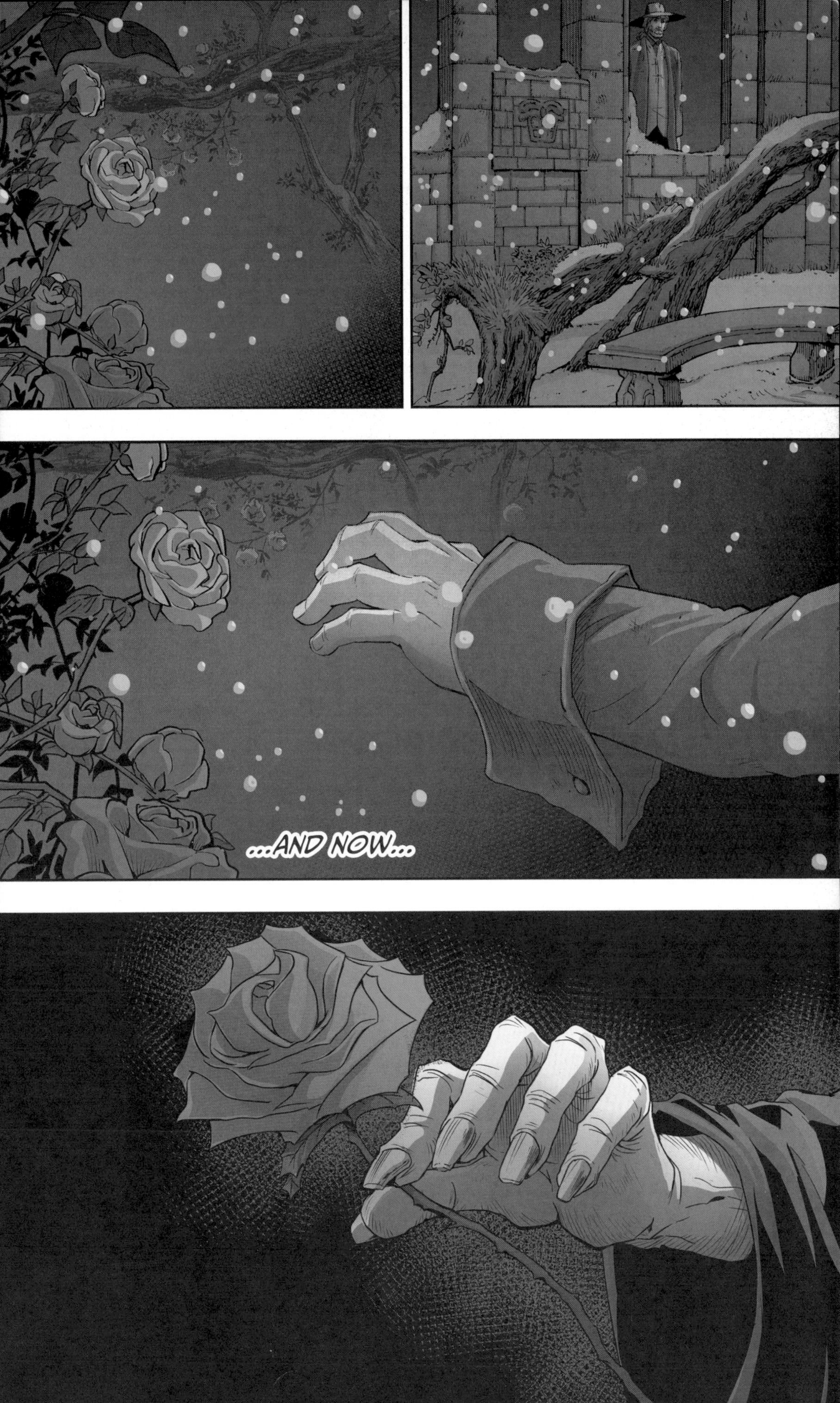
...AND NOW...

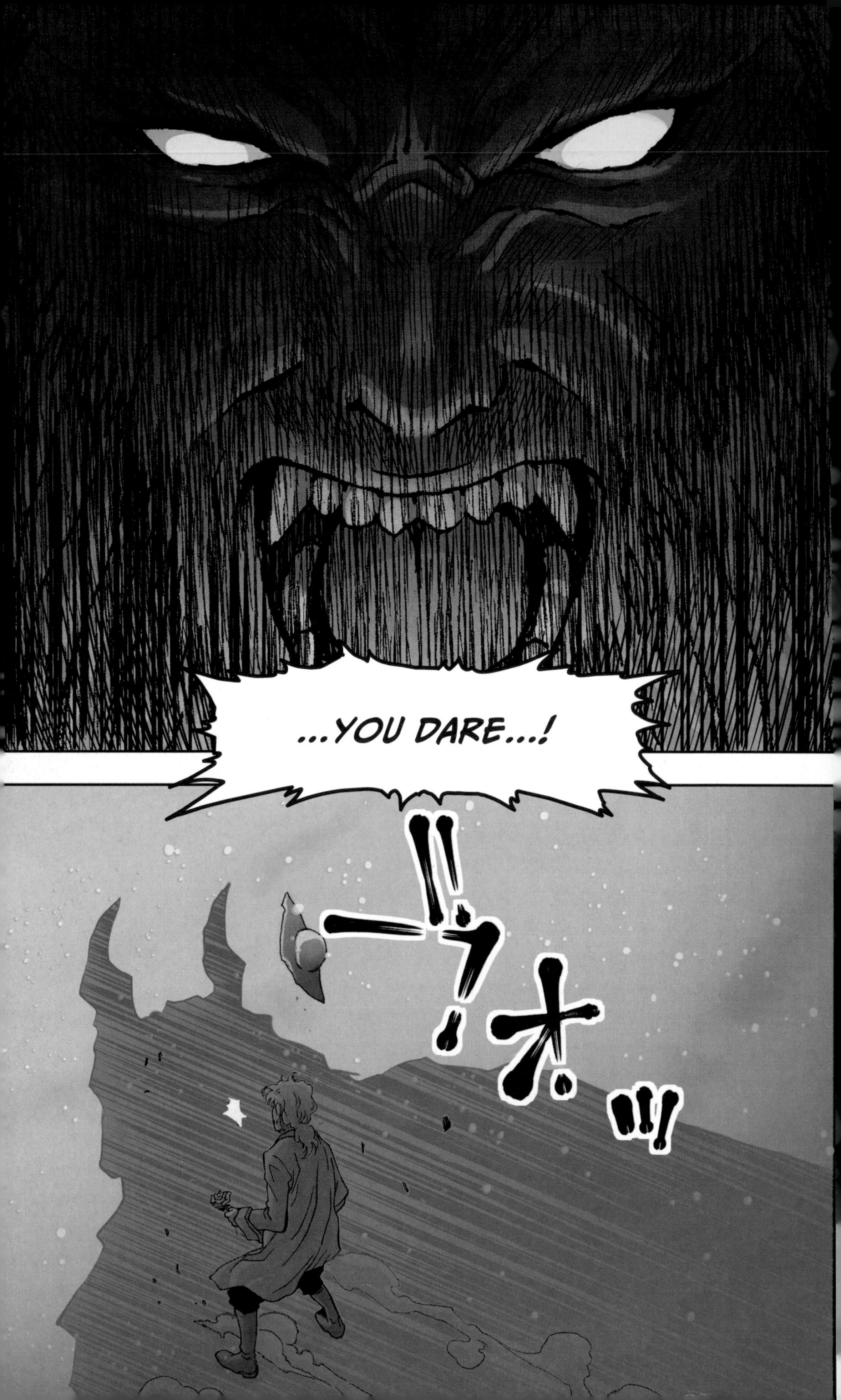
...YOU DARE...!
ゴッ!オッ!!

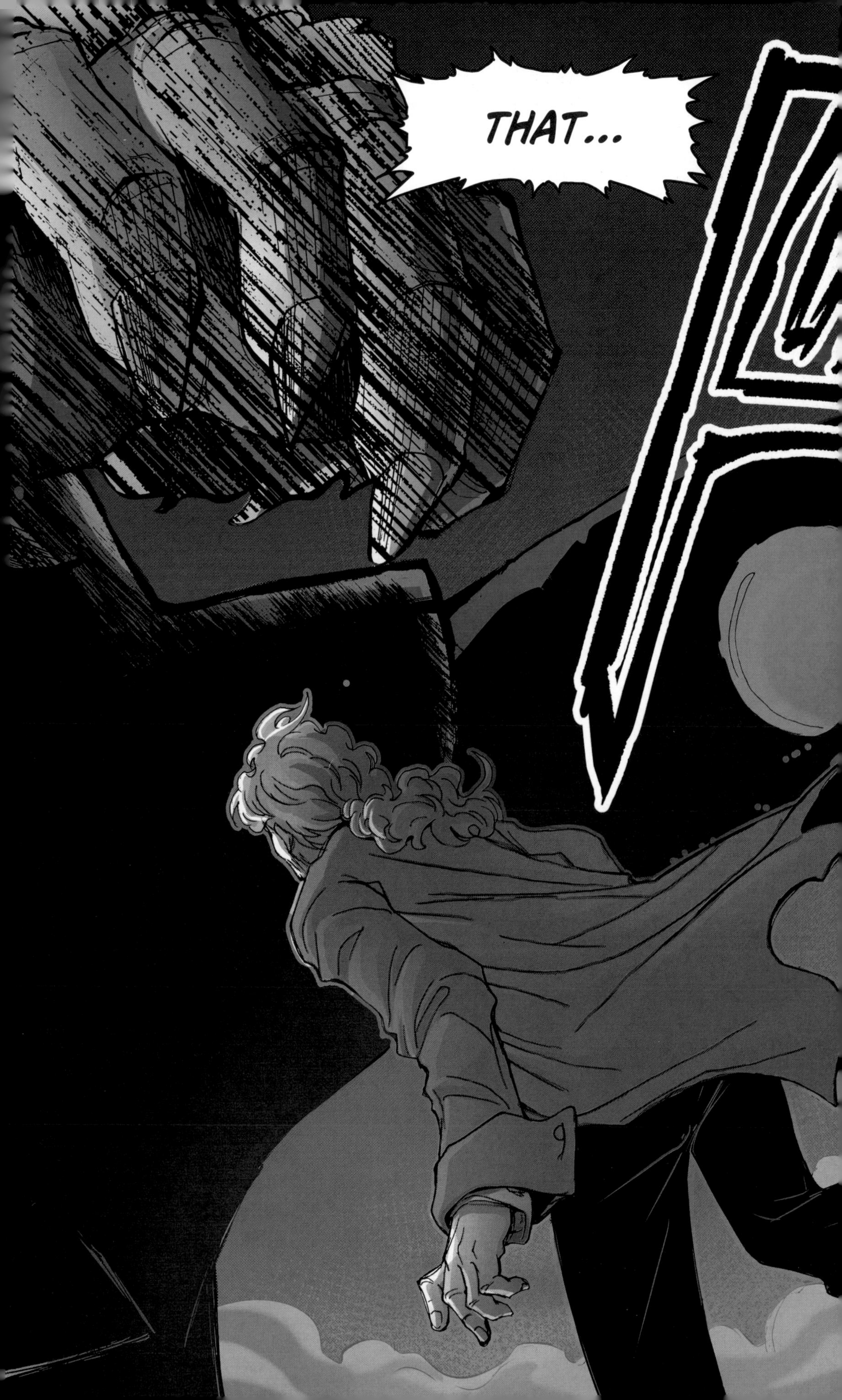
THAT...

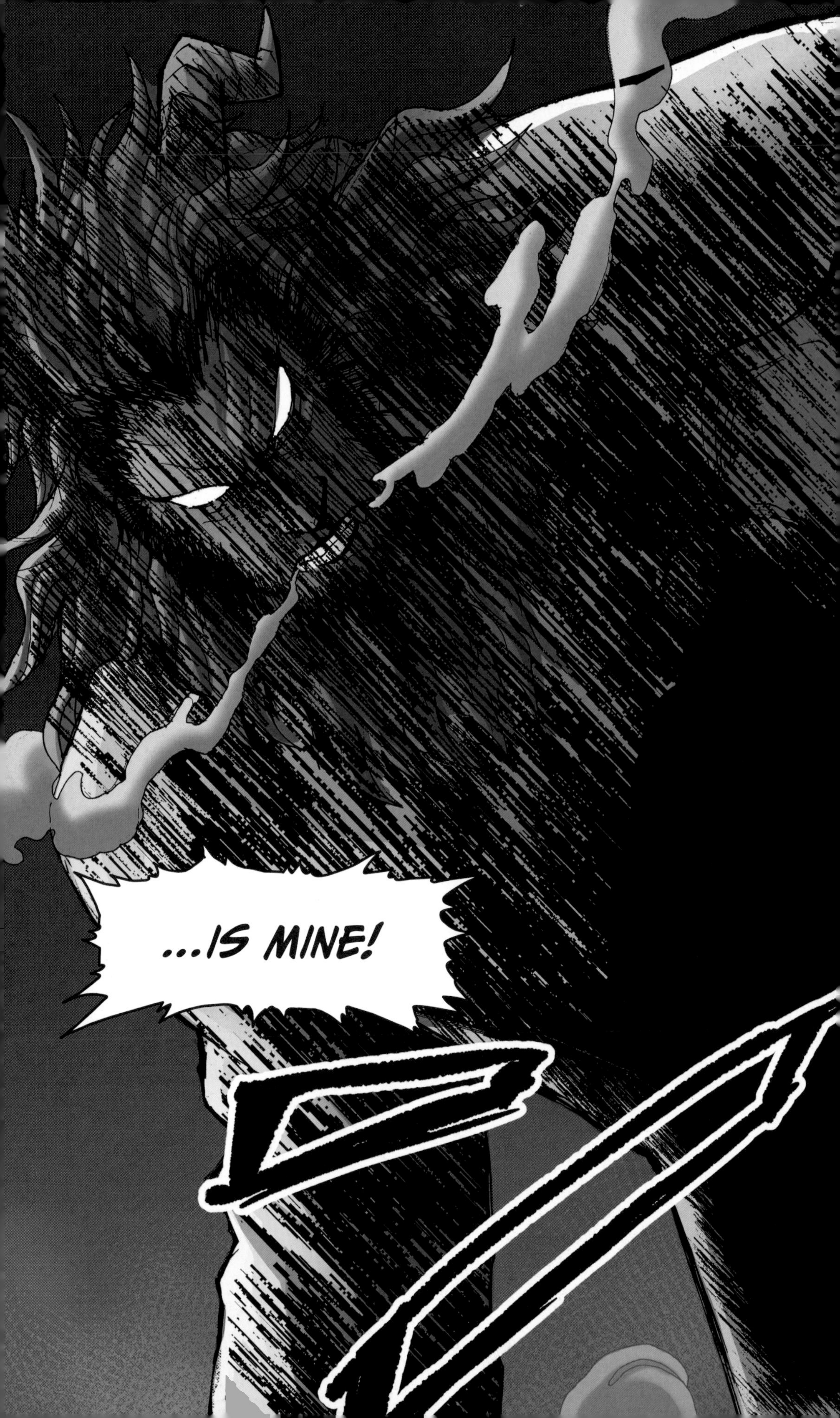
...IS MINE!

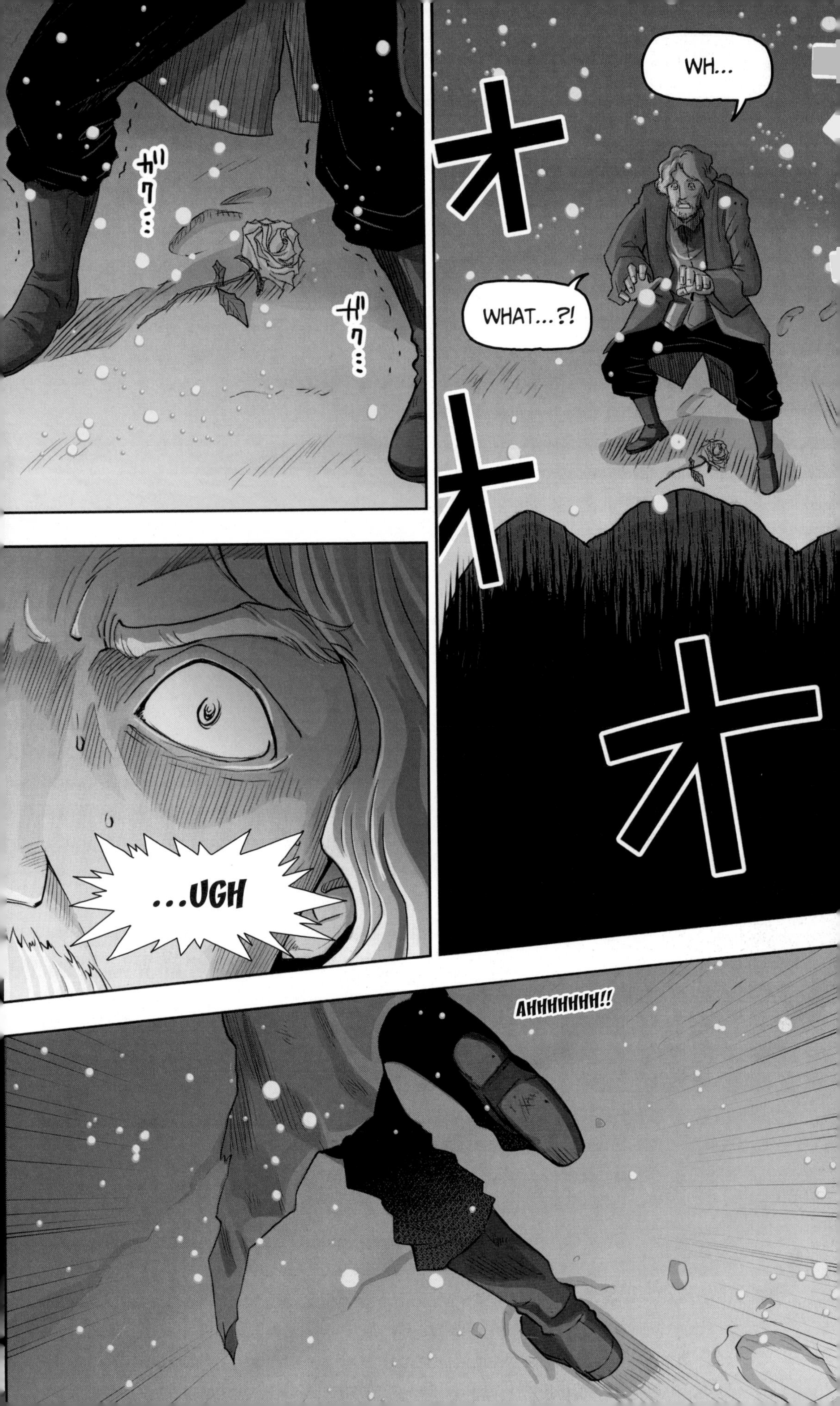
オ
WH...
WHAT...?!
オ
オ
ガク…
ガク…
...UGH
AHHHHHHH!!

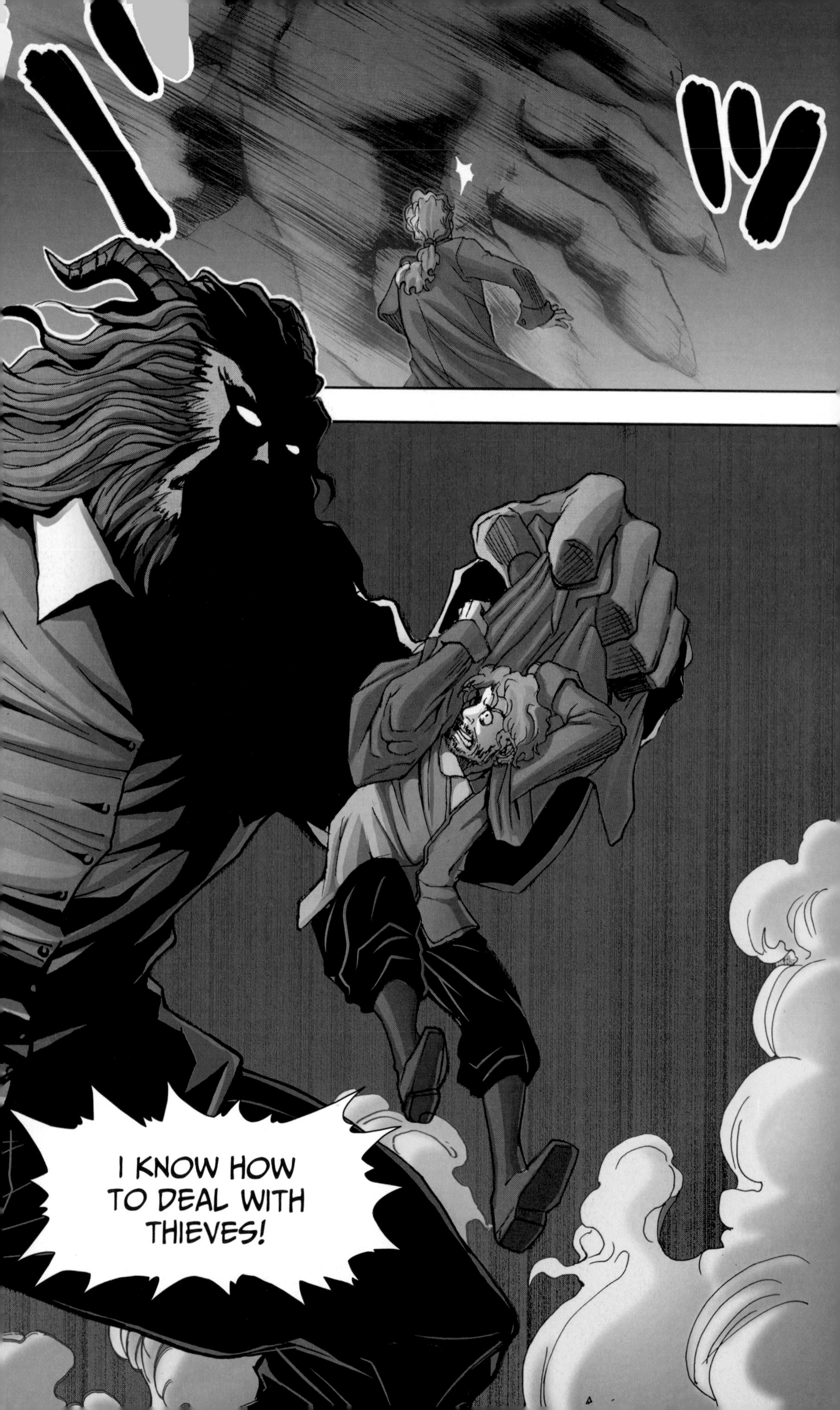
I KNOW HOW TO DEAL WITH THIEVES!

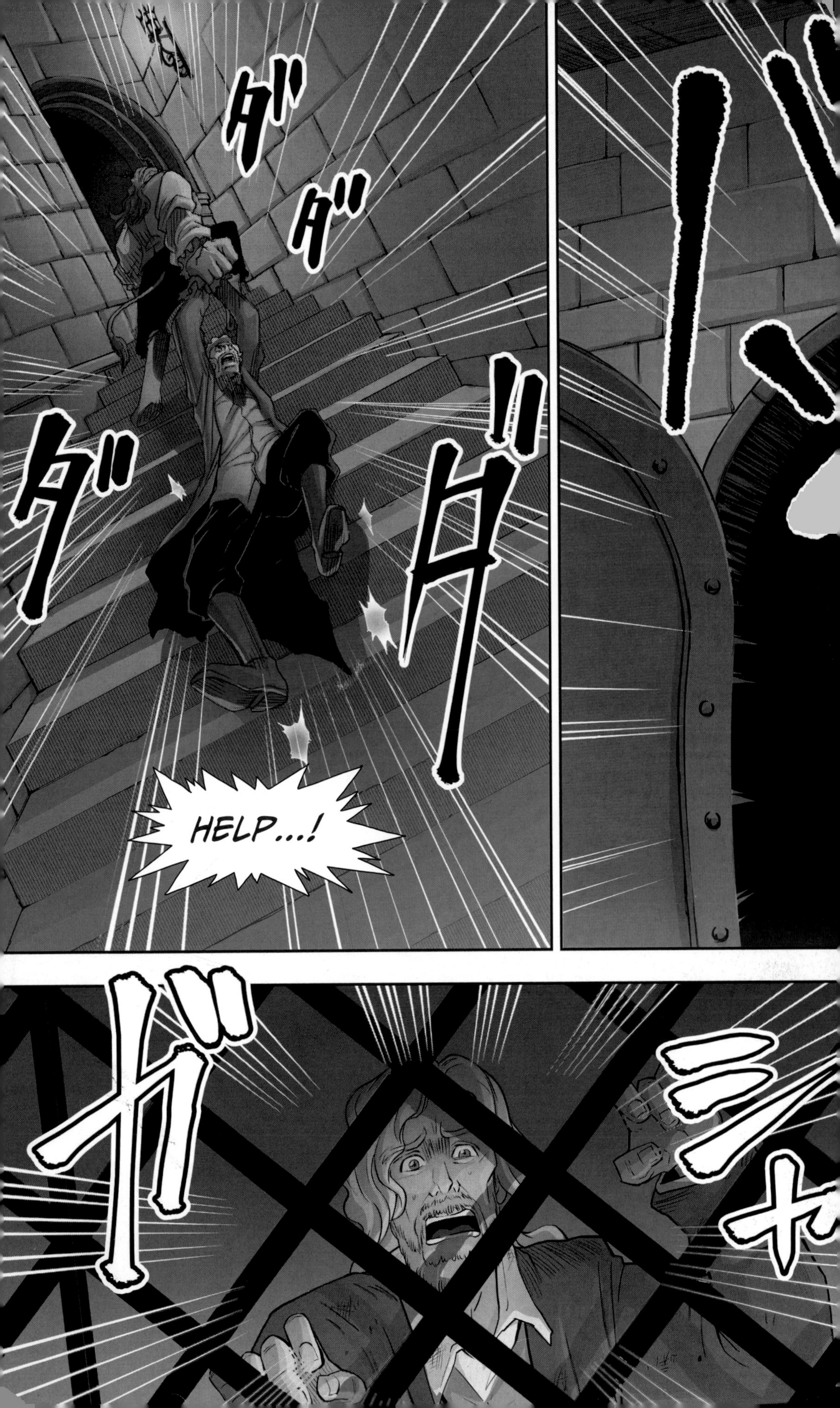
ダ
ダ
ダ
ダ
HELP...!
ガ

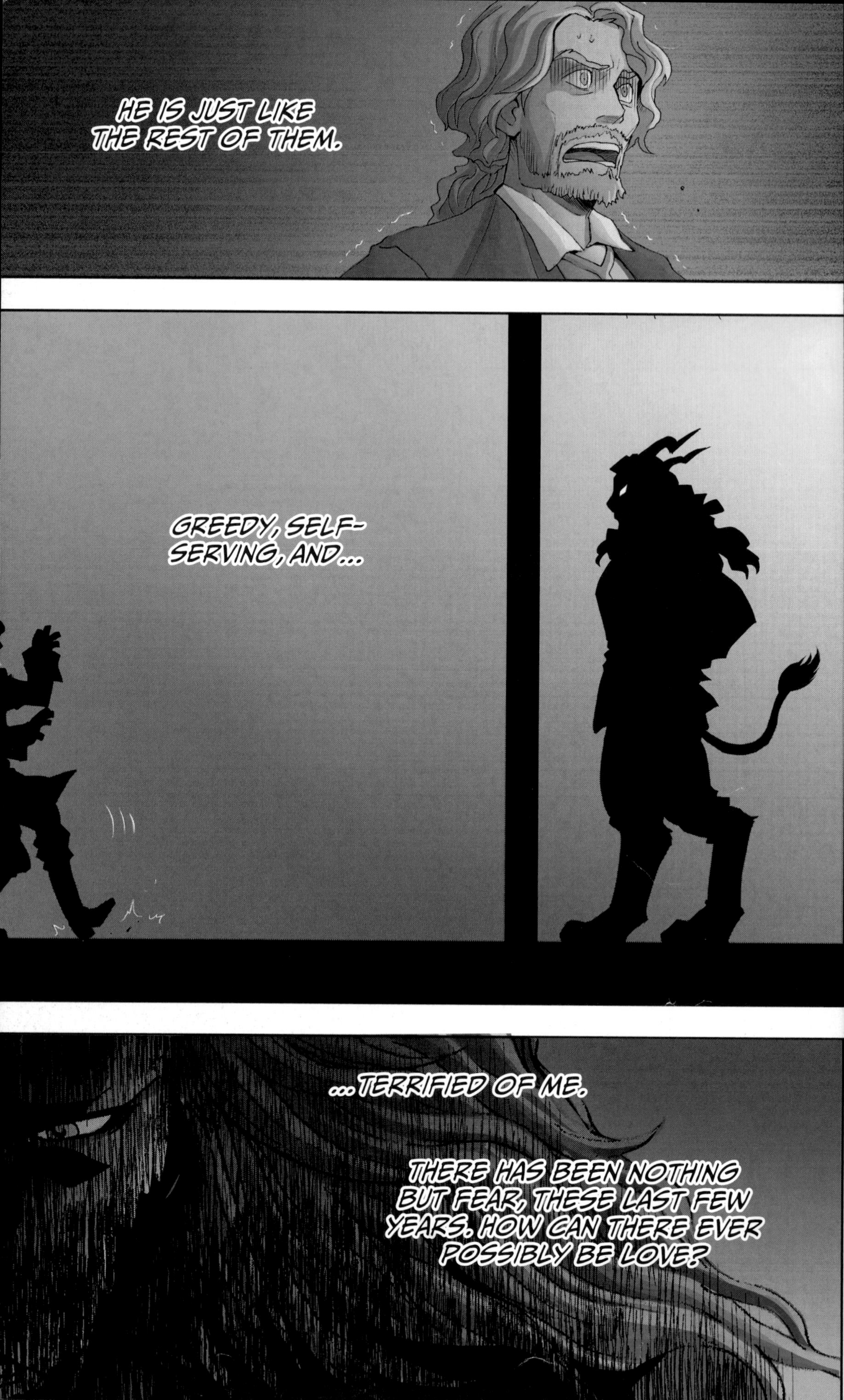
HE IS JUST LIKE THE REST OF THEM.
GREEDY, SELF-SERVING, AND...
...TERRIFIED OF ME.
THERE HAS BEEN NOTHING BUT FEAR, THESE LAST FEW YEARS. HOW CAN THERE EVER POSSIBLY BE LOVE?

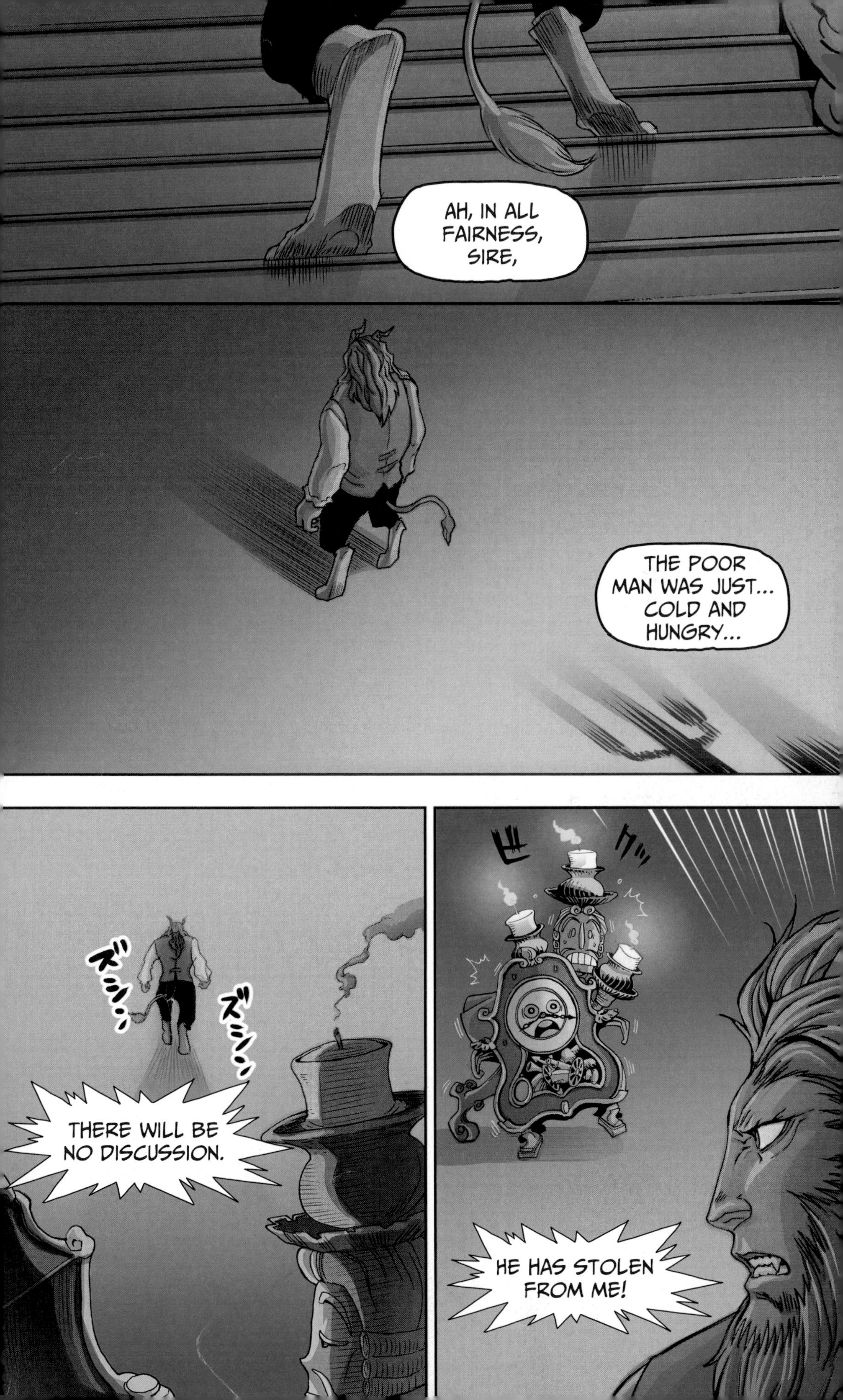
AH, IN ALL FAIRNESS, SIRE,
THE POOR MAN WAS JUST... COLD AND HUNGRY...
HE HAS STOLEN FROM ME!
ズシン、
ズシン、
THERE WILL BE NO DISCUSSION.

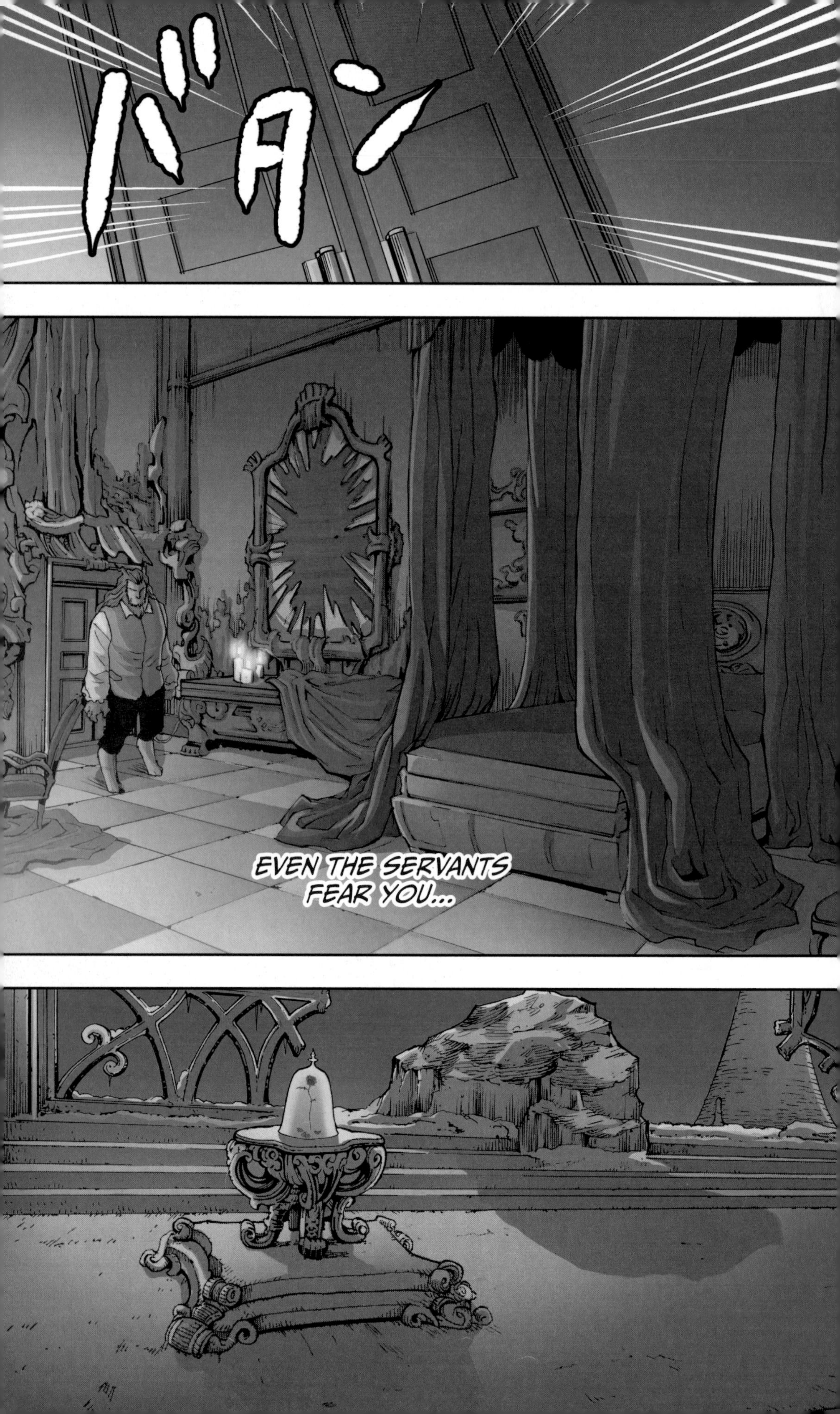
バタン
EVEN THE SERVANTS FEAR YOU...

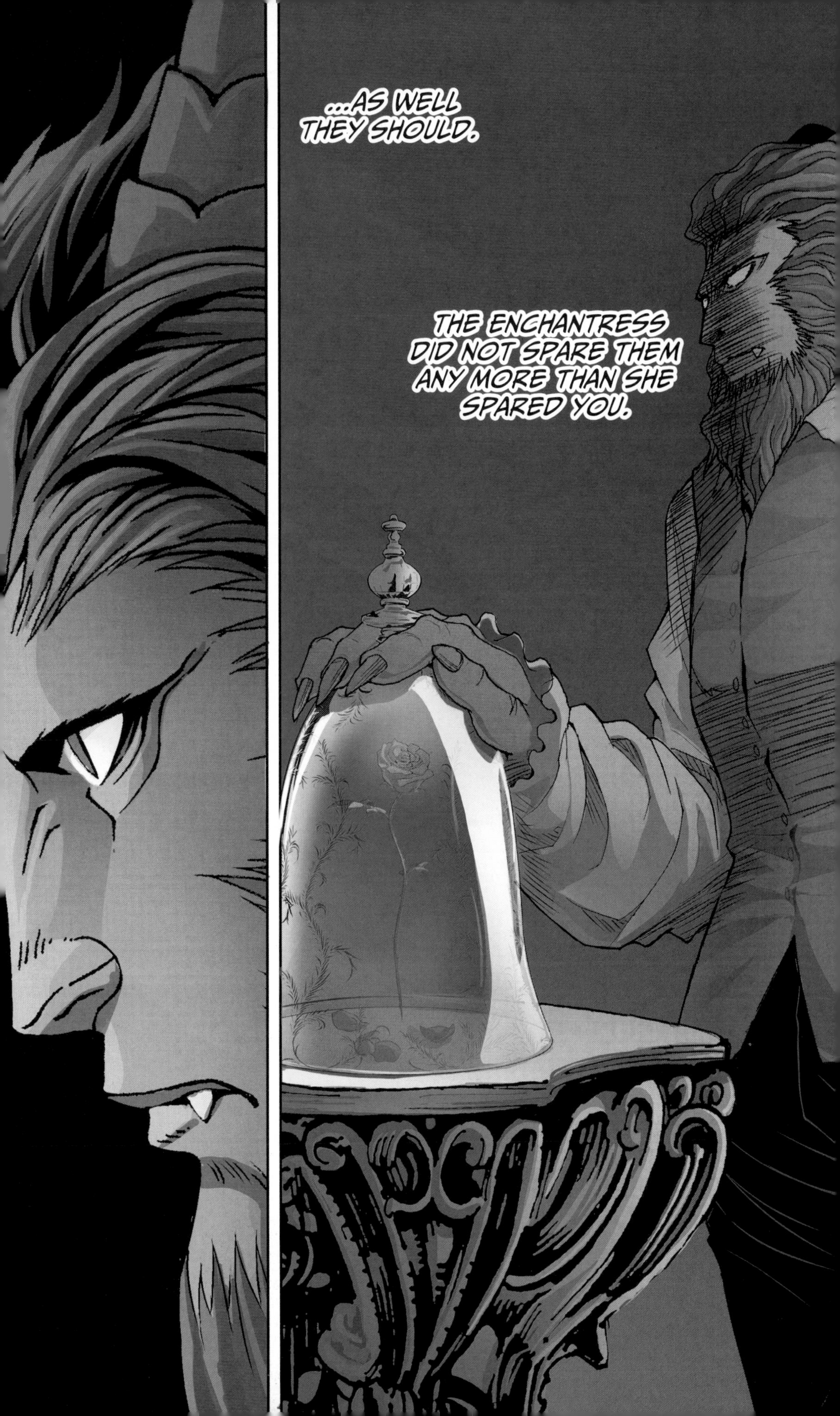
...AS WELL THEY SHOULD.
THE ENCHANTRESS DID NOT SPARE THEM ANY MORE THAN SHE SPARED YOU.

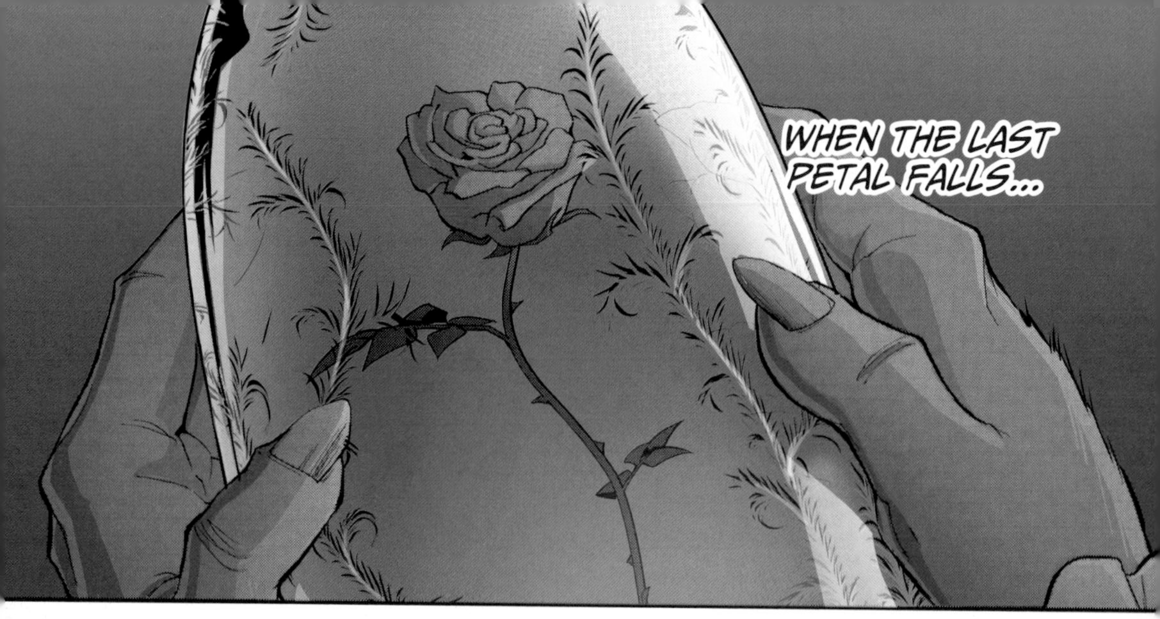
WHEN THE LAST PETAL FALLS...

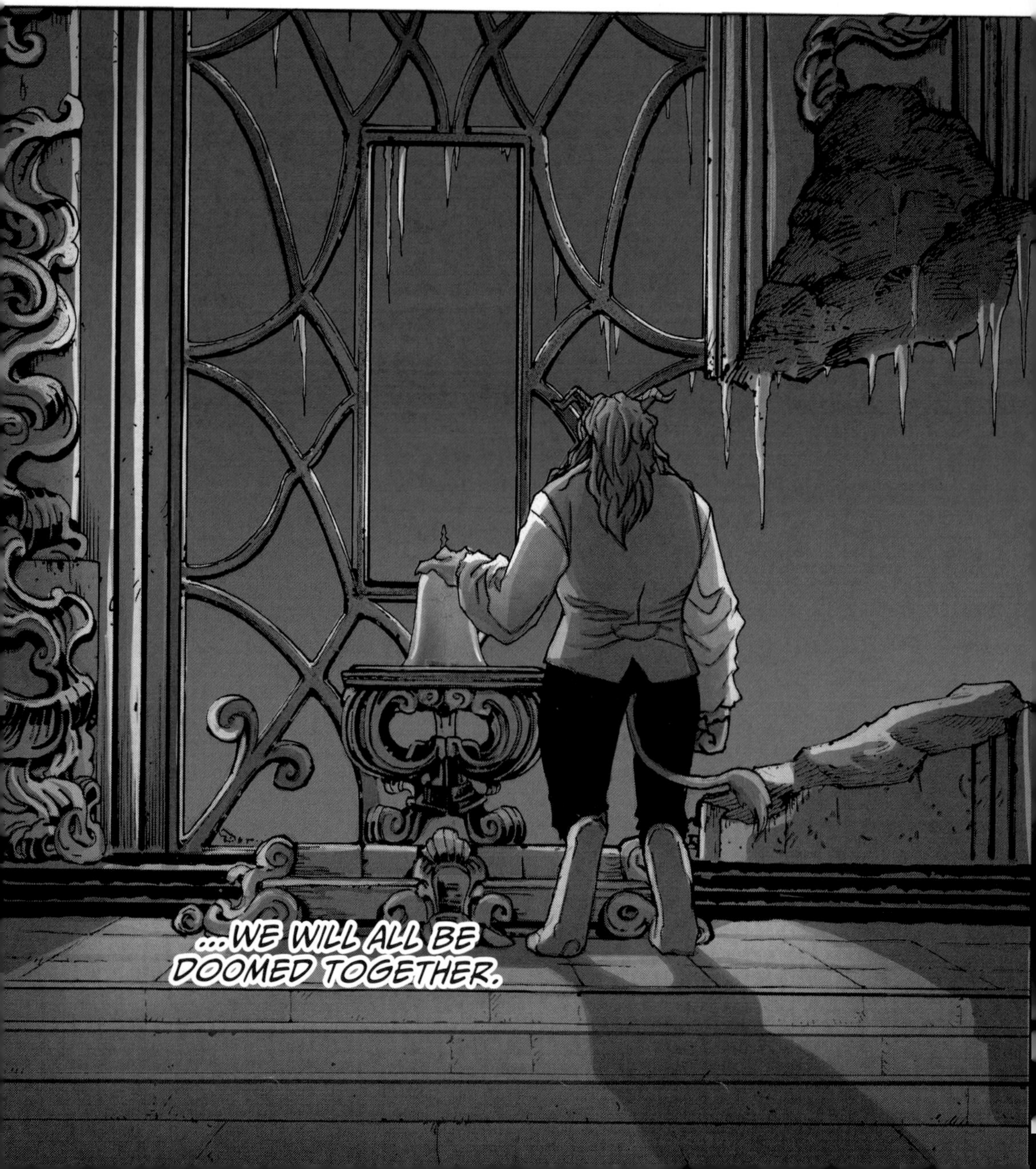
...WE WILL ALL BE DOOMED TOGETHER.

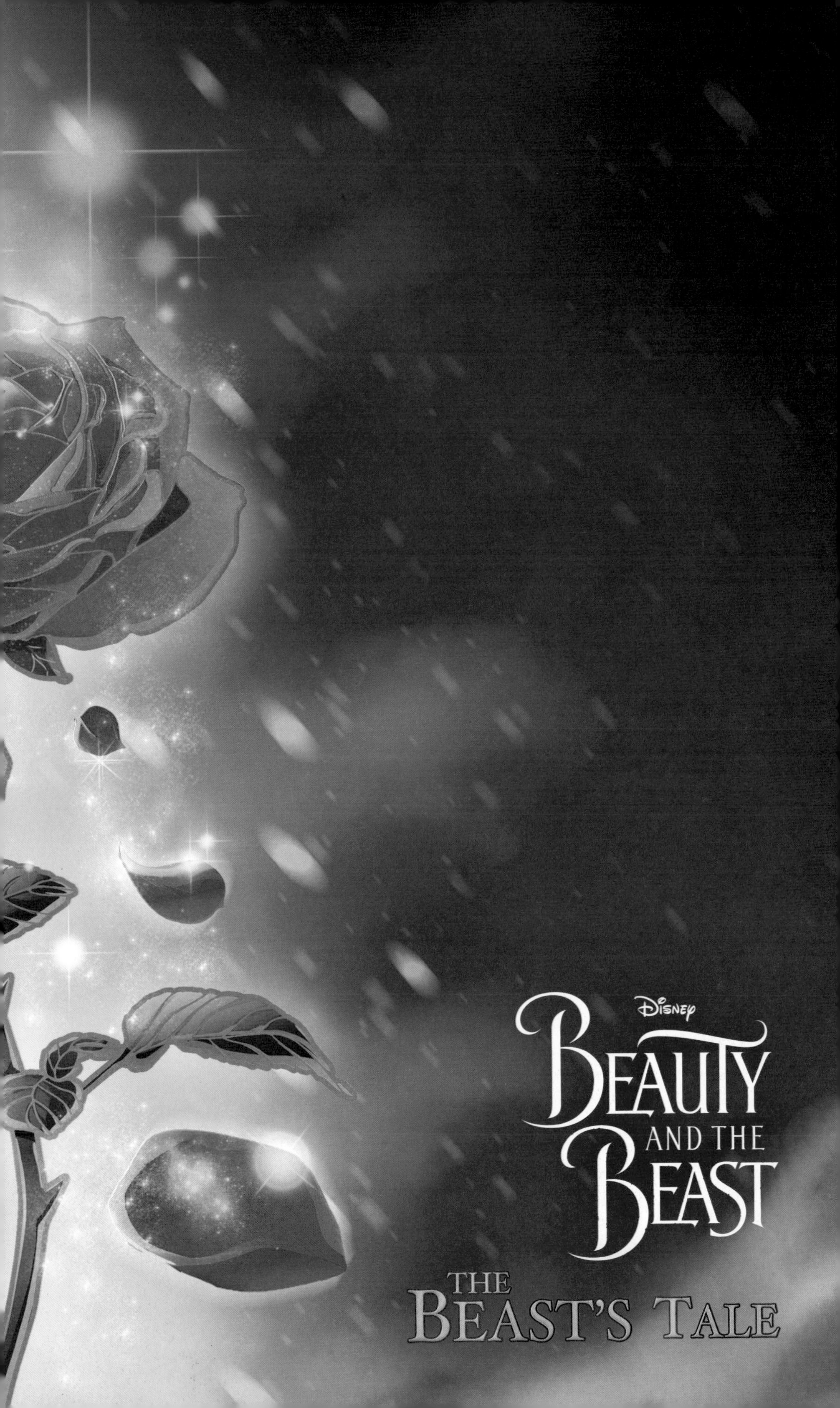
Disney
Beauty and the Beast
The Beast's Tale

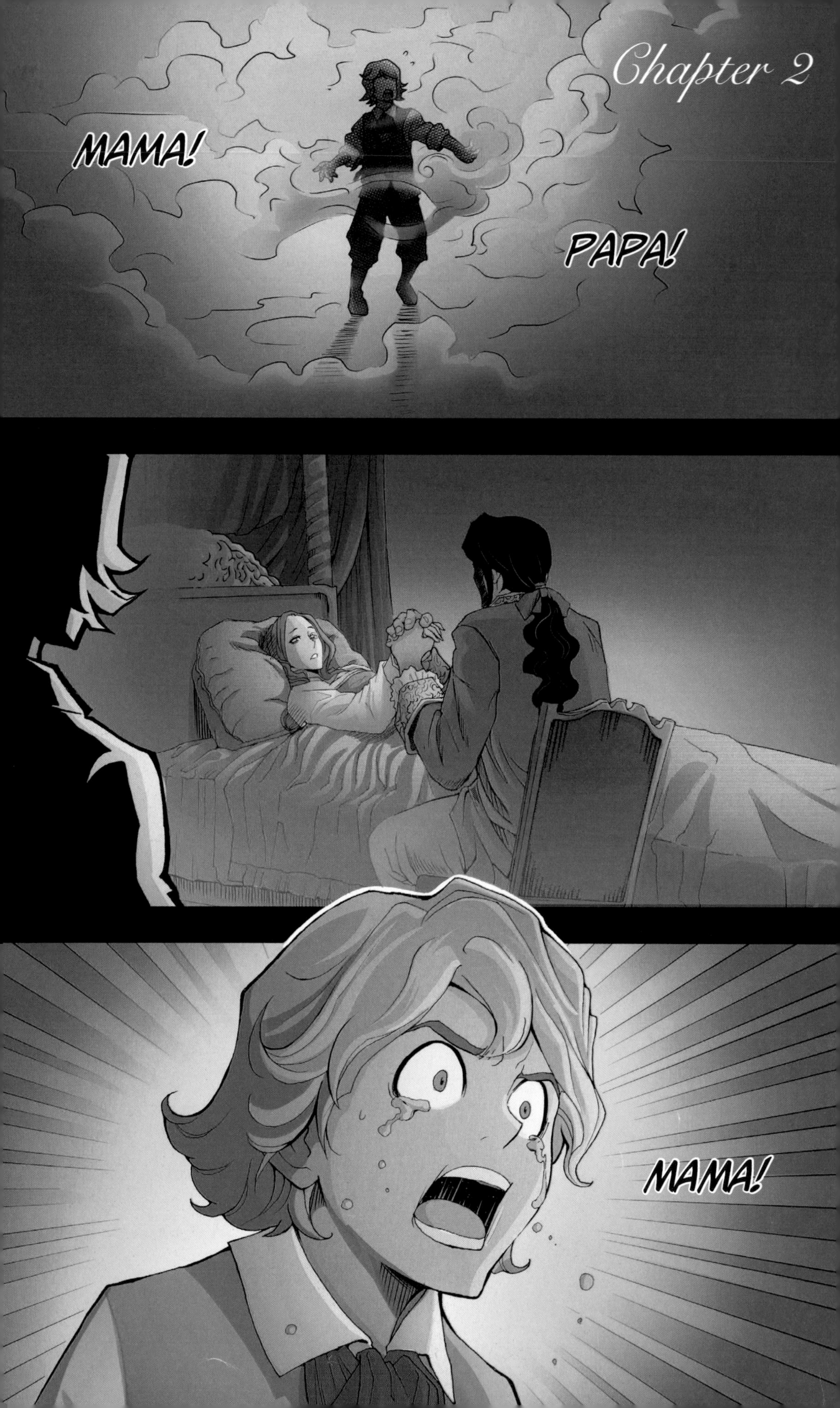
Chapter 2
MAMA!
PAPA!
MAMA!

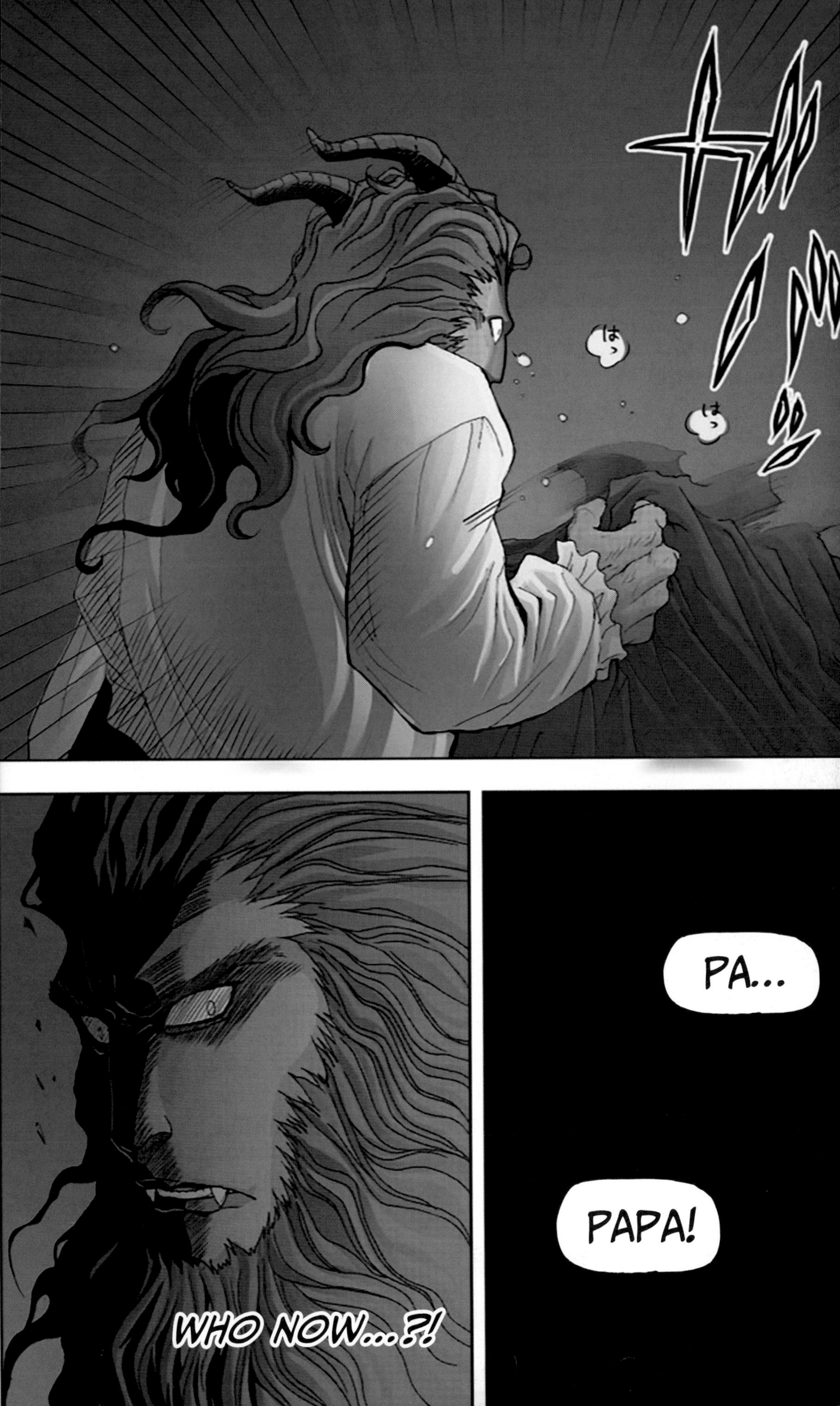
ガバッ
はっ
はっ
PA...
PAPA!
WHO NOW...?!

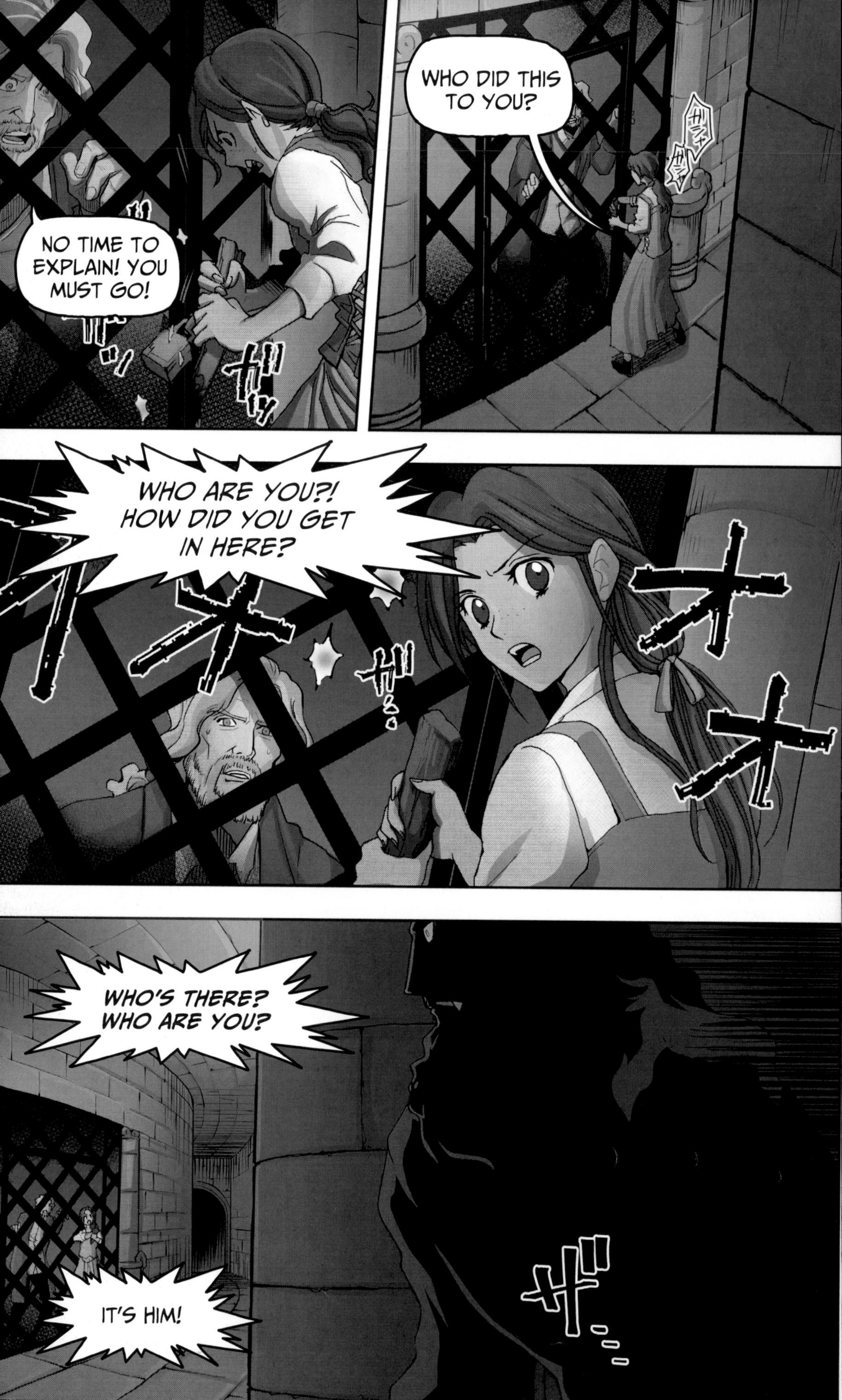
WHO DID THIS TO YOU?
NO TIME TO EXPLAIN! YOU MUST GO!
WHO ARE YOU?! HOW DID YOU GET IN HERE?
WHO'S THERE? WHO ARE YOU?
IT'S HIM!

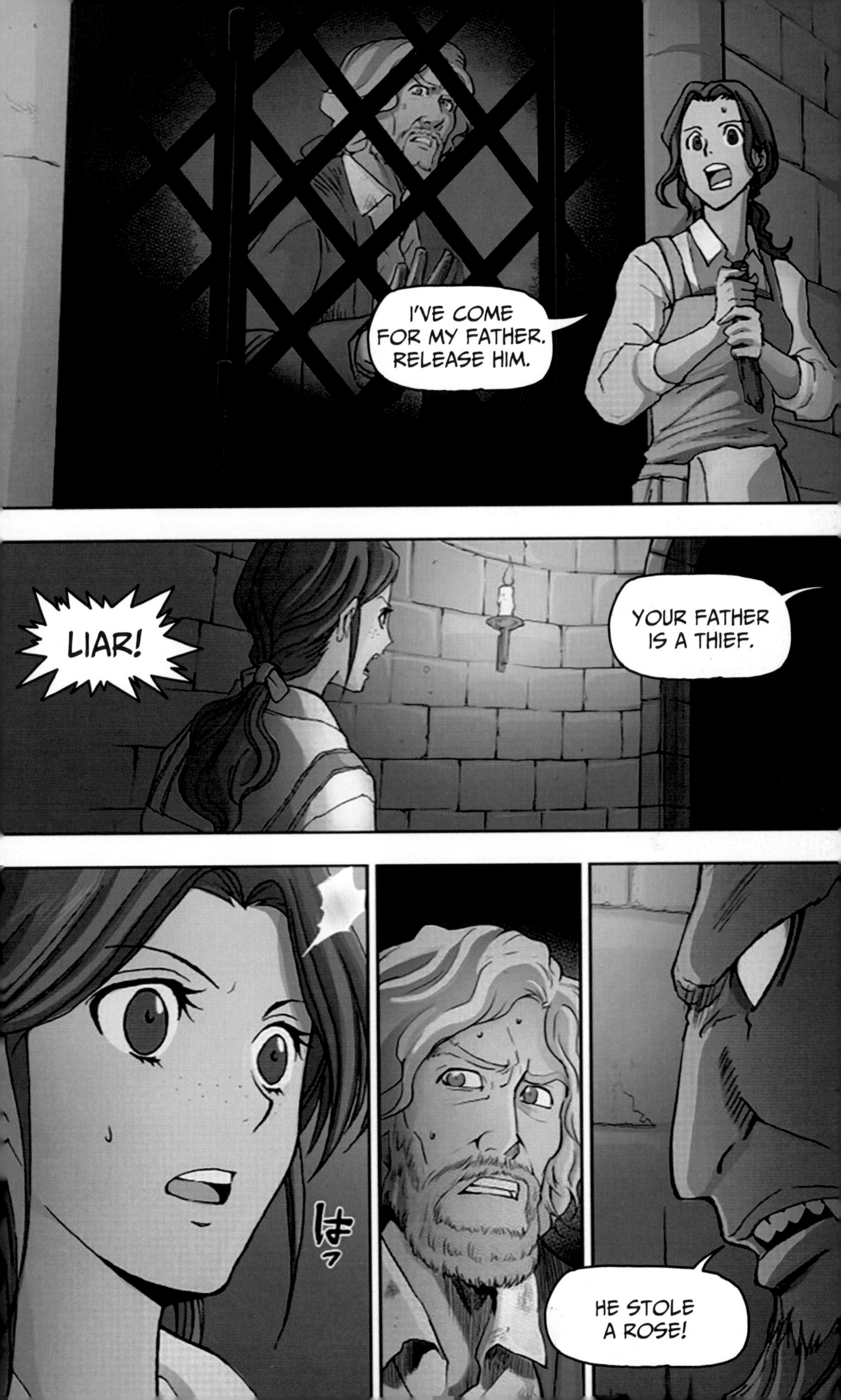
I'VE COME FOR MY FATHER. RELEASE HIM.
YOUR FATHER IS A THIEF.
LIAR!
HE STOLE A ROSE!
はっ

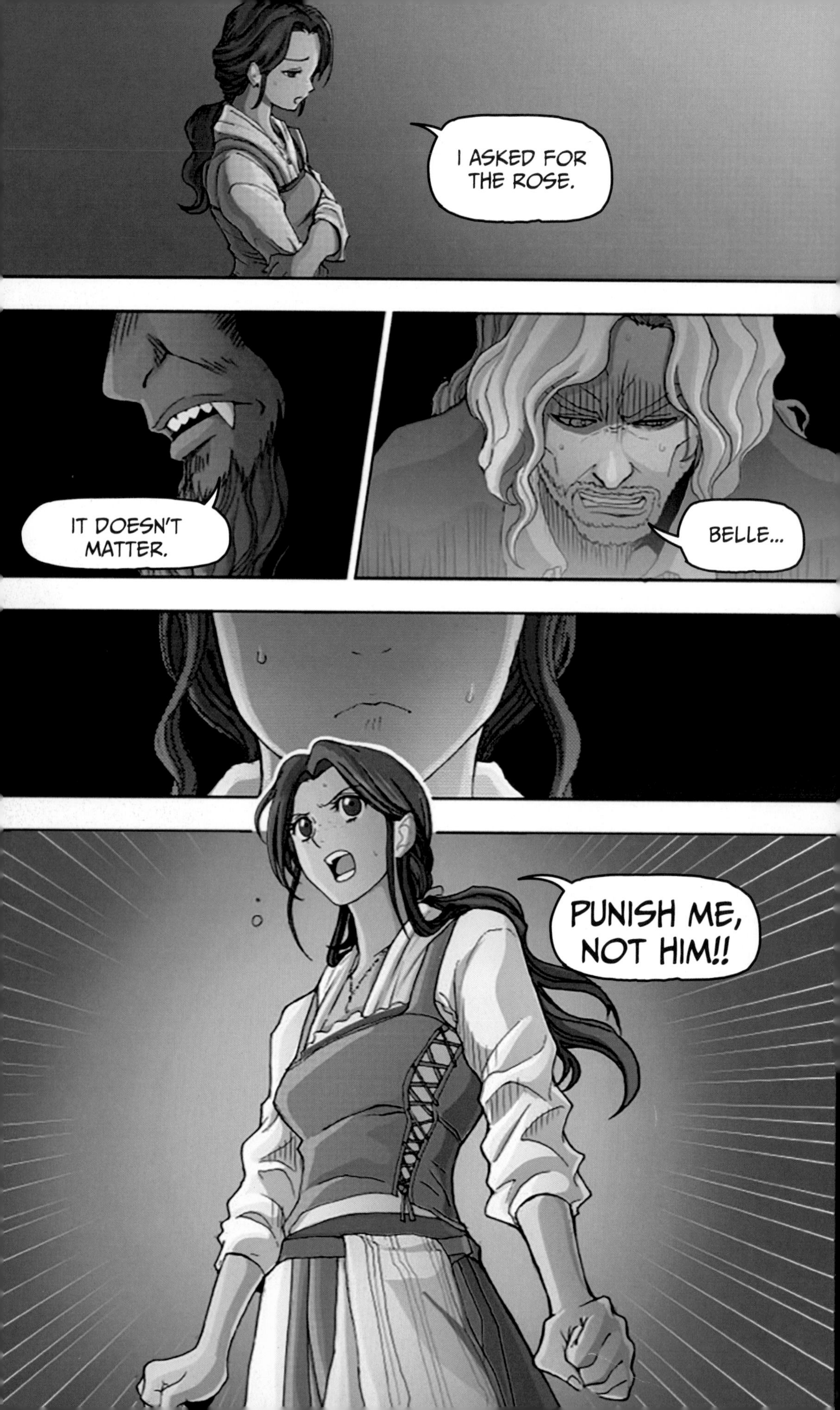
I ASKED FOR THE ROSE.
BELLE...
IT DOESN'T MATTER.
PUNISH ME, NOT HIM!!

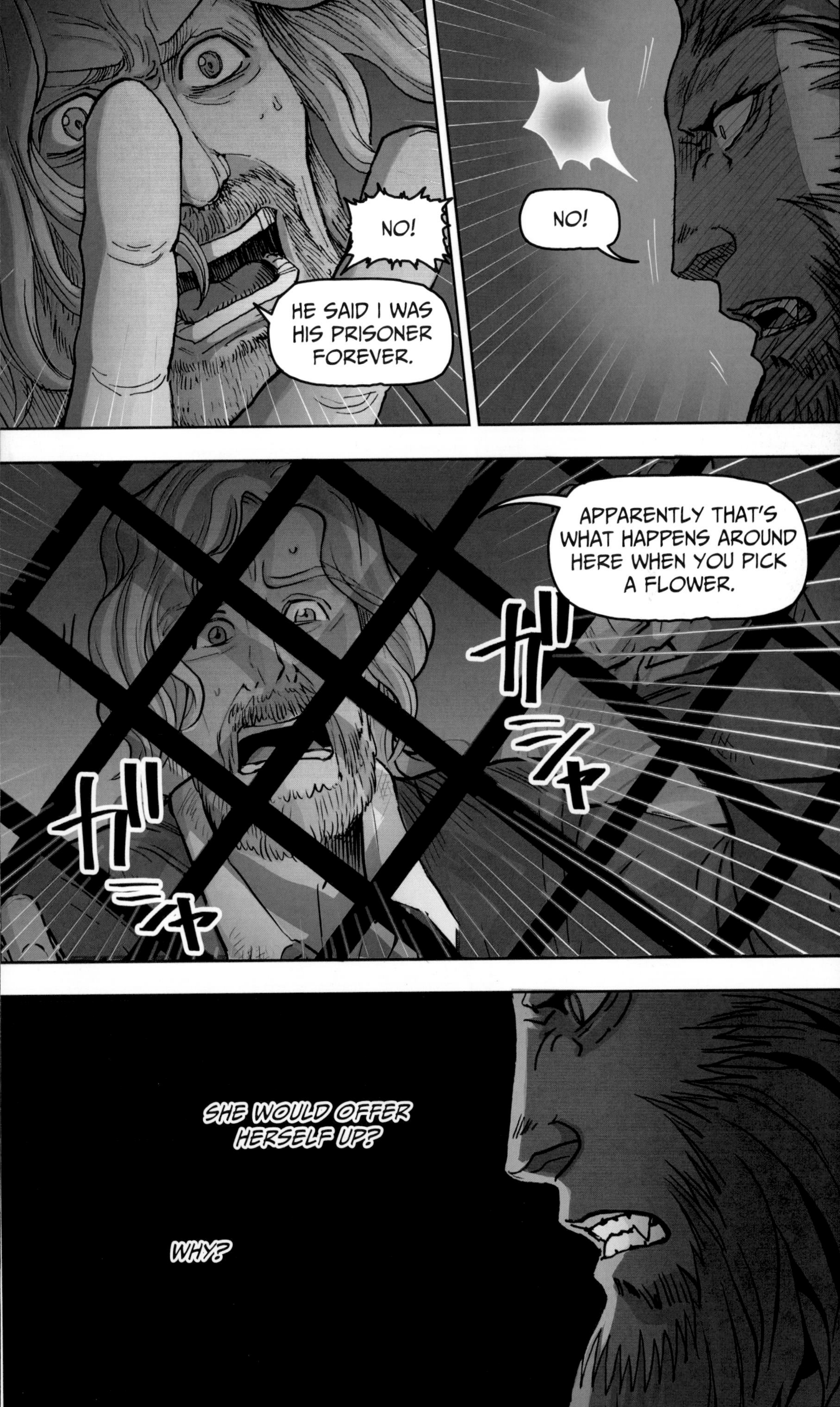
NO!
NO!
HE SAID I WAS HIS PRISONER FOREVER.
APPARENTLY THAT'S WHAT HAPPENS AROUND HERE WHEN YOU PICK A FLOWER.
ガシャ
ガシャ
SHE WOULD OFFER HERSELF UP?
WHY?

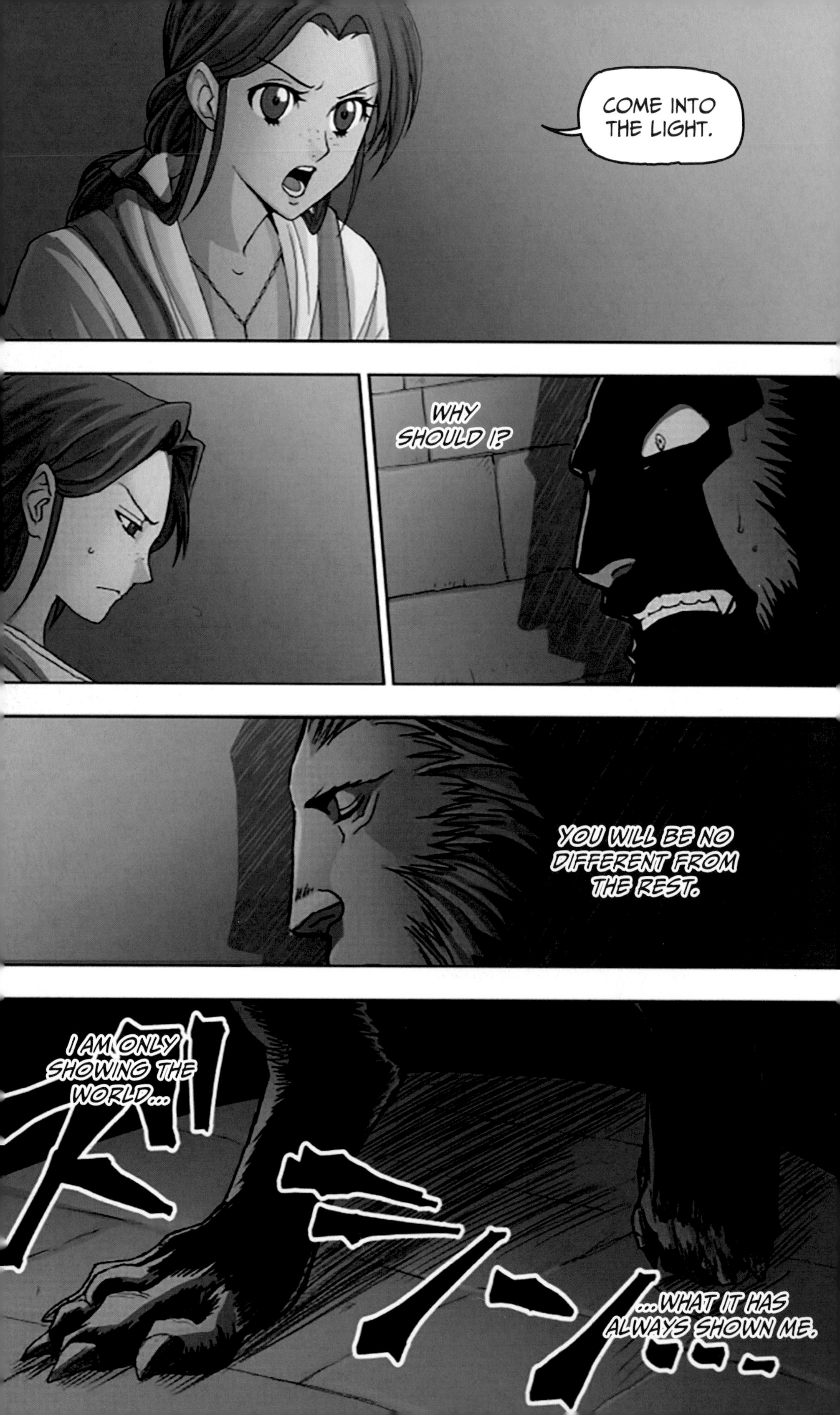
COME INTO THE LIGHT.
WHY SHOULD I?
YOU WILL BE NO DIFFERENT FROM THE REST.
I AM ONLY SHOWING THE WORLD...
...WHAT IT HAS ALWAYS SHOWN ME.

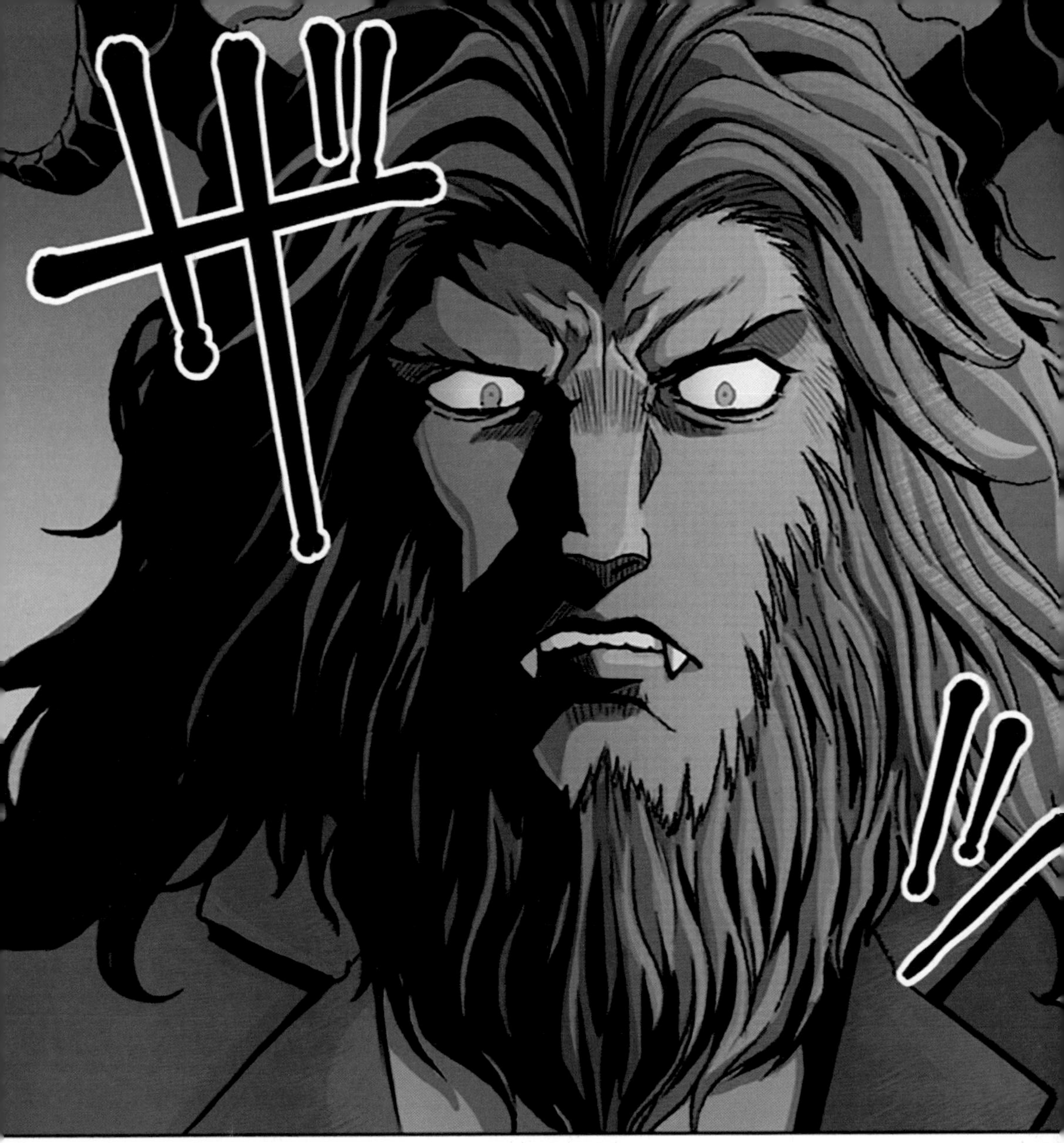
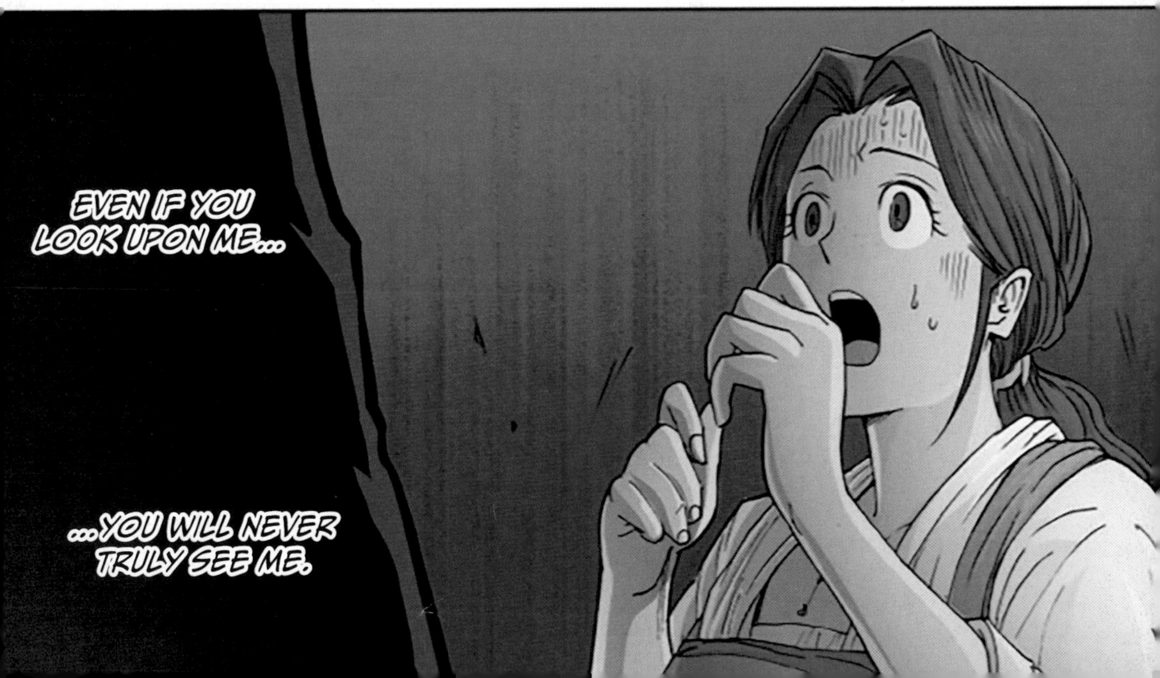
EVEN IF YOU LOOK UPON ME...
...YOU WILL NEVER TRULY SEE ME.

CHOOSE!

BELLE, I WON'T LET YOU DO THIS!

BUT YOU'LL DIE HERE!

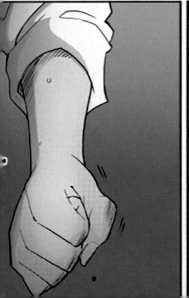

NO, BELLE... I COULDN'T SAVE YOUR MOTHER...

BUT I CAN SAVE YOU. NOW GO!

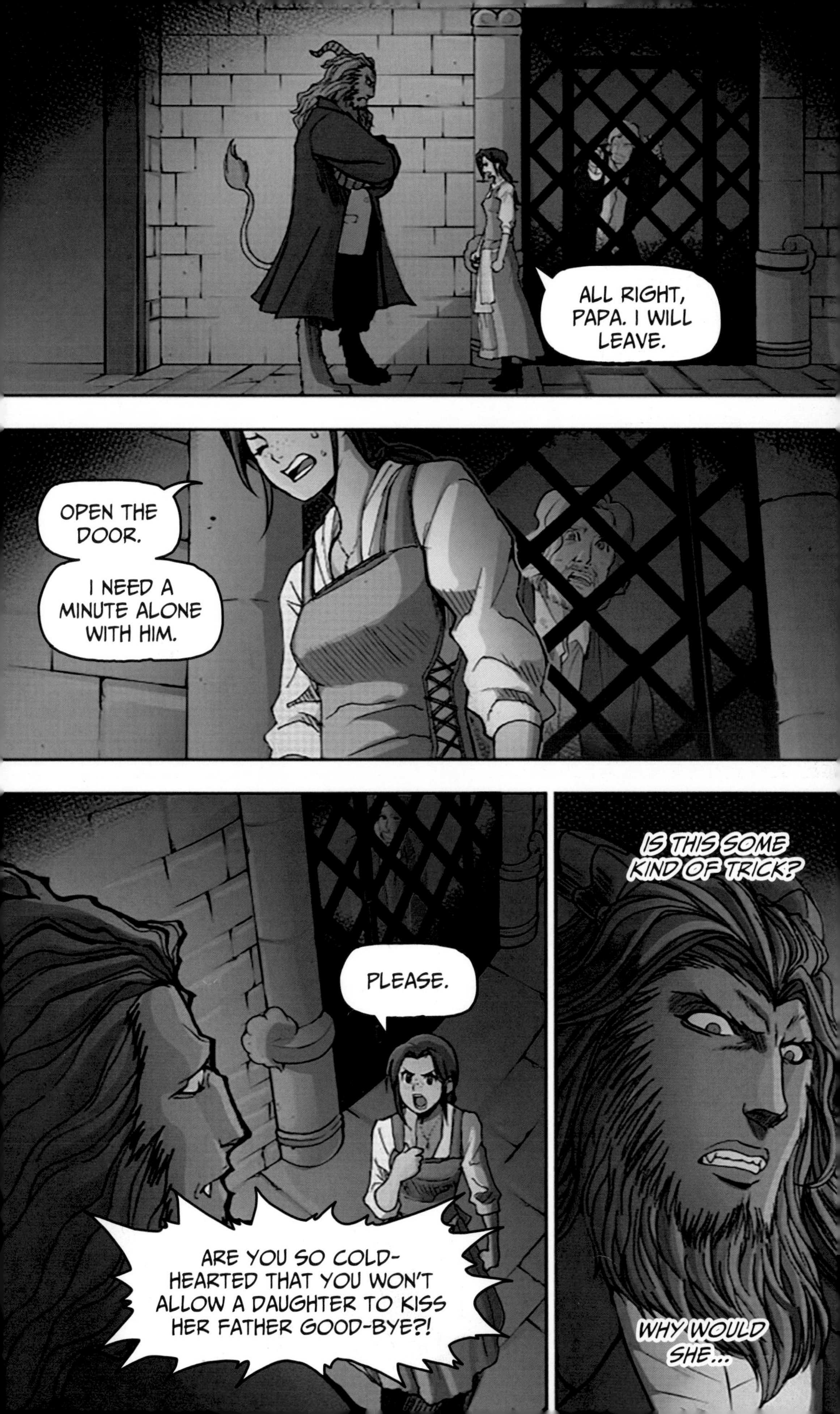
ALL RIGHT, PAPA. I WILL LEAVE.
OPEN THE DOOR.
I NEED A MINUTE ALONE WITH HIM.
IS THIS SOME KIND OF TRICK?
WHY WOULD SHE...
PLEASE.
ARE YOU SO COLD-HEARTED THAT YOU WON'T ALLOW A DAUGHTER TO KISS HER FATHER GOOD-BYE?!

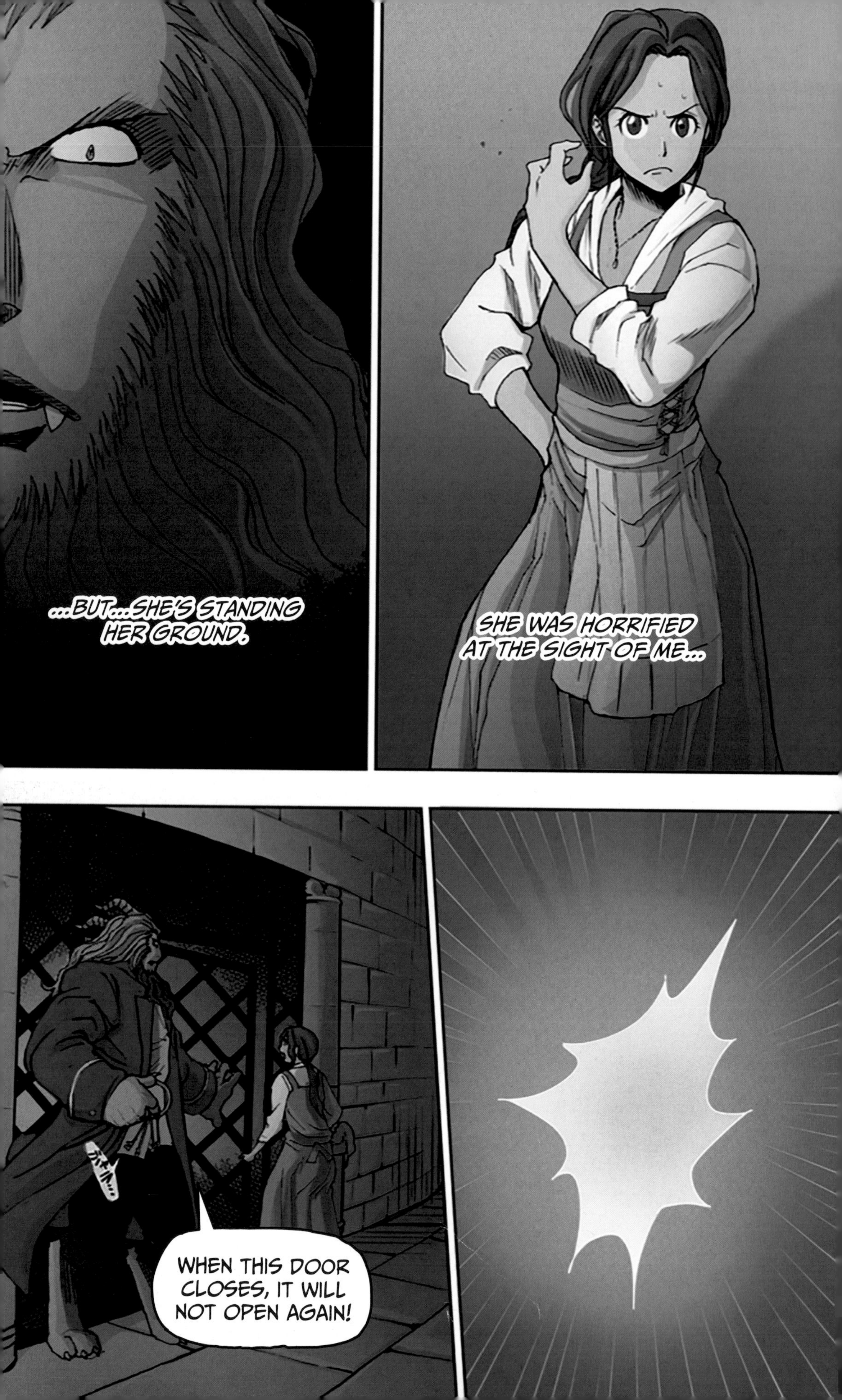
SHE WAS HORRIFIED AT THE SIGHT OF ME...
...BUT...SHE'S STANDING HER GROUND.
WHEN THIS DOOR CLOSES, IT WILL NOT OPEN AGAIN!

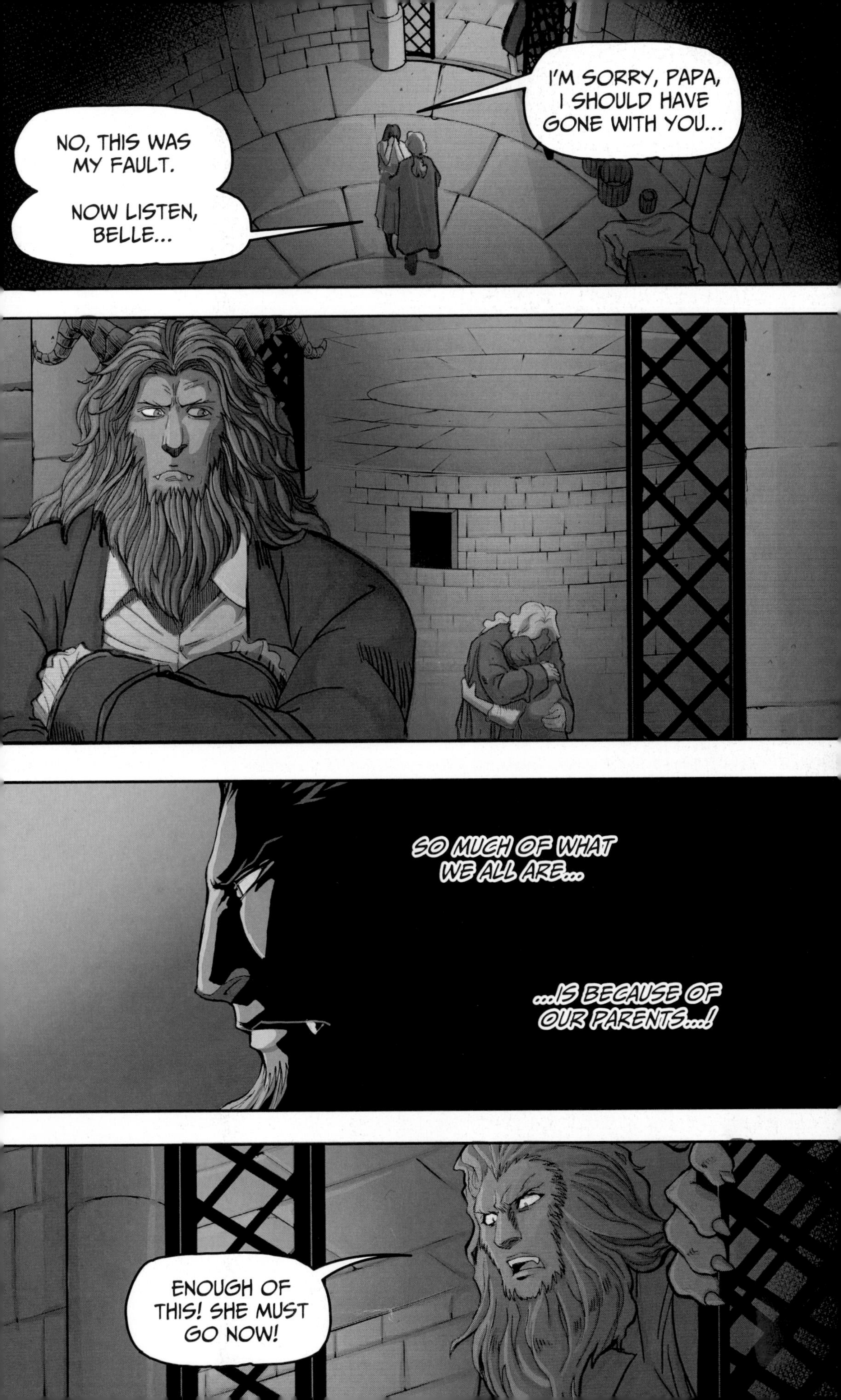
I'M SORRY, PAPA, I SHOULD HAVE GONE WITH YOU...
NO, THIS WAS MY FAULT.
NOW LISTEN, BELLE...
SO MUCH OF WHAT WE ALL ARE...
...IS BECAUSE OF OUR PARENTS...!
ENOUGH OF THIS! SHE MUST GO NOW!

YOU TOOK HIS PLACE—WHY?

OPEN THE DOOR

BELLE!

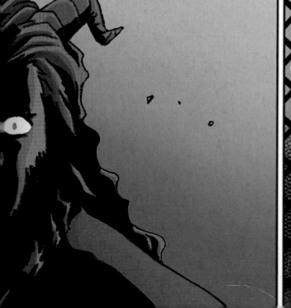

HE IS MY FATHER.

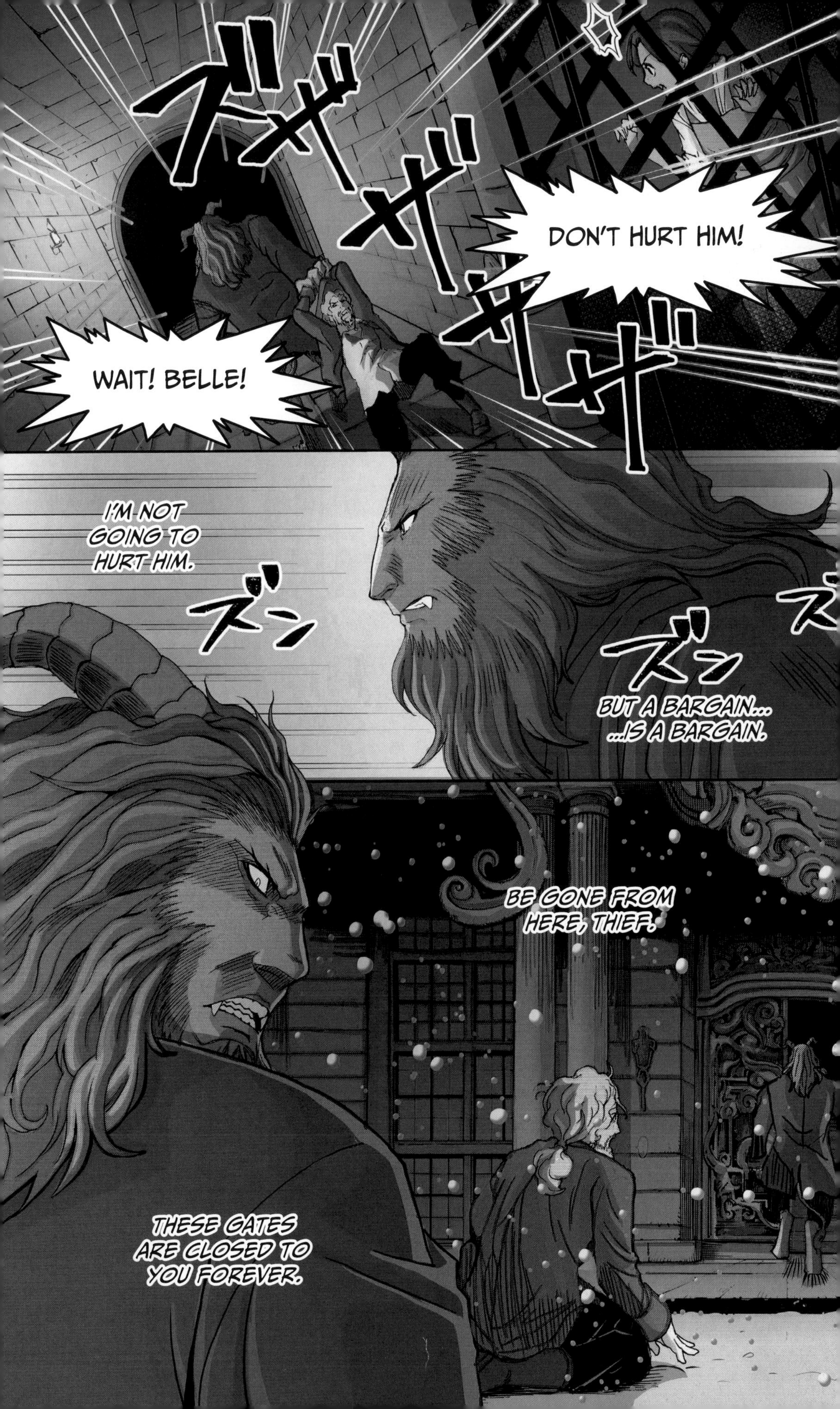
ズザザザ
DON'T HURT HIM!
WAIT! BELLE!
ズ
ズン
I'M NOT GOING TO HURT HIM.
ズン
BUT A BARGAIN... ...IS A BARGAIN.
BE GONE FROM HERE, THIEF.
THESE GATES ARE CLOSED TO YOU FOREVER.

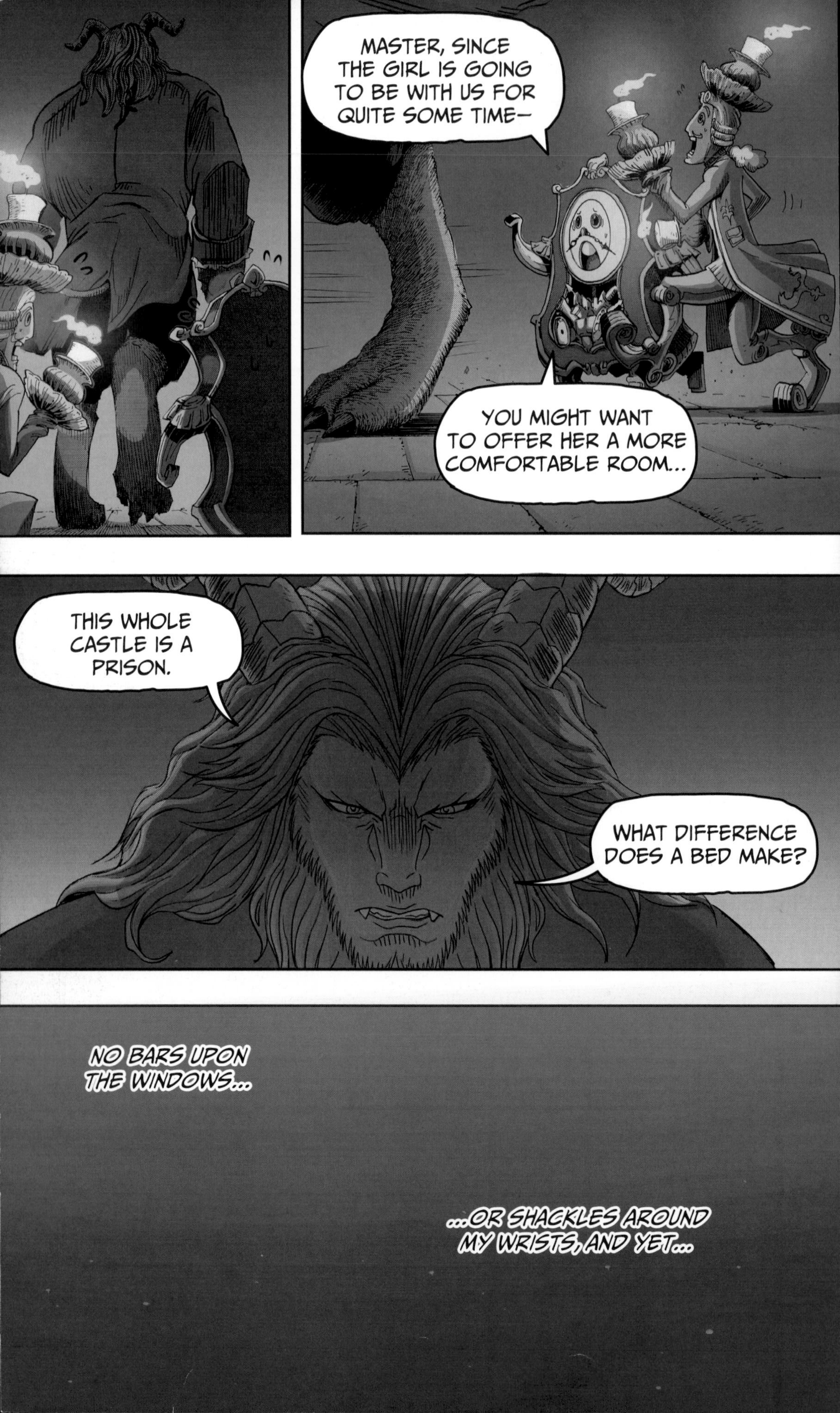
MASTER, SINCE THE GIRL IS GOING TO BE WITH US FOR QUITE SOME TIME–
YOU MIGHT WANT TO OFFER HER A MORE COMFORTABLE ROOM...
THIS WHOLE CASTLE IS A PRISON.
WHAT DIFFERENCE DOES A BED MAKE?
NO BARS UPON THE WINDOWS...
...OR SHACKLES AROUND MY WRISTS, AND YET...

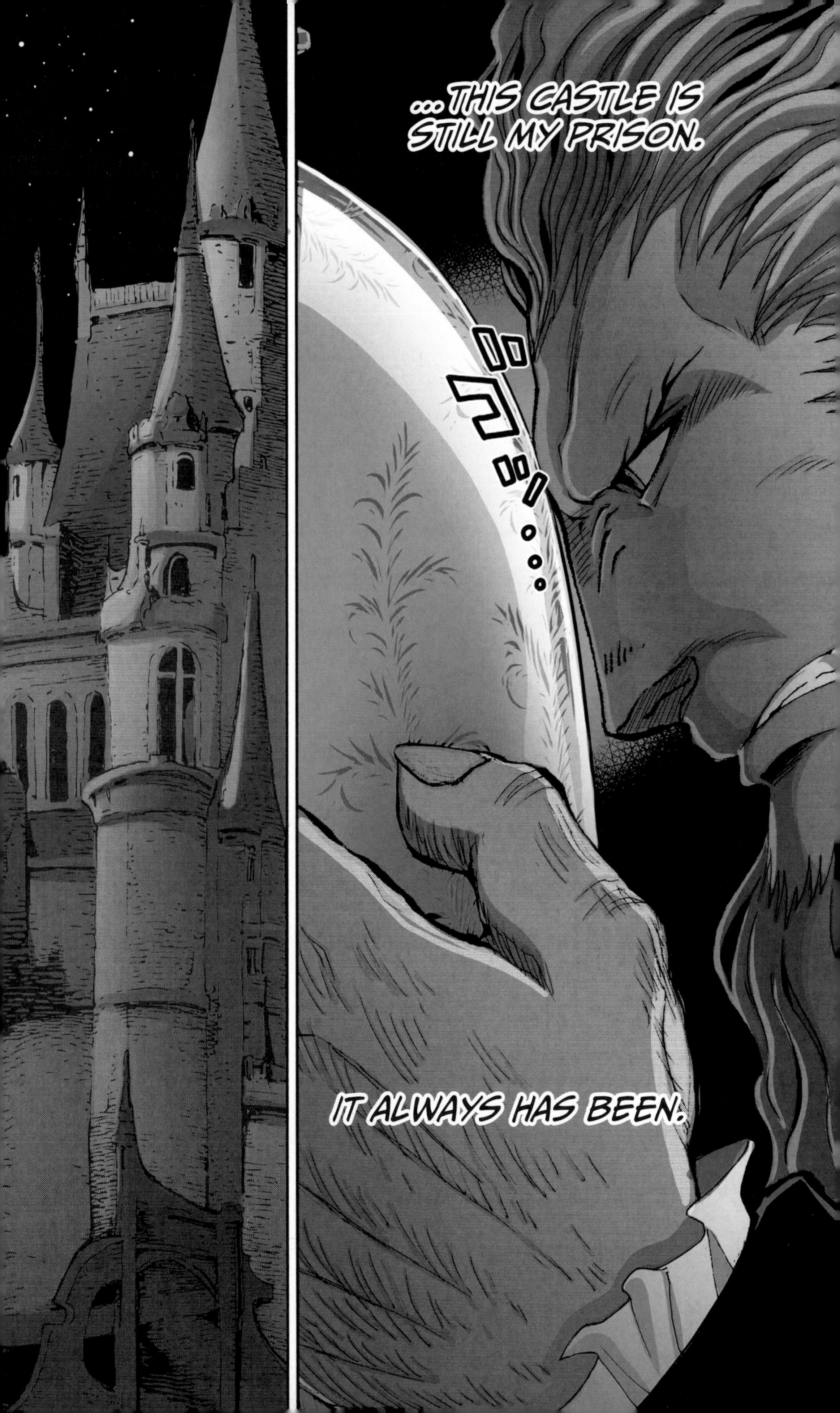
...THIS CASTLE IS STILL MY PRISON.
IT ALWAYS HAS BEEN.

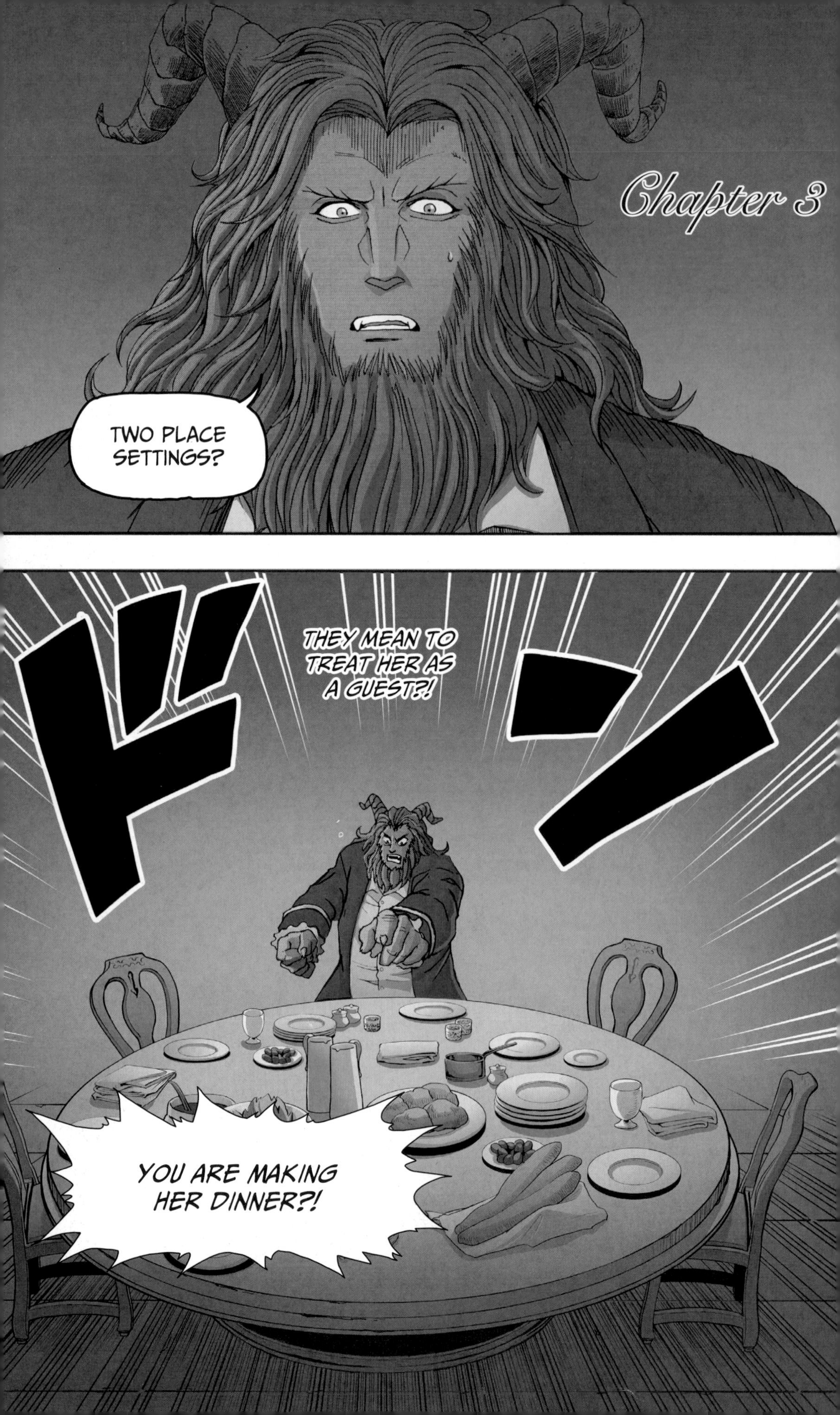
Chapter 3
TWO PLACE SETTINGS?
ドン
THEY MEAN TO TREAT HER AS A GUEST?!
YOU ARE MAKING HER DINNER?!

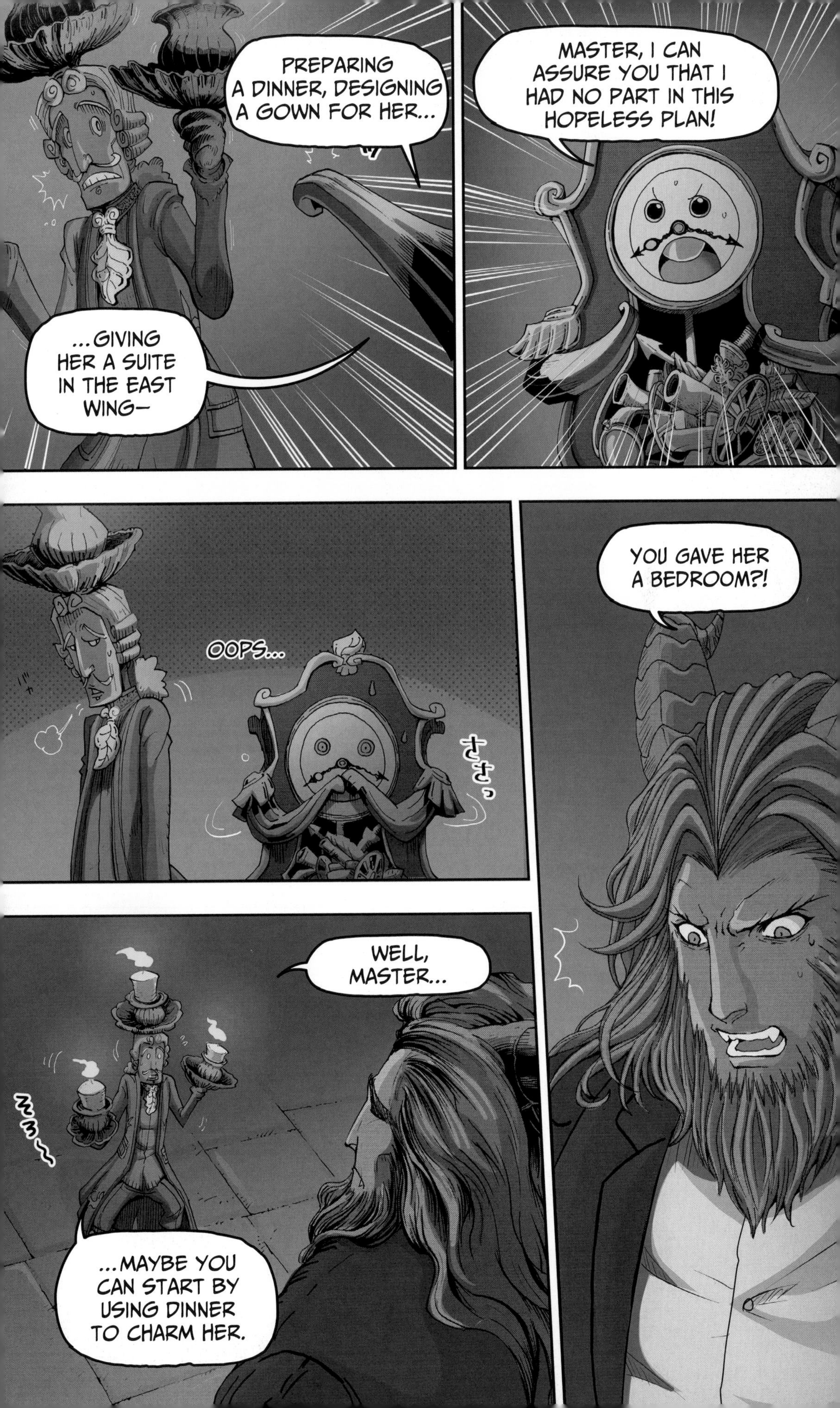
MASTER, I CAN ASSURE YOU THAT I HAD NO PART IN THIS HOPELESS PLAN!
PREPARING A DINNER, DESIGNING A GOWN FOR HER...
...GIVING HER A SUITE IN THE EAST WING—
YOU GAVE HER A BEDROOM?!
OOPS...
ささっ
WELL, MASTER...
...MAYBE YOU CAN START BY USING DINNER TO CHARM HER.

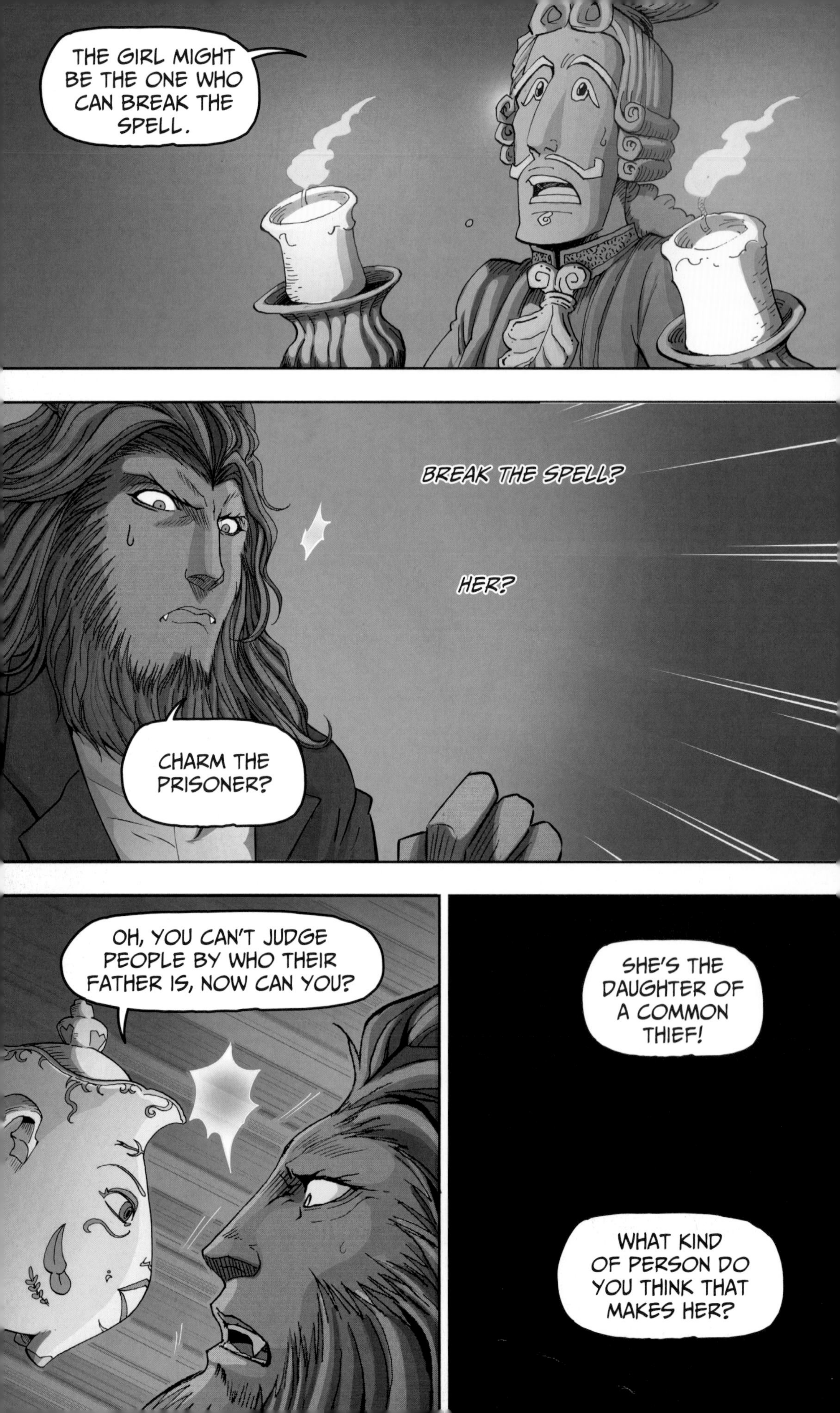
THE GIRL MIGHT BE THE ONE WHO CAN BREAK THE SPELL.
BREAK THE SPELL?
HER?
CHARM THE PRISONER?
SHE'S THE DAUGHTER OF A COMMON THIEF!
WHAT KIND OF PERSON DO YOU THINK THAT MAKES HER?
OH, YOU CAN'T JUDGE PEOPLE BY WHO THEIR FATHER IS, NOW CAN YOU?

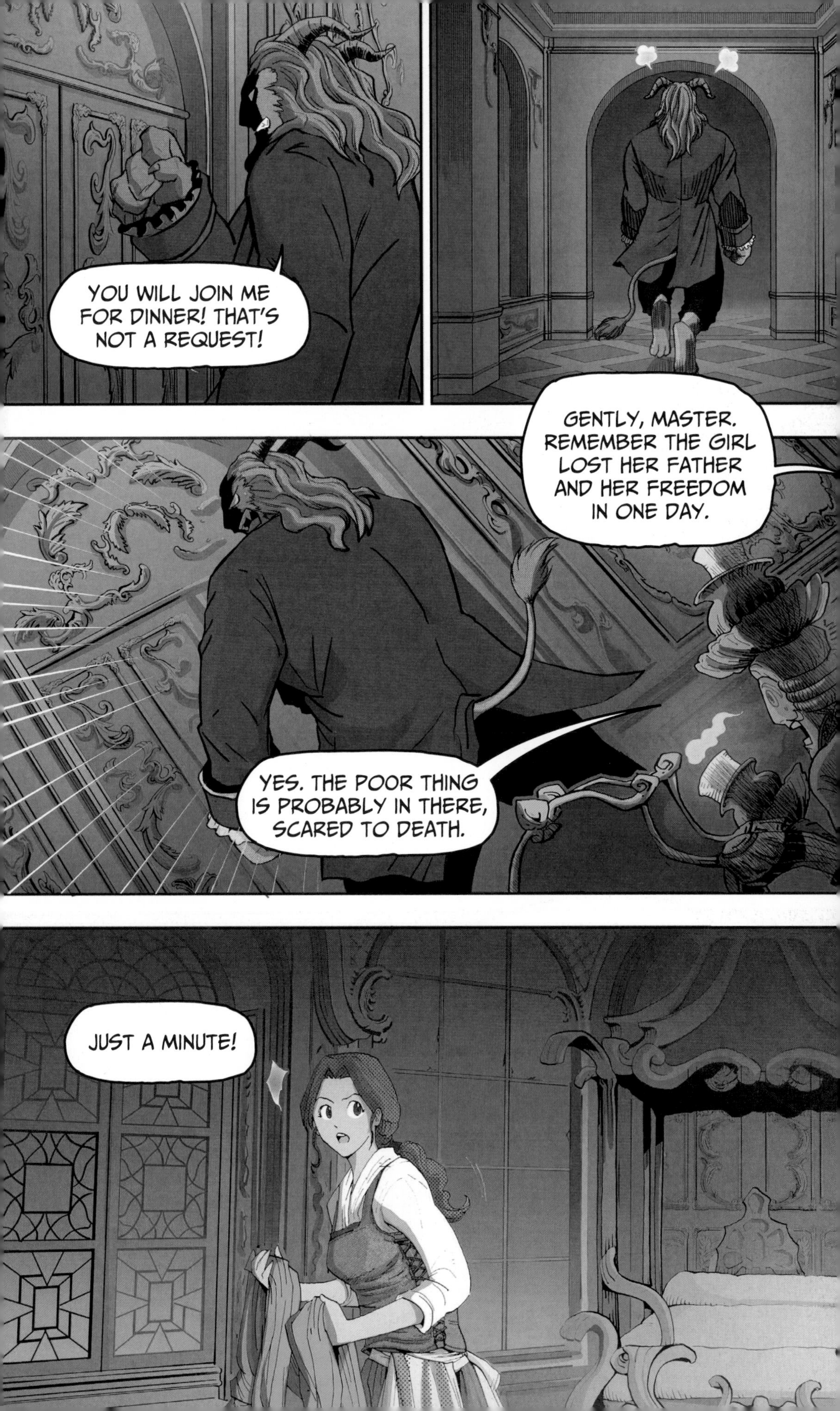
YOU WILL JOIN ME FOR DINNER! THAT'S NOT A REQUEST!
GENTLY, MASTER. REMEMBER THE GIRL LOST HER FATHER AND HER FREEDOM IN ONE DAY.
YES. THE POOR THING IS PROBABLY IN THERE, SCARED TO DEATH.
JUST A MINUTE!

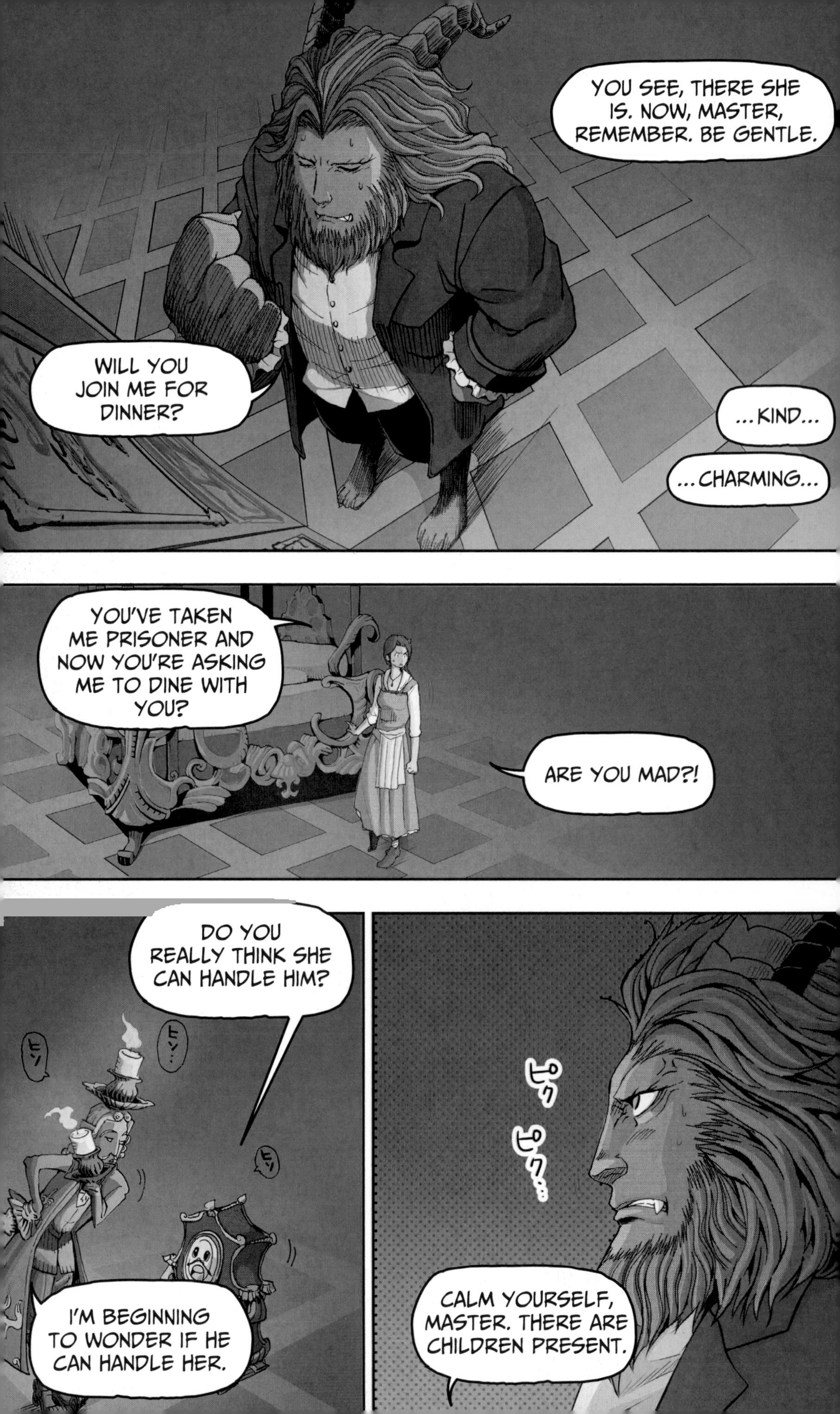
YOU SEE, THERE SHE IS. NOW, MASTER, REMEMBER. BE GENTLE.
...KIND...
...CHARMING...
WILL YOU JOIN ME FOR DINNER?
YOU'VE TAKEN ME PRISONER AND NOW YOU'RE ASKING ME TO DINE WITH YOU?
ARE YOU MAD?!
ピク
ピク…
CALM YOURSELF, MASTER. THERE ARE CHILDREN PRESENT.
DO YOU REALLY THINK SHE CAN HANDLE HIM?
ヒソ…
ヒソ
ヒソ
I'M BEGINNING TO WONDER IF HE CAN HANDLE HER.

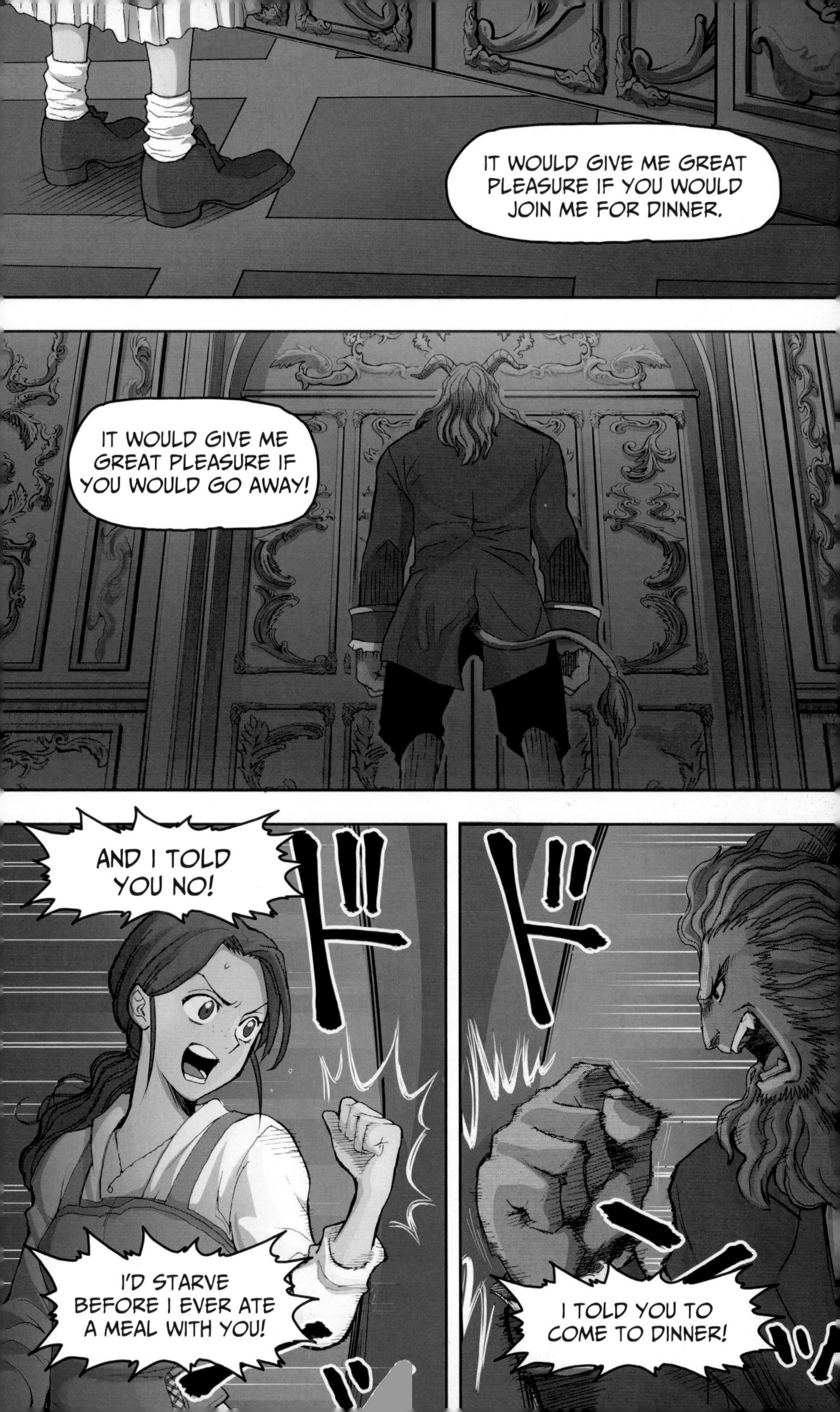

IT WOULD GIVE ME GREAT PLEASURE IF YOU WOULD JOIN ME FOR DINNER.
IT WOULD GIVE ME GREAT PLEASURE IF YOU WOULD GO AWAY!
ド
I TOLD YOU TO COME TO DINNER!
AND I TOLD YOU NO!
ド
I'D STARVE BEFORE I EVER ATE A MEAL WITH YOU!

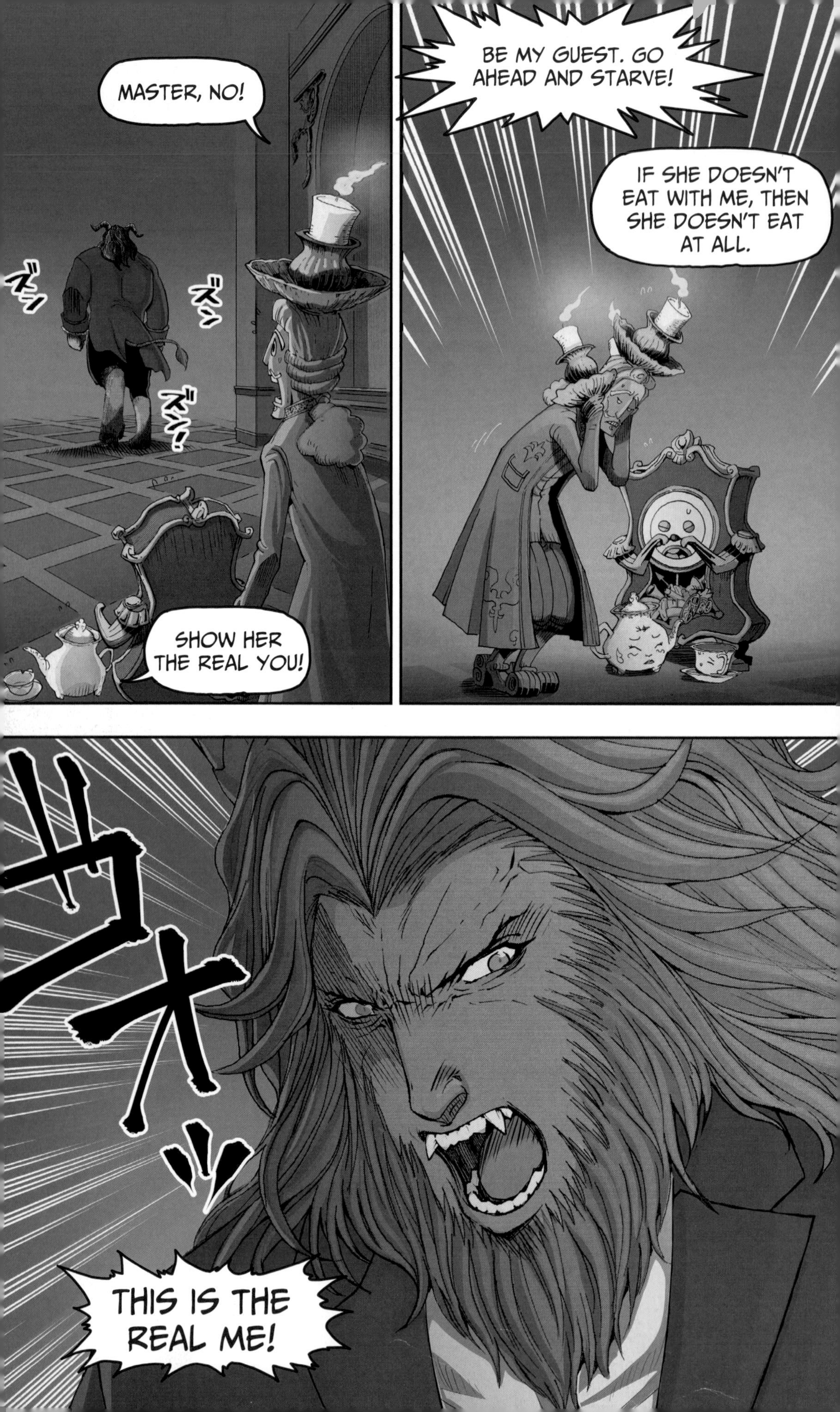
BE MY GUEST. GO AHEAD AND STARVE!
IF SHE DOESN'T EAT WITH ME, THEN SHE DOESN'T EAT AT ALL.
MASTER, NO!
ズン
ズン
ズン!
SHOW HER THE REAL YOU!
THIS IS THE REAL ME!

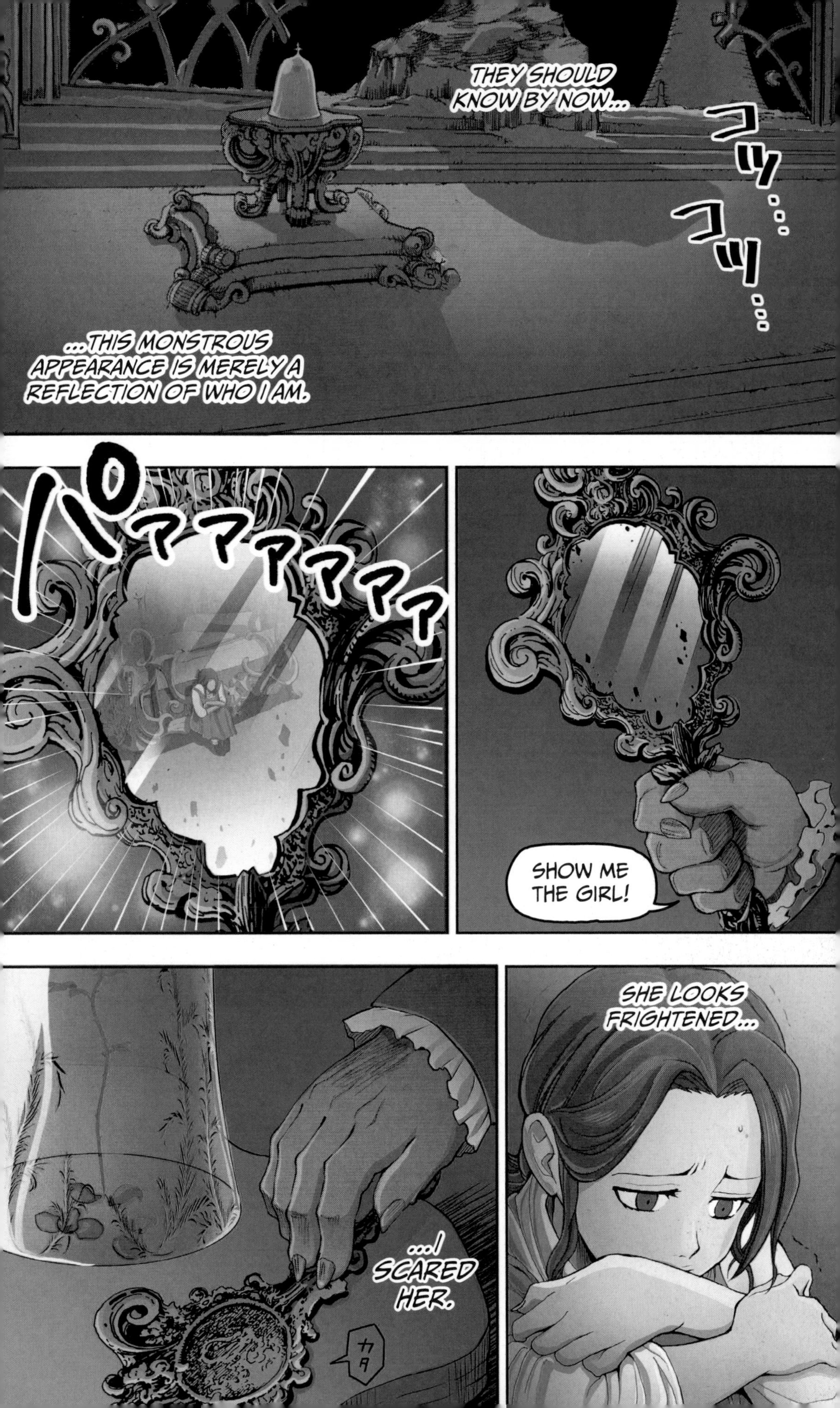
THEY SHOULD KNOW BY NOW...
コツ...
コツ...
...THIS MONSTROUS APPEARANCE IS MERELY A REFLECTION OF WHO I AM.
SHOW ME THE GIRL!
パァァァァァァ
SHE LOOKS FRIGHTENED...
...I SCARED HER.
カタ

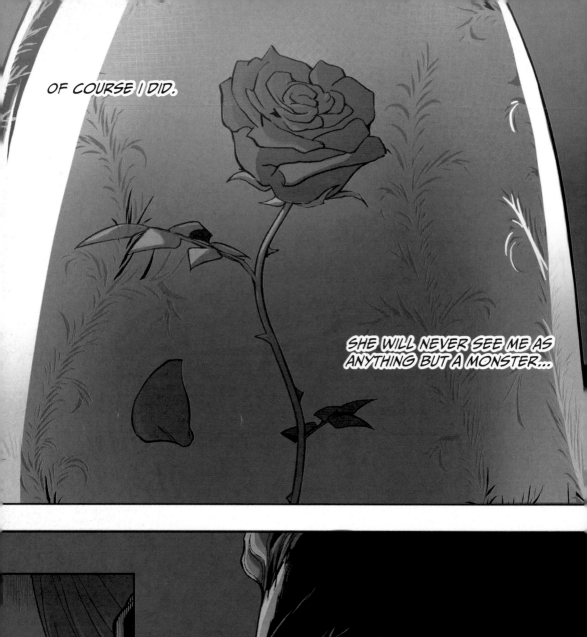

OF COURSE I DID.

SHE WILL NEVER SEE ME AS ANYTHING BUT A MONSTER...

...BECAUSE I HAVE NEVER BEEN ANYTHING MORE.

MOTHER...

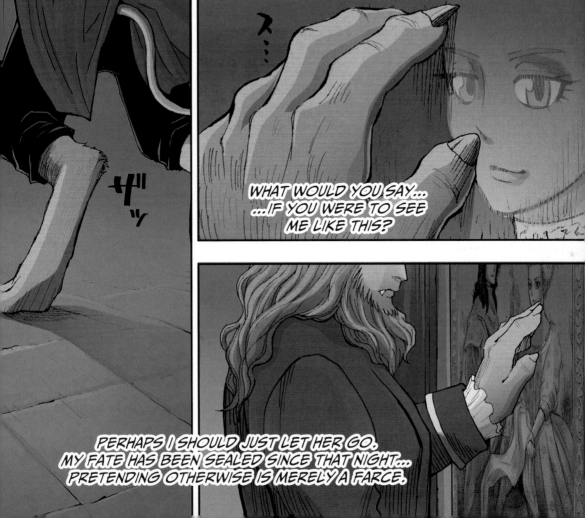

WHAT WOULD YOU SAY...
...IF YOU WERE TO SEE
ME LIKE THIS?

PERHAPS I SHOULD JUST LET HER GO.
MY FATE HAS BEEN SEALED SINCE THAT NIGHT...
PRETENDING OTHERWISE IS MERELY A FARCE.

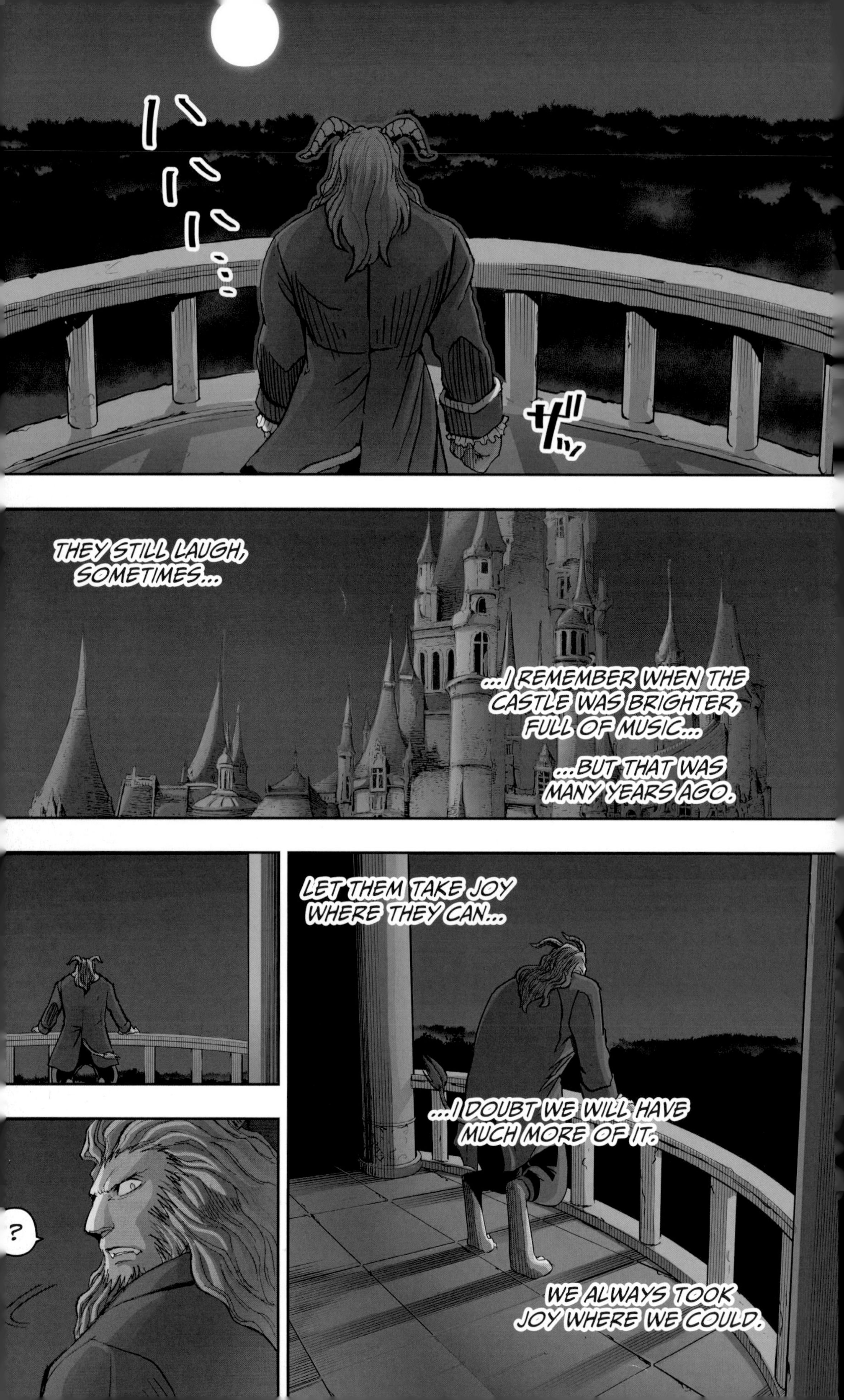
ハハハ…
ザッ
THEY STILL LAUGH, SOMETIMES...
...I REMEMBER WHEN THE CASTLE WAS BRIGHTER, FULL OF MUSIC...
...BUT THAT WAS MANY YEARS AGO.
LET THEM TAKE JOY WHERE THEY CAN...
...I DOUBT WE WILL HAVE MUCH MORE OF IT.
WE ALWAYS TOOK JOY WHERE WE COULD.
?

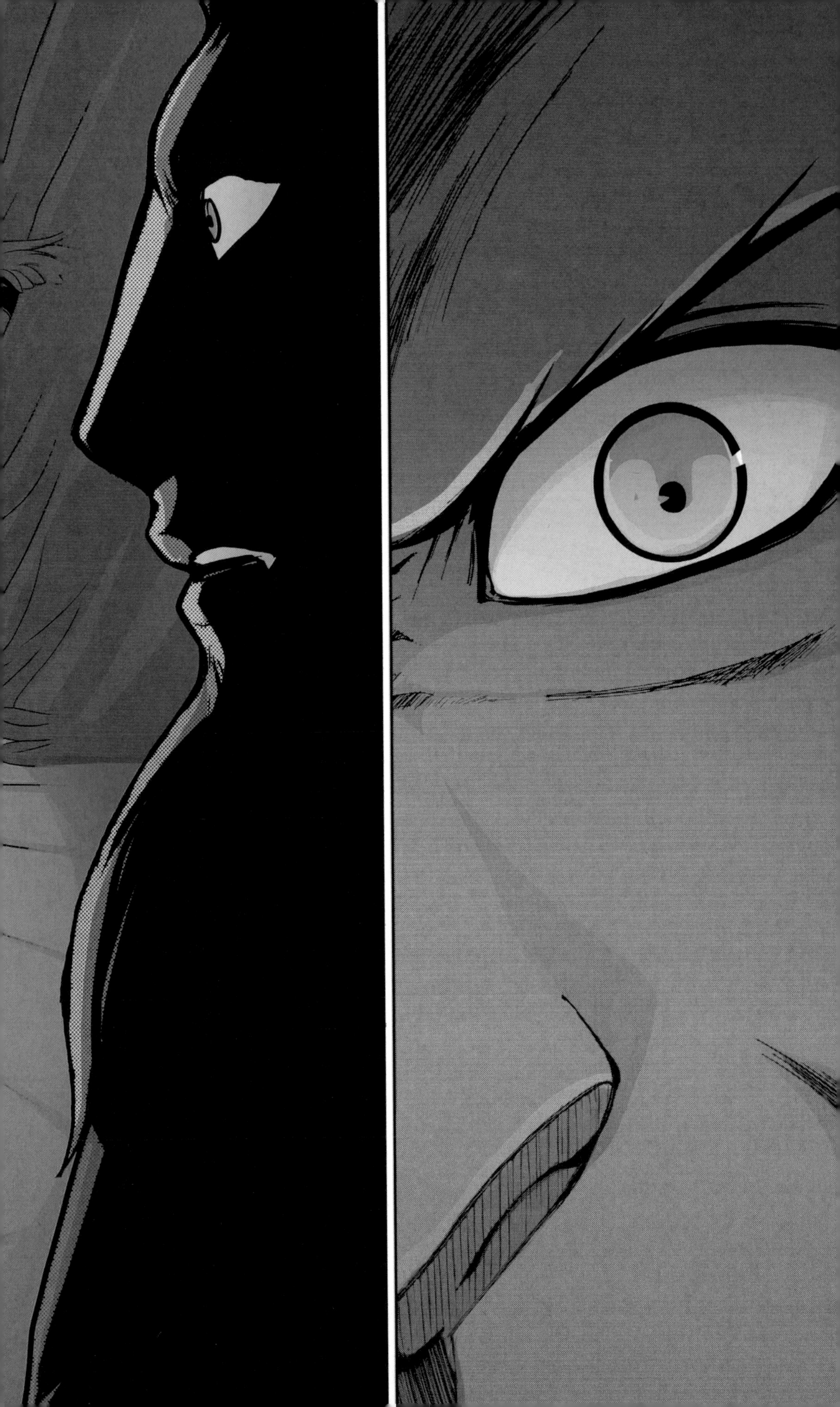

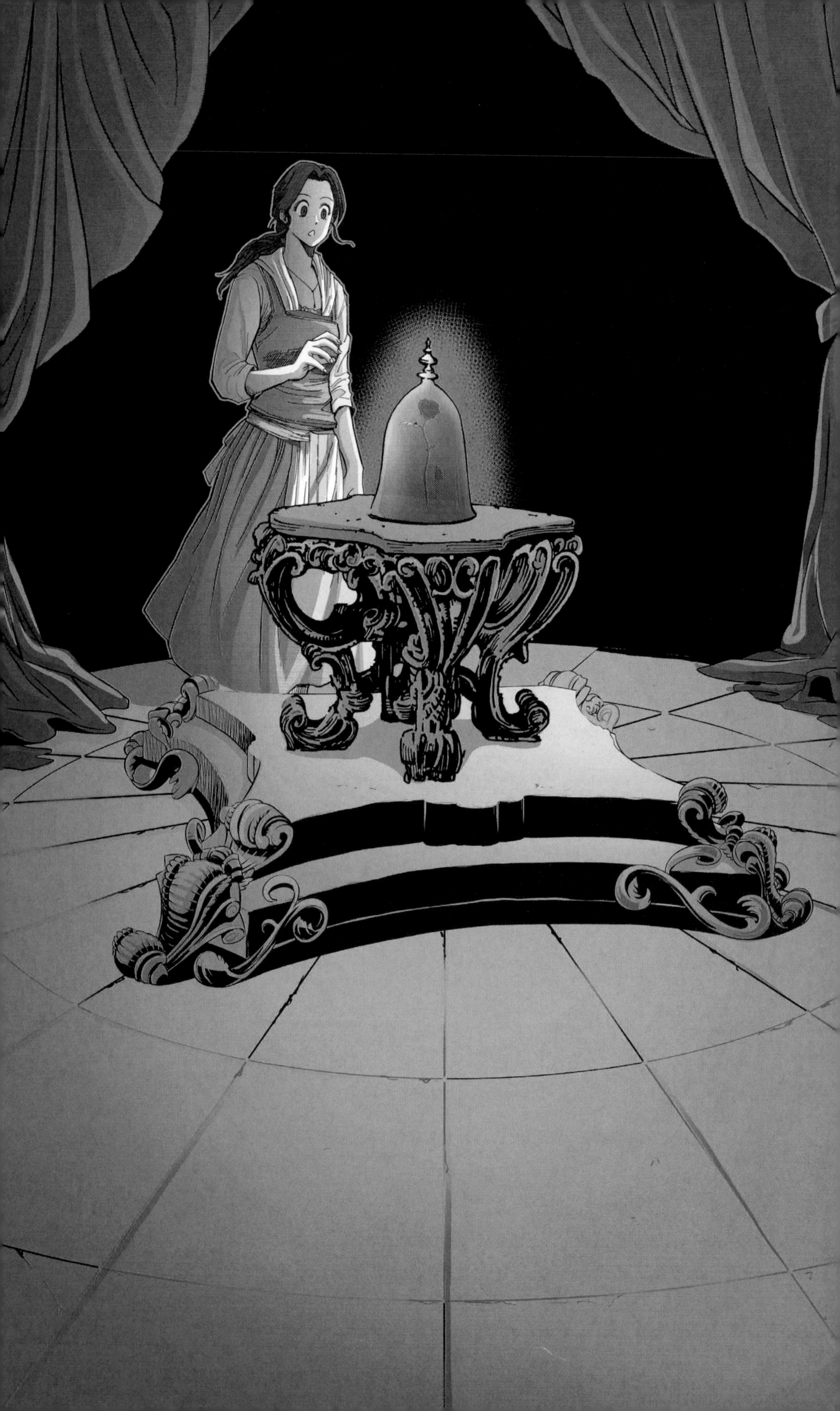

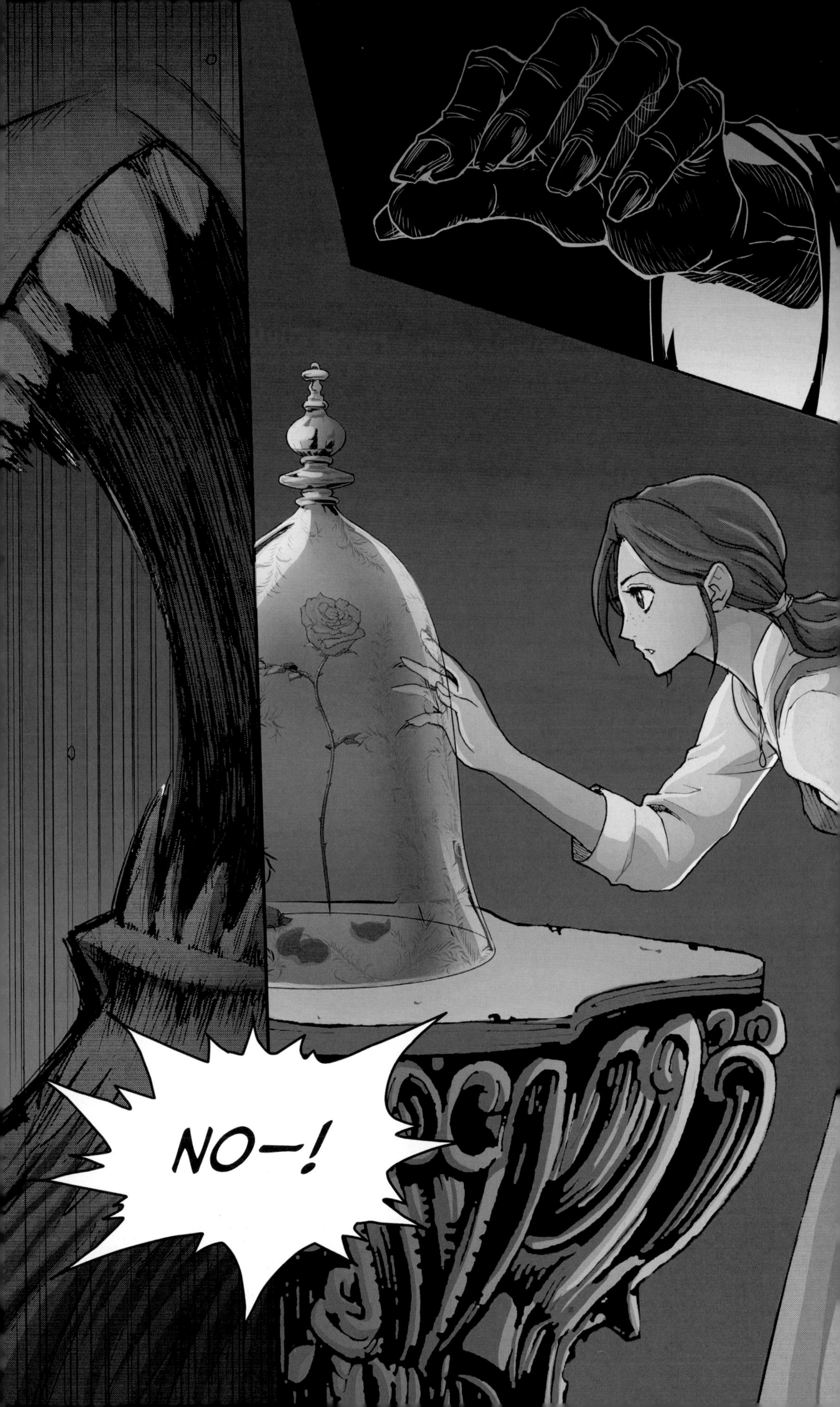
NO—!

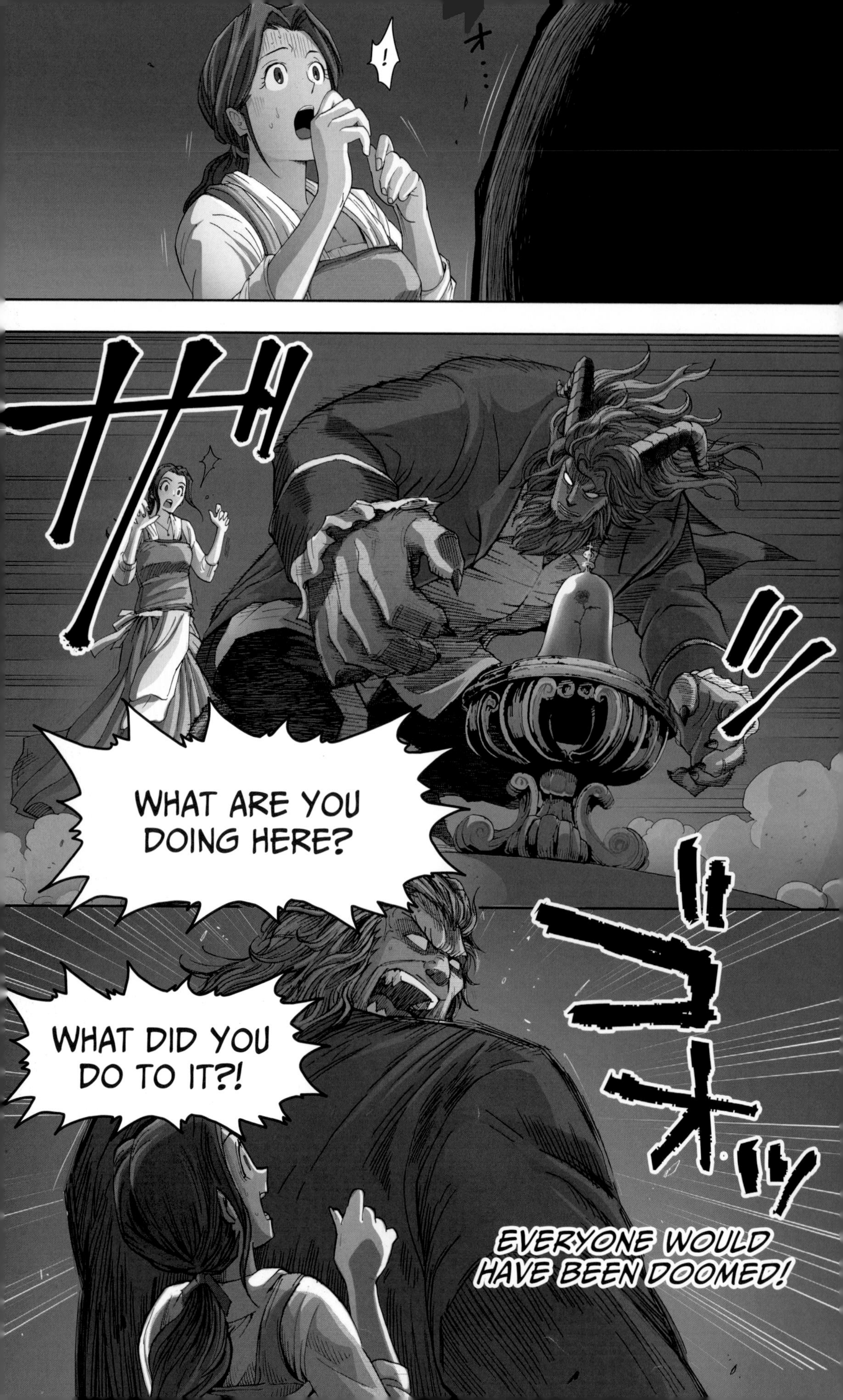
!
WHAT ARE YOU DOING HERE?
WHAT DID YOU DO TO IT?!
EVERYONE WOULD HAVE BEEN DOOMED!

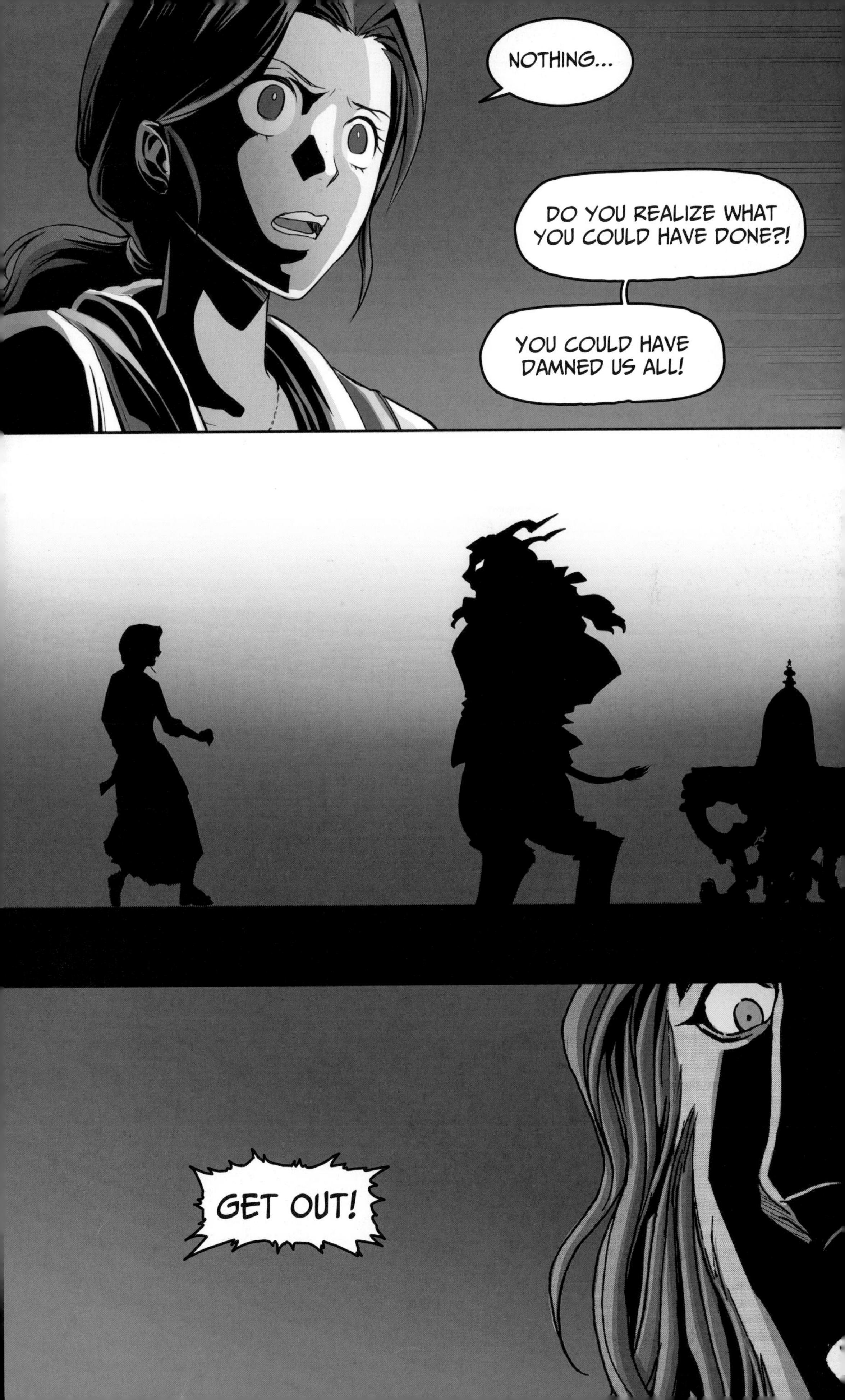
NOTHING...
DO YOU REALIZE WHAT YOU COULD HAVE DONE?!
YOU COULD HAVE DAMNED US ALL!
GET OUT!

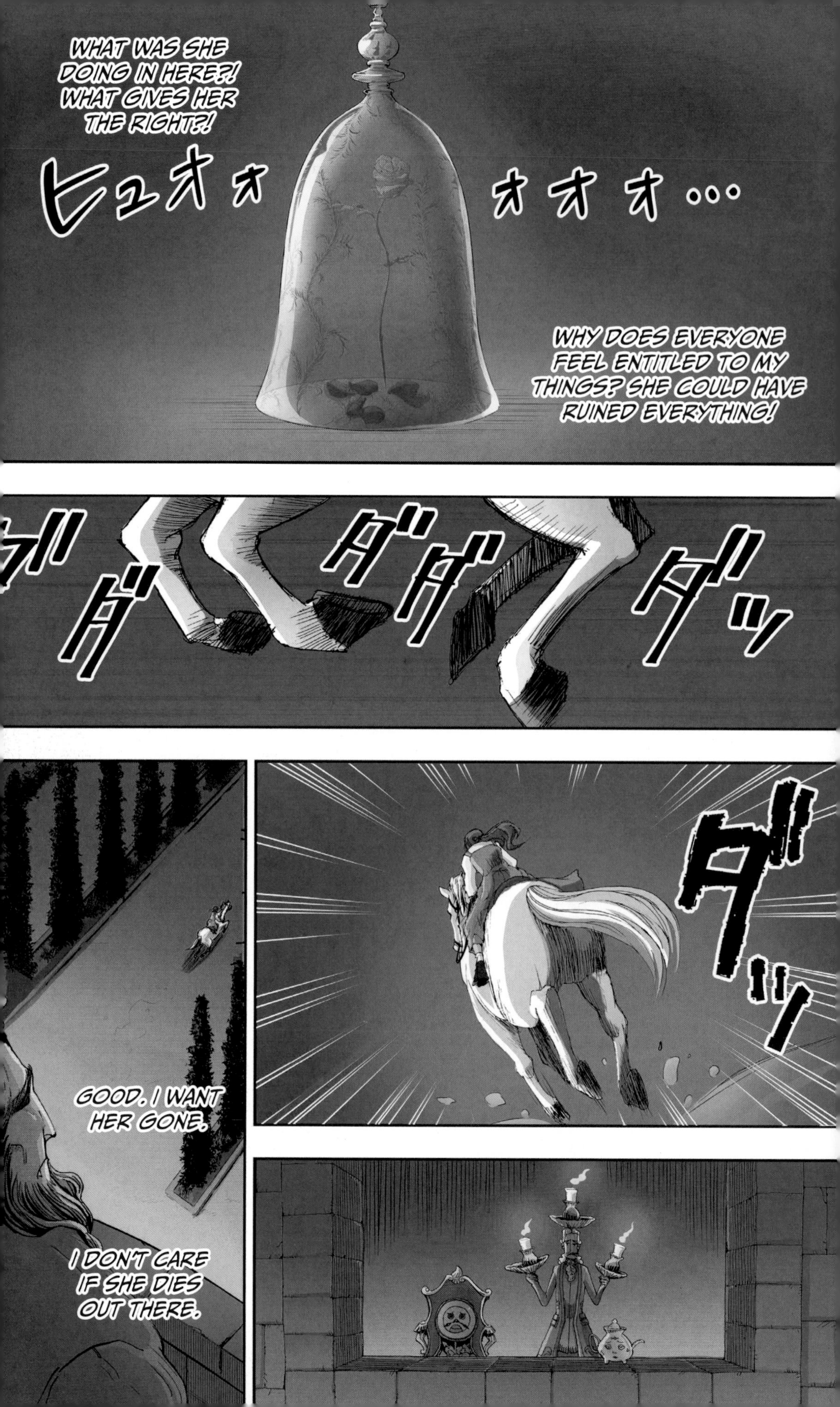
WHAT WAS SHE DOING IN HERE?! WHAT GIVES HER THE RIGHT?!
ヒュオォ
オオオ…
WHY DOES EVERYONE FEEL ENTITLED TO MY THINGS? SHE COULD HAVE RUINED EVERYTHING!
ダッ
ダダ
ダダ
ダッ
GOOD. I WANT HER GONE.
I DON'T CARE IF SHE DIES OUT THERE.

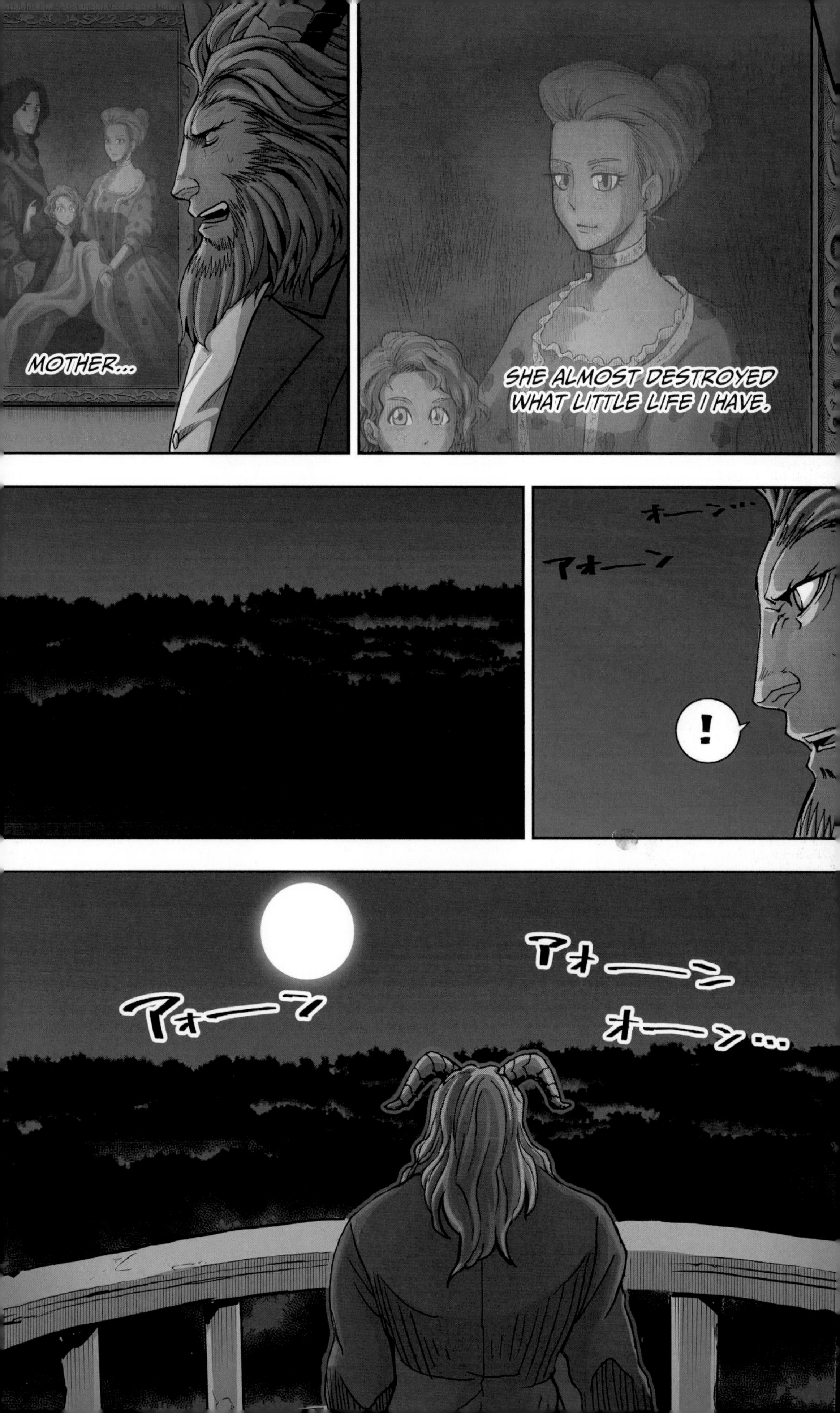
SHE ALMOST DESTROYED WHAT LITTLE LIFE I HAVE.
MOTHER...
オーン‥
アオーン
!
アオーン
オーン…
アオーン

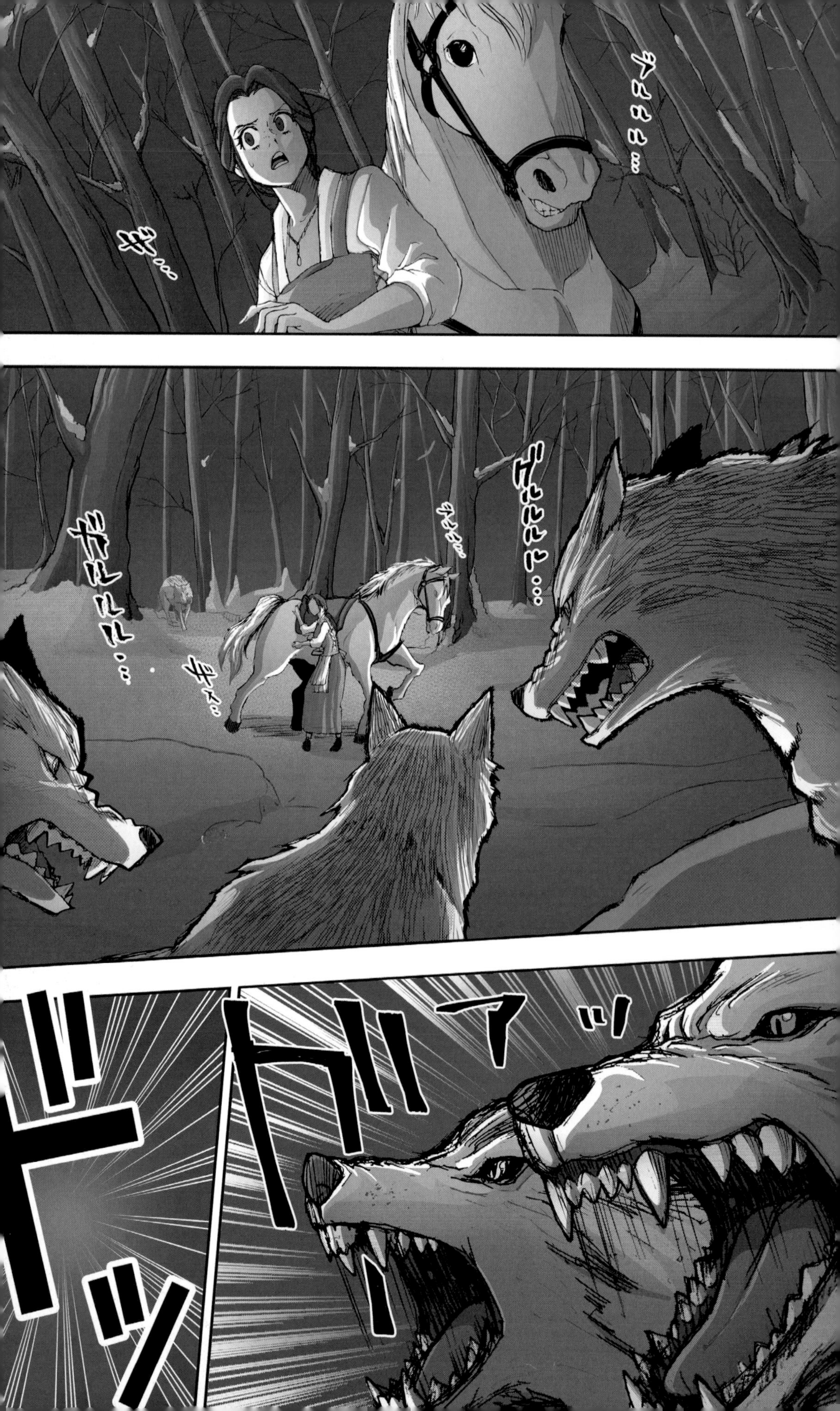
ブルルル…
ザ…
グルルルル…
ブルル…
ガルルルル…
ザス…
ガアァッ
ドッ

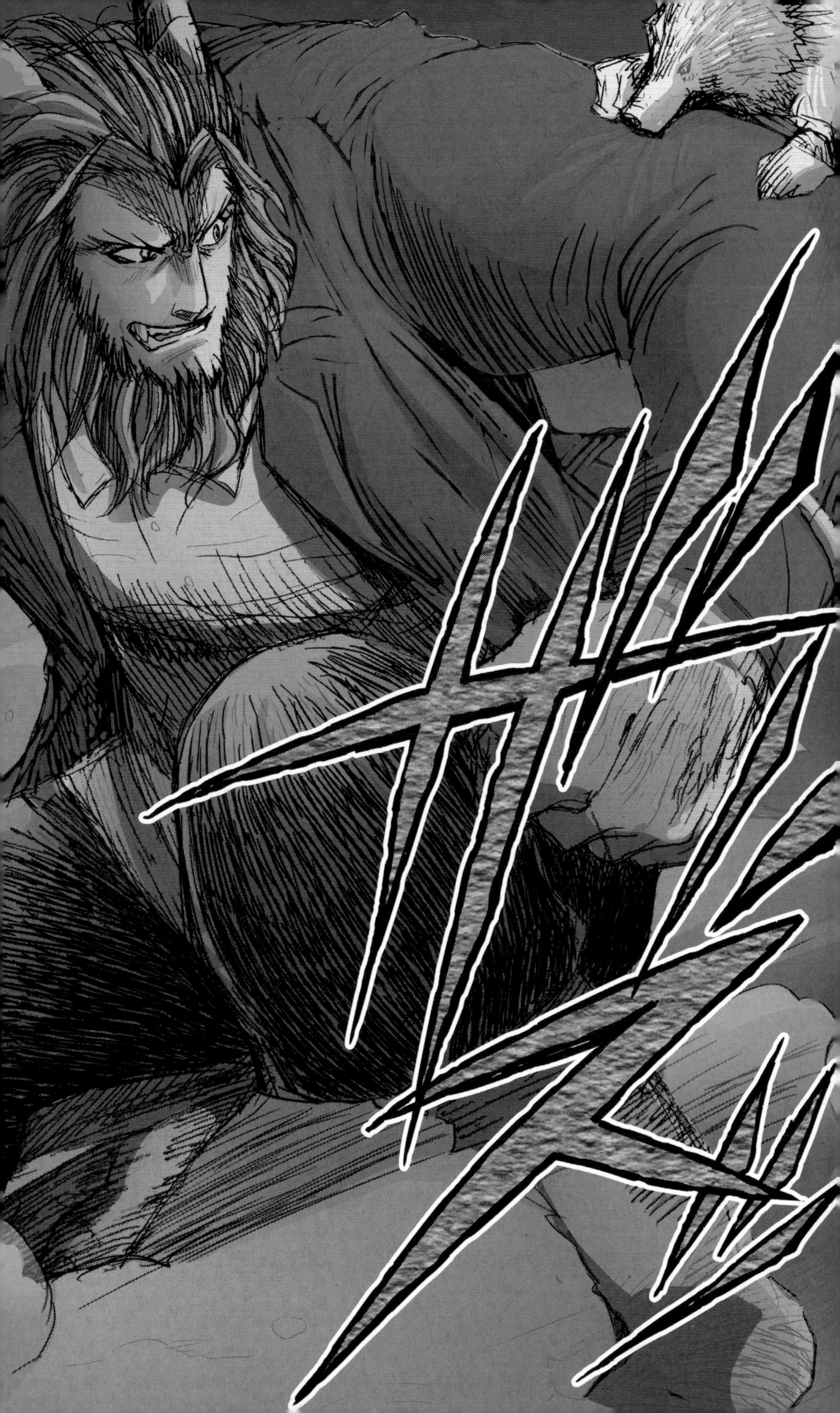

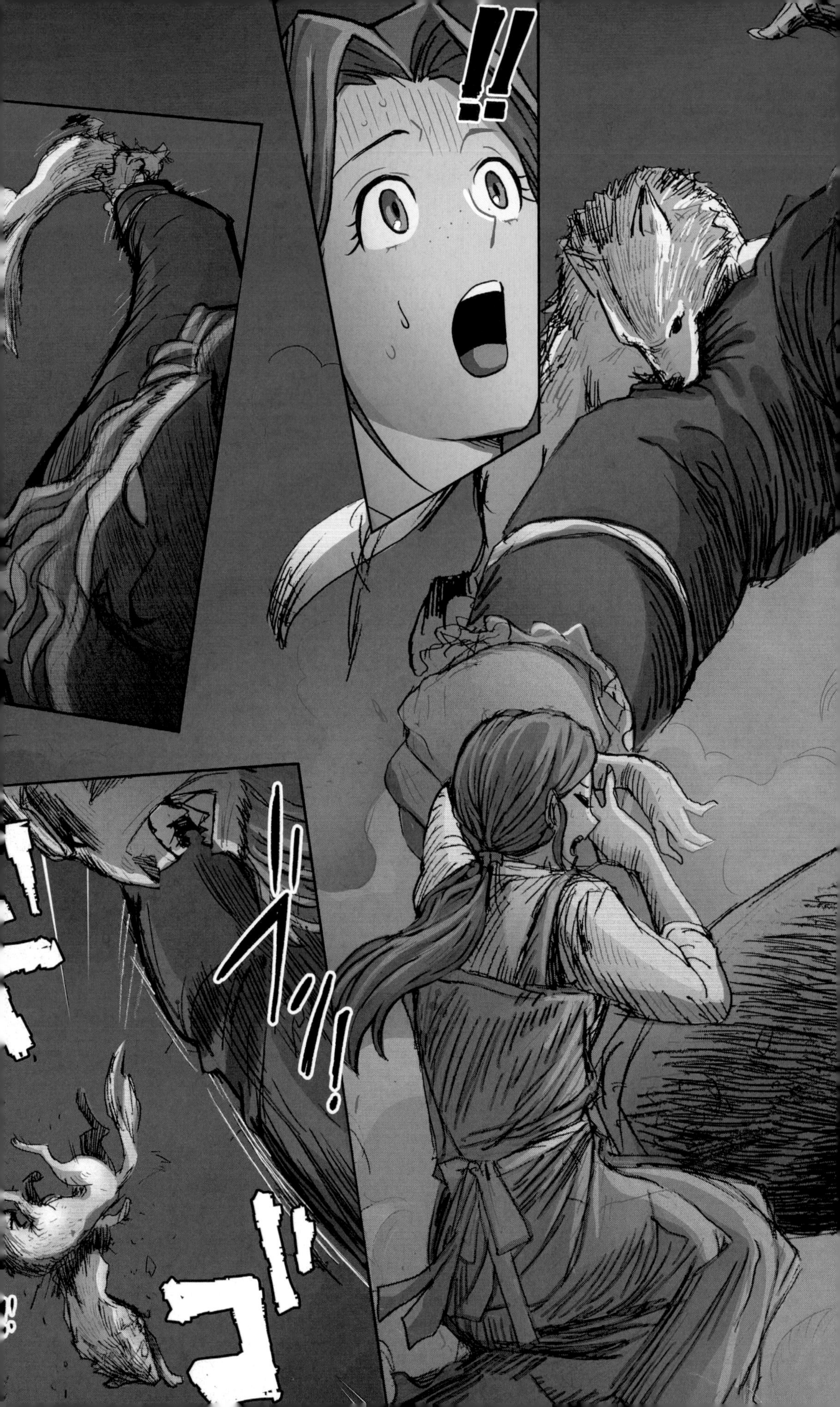
!!

THIS IS THE FIRST TIME...

...I HAVE EVER USED IT TO HELP SOMEONE.

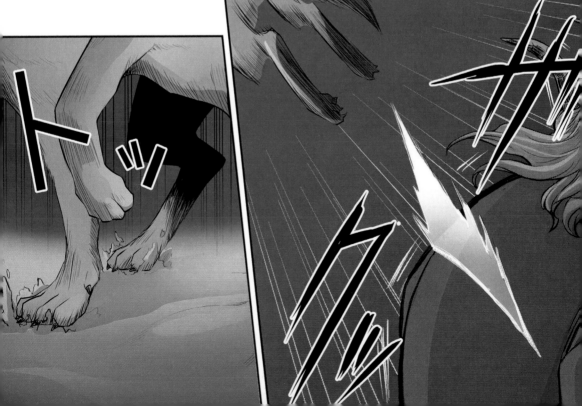

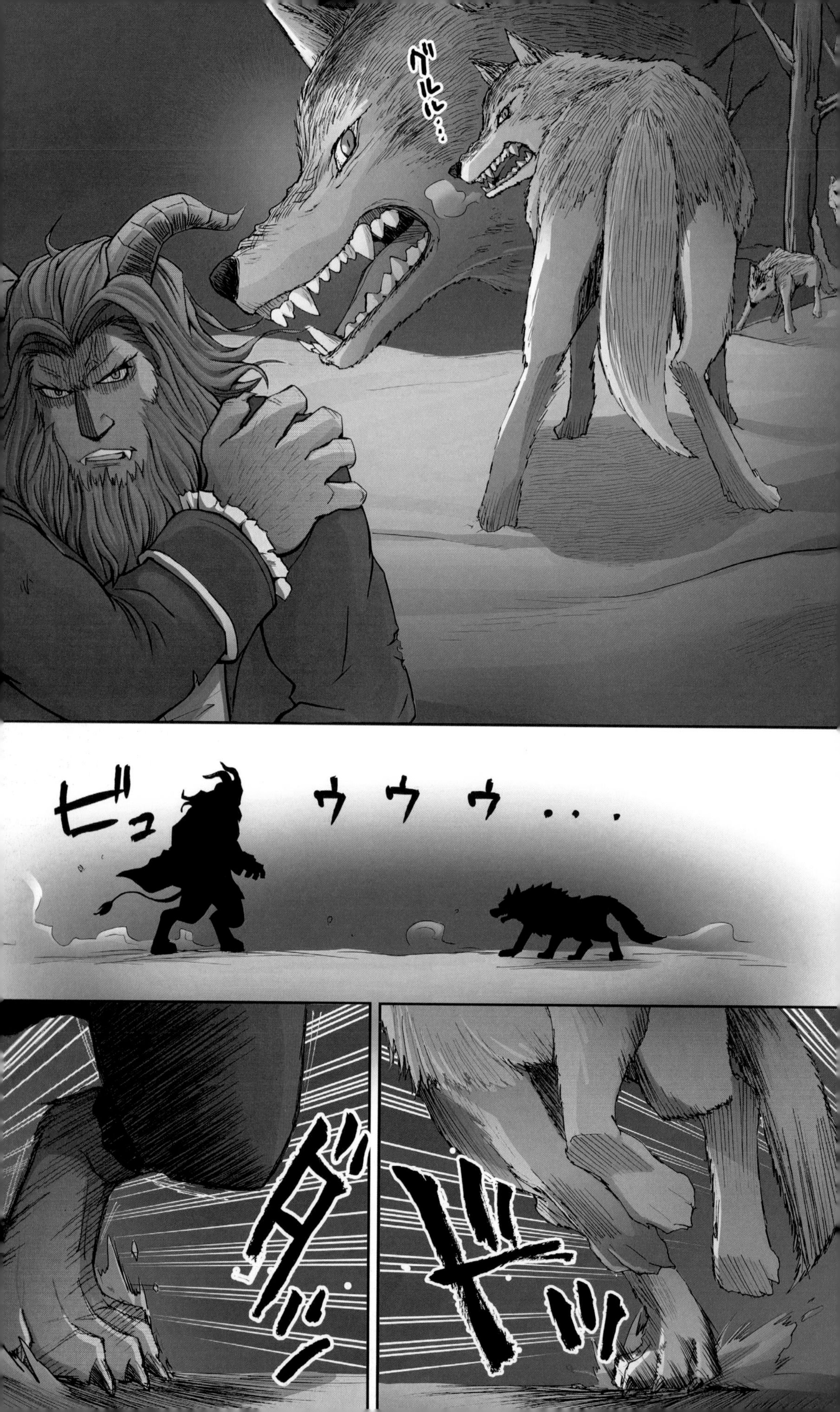
グルル・・・
ビュウウウ・・・
ザッ
ダッ

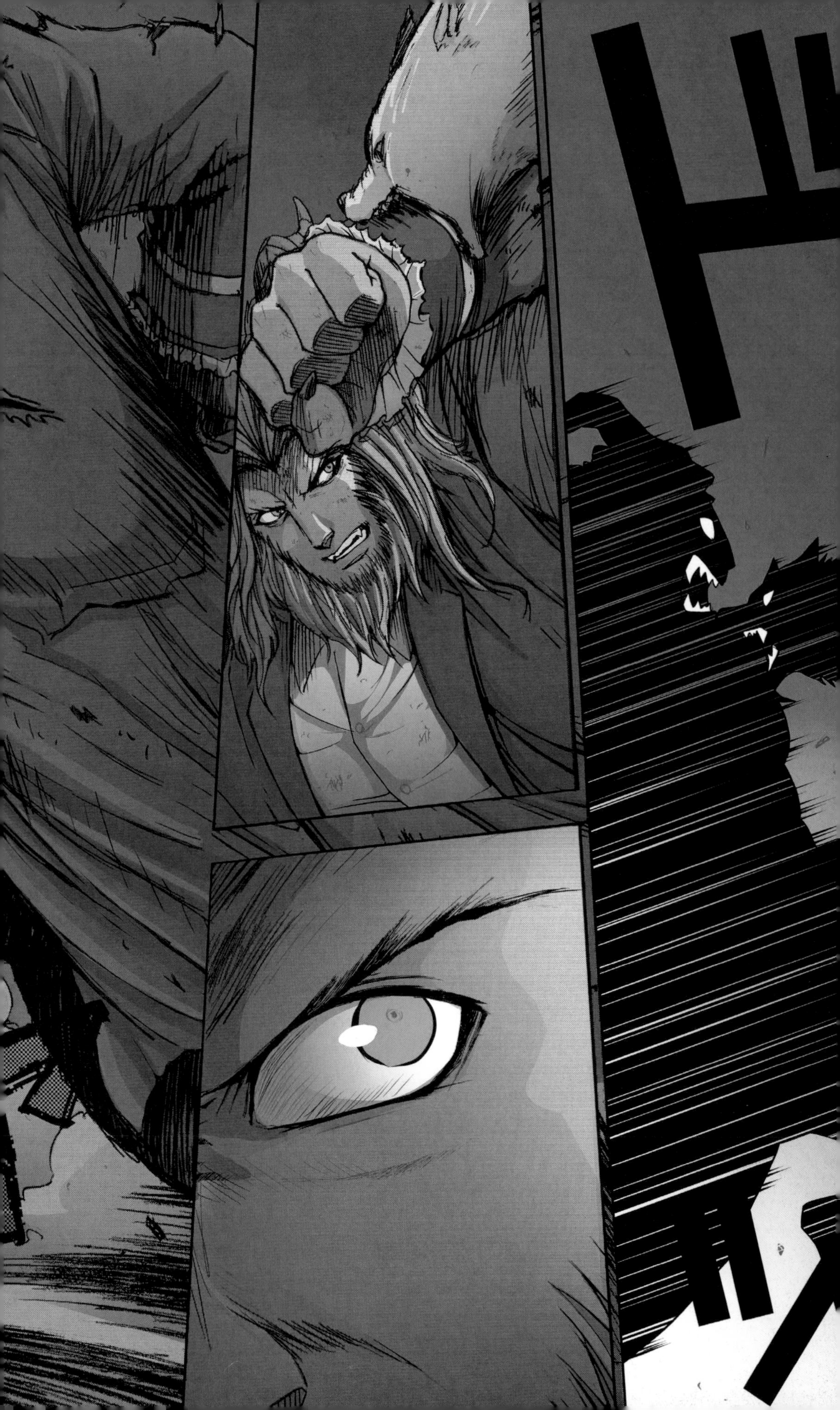

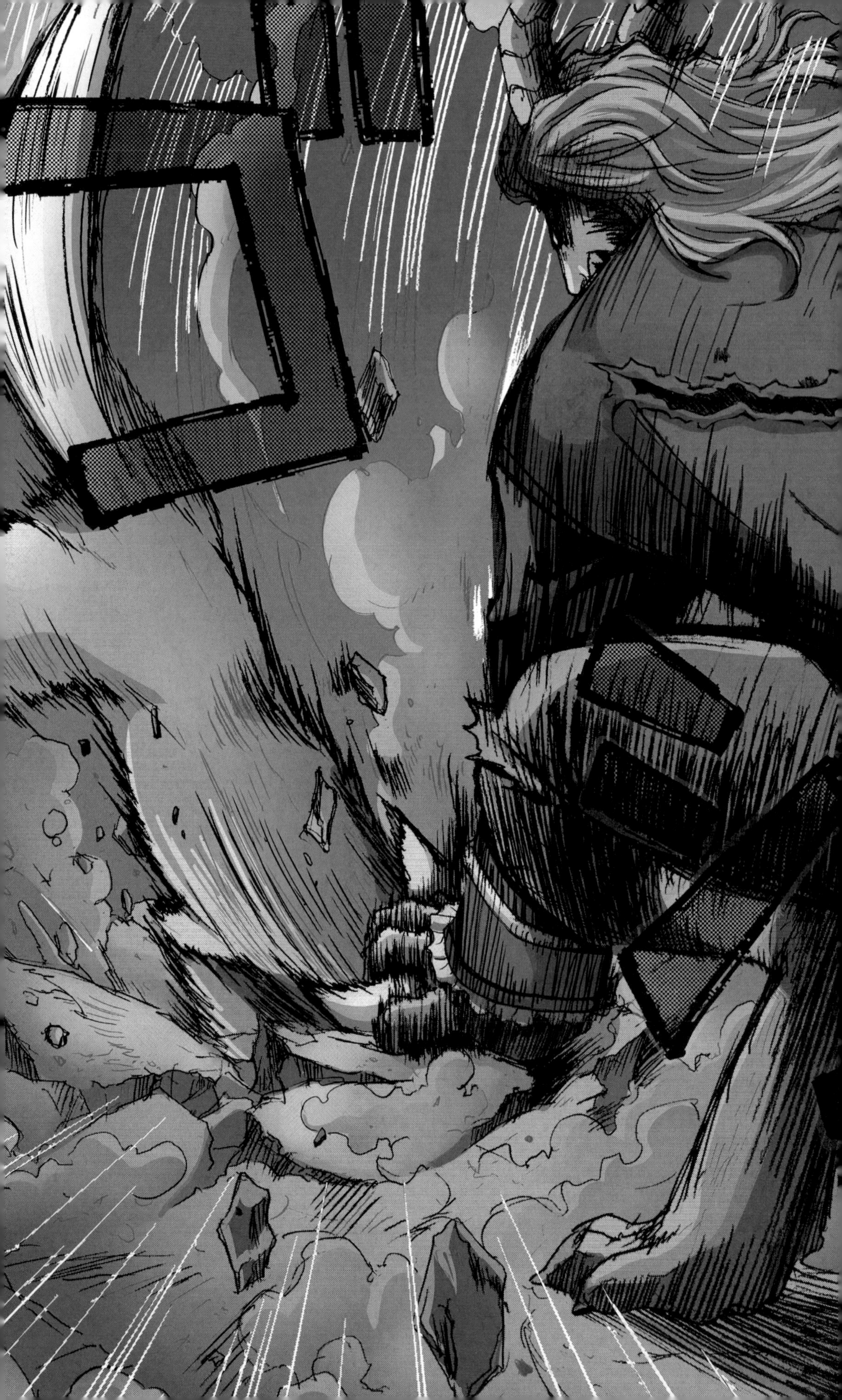

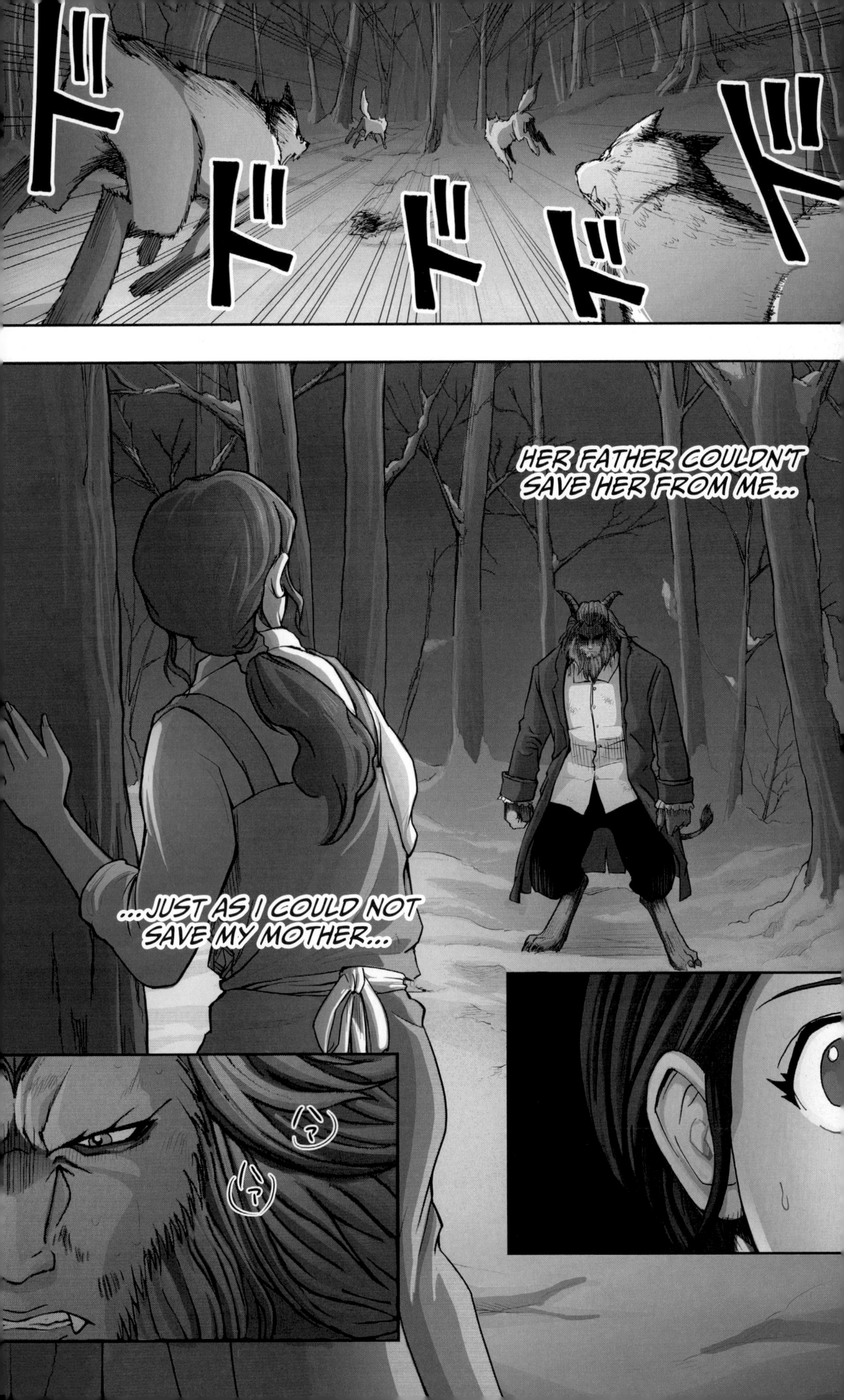
ドドドドド
HER FATHER COULDN'T SAVE HER FROM ME...
...JUST AS I COULD NOT SAVE MY MOTHER...

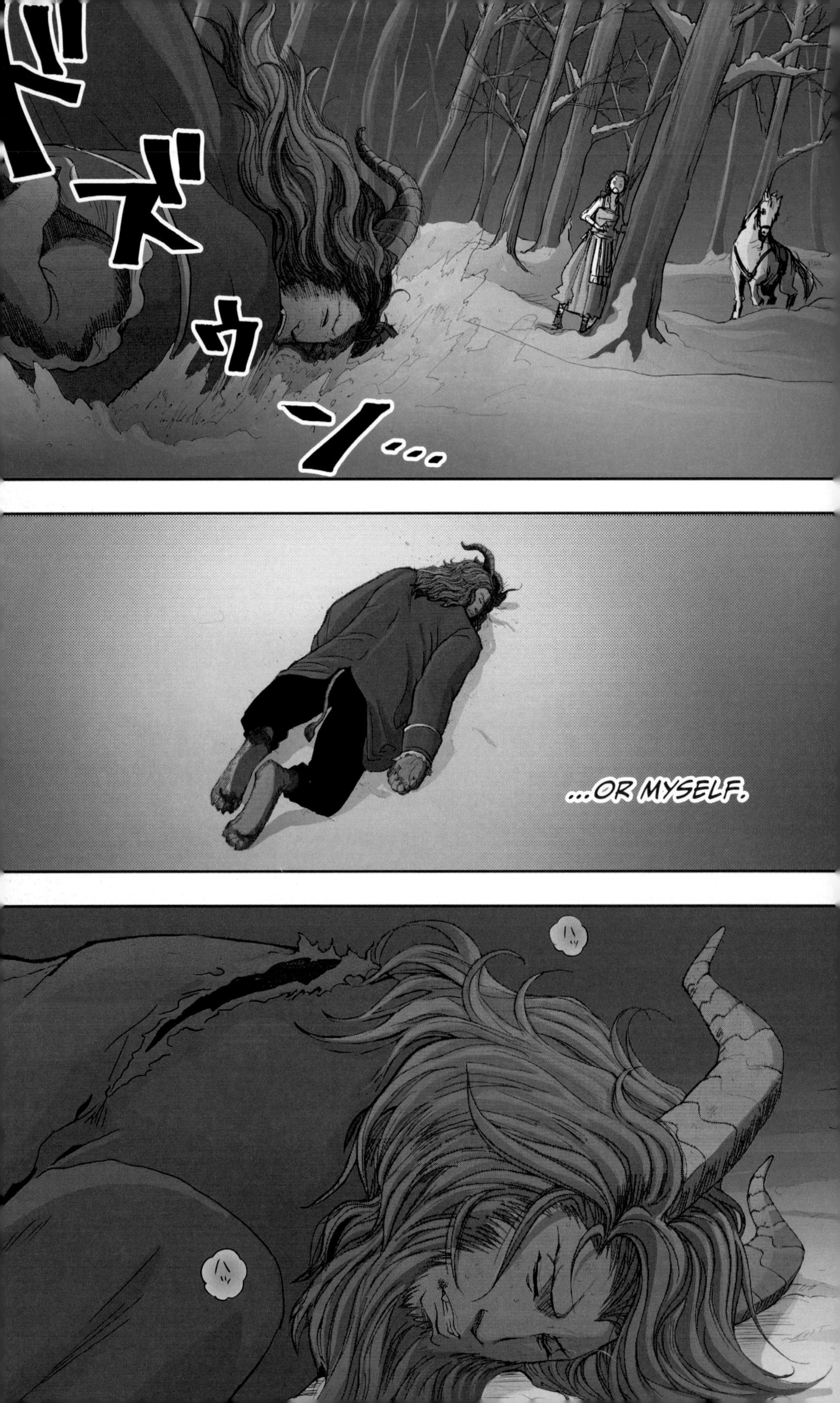
ズゥン…
...OR MYSELF.
ハッ
ハッ

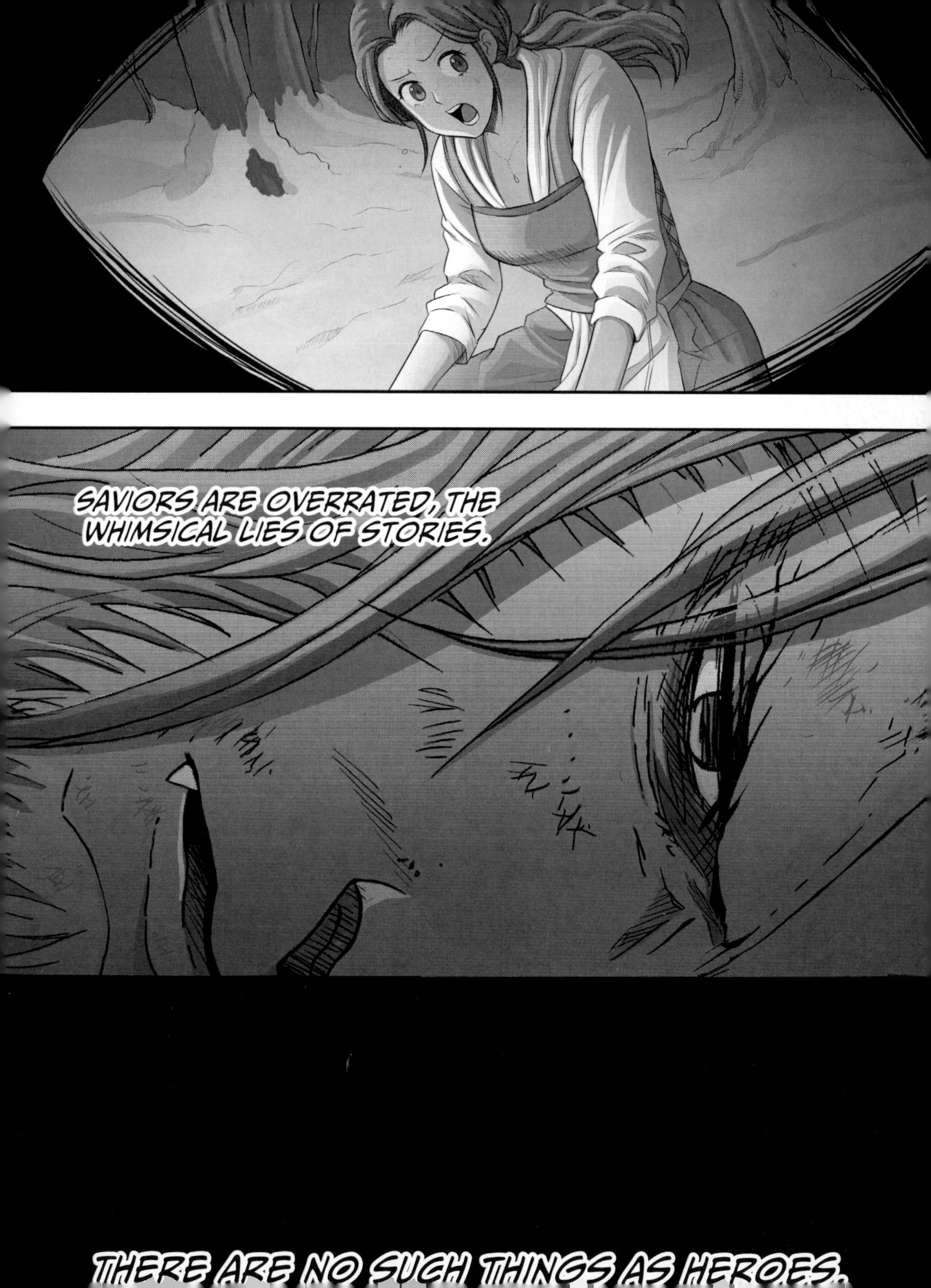
SAVIORS ARE OVERRATED, THE WHIMSICAL LIES OF STORIES.
THERE ARE NO SUCH THINGS AS HEROES.

I'M...

...WARM?

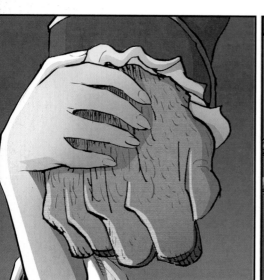

SHE...

...DIDN'T LEAVE...?

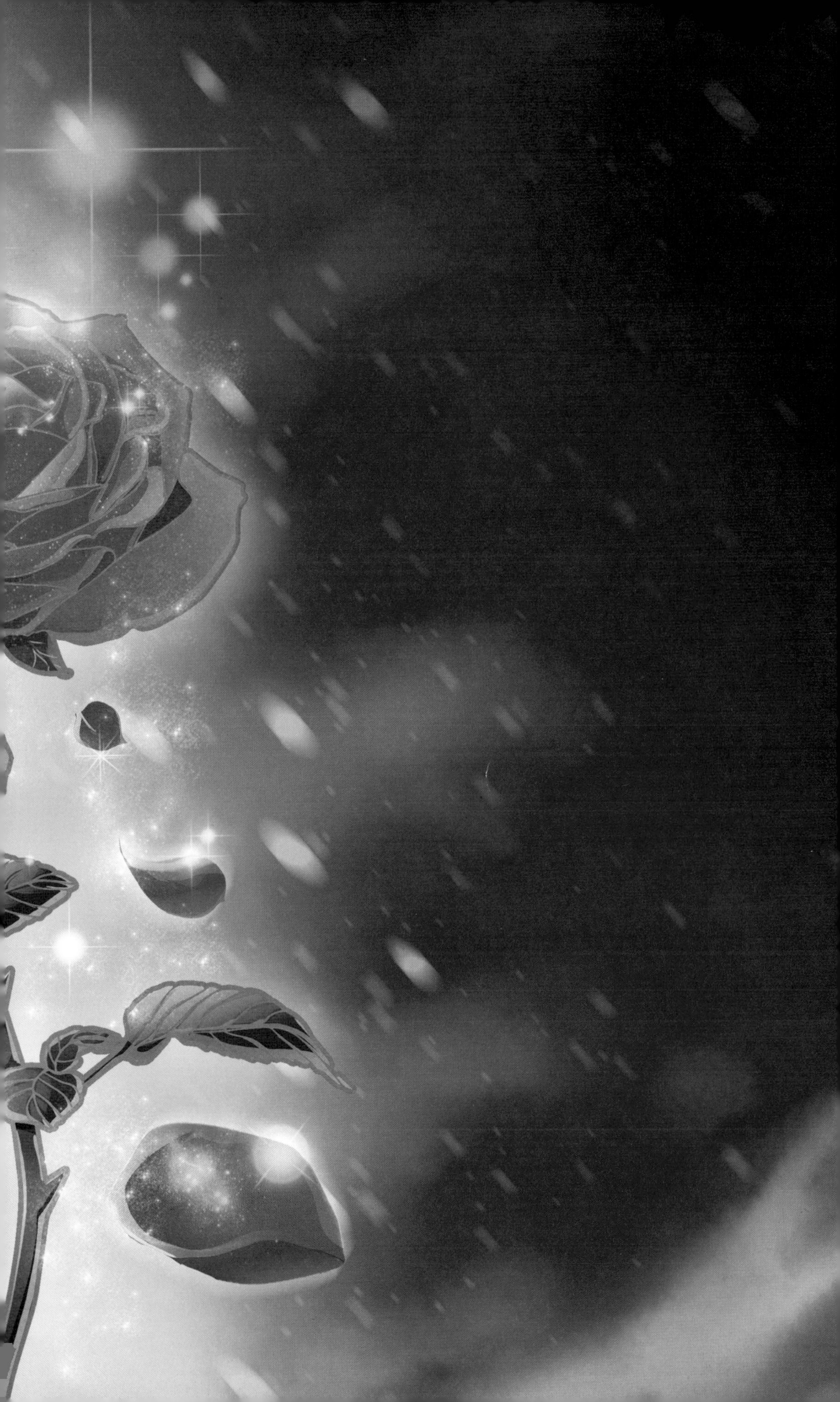

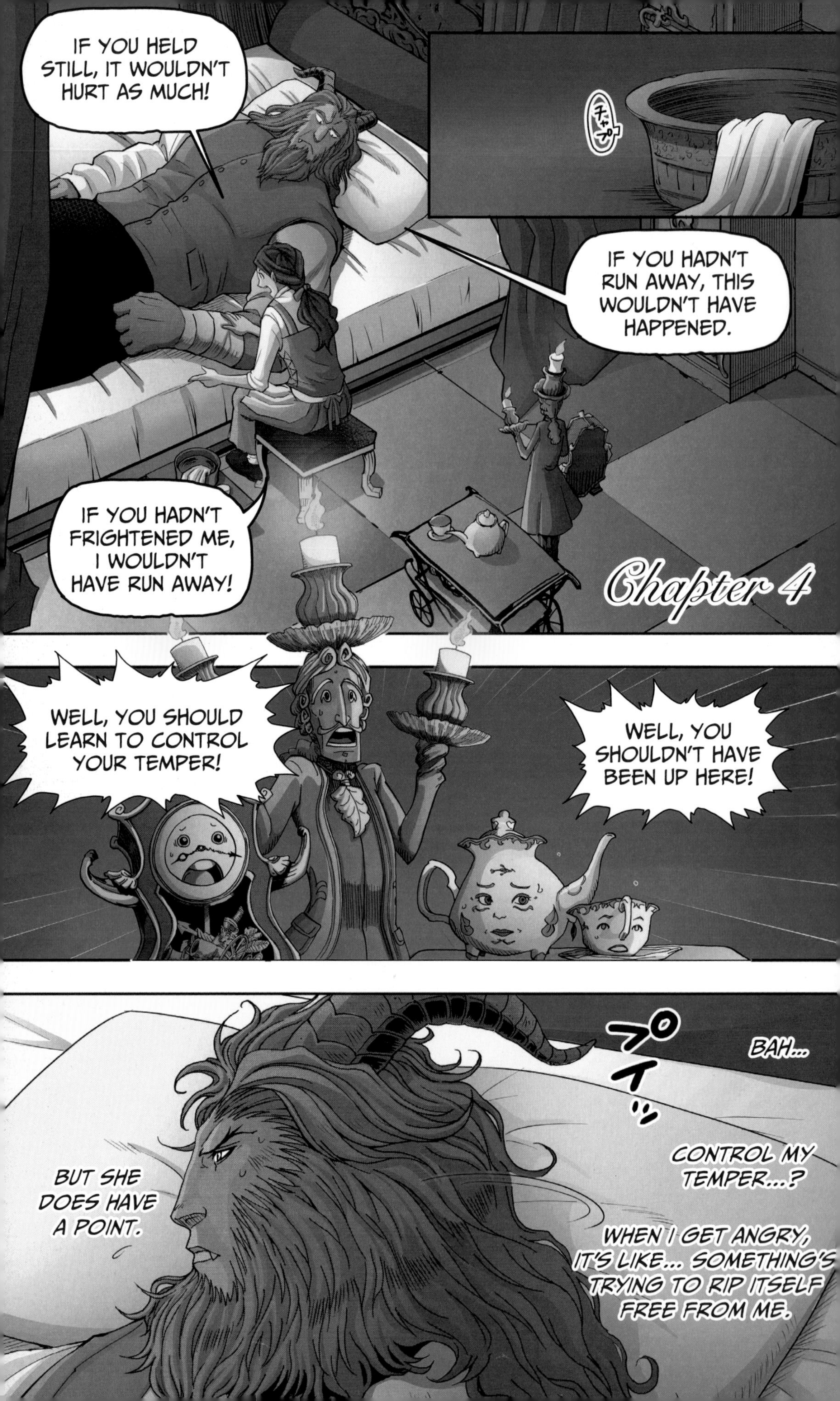

チャプ
IF YOU HELD STILL, IT WOULDN'T HURT AS MUCH!
IF YOU HADN'T RUN AWAY, THIS WOULDN'T HAVE HAPPENED.
IF YOU HADN'T FRIGHTENED ME, I WOULDN'T HAVE RUN AWAY!
Chapter 4
WELL, YOU SHOULDN'T HAVE BEEN UP HERE!
WELL, YOU SHOULD LEARN TO CONTROL YOUR TEMPER!
プイッ
BAH...
CONTROL MY TEMPER...?
WHEN I GET ANGRY, IT'S LIKE... SOMETHING'S TRYING TO RIP ITSELF FREE FROM ME.
BUT SHE DOES HAVE A POINT.

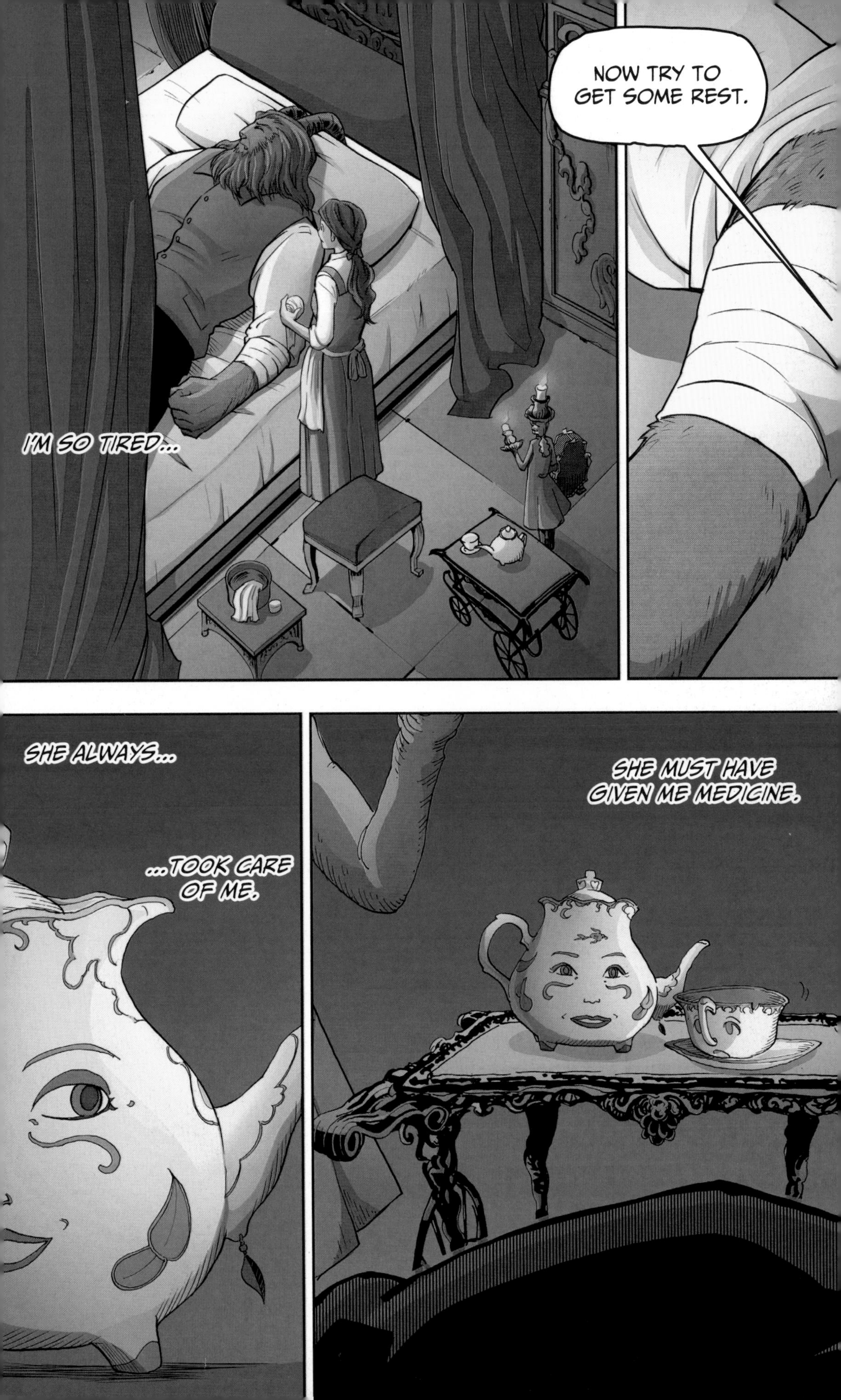
NOW TRY TO GET SOME REST.
I'M SO TIRED...
SHE MUST HAVE GIVEN ME MEDICINE.
SHE ALWAYS...
...TOOK CARE OF ME.

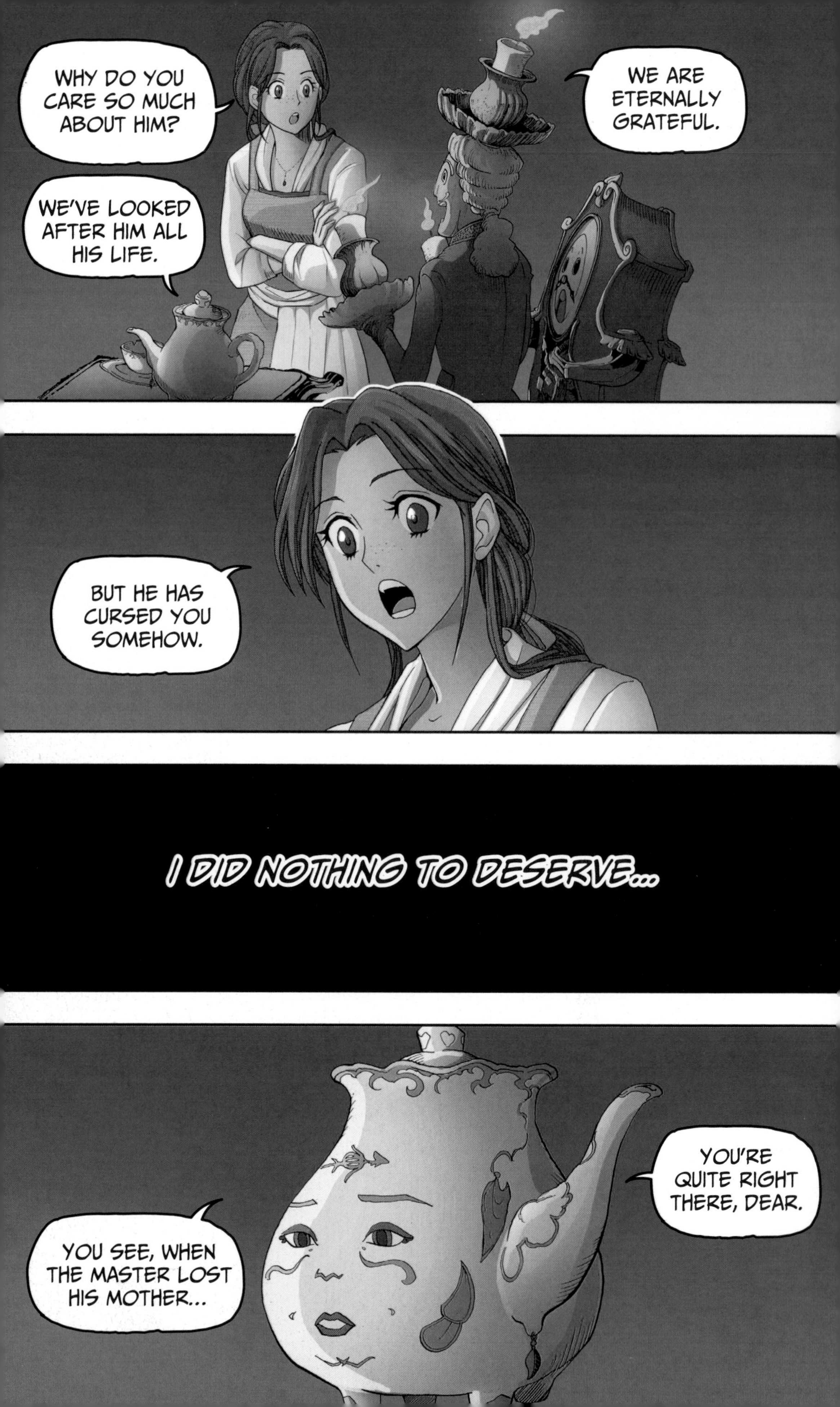
WE ARE ETERNALLY GRATEFUL.
WHY DO YOU CARE SO MUCH ABOUT HIM?
WE'VE LOOKED AFTER HIM ALL HIS LIFE.
BUT HE HAS CURSED YOU SOMEHOW.
I DID NOTHING TO DESERVE...
YOU'RE QUITE RIGHT THERE, DEAR.
YOU SEE, WHEN THE MASTER LOST HIS MOTHER...

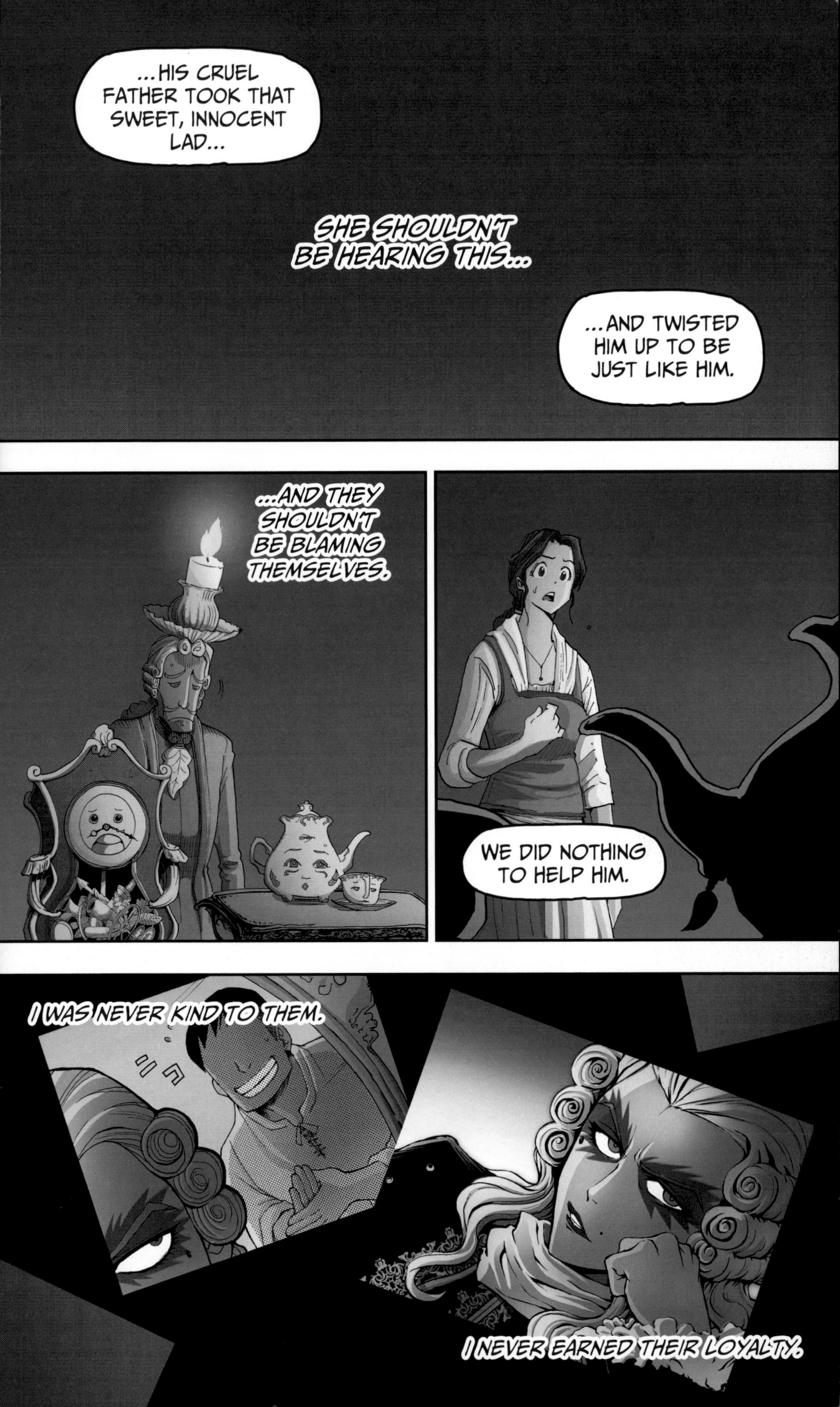
...HIS CRUEL FATHER TOOK THAT SWEET, INNOCENT LAD...
SHE SHOULDN'T BE HEARING THIS...
...AND TWISTED HIM UP TO BE JUST LIKE HIM.
WE DID NOTHING TO HELP HIM.
...AND THEY SHOULDN'T BE BLAMING THEMSELVES.
I WAS NEVER KIND TO THEM.
I NEVER EARNED THEIR LOYALTY.

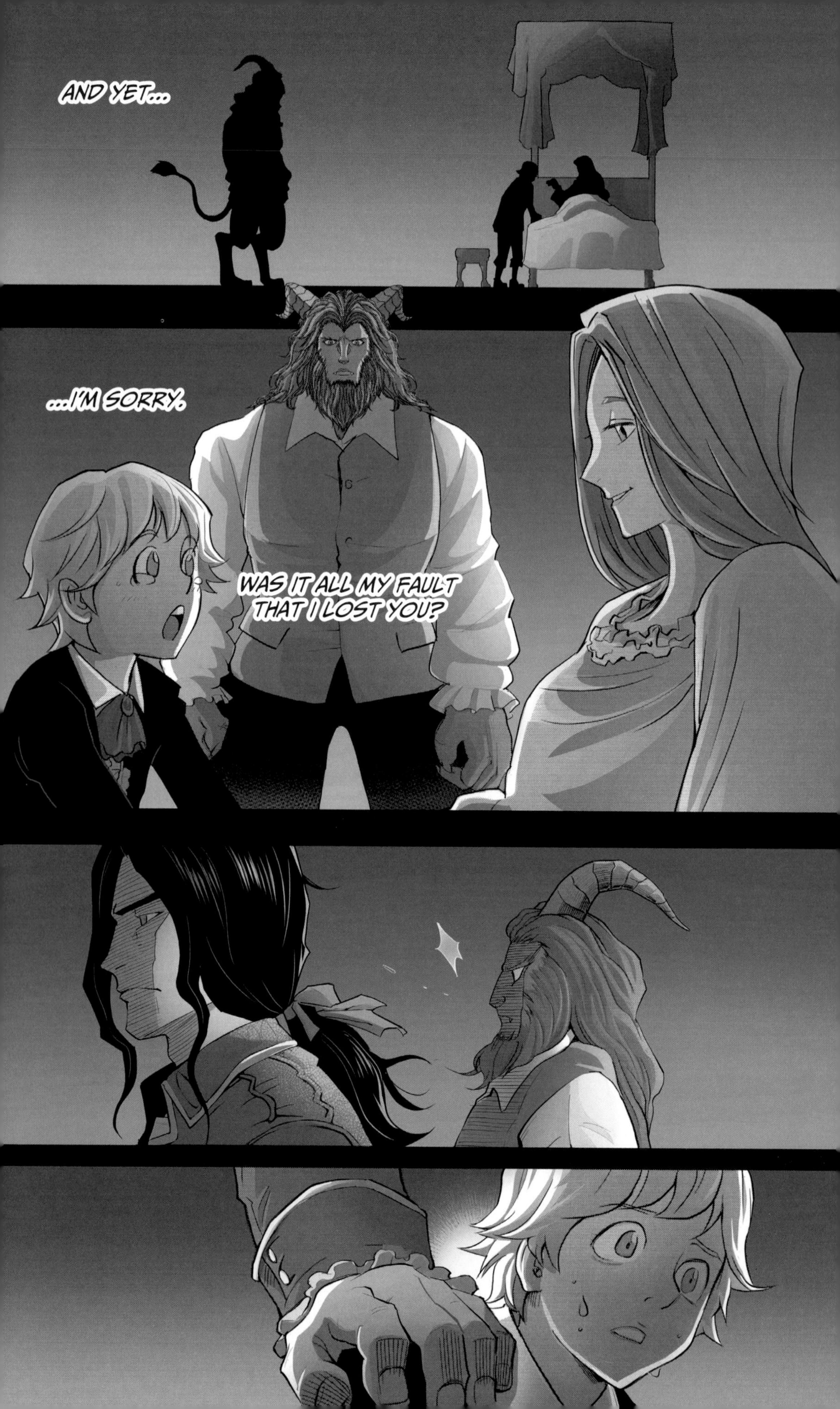
AND YET...
...I'M SORRY.
WAS IT ALL MY FAULT THAT I LOST YOU?

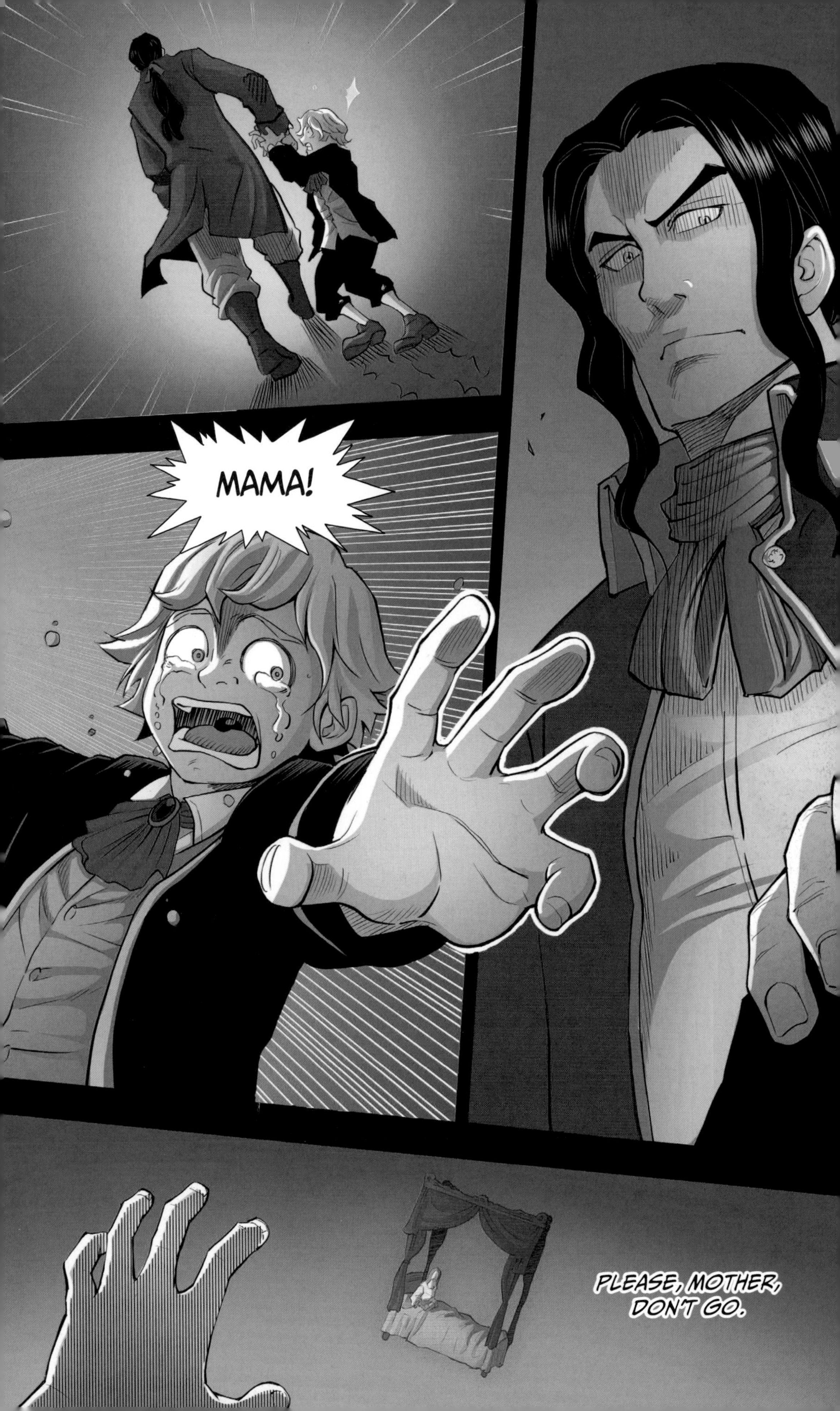
MAMA!
PLEASE, MOTHER, DON'T GO.

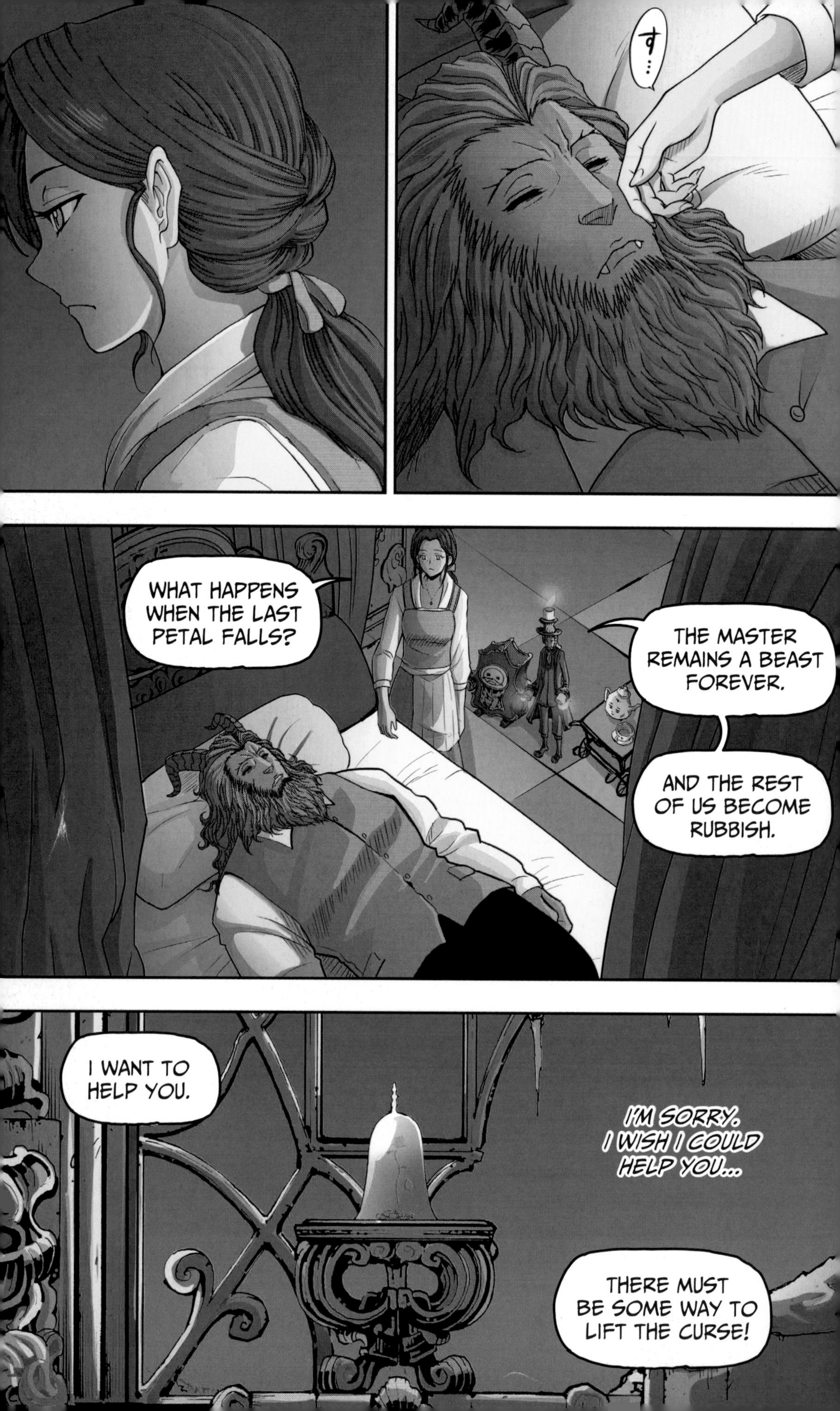
す…
WHAT HAPPENS WHEN THE LAST PETAL FALLS?
THE MASTER REMAINS A BEAST FOREVER.
AND THE REST OF US BECOME RUBBISH.
I WANT TO HELP YOU.
I'M SORRY. I WISH I COULD HELP YOU...
THERE MUST BE SOME WAY TO LIFT THE CURSE!

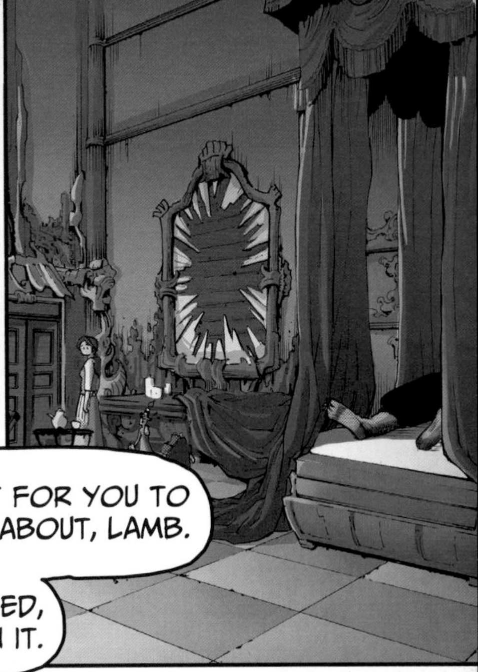
IT'S NOT FOR YOU TO WORRY ABOUT, LAMB.
WE'VE MADE OUR BED, AND WE MUST LIE IN IT.

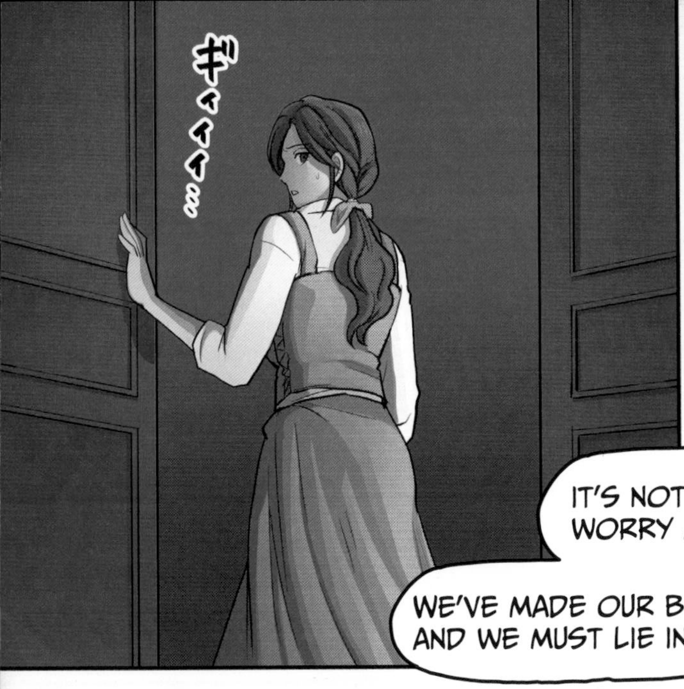
ギィィィ…

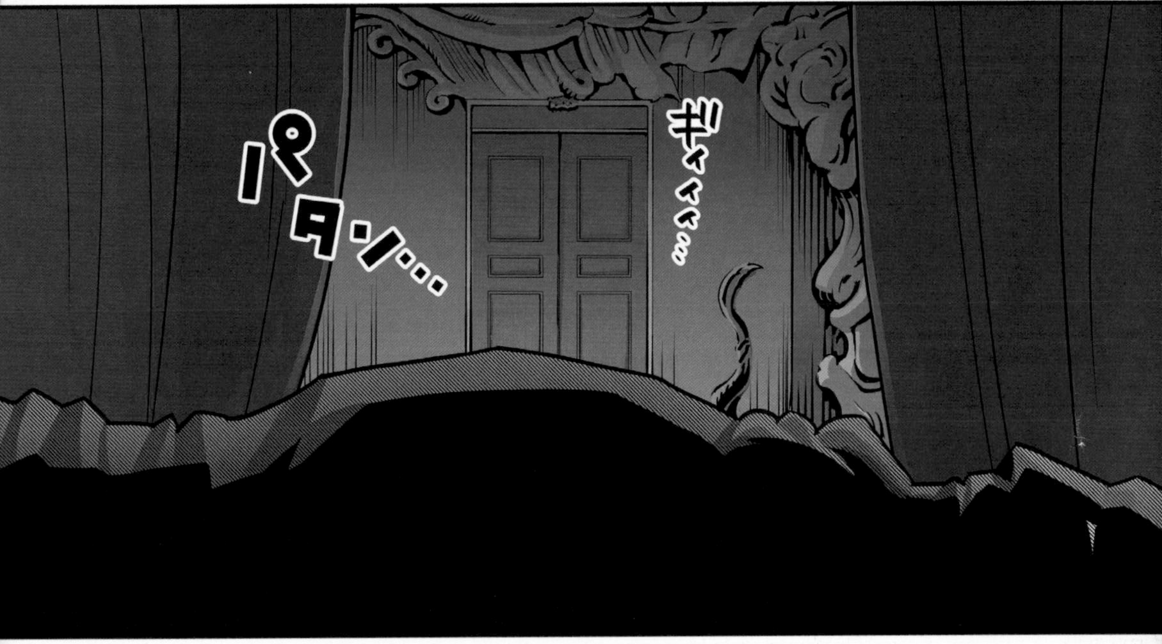
ギィィィ…
パタン…

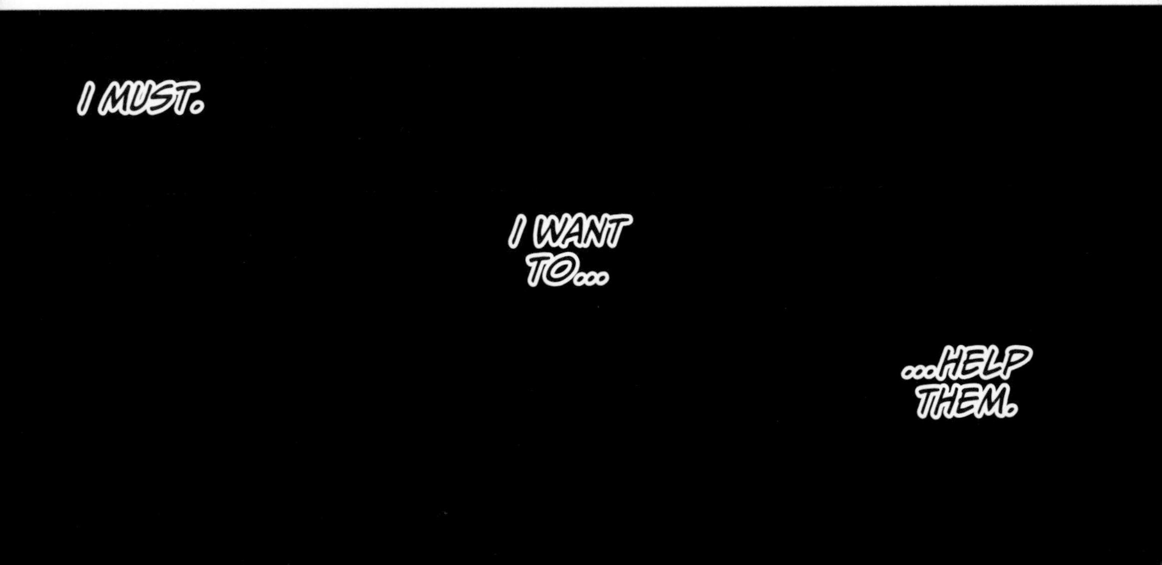
I MUST.
I WANT TO...
...HELP THEM.

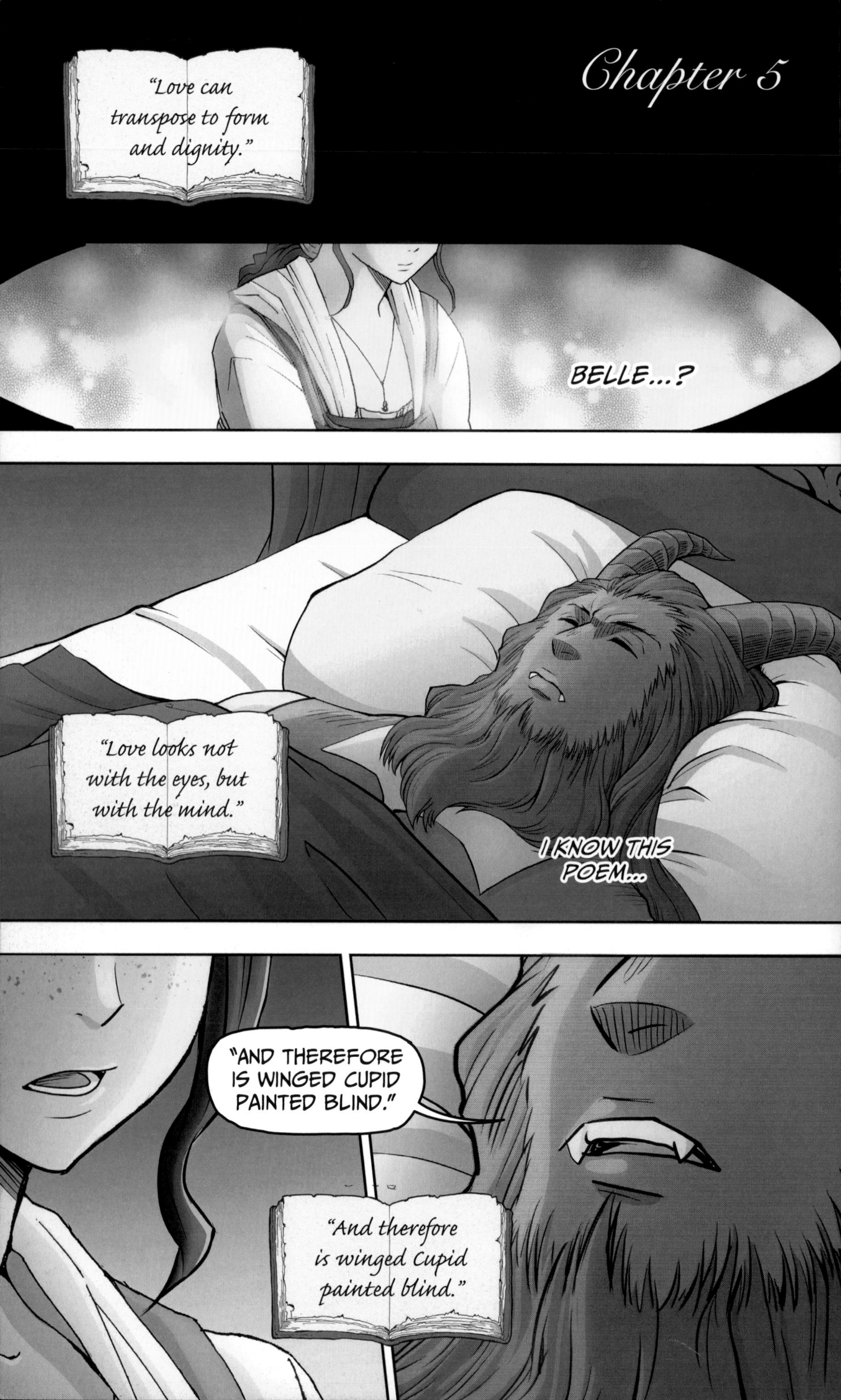
Chapter 5
"Love can transpose to form and dignity."
BELLE...?
I KNOW THIS POEM...
"Love looks not with the eyes, but with the mind."
"AND THEREFORE IS WINGED CUPID PAINTED BLIND."
"And therefore is winged Cupid painted blind."

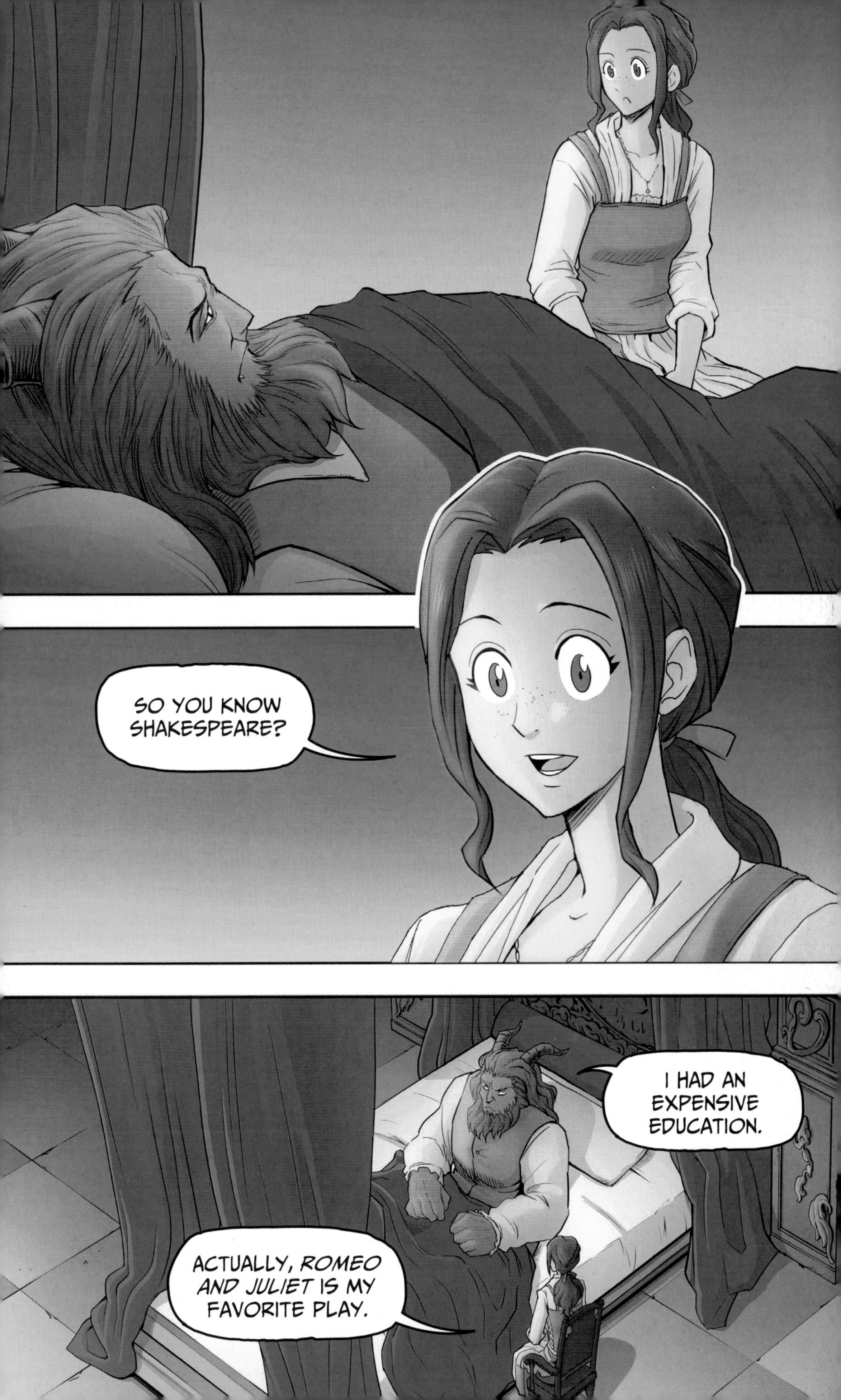
SO YOU KNOW SHAKESPEARE?
I HAD AN EXPENSIVE EDUCATION.
ACTUALLY, *ROMEO AND JULIET* IS MY FAVORITE PLAY.

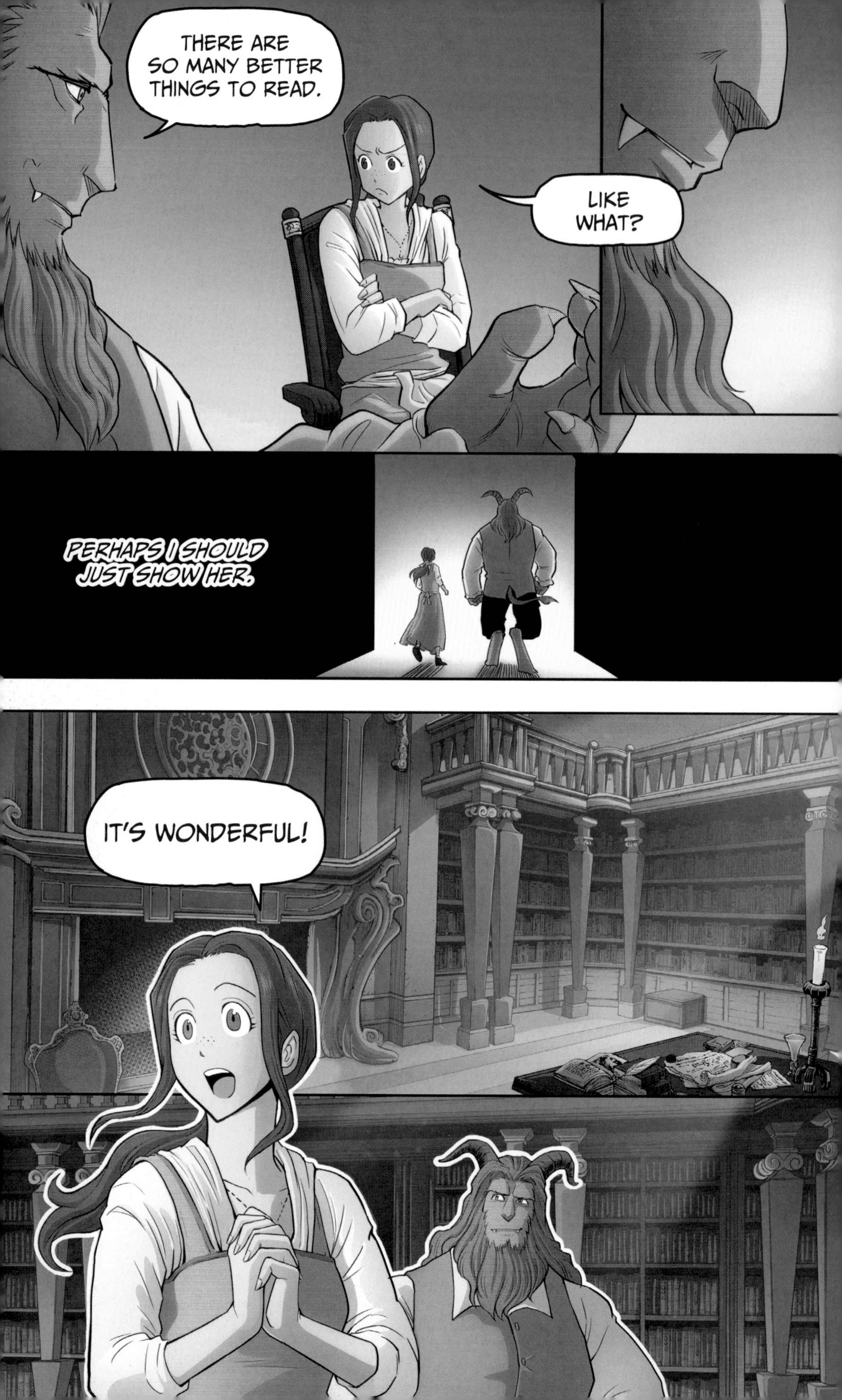
THERE ARE SO MANY BETTER THINGS TO READ.
LIKE WHAT?
PERHAPS I SHOULD JUST SHOW HER.
IT'S WONDERFUL!

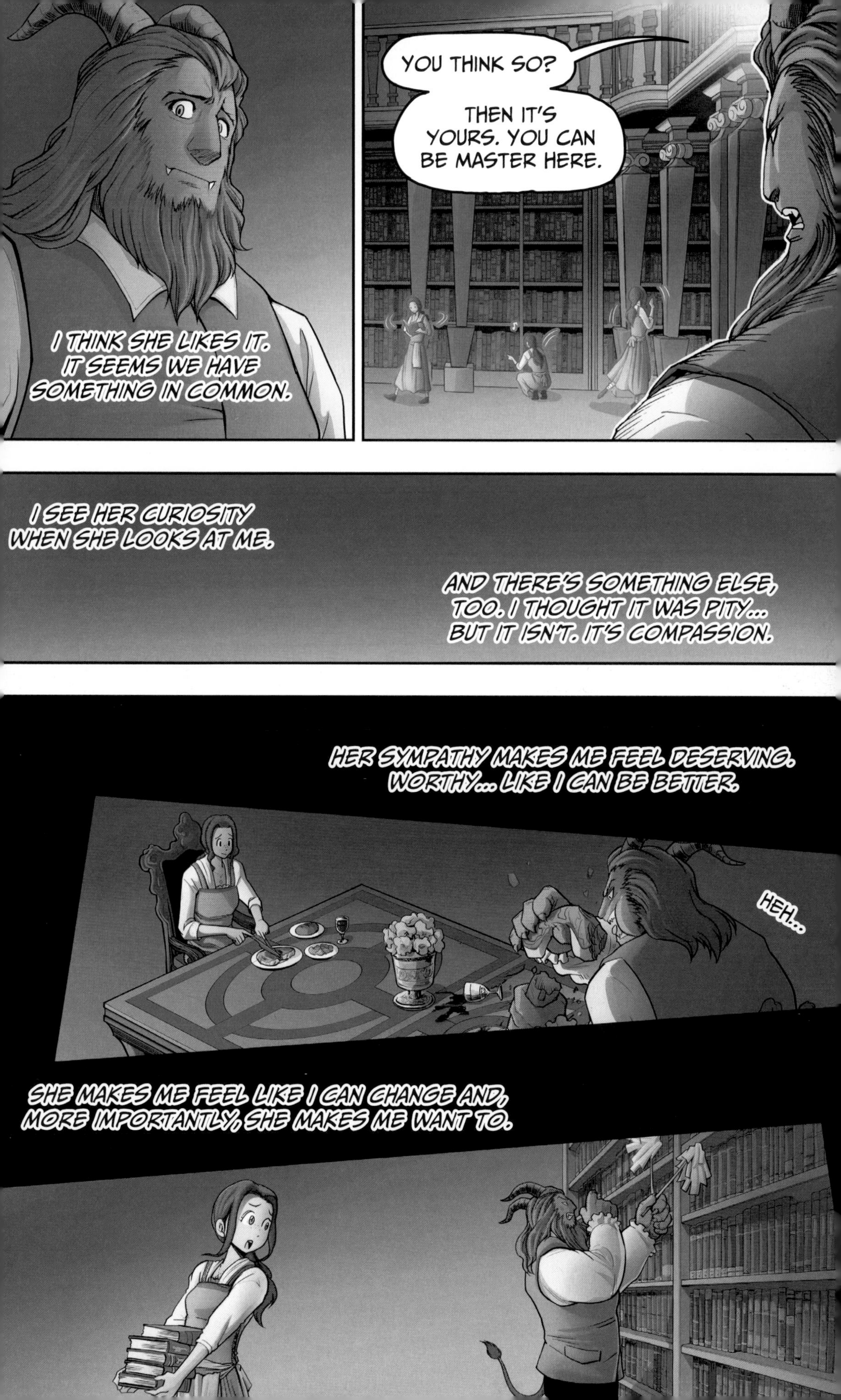
I THINK SHE LIKES IT. IT SEEMS WE HAVE SOMETHING IN COMMON.
YOU THINK SO?
THEN IT'S YOURS. YOU CAN BE MASTER HERE.
I SEE HER CURIOSITY WHEN SHE LOOKS AT ME.
AND THERE'S SOMETHING ELSE, TOO. I THOUGHT IT WAS PITY... BUT IT ISN'T. IT'S COMPASSION.
HER SYMPATHY MAKES ME FEEL DESERVING. WORTHY... LIKE I CAN BE BETTER.
HEH...
SHE MAKES ME FEEL LIKE I CAN CHANGE AND, MORE IMPORTANTLY, SHE MAKES ME WANT TO.

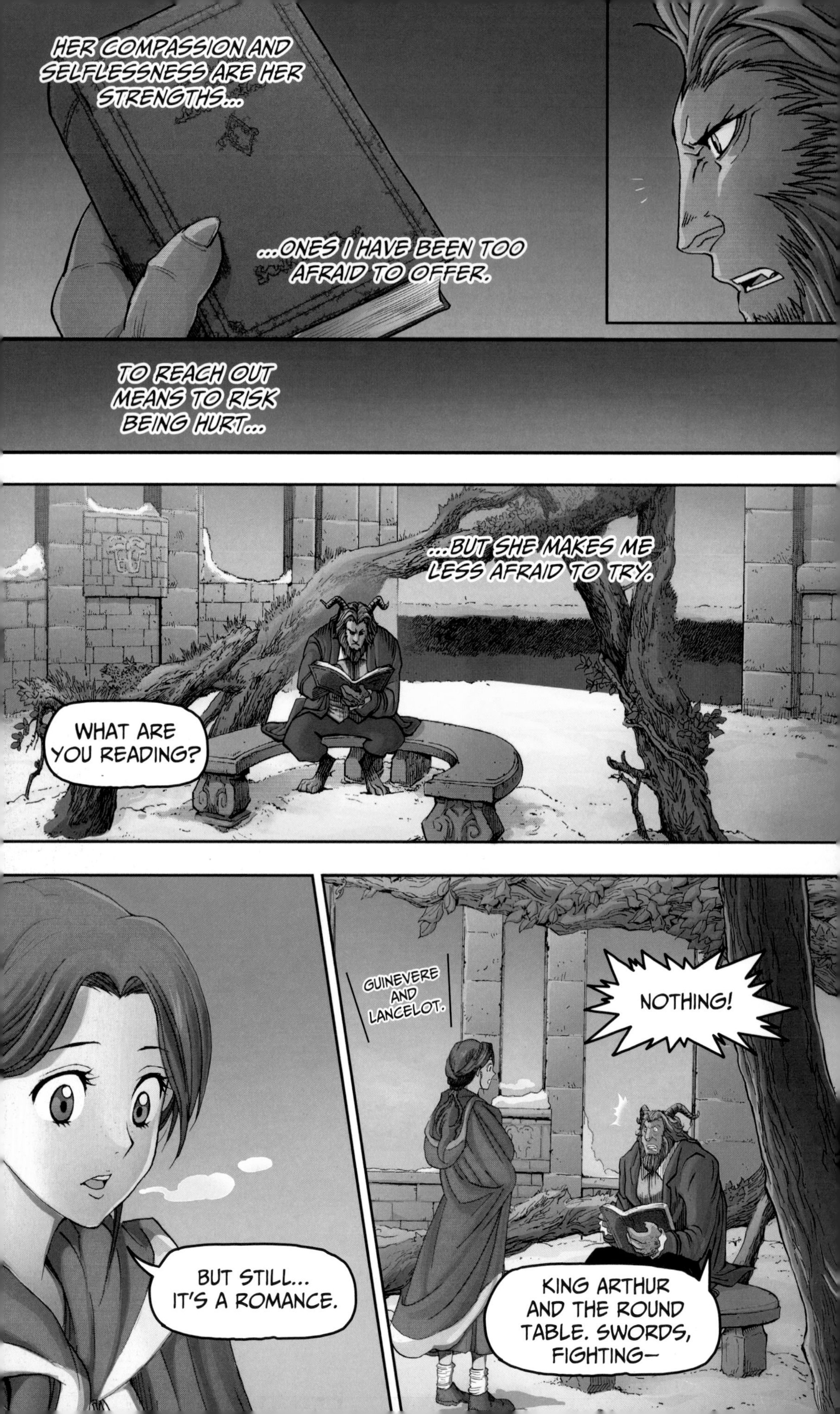
HER COMPASSION AND SELFLESSNESS ARE HER STRENGTHS...
...ONES I HAVE BEEN TOO AFRAID TO OFFER.
TO REACH OUT MEANS TO RISK BEING HURT...
...BUT SHE MAKES ME LESS AFRAID TO TRY.
WHAT ARE YOU READING?
NOTHING!
KING ARTHUR AND THE ROUND TABLE. SWORDS, FIGHTING—
GUINEVERE AND LANCELOT.
BUT STILL... IT'S A ROMANCE.

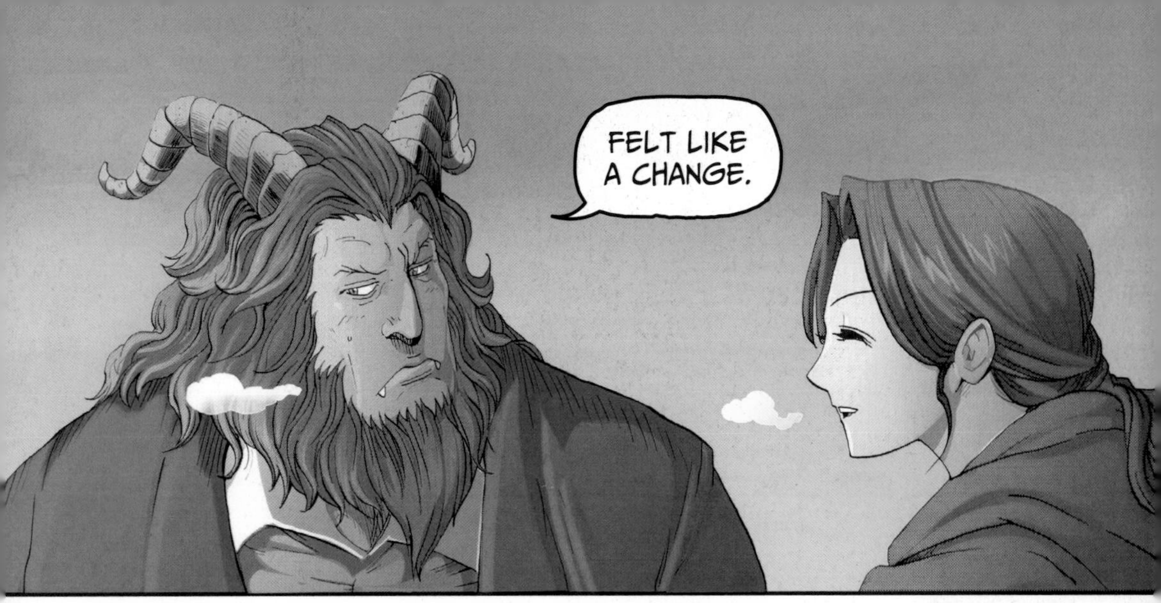
FELT LIKE A CHANGE.

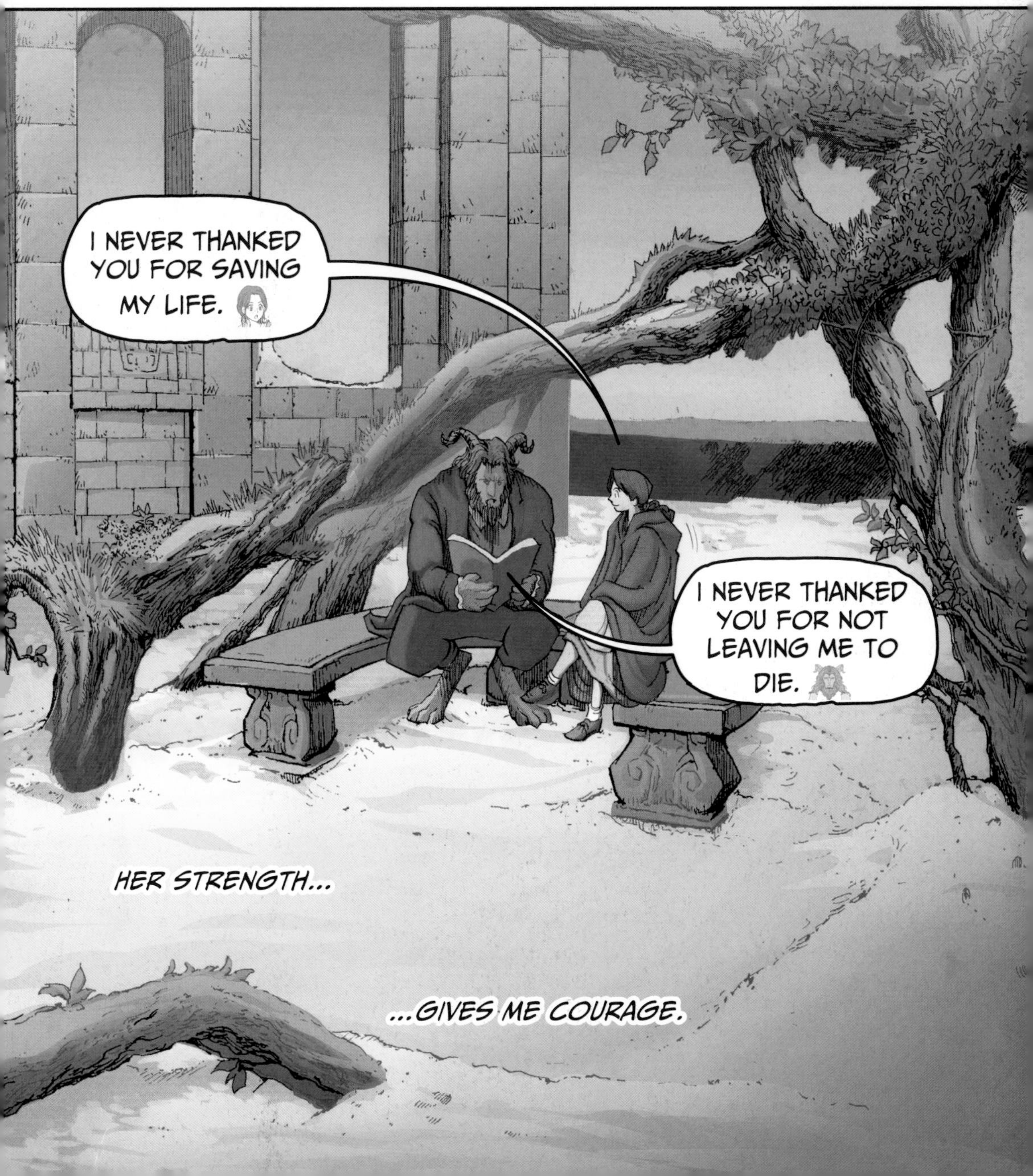
I NEVER THANKED YOU FOR SAVING MY LIFE.
I NEVER THANKED YOU FOR NOT LEAVING ME TO DIE.
HER STRENGTH...
...GIVES ME COURAGE.

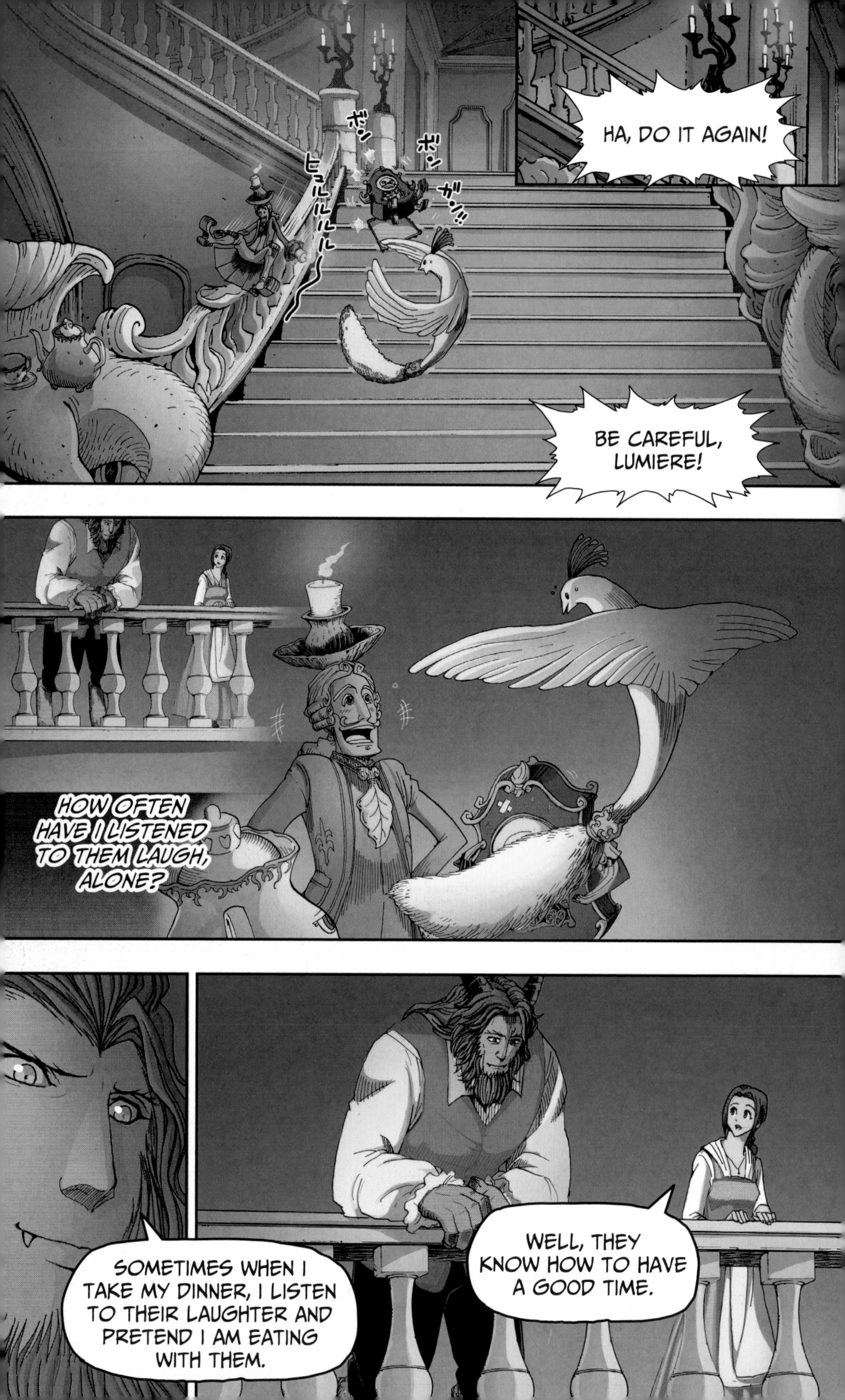
HA, DO IT AGAIN!
ボン
ボン
ガン!!
ヒュルルルル~
BE CAREFUL, LUMIERE!
HOW OFTEN HAVE I LISTENED TO THEM LAUGH, ALONE?
WELL, THEY KNOW HOW TO HAVE A GOOD TIME.
SOMETIMES WHEN I TAKE MY DINNER, I LISTEN TO THEIR LAUGHTER AND PRETEND I AM EATING WITH THEM.

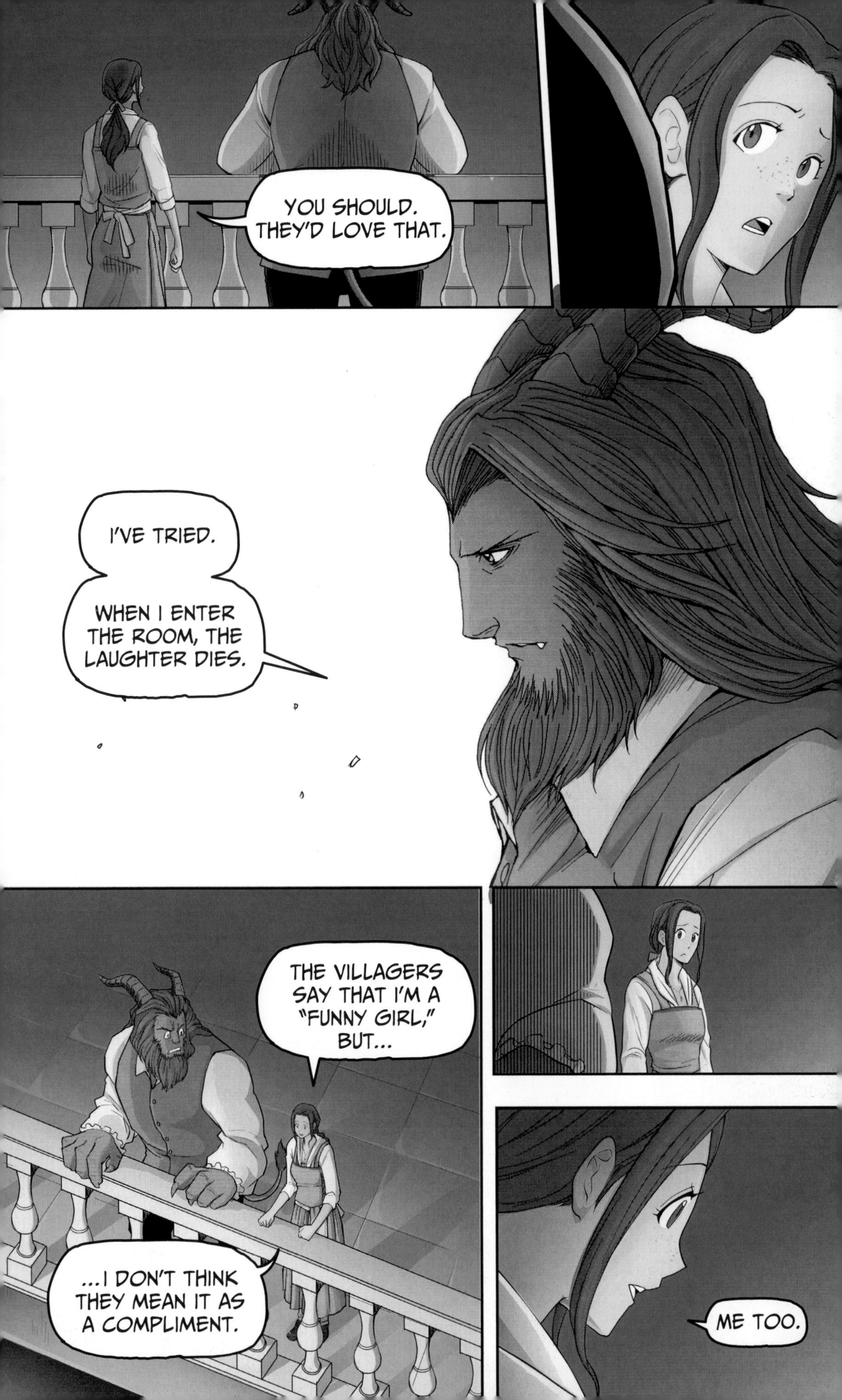
YOU SHOULD. THEY'D LOVE THAT.
I'VE TRIED.
WHEN I ENTER THE ROOM, THE LAUGHTER DIES.
ME TOO.
THE VILLAGERS SAY THAT I'M A "FUNNY GIRL," BUT...
...I DON'T THINK THEY MEAN IT AS A COMPLIMENT.

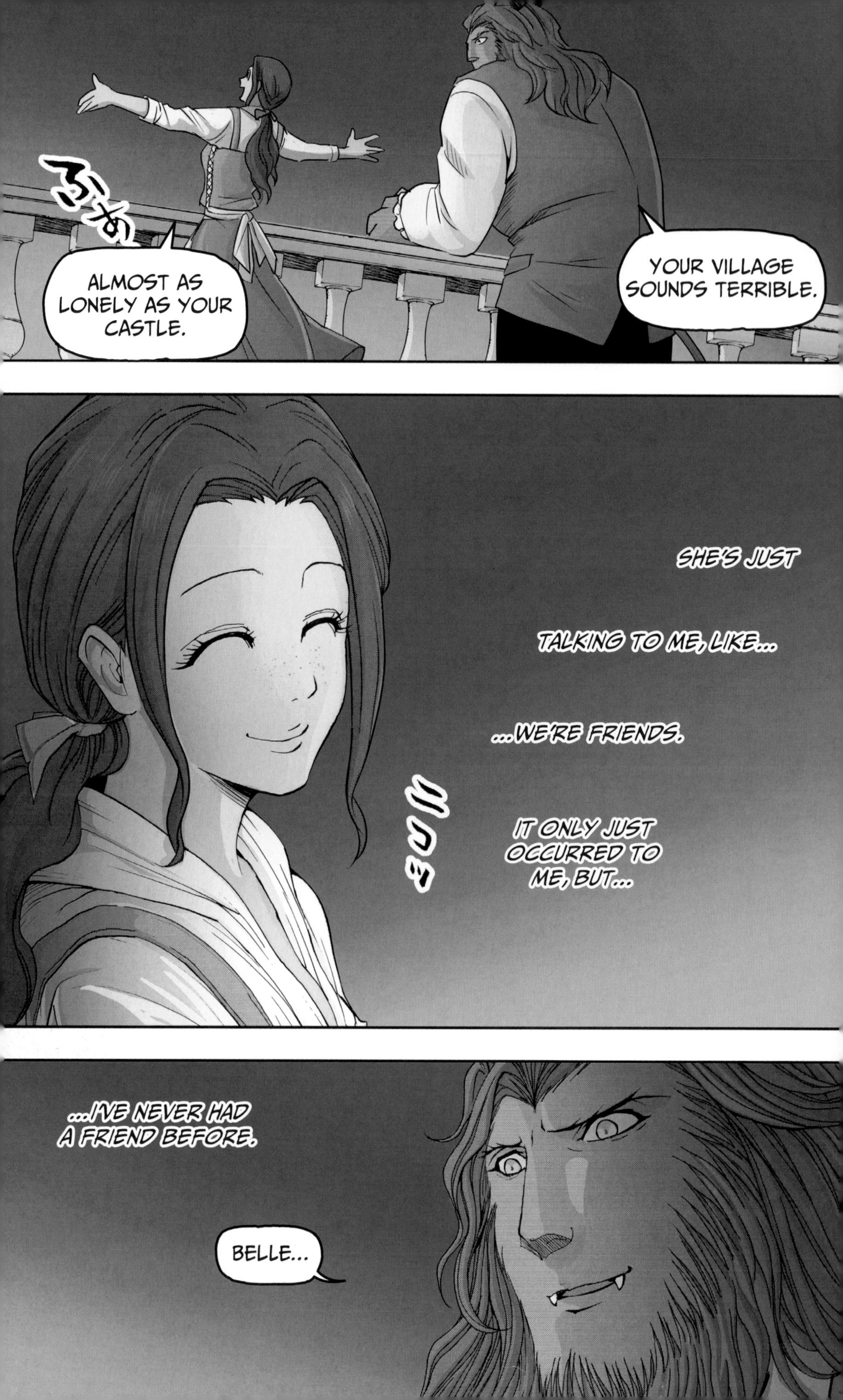
YOUR VILLAGE SOUNDS TERRIBLE.
ふぁ
ALMOST AS LONELY AS YOUR CASTLE.
SHE'S JUST
TALKING TO ME, LIKE...
...WE'RE FRIENDS.
IT ONLY JUST OCCURRED TO ME, BUT...
ニコッ
...I'VE NEVER HAD A FRIEND BEFORE.
BELLE...

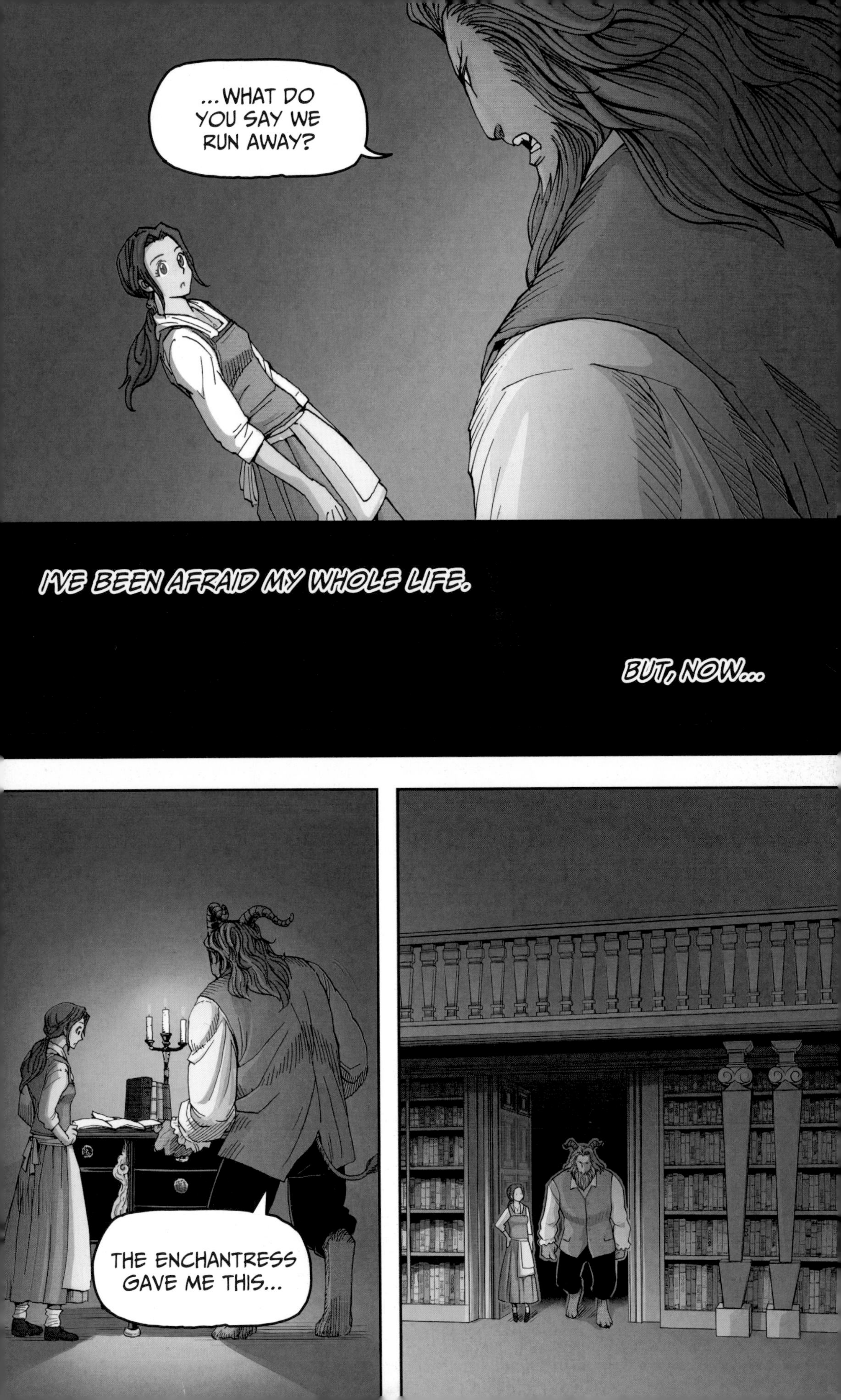
...WHAT DO YOU SAY WE RUN AWAY?
I'VE BEEN AFRAID MY WHOLE LIFE.
BUT, NOW...
THE ENCHANTRESS GAVE ME THIS...

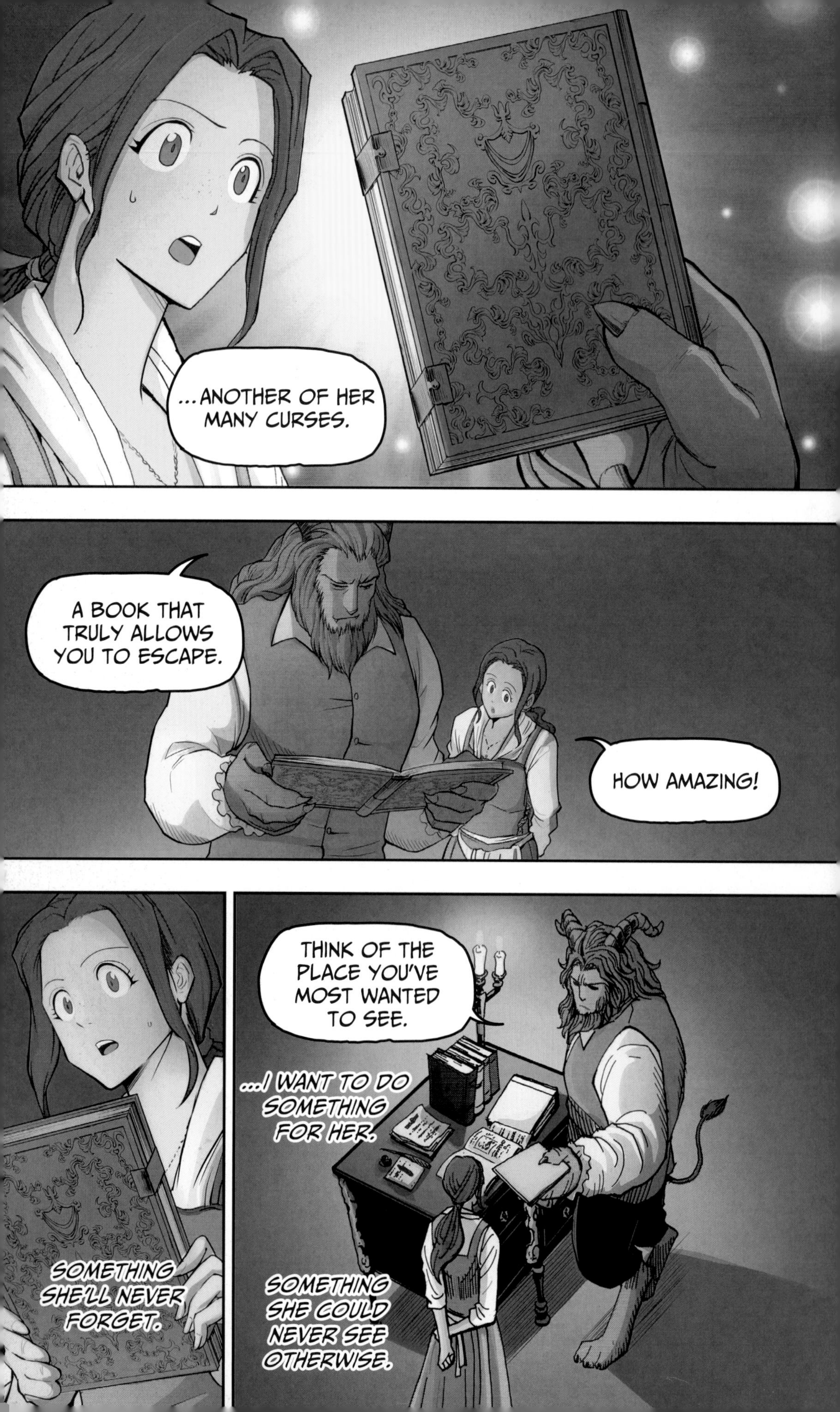
...ANOTHER OF HER MANY CURSES.
A BOOK THAT TRULY ALLOWS YOU TO ESCAPE.
HOW AMAZING!
THINK OF THE PLACE YOU'VE MOST WANTED TO SEE.
...I WANT TO DO SOMETHING FOR HER.
SOMETHING SHE COULD NEVER SEE OTHERWISE.
SOMETHING SHE'LL NEVER FORGET.

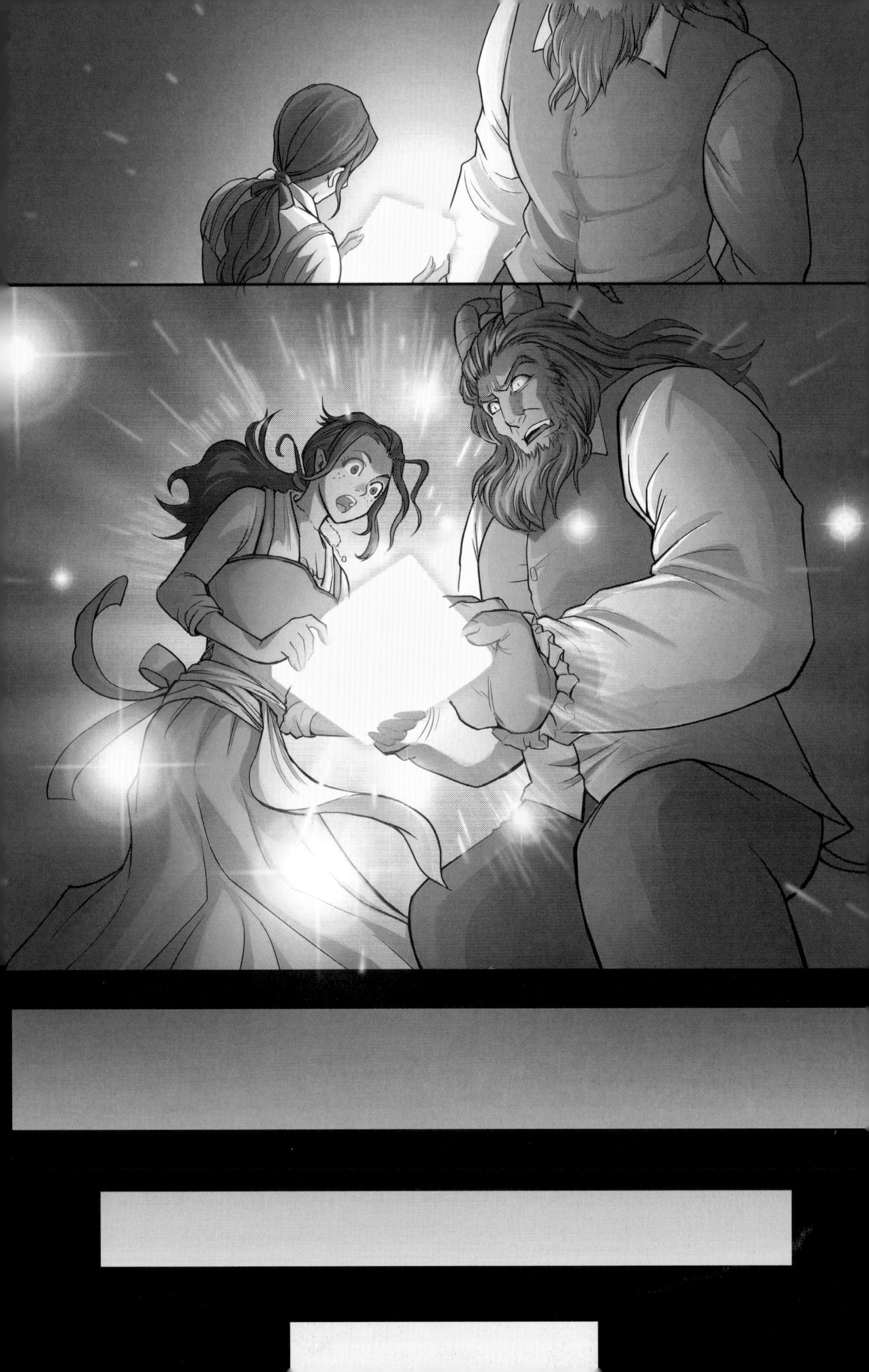

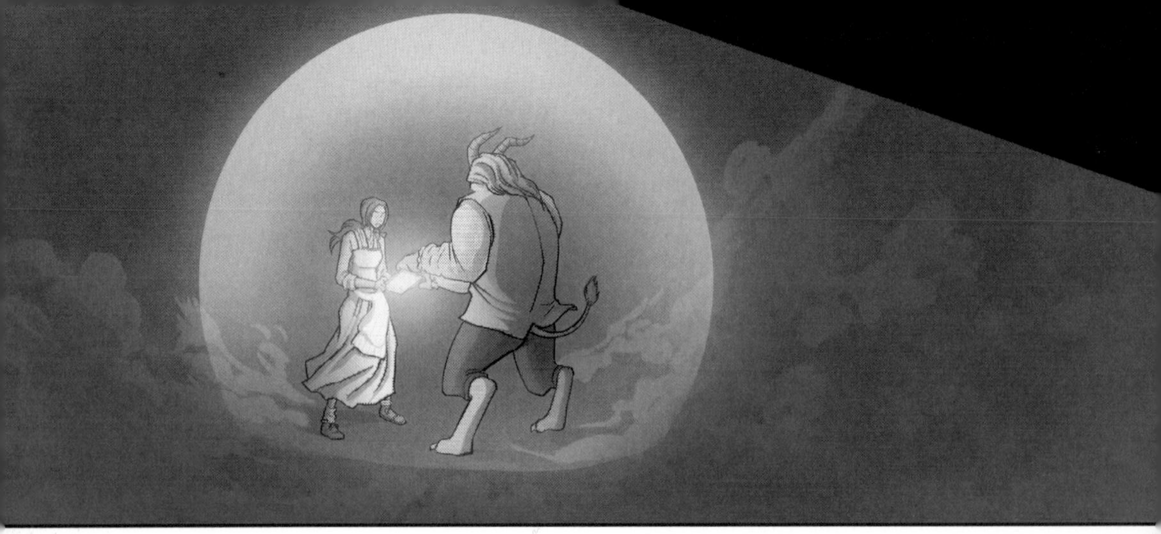

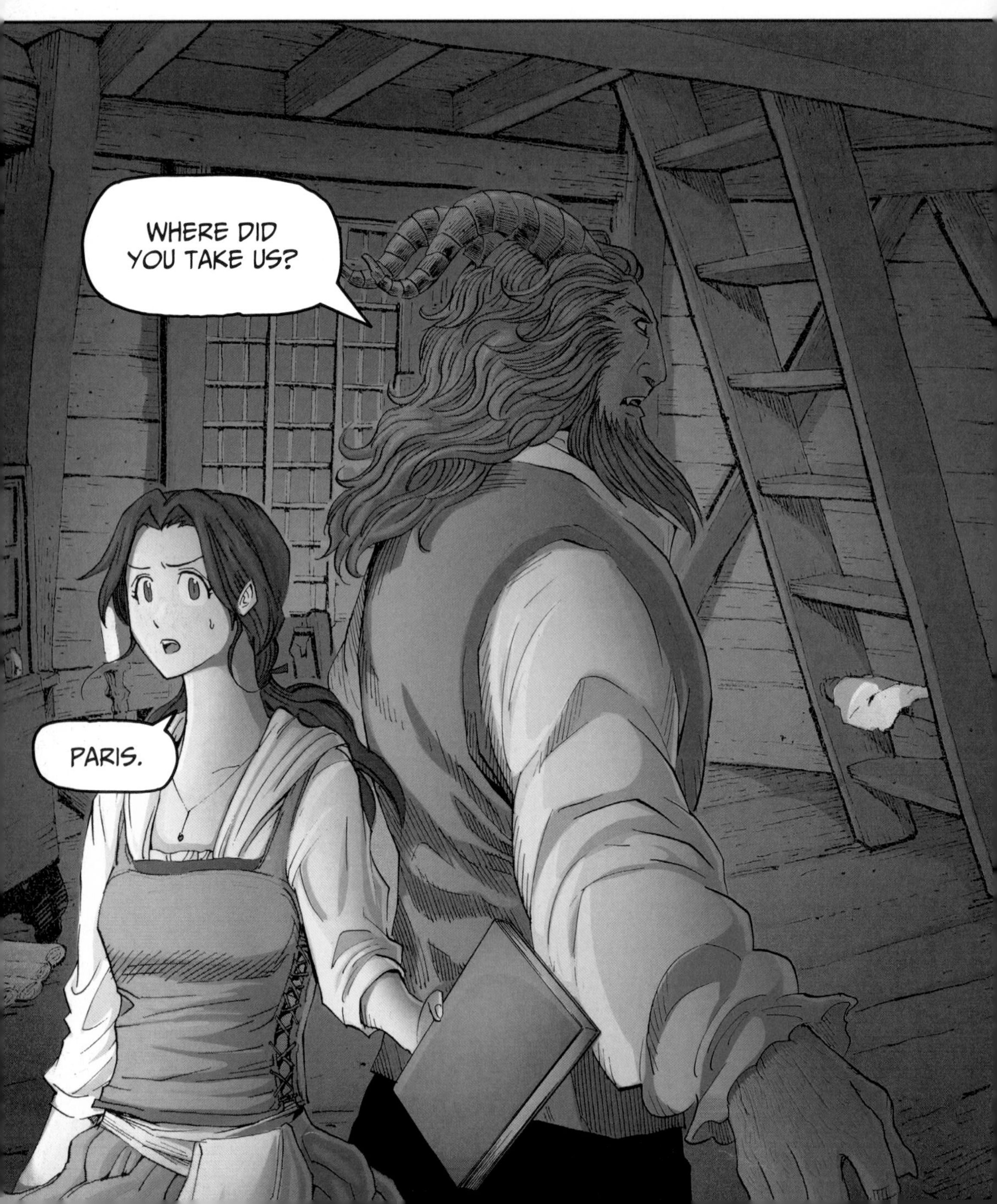
WHERE DID YOU TAKE US?
PARIS.

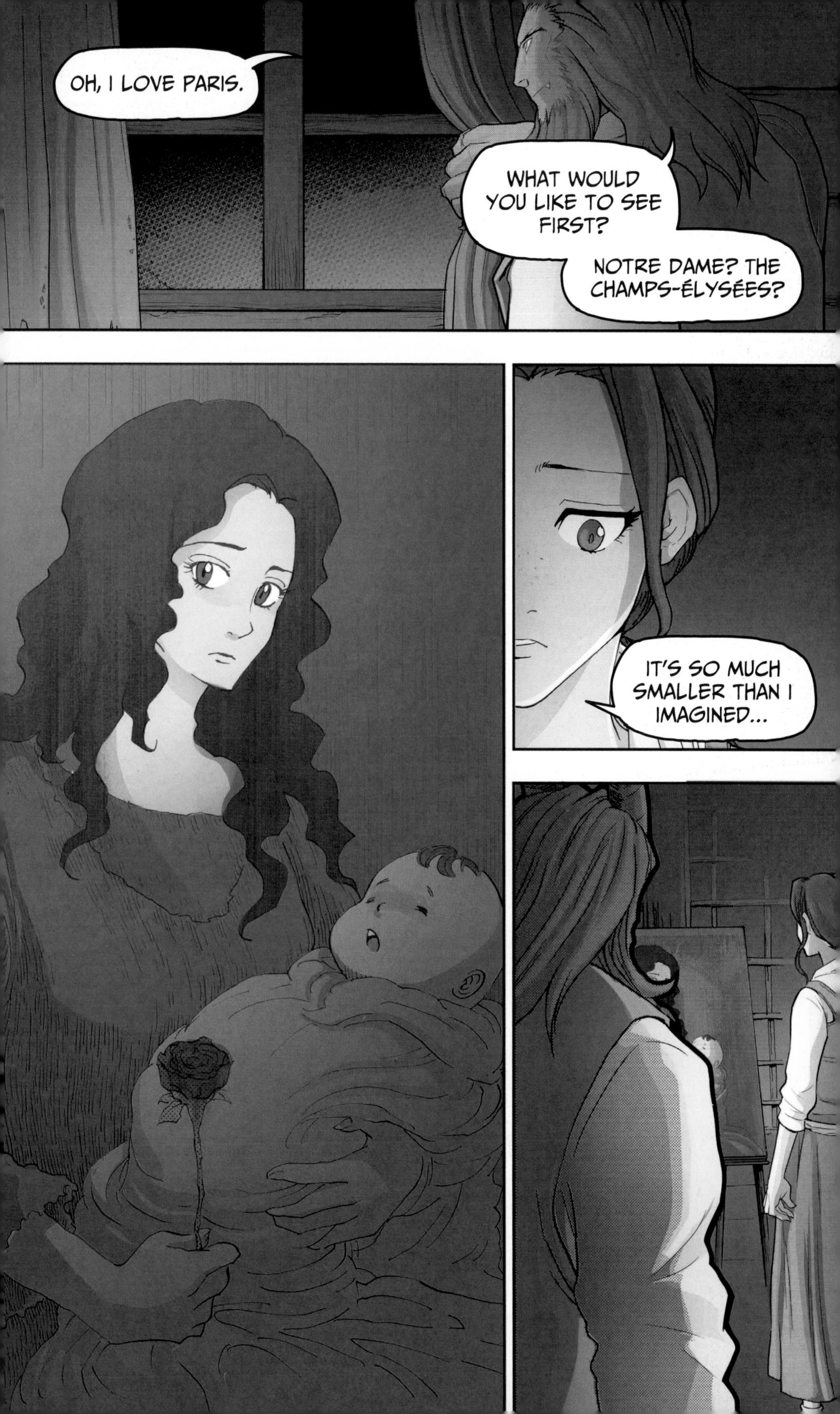
OH, I LOVE PARIS.
WHAT WOULD YOU LIKE TO SEE FIRST?
NOTRE DAME? THE CHAMPS-ÉLYSÉES?
IT'S SO MUCH SMALLER THAN I IMAGINED...

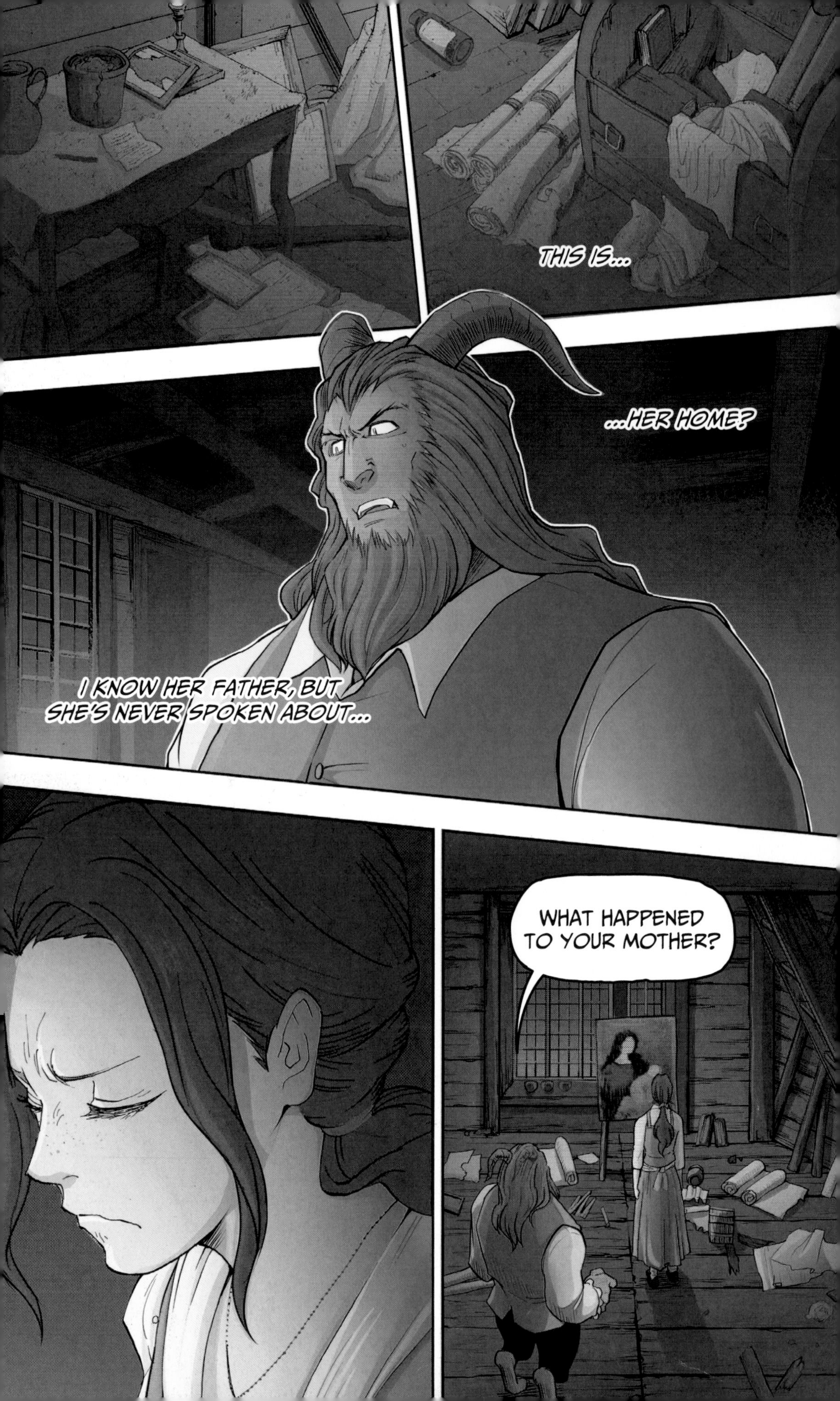
THIS IS...
...HER HOME?
I KNOW HER FATHER, BUT SHE'S NEVER SPOKEN ABOUT...
WHAT HAPPENED TO YOUR MOTHER?

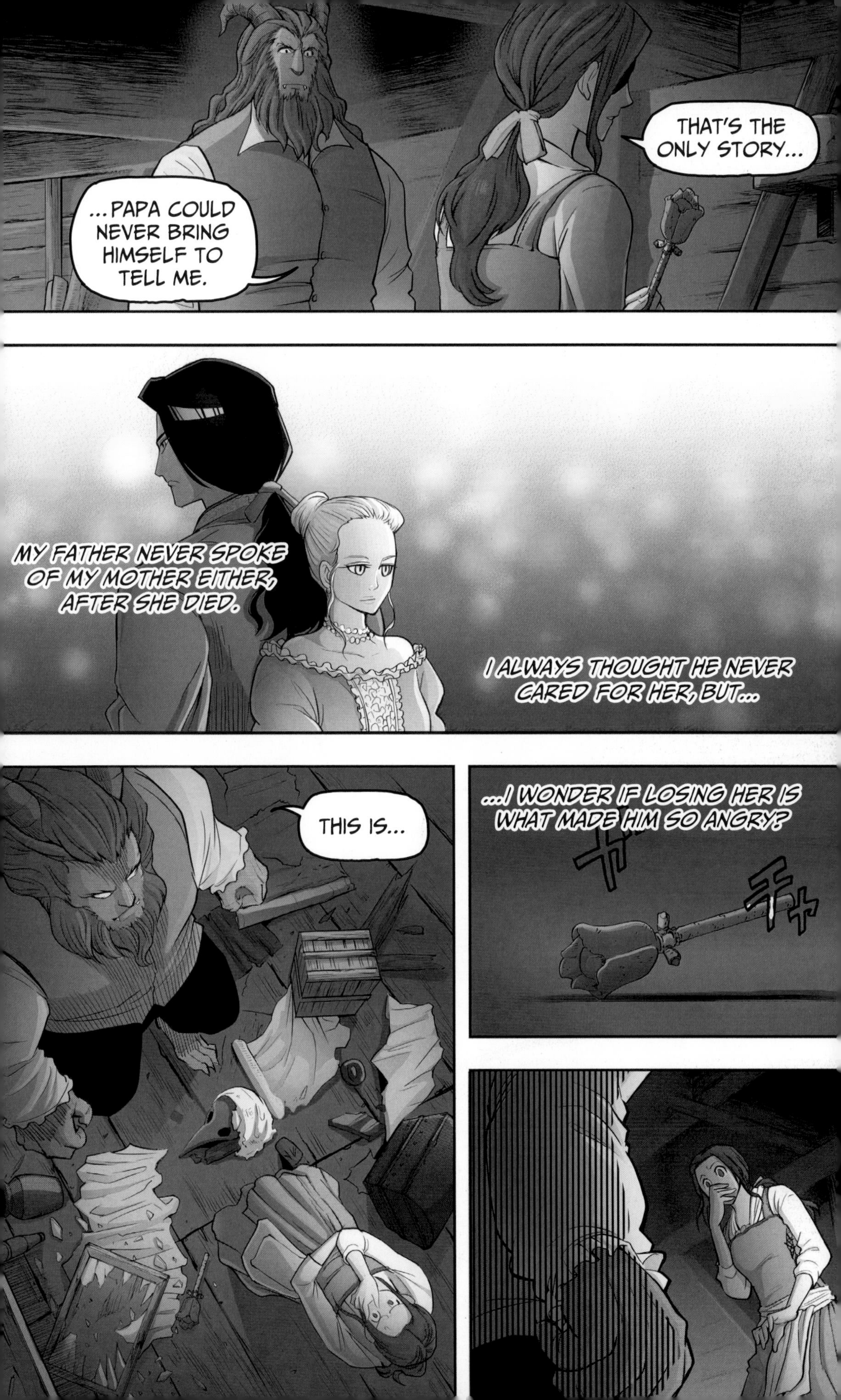
THAT'S THE ONLY STORY...
...PAPA COULD NEVER BRING HIMSELF TO TELL ME.
MY FATHER NEVER SPOKE OF MY MOTHER EITHER, AFTER SHE DIED.
I ALWAYS THOUGHT HE NEVER CARED FOR HER, BUT...
...I WONDER IF LOSING HER IS WHAT MADE HIM SO ANGRY?
THIS IS...

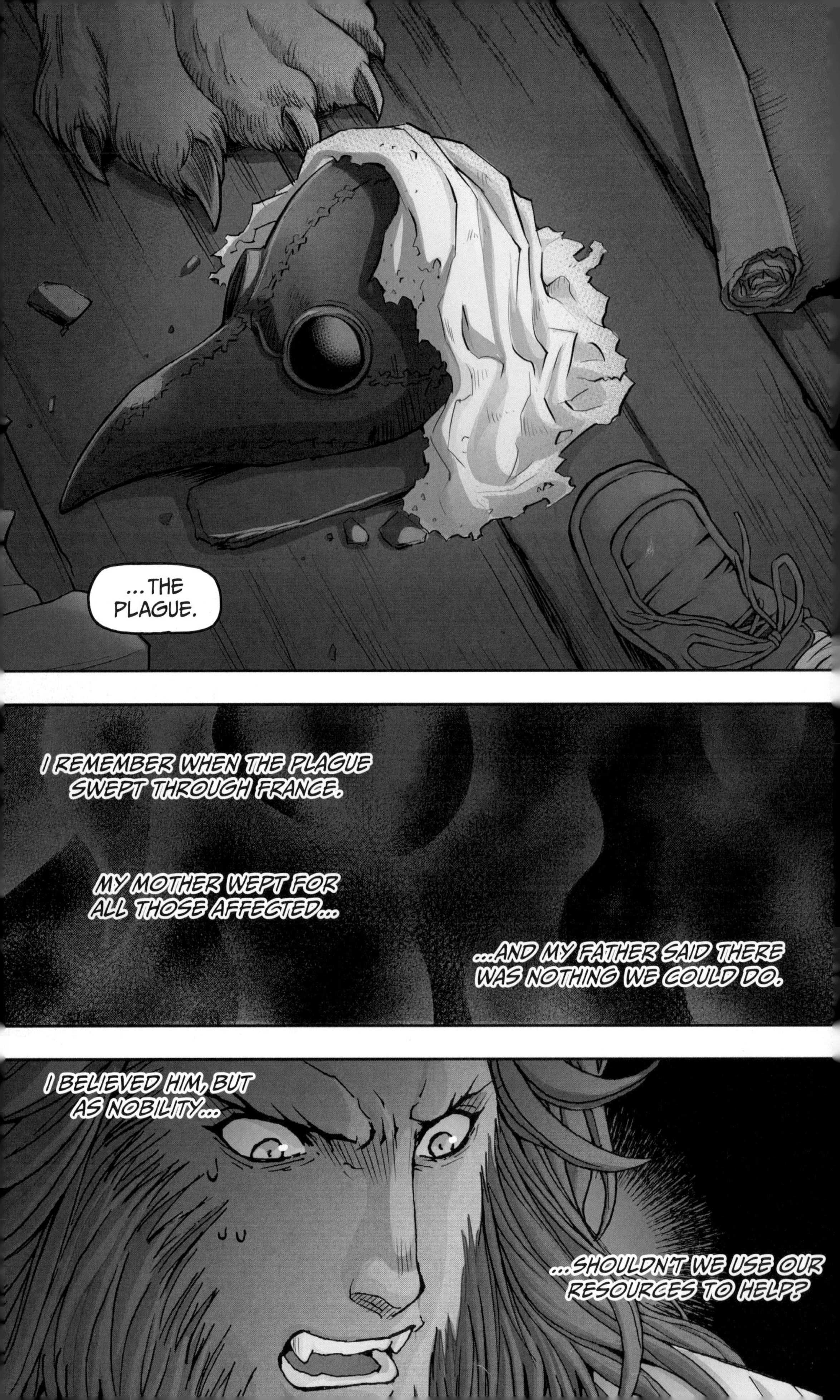
...THE PLAGUE.
I REMEMBER WHEN THE PLAGUE SWEPT THROUGH FRANCE.
MY MOTHER WEPT FOR ALL THOSE AFFECTED...
...AND MY FATHER SAID THERE WAS NOTHING WE COULD DO.
I BELIEVED HIM, BUT AS NOBILITY...
...SHOULDN'T WE USE OUR RESOURCES TO HELP?

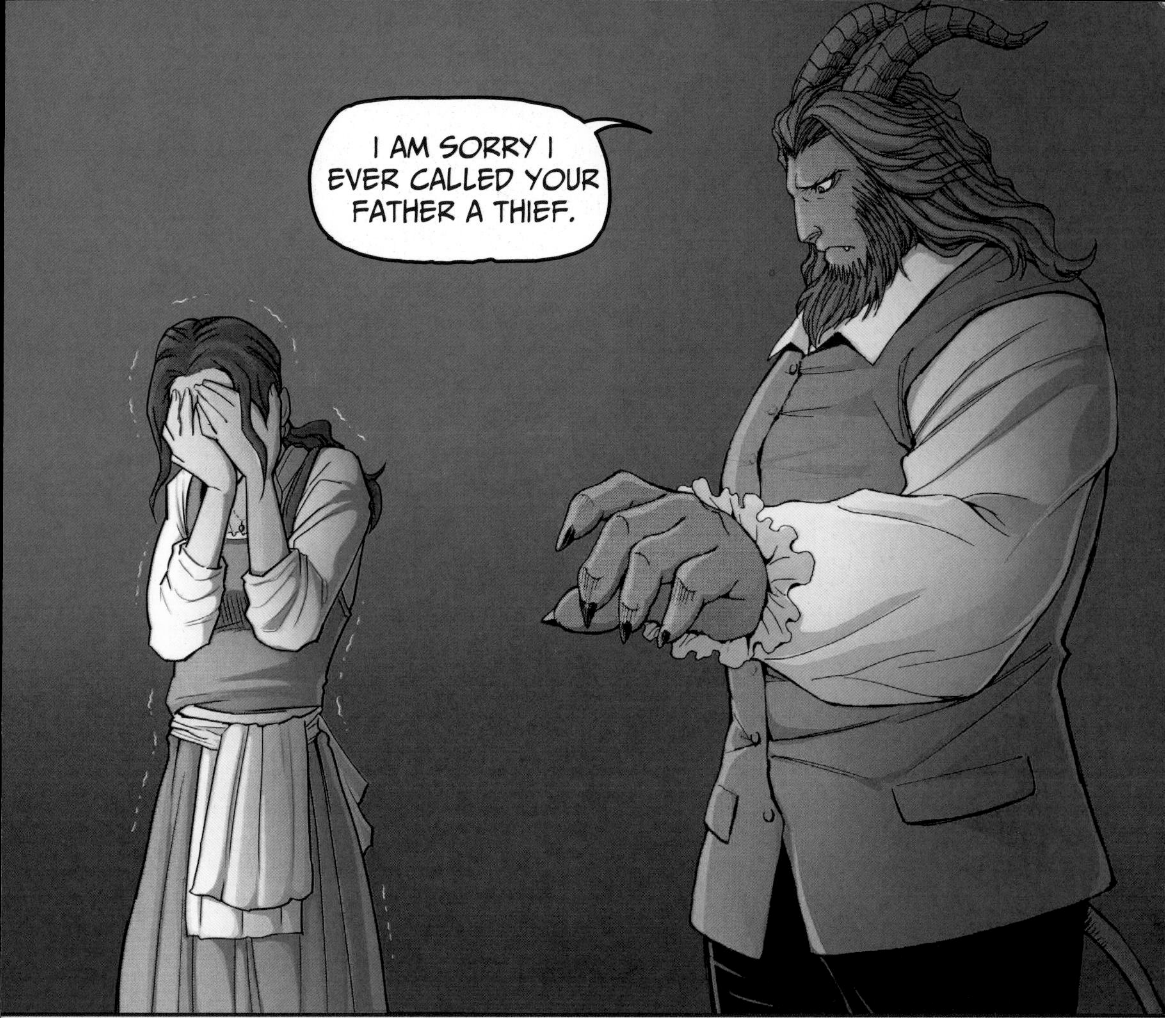
I AM SORRY I EVER CALLED YOUR FATHER A THIEF.

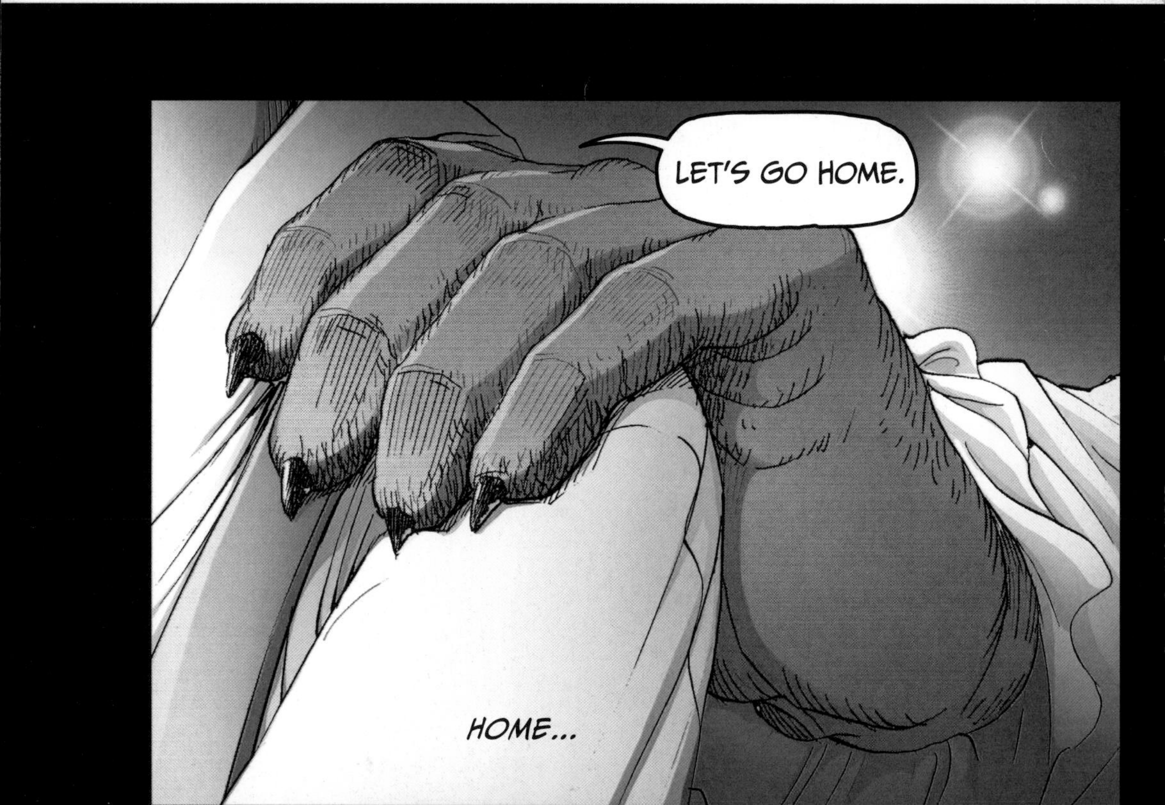
LET'S GO HOME.
HOME...

Chapter 6

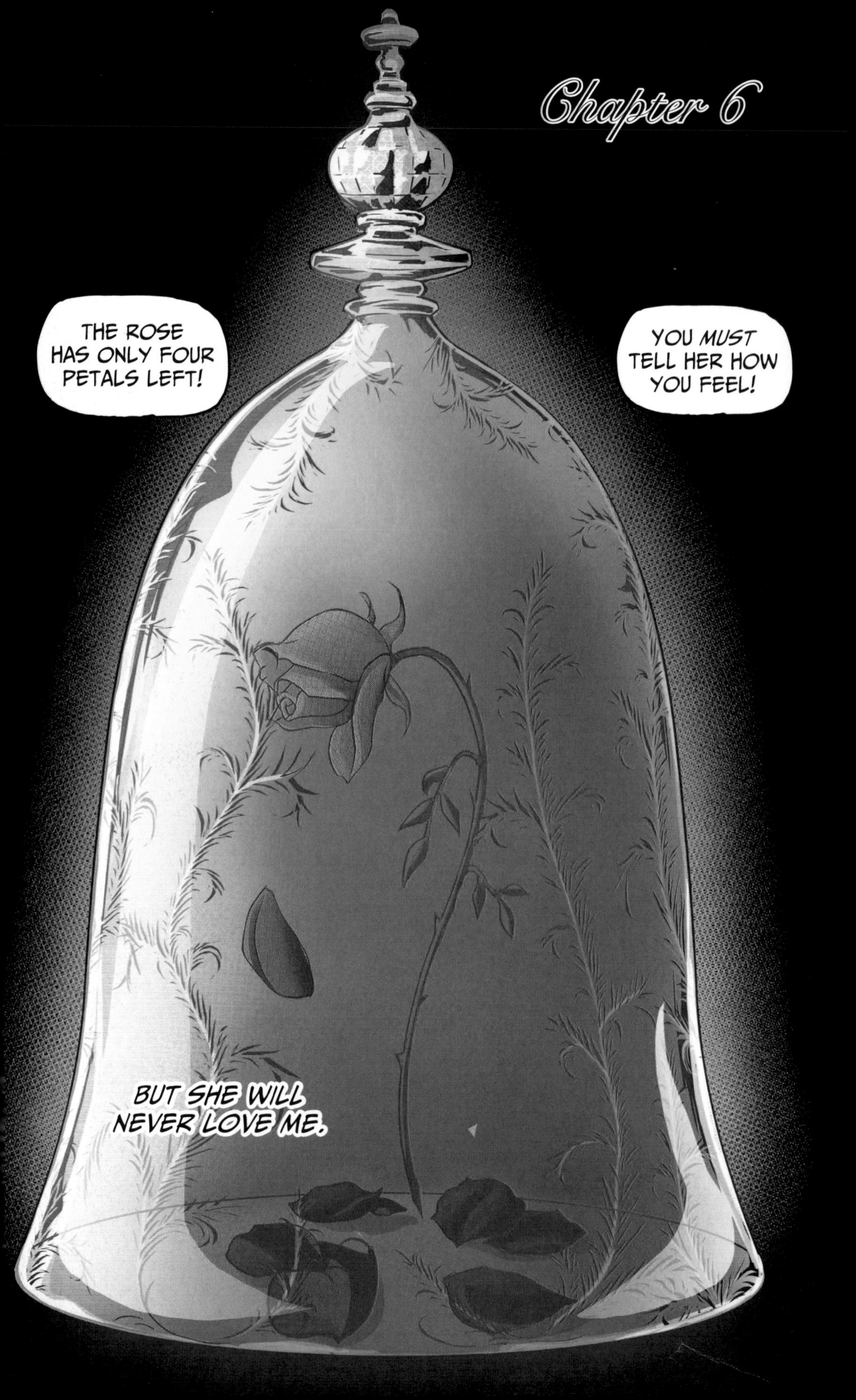
THE ROSE HAS ONLY FOUR PETALS LEFT!
YOU *MUST* TELL HER HOW YOU FEEL!
BUT SHE WILL NEVER LOVE ME.

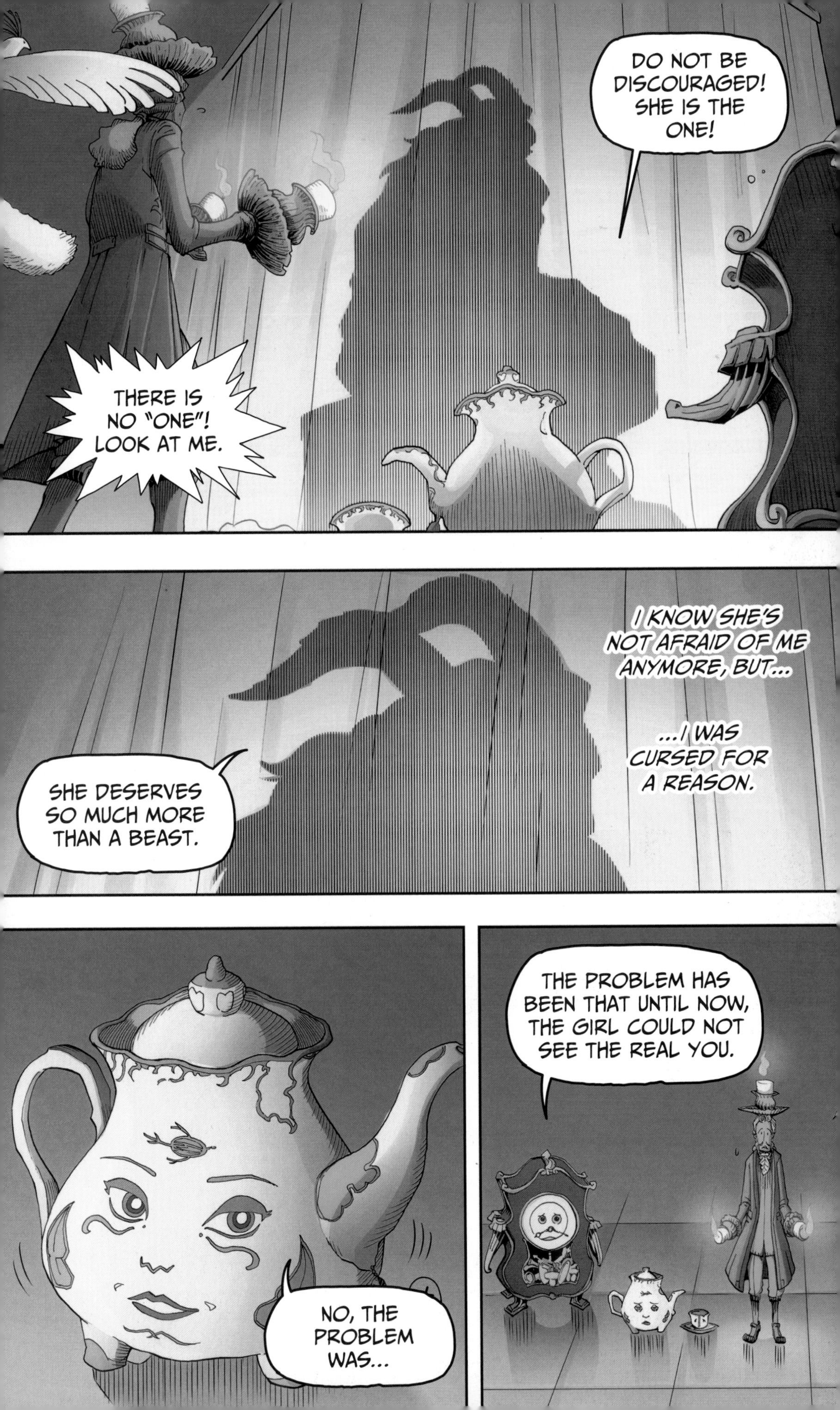
DO NOT BE DISCOURAGED! SHE IS THE ONE!
THERE IS NO "ONE"! LOOK AT ME.
I KNOW SHE'S NOT AFRAID OF ME ANYMORE, BUT...
...I WAS CURSED FOR A REASON.
SHE DESERVES SO MUCH MORE THAN A BEAST.
THE PROBLEM HAS BEEN THAT UNTIL NOW, THE GIRL COULD NOT SEE THE REAL YOU.
NO, THE PROBLEM WAS...

...SHE COULD.

FOR YEARS, WE HAVE HOPED AGAINST HOPE THAT THIS CURSE WOULD MAKE YOU A BETTER MAN....

WHAT?

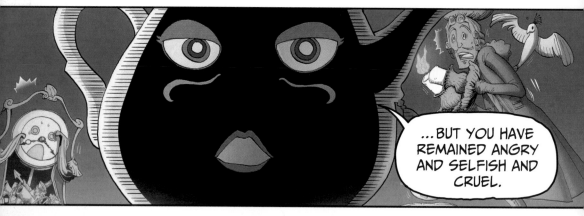

...BUT YOU HAVE REMAINED ANGRY AND SELFISH AND CRUEL.

SHE'S RIGHT.

THAT GIRL HAS BROUGHT ABOUT A CHANGE IN YOU...

...AND WE'RE ALL GLAD TO SEE IT.

WE LOVE YOU, MASTER.

WHAT...?

SO STOP BEING A COWARD, AND TELL BELLE HOW YOU FEEL!

AND IF YOU DON'T, I PROMISE YOU'LL BE DRINKING COLD TEA FOR THE REST OF YOUR LIFE!

I HAVEN'T...

...FELT THIS WAY IN A LONG TIME.

I FEEL LOVED.

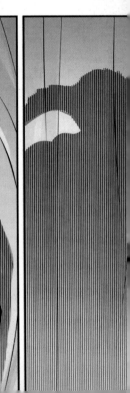

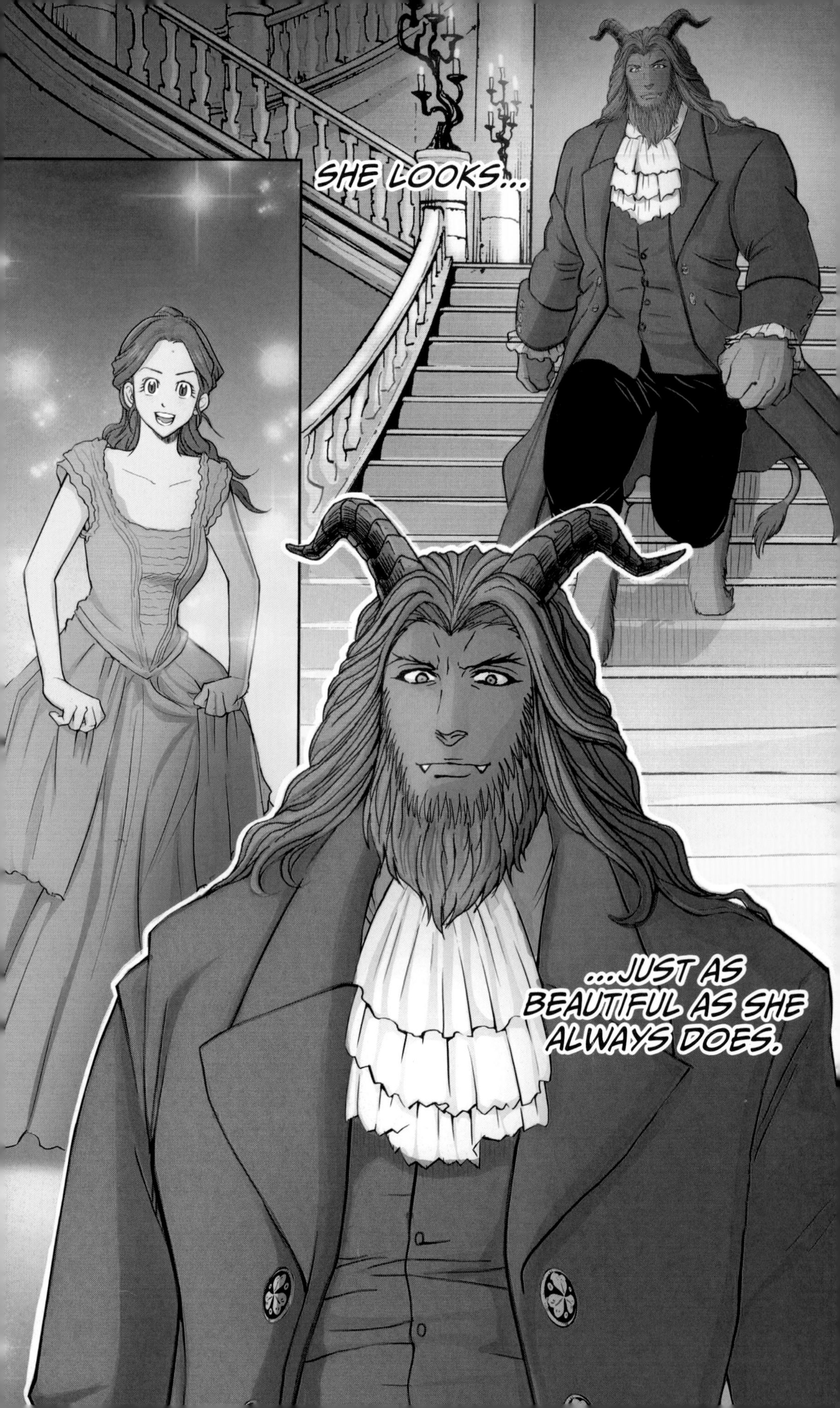
SHE LOOKS...
...JUST AS BEAUTIFUL AS SHE ALWAYS DOES.

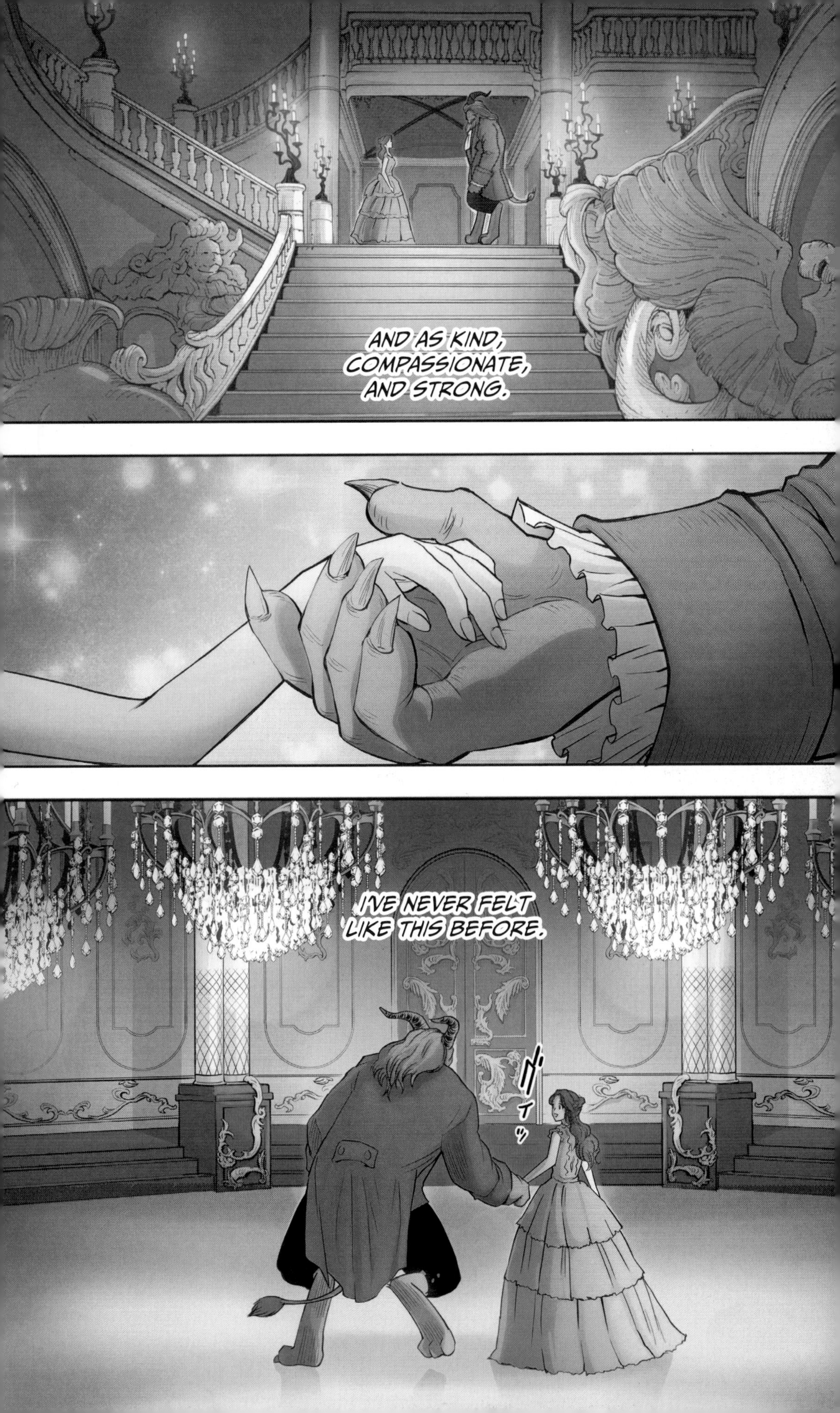
AND AS KIND, COMPASSIONATE, AND STRONG.
I'VE NEVER FELT LIKE THIS BEFORE.

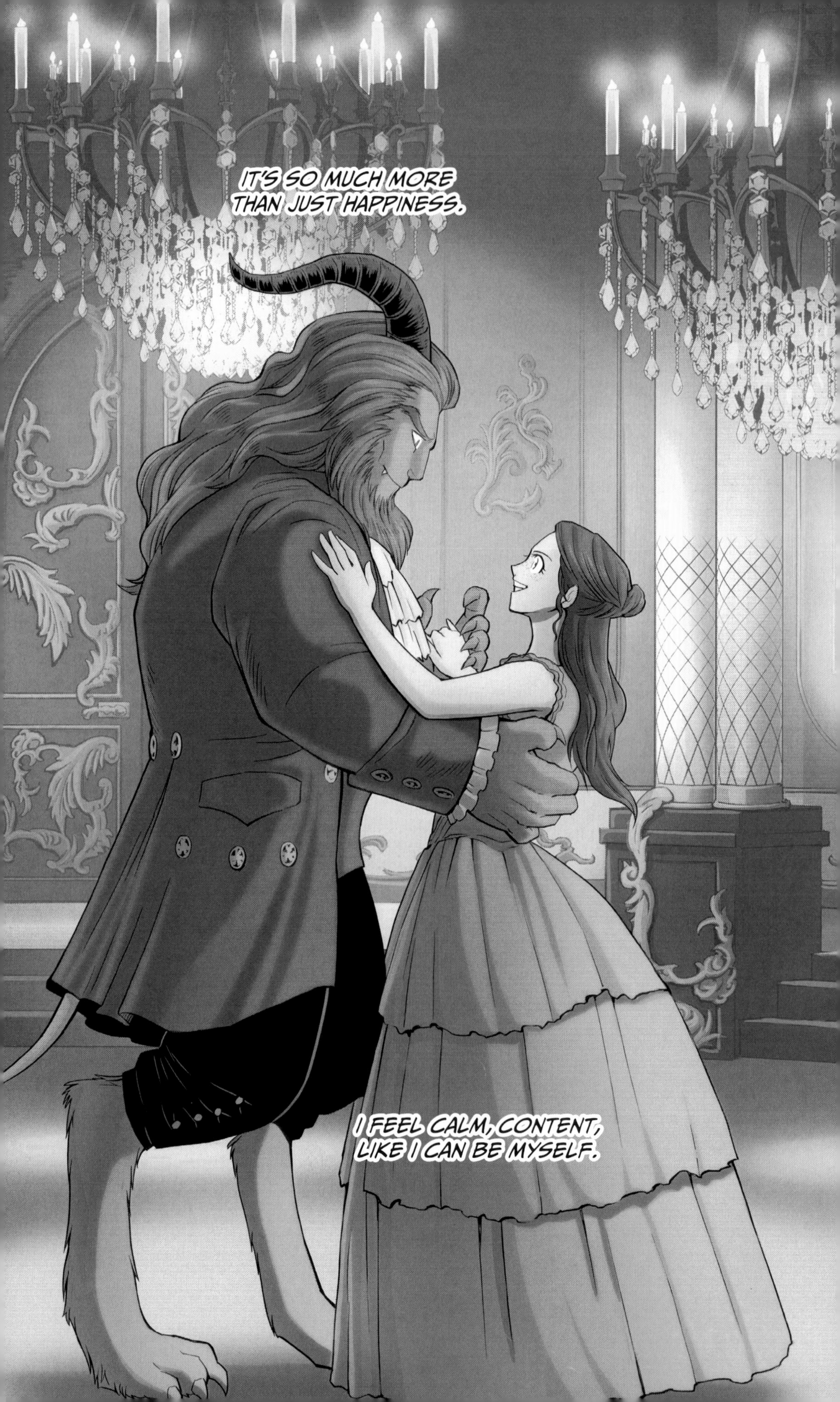
IT'S SO MUCH MORE THAN JUST HAPPINESS.
I FEEL CALM, CONTENT, LIKE I CAN BE MYSELF.

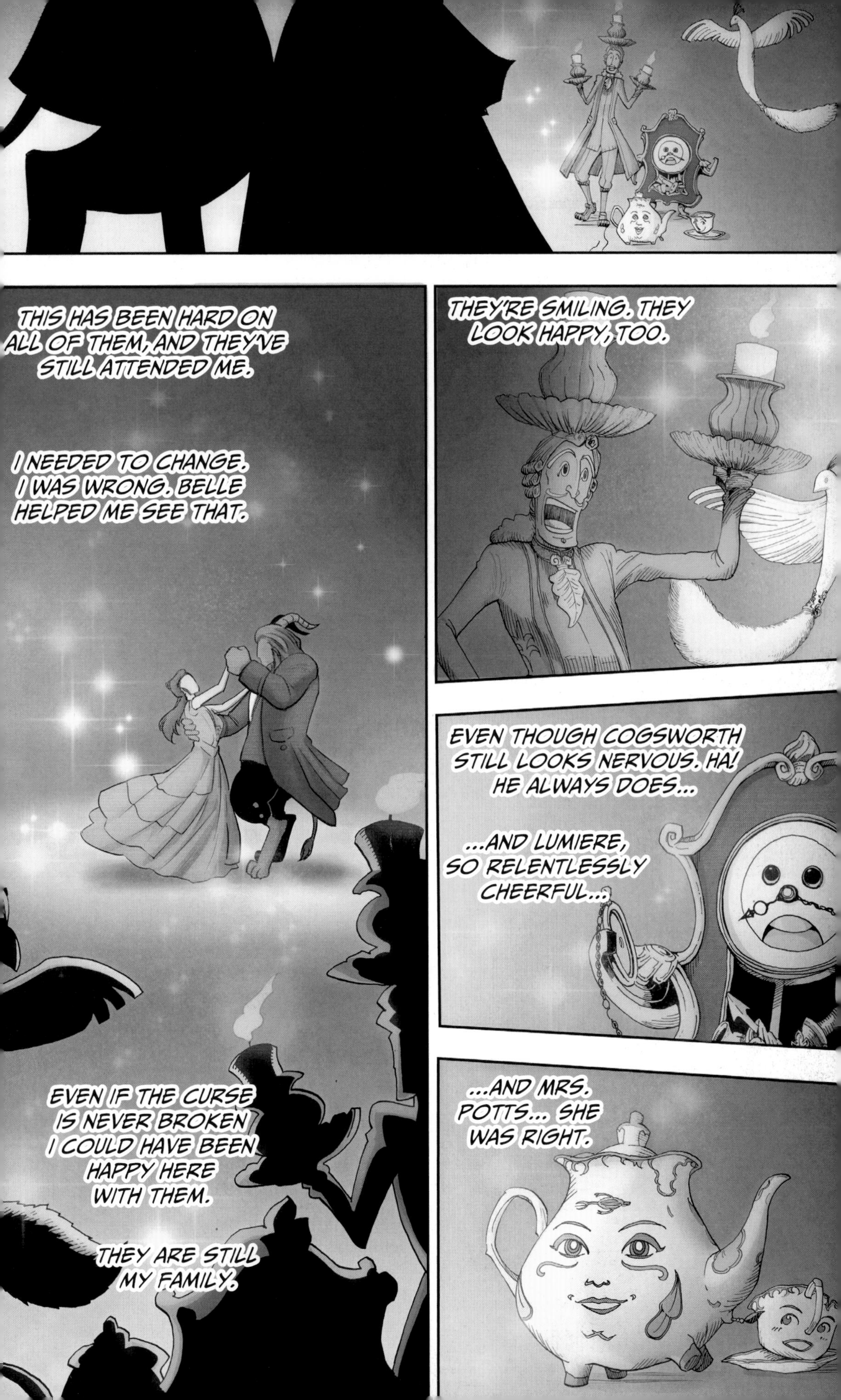
THEY'RE SMILING. THEY LOOK HAPPY, TOO.
EVEN THOUGH COGSWORTH STILL LOOKS NERVOUS. HA! HE ALWAYS DOES...
...AND LUMIERE, SO RELENTLESSLY CHEERFUL...
...AND MRS. POTTS... SHE WAS RIGHT.
THIS HAS BEEN HARD ON ALL OF THEM, AND THEY'VE STILL ATTENDED ME.
I NEEDED TO CHANGE. I WAS WRONG. BELLE HELPED ME SEE THAT.
EVEN IF THE CURSE IS NEVER BROKEN I COULD HAVE BEEN HAPPY HERE WITH THEM.
THEY ARE STILL MY FAMILY.

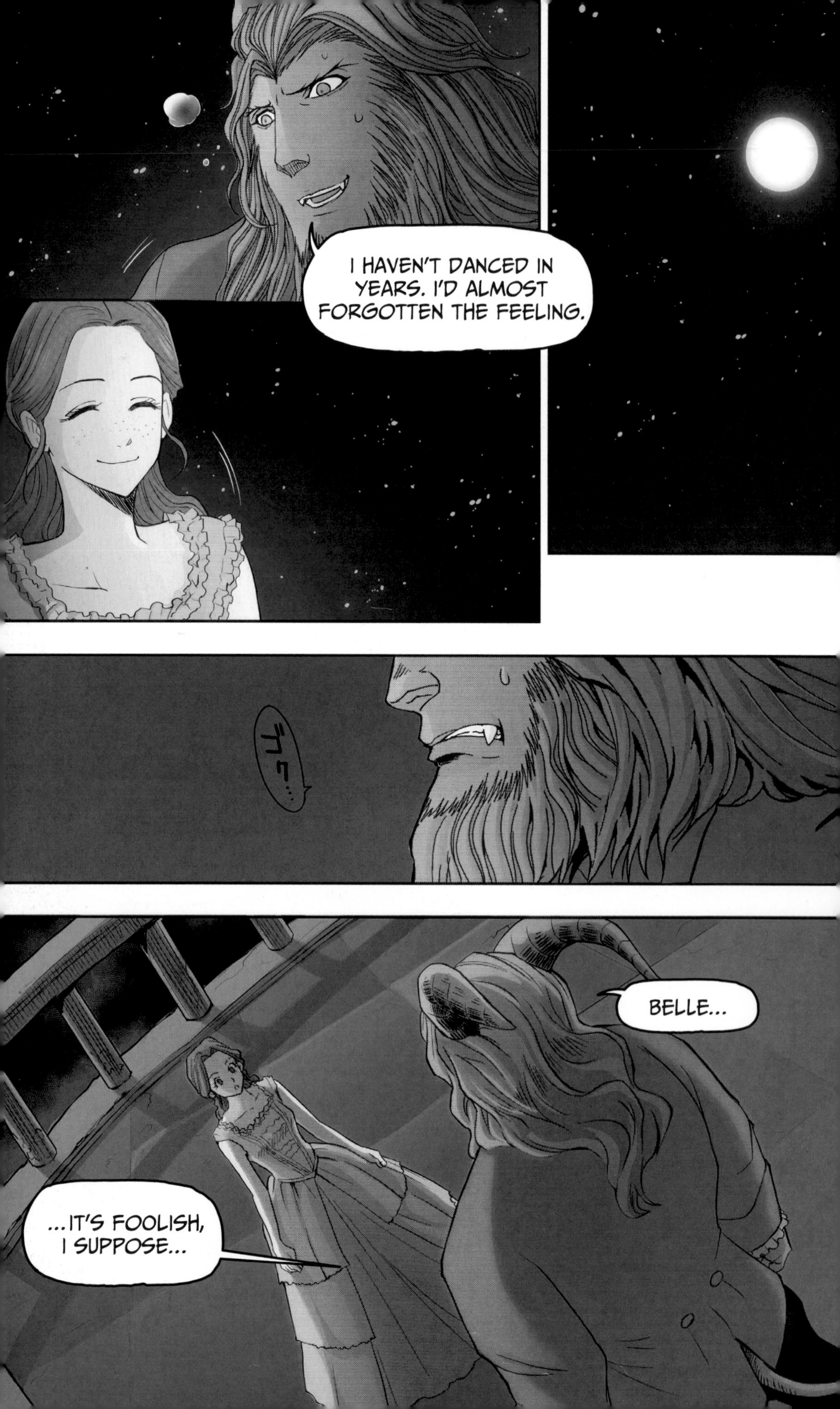
I HAVEN'T DANCED IN YEARS. I'D ALMOST FORGOTTEN THE FEELING.
ゴク…
BELLE...
...IT'S FOOLISH, I SUPPOSE...

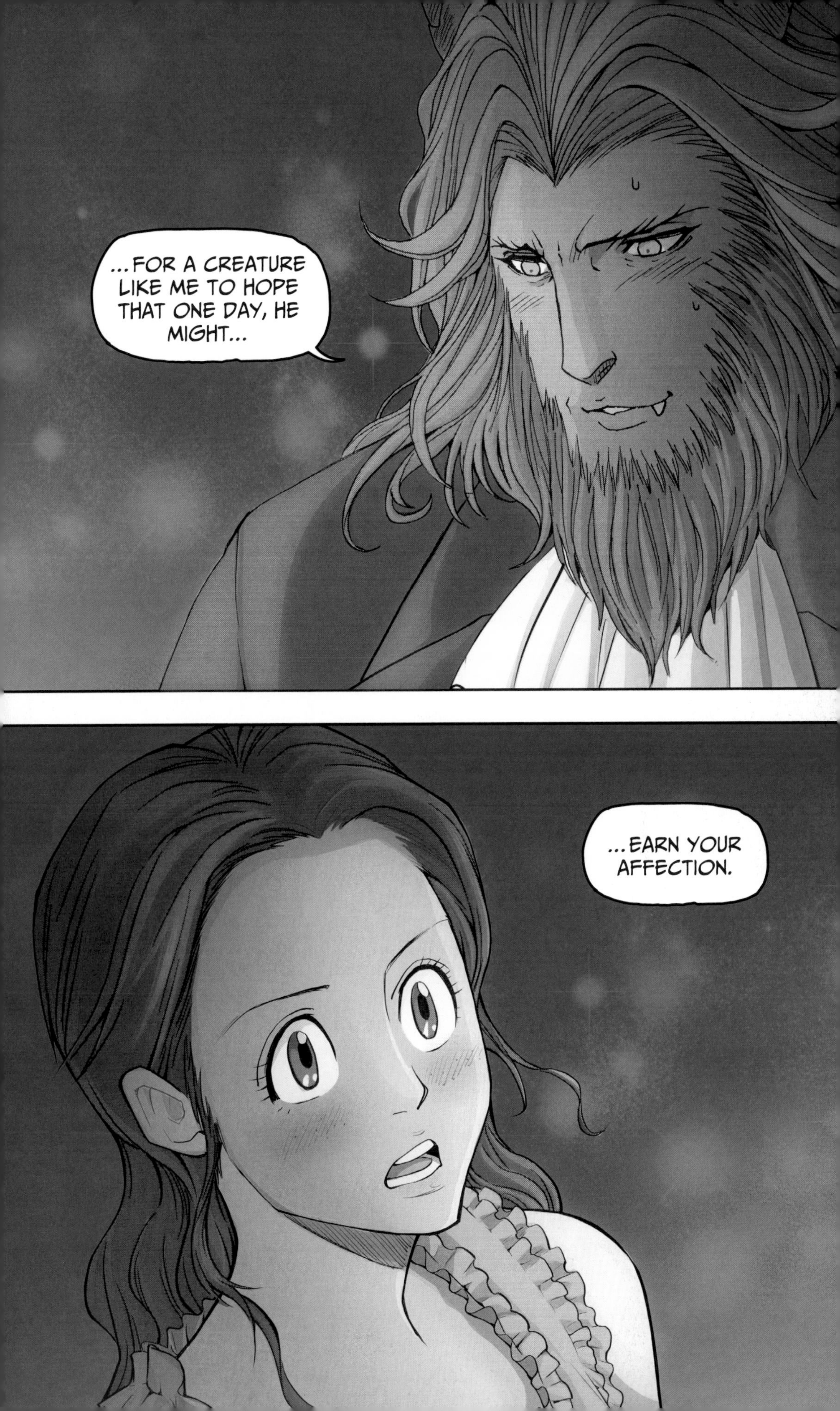
...FOR A CREATURE LIKE ME TO HOPE THAT ONE DAY, HE MIGHT...
...EARN YOUR AFFECTION.

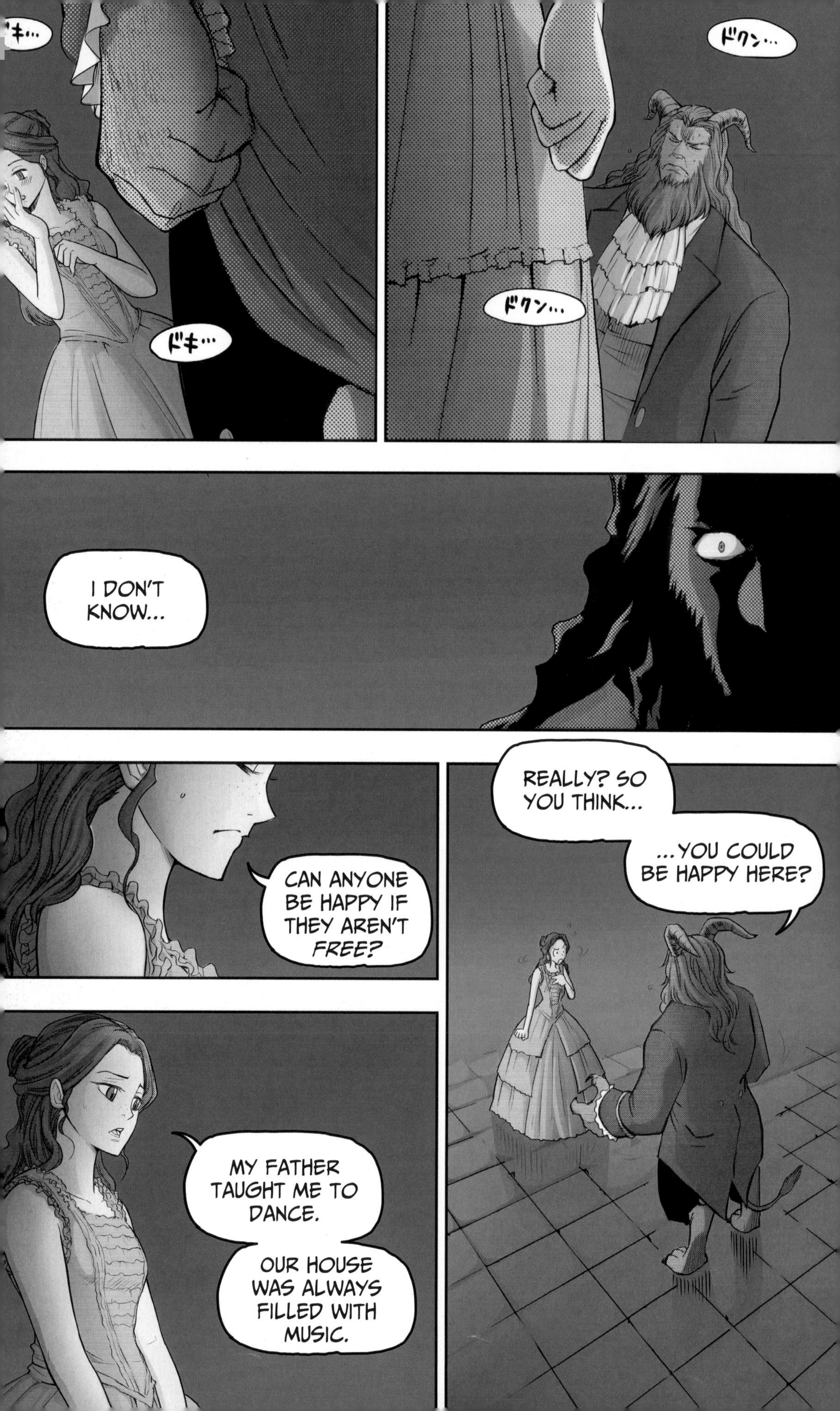
ドクン…
ドクン…
キ…
ドキ…
I DON'T KNOW...
REALLY? SO YOU THINK...
...YOU COULD BE HAPPY HERE?
CAN ANYONE BE HAPPY IF THEY AREN'T *FREE?*
MY FATHER TAUGHT ME TO DANCE.
OUR HOUSE WAS ALWAYS FILLED WITH MUSIC.

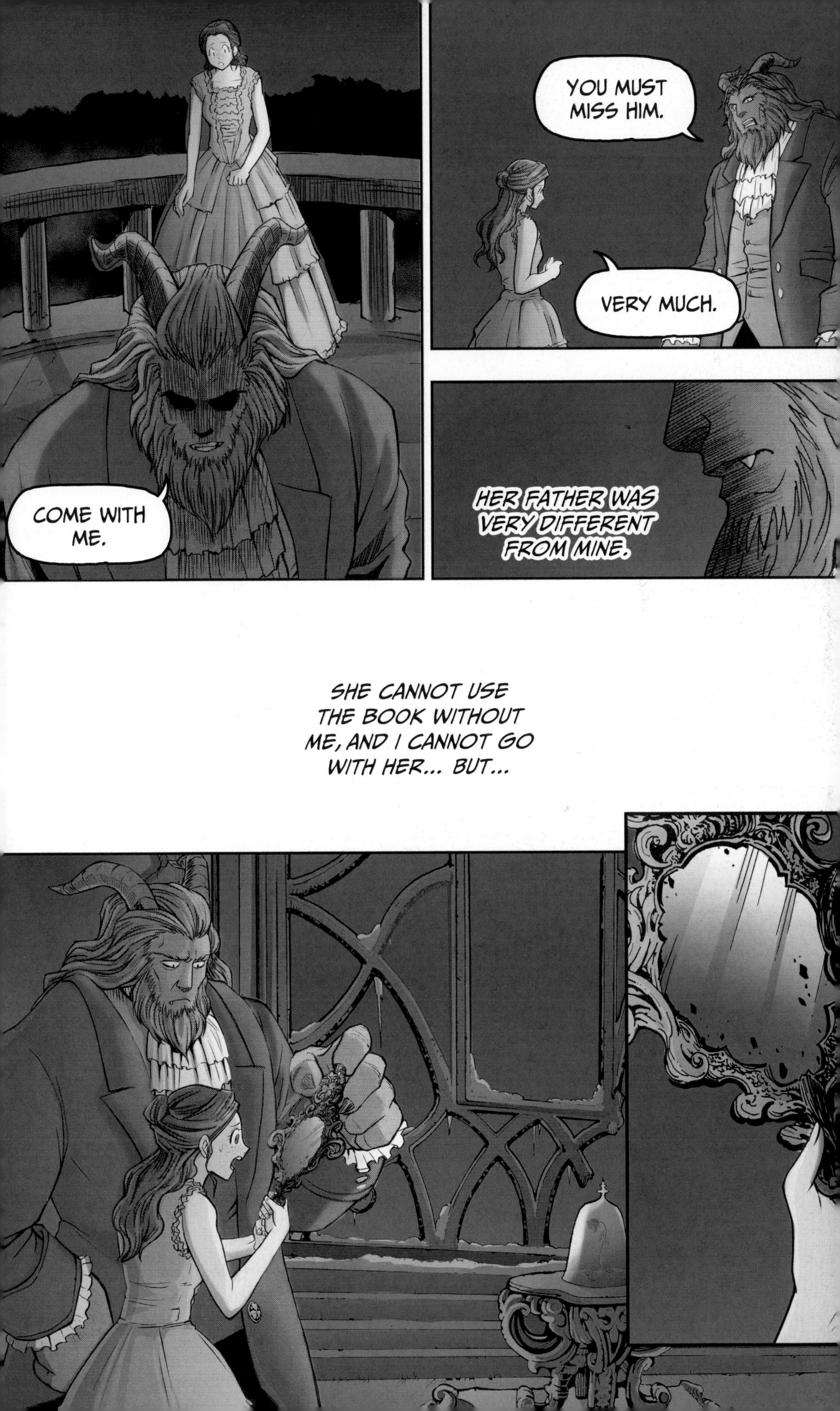
YOU MUST MISS HIM.
VERY MUCH.
HER FATHER WAS VERY DIFFERENT FROM MINE.
COME WITH ME.
SHE CANNOT USE THE BOOK WITHOUT ME, AND I CANNOT GO WITH HER... BUT...

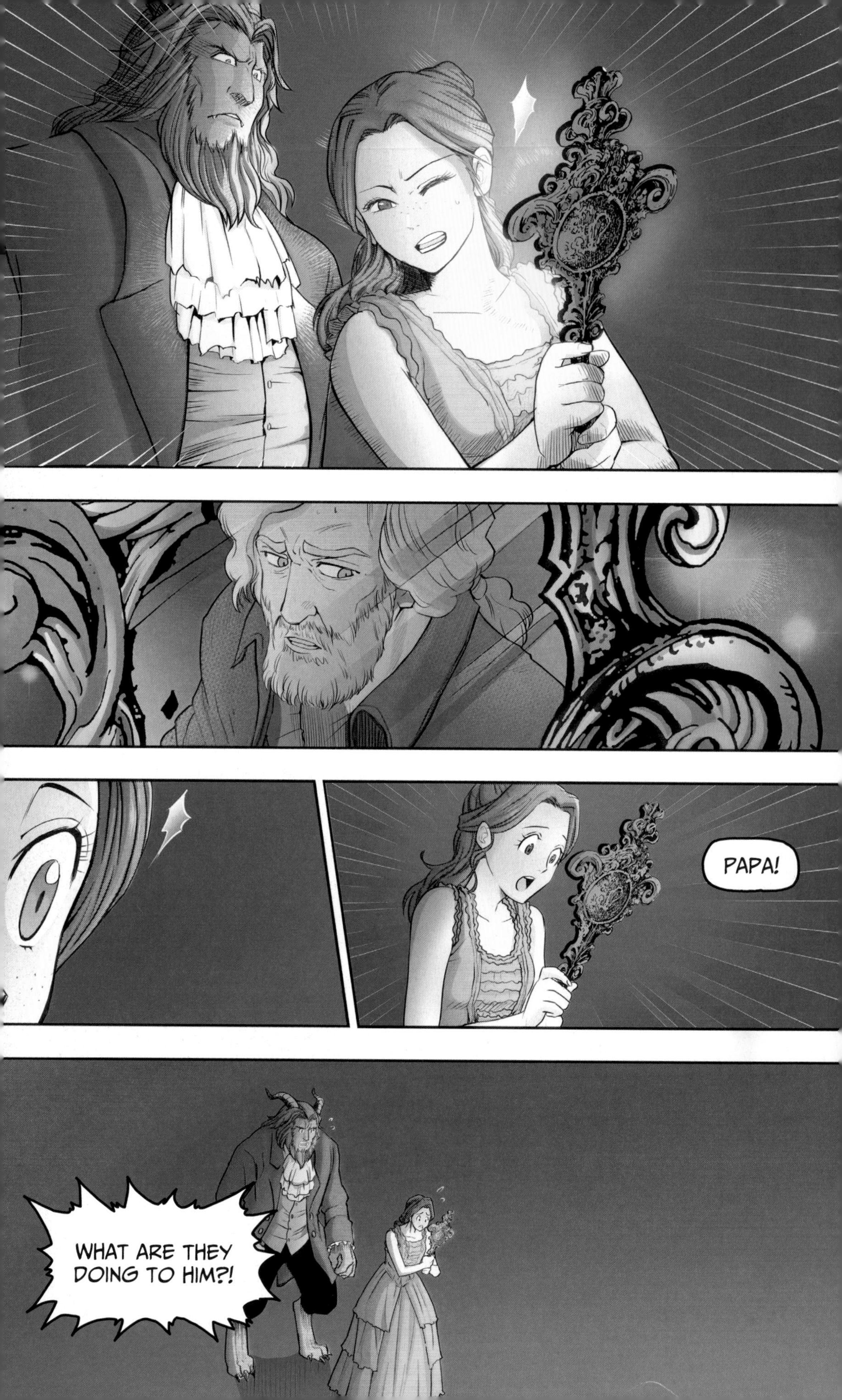
PAPA!
WHAT ARE THEY DOING TO HIM?!

THE VILLAGERS ARE...

...LOCKING HIM UP?

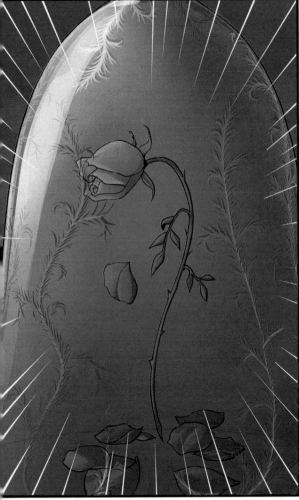

THERE IS NOTHING I CAN DO.

EXCEPT...

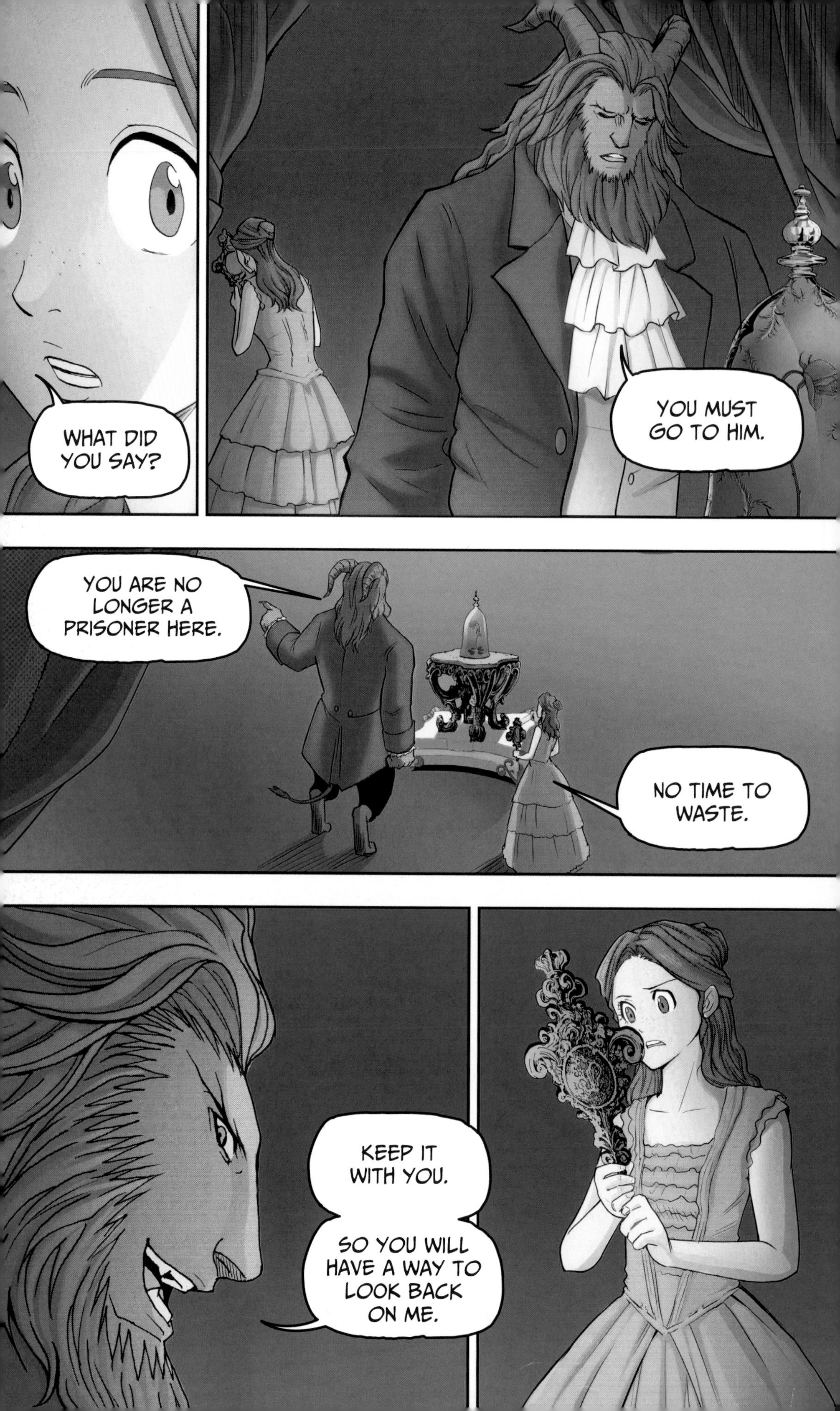
YOU MUST GO TO HIM.
WHAT DID YOU SAY?
YOU ARE NO LONGER A PRISONER HERE.
NO TIME TO WASTE.
KEEP IT WITH YOU.
SO YOU WILL HAVE A WAY TO LOOK BACK ON ME.

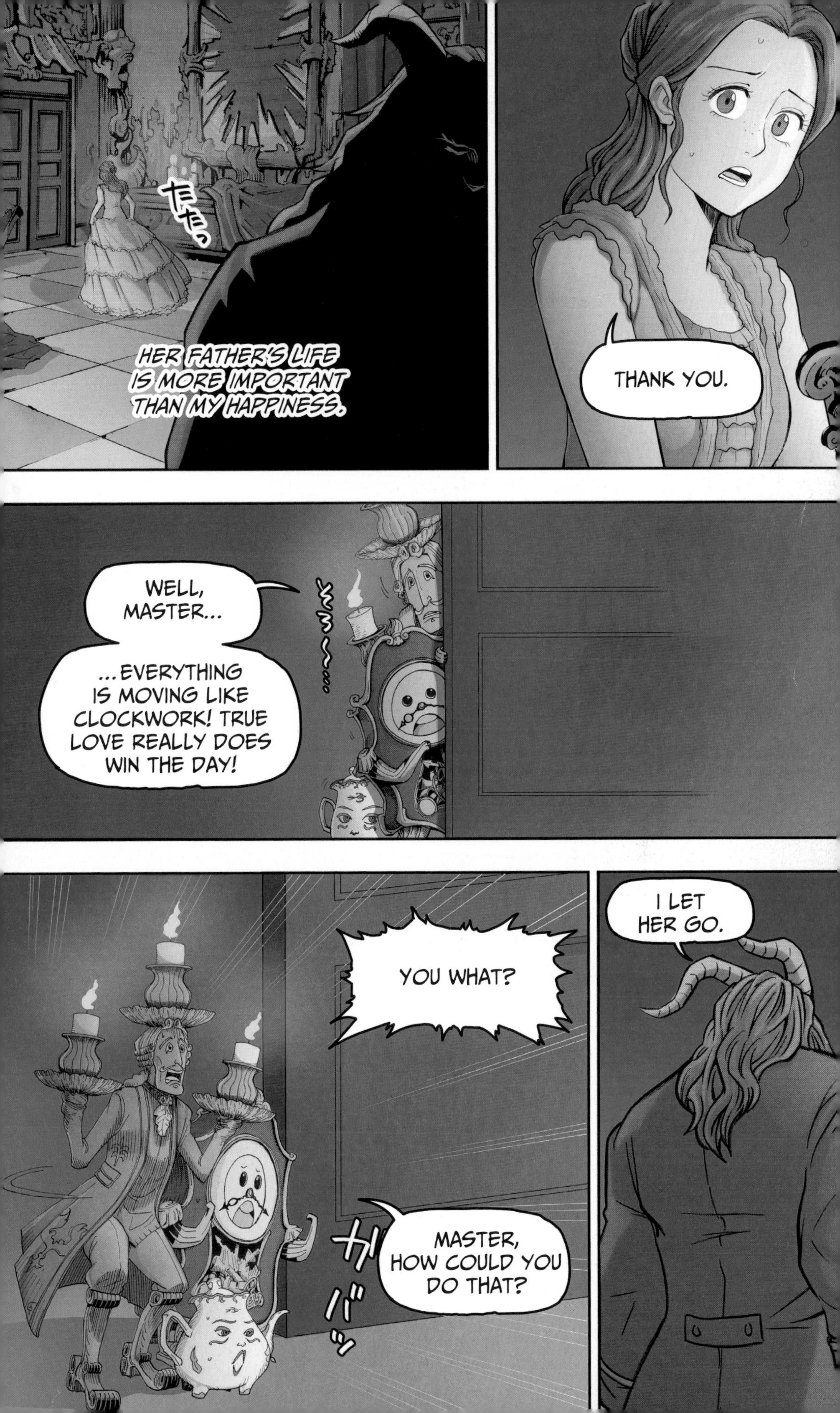
THANK YOU.
HER FATHER'S LIFE IS MORE IMPORTANT THAN MY HAPPINESS.
たたっ
WELL, MASTER...
...EVERYTHING IS MOVING LIKE CLOCKWORK! TRUE LOVE REALLY DOES WIN THE DAY!
I LET HER GO.
YOU WHAT?
MASTER, HOW COULD YOU DO THAT?

BECAUSE HE LOVES HER.

I HAD TO.

I SET HER FREE.

I'M SORRY I COULDN'T DO THE SAME FOR YOU.

BUT WHY?

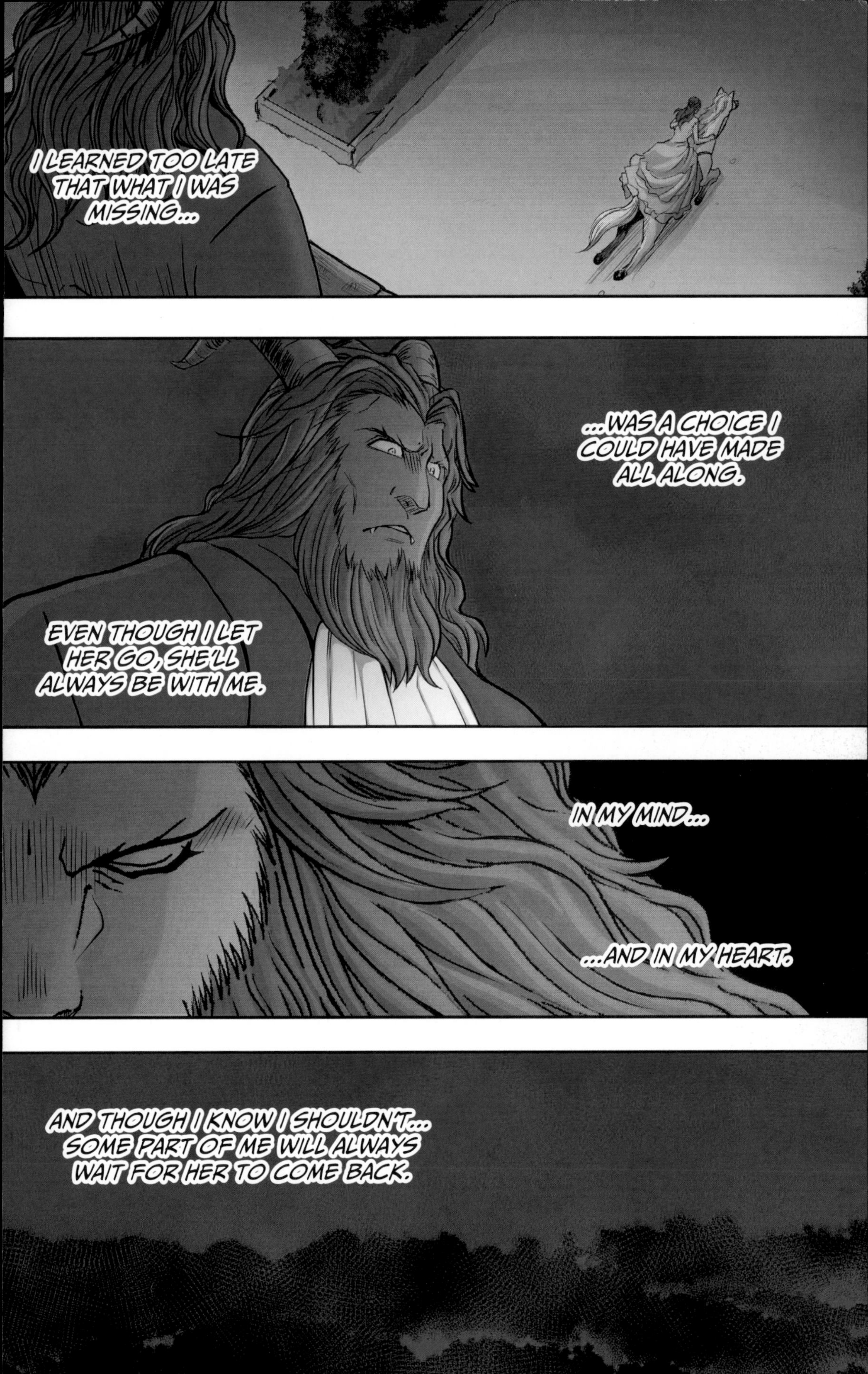
I LEARNED TOO LATE THAT WHAT I WAS MISSING...
...WAS A CHOICE I COULD HAVE MADE ALL ALONG.
EVEN THOUGH I LET HER GO, SHE'LL ALWAYS BE WITH ME.
IN MY MIND...
...AND IN MY HEART.
AND THOUGH I KNOW I SHOULDN'T... SOME PART OF ME WILL ALWAYS WAIT FOR HER TO COME BACK.

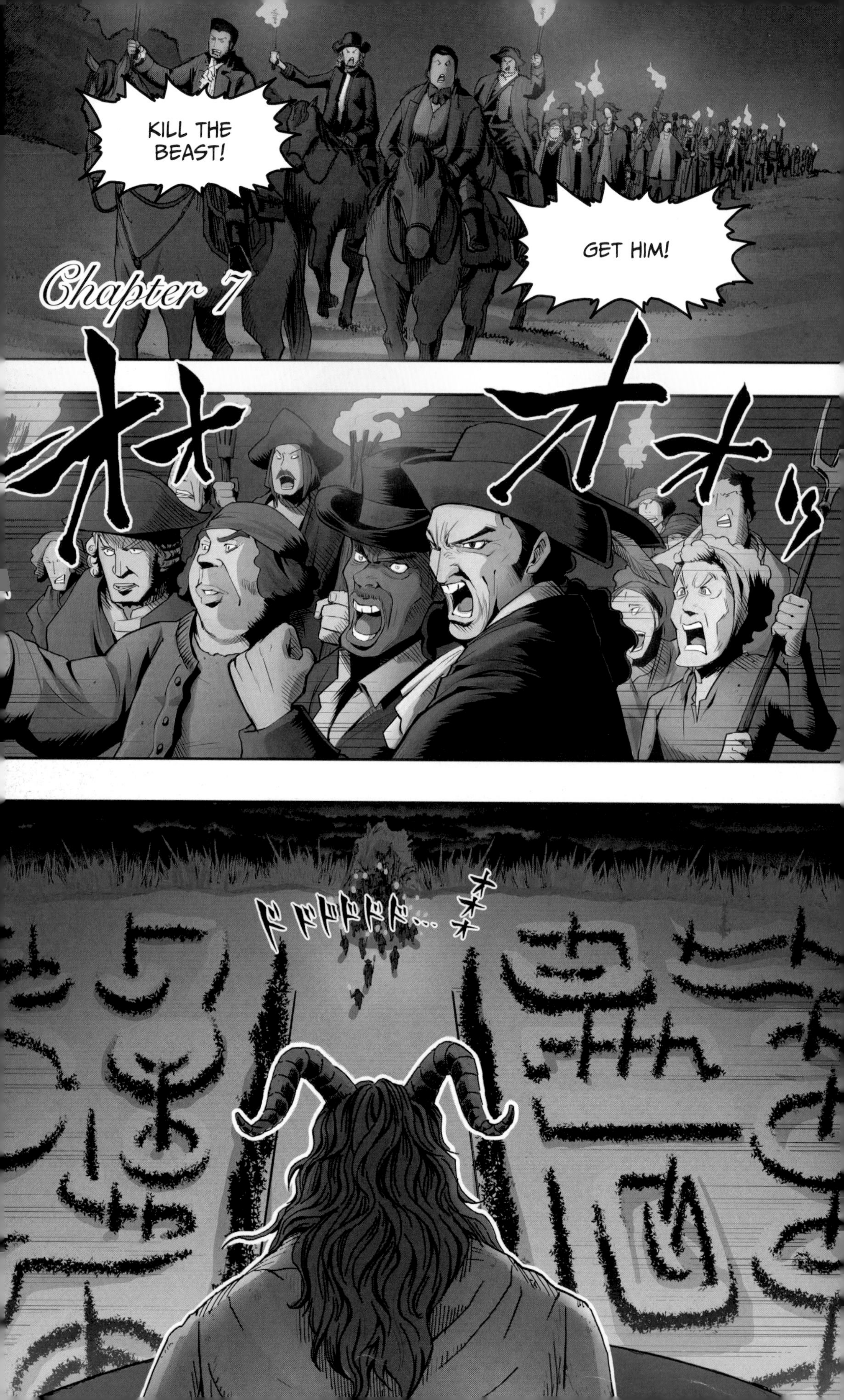
Chapter 7
GET HIM!
KILL THE BEAST!
オオオオオオッ
ドドドドドド…
オオオ

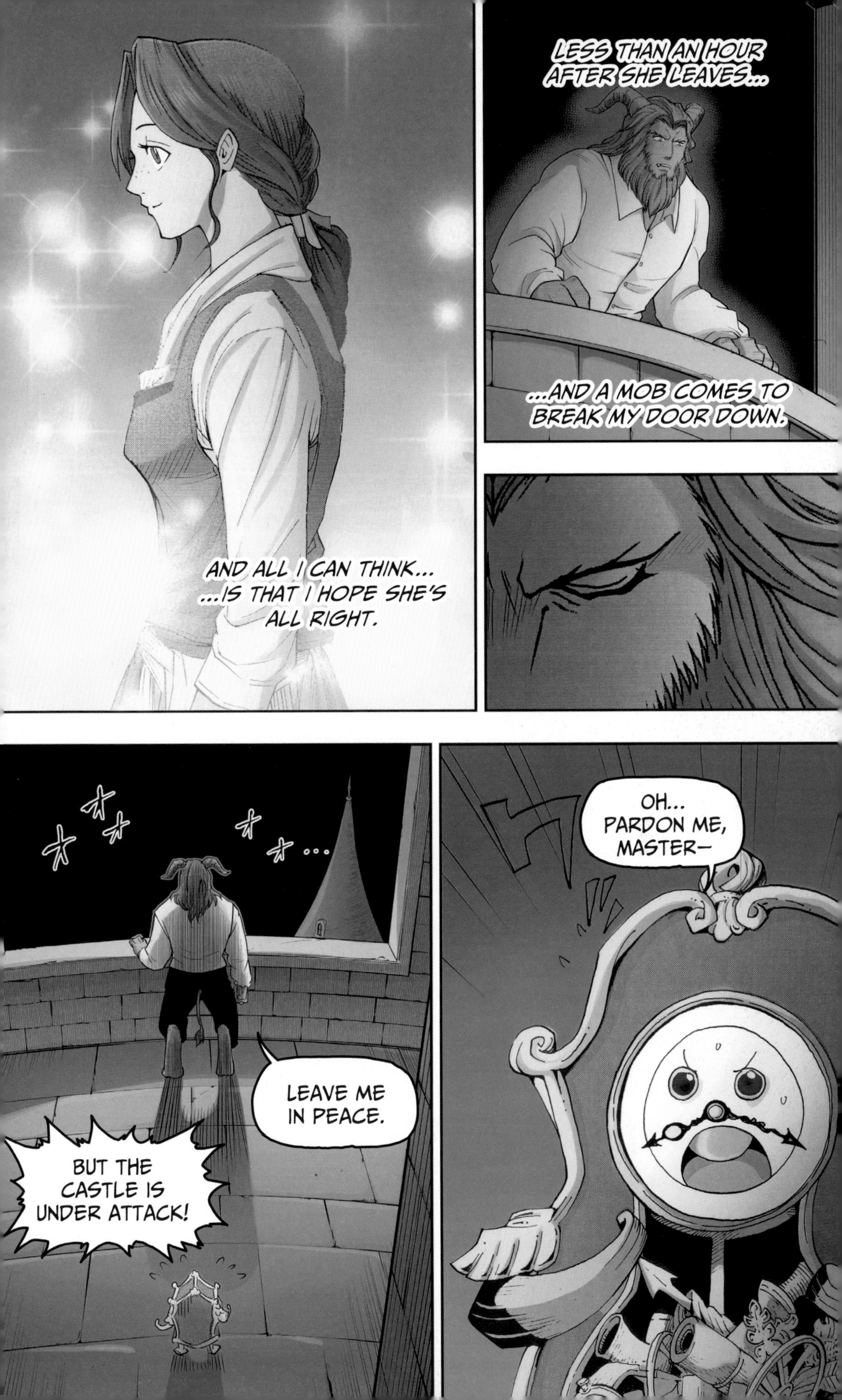
LESS THAN AN HOUR AFTER SHE LEAVES...
...AND A MOB COMES TO BREAK MY DOOR DOWN.
AND ALL I CAN THINK... ...IS THAT I HOPE SHE'S ALL RIGHT.
OH... PARDON ME, MASTER—
LEAVE ME IN PEACE.
BUT THE CASTLE IS UNDER ATTACK!

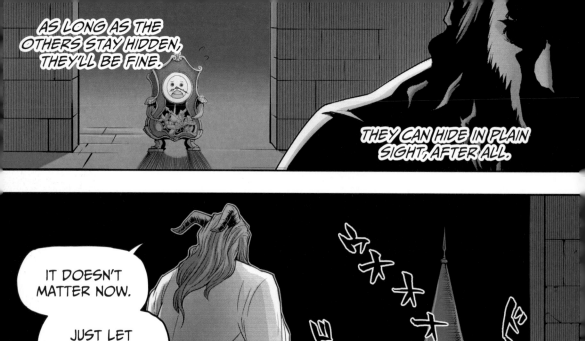

AS LONG AS THE OTHERS STAY HIDDEN, THEY'LL BE FINE.

THEY CAN HIDE IN PLAIN SIGHT, AFTER ALL.

IT DOESN'T MATTER NOW.

JUST LET THEM COME.

WHY FIGHT?! WHY INDEED!

WHY DO ANY BLOODY THING AT ALL?!

I'M SORRY, OLD FRIEND.

BUT SOON ENOUGH, IT WON'T MATTER.

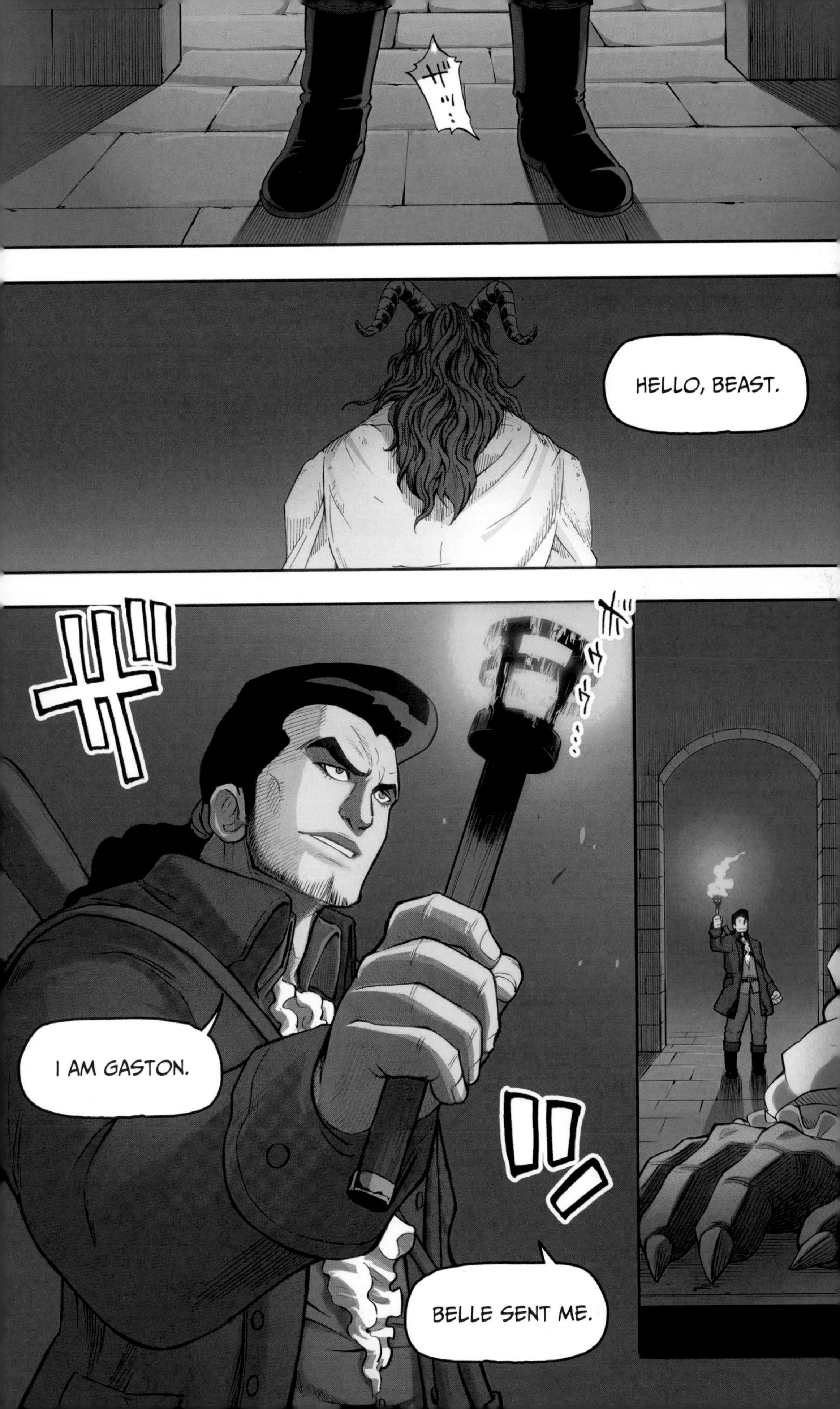
HELLO, BEAST.
I AM GASTON.
BELLE SENT ME.

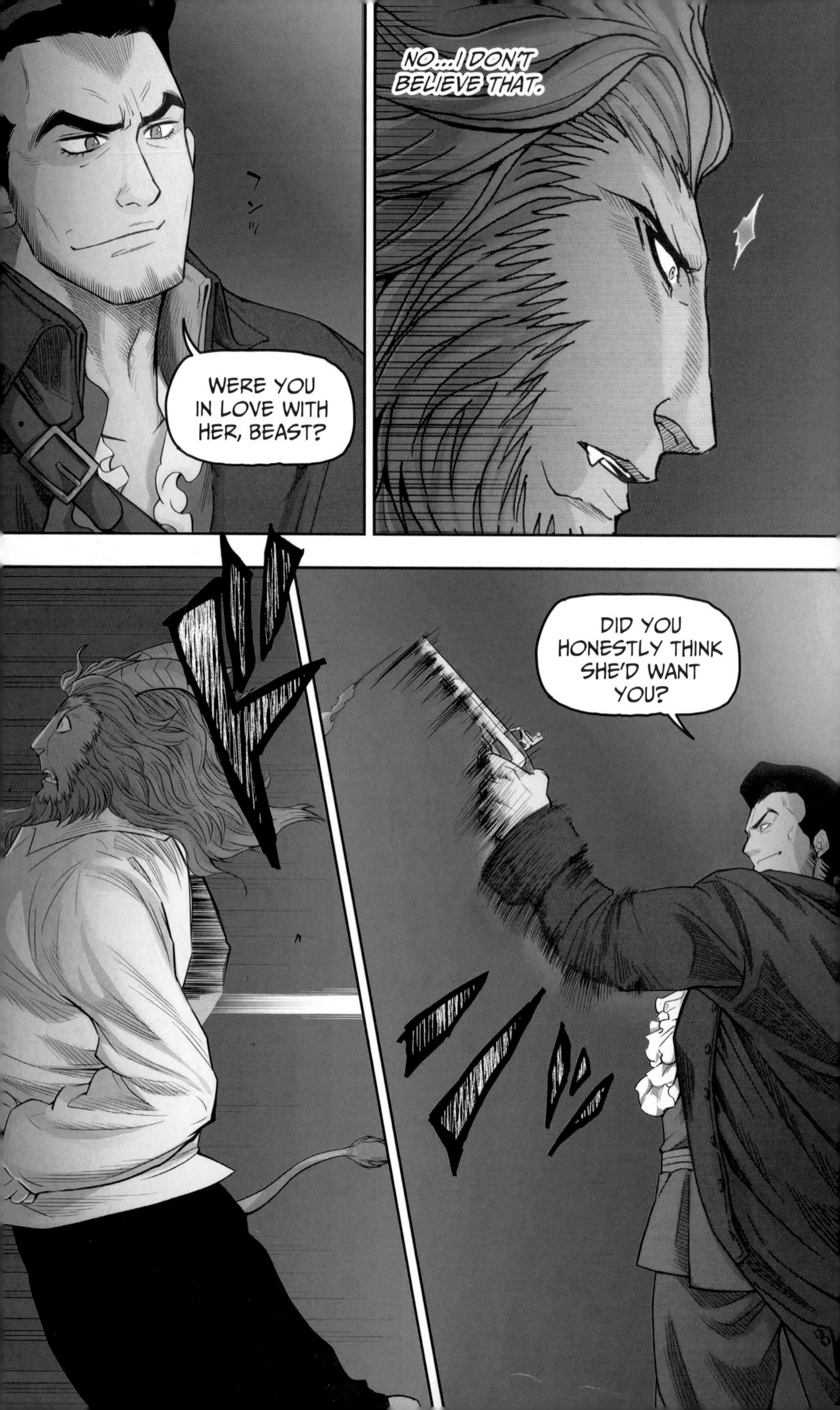
NO...I DON'T BELIEVE THAT.
WERE YOU IN LOVE WITH HER, BEAST?
DID YOU HONESTLY THINK SHE'D WANT YOU?

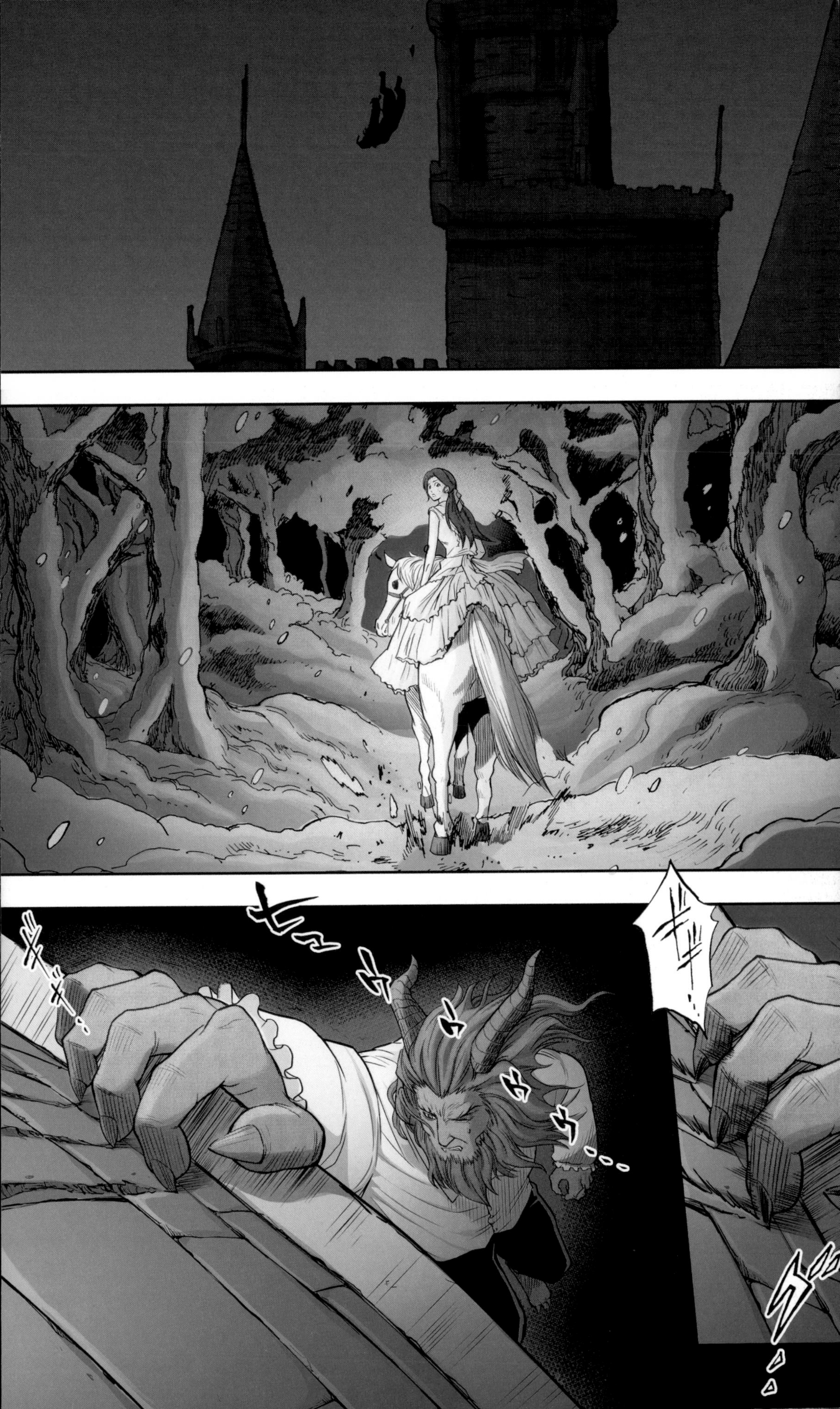

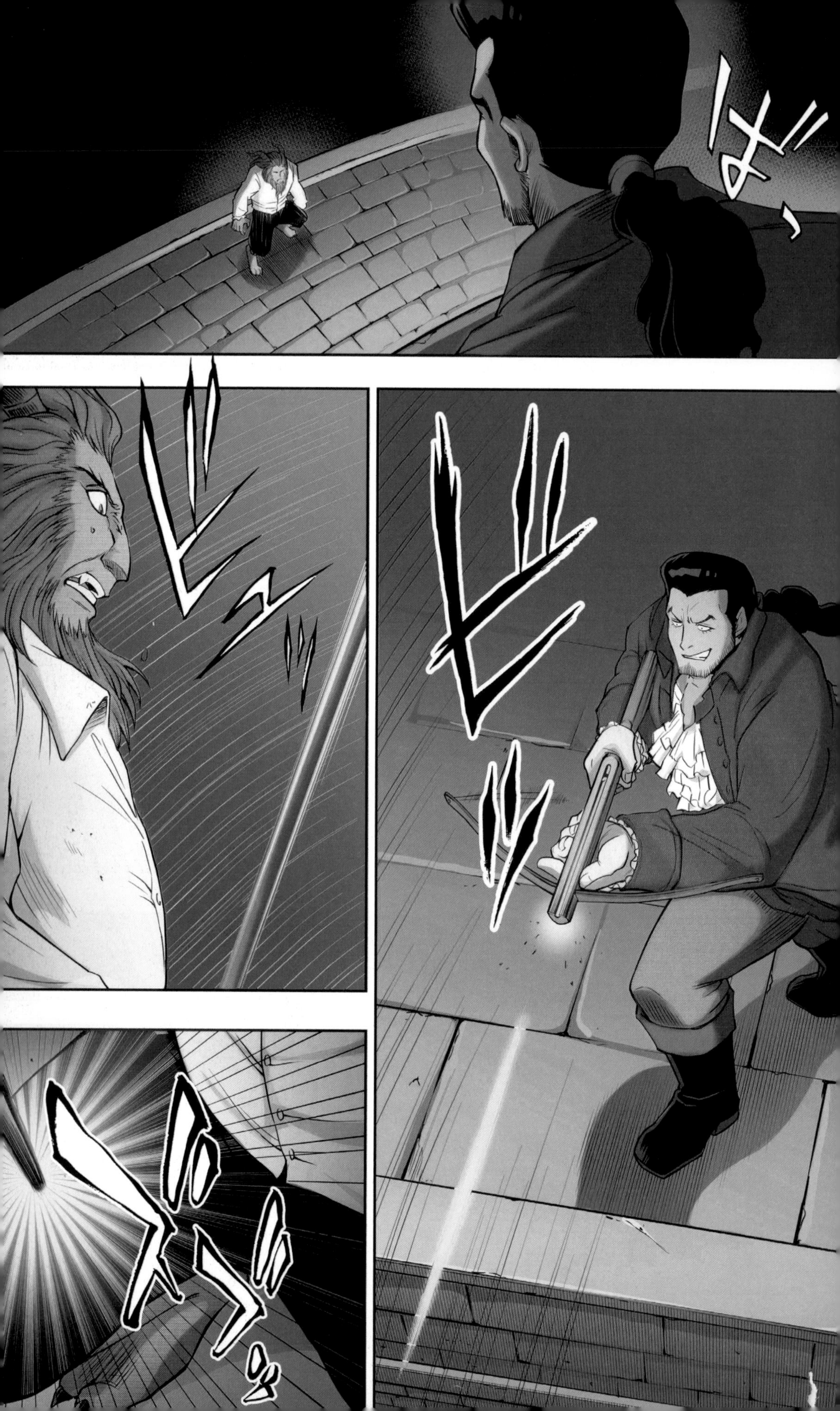
ば
ビッ
ビュッ

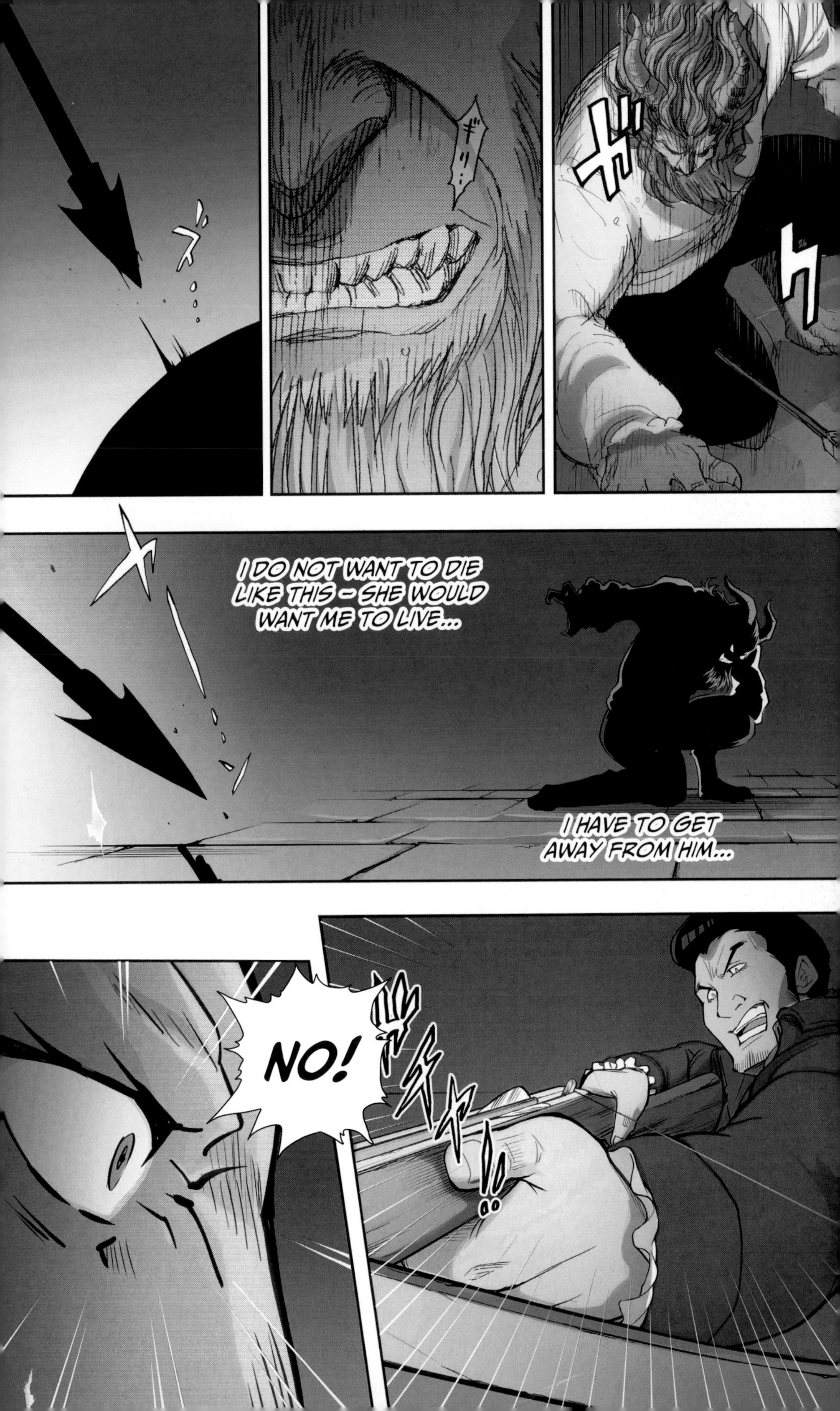
I DO NOT WANT TO DIE LIKE THIS – SHE WOULD WANT ME TO LIVE...
I HAVE TO GET AWAY FROM HIM...
NO!

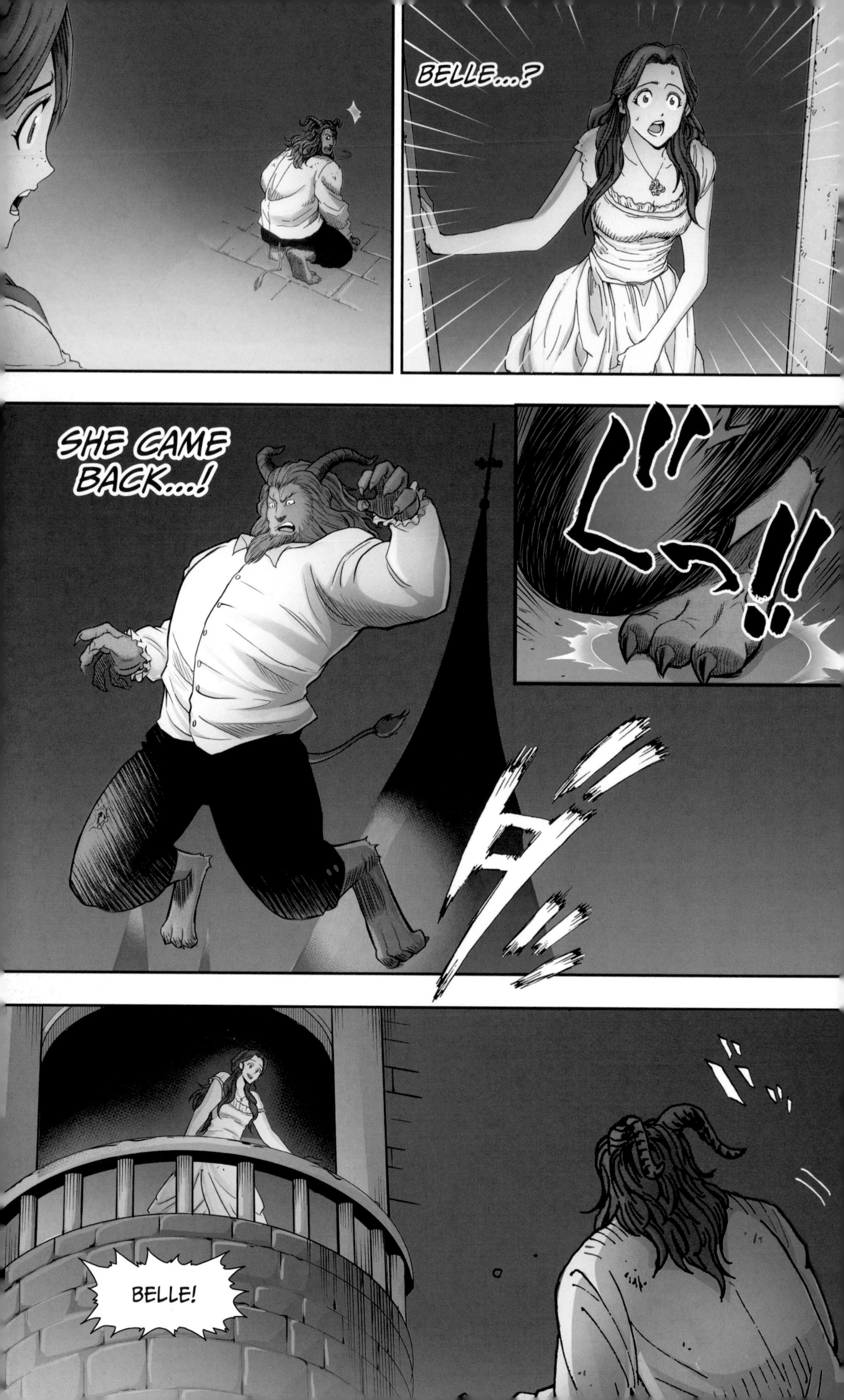
BELLE...?
SHE CAME BACK...!
BELLE!

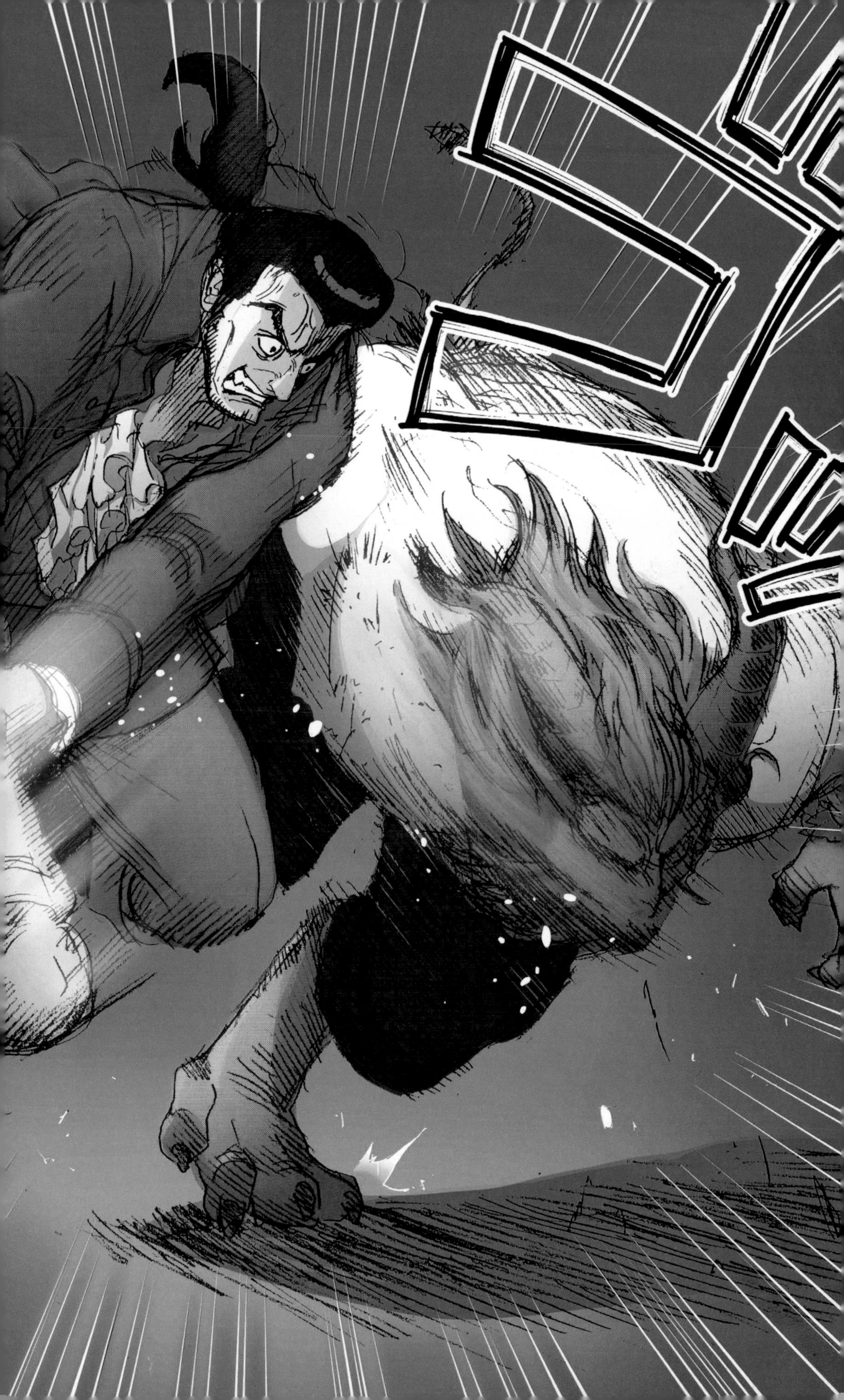

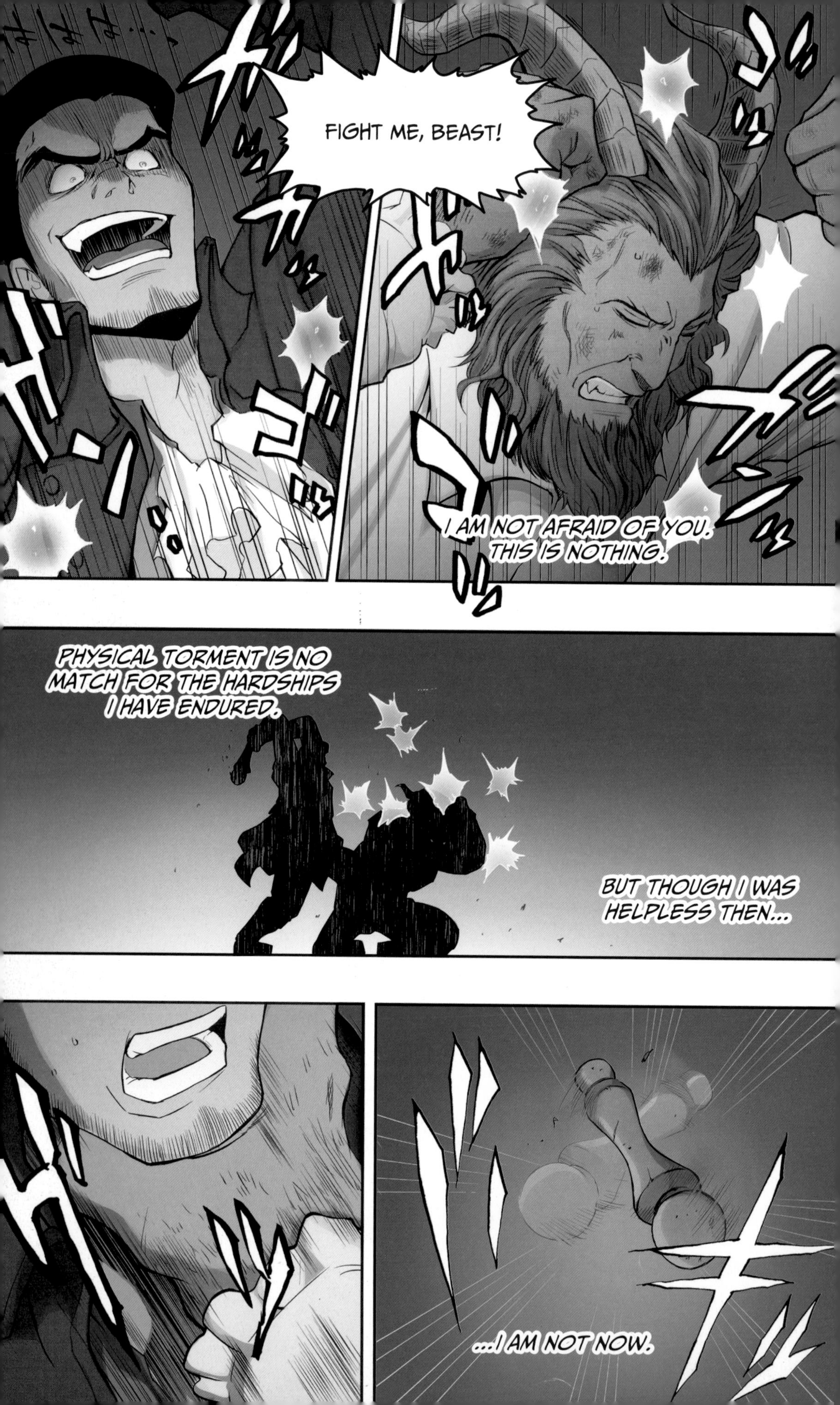

FIGHT ME, BEAST!
I AM NOT AFRAID OF YOU. THIS IS NOTHING.
PHYSICAL TORMENT IS NO MATCH FOR THE HARDSHIPS I HAVE ENDURED.
BUT THOUGH I WAS HELPLESS THEN...
...I AM NOT NOW.

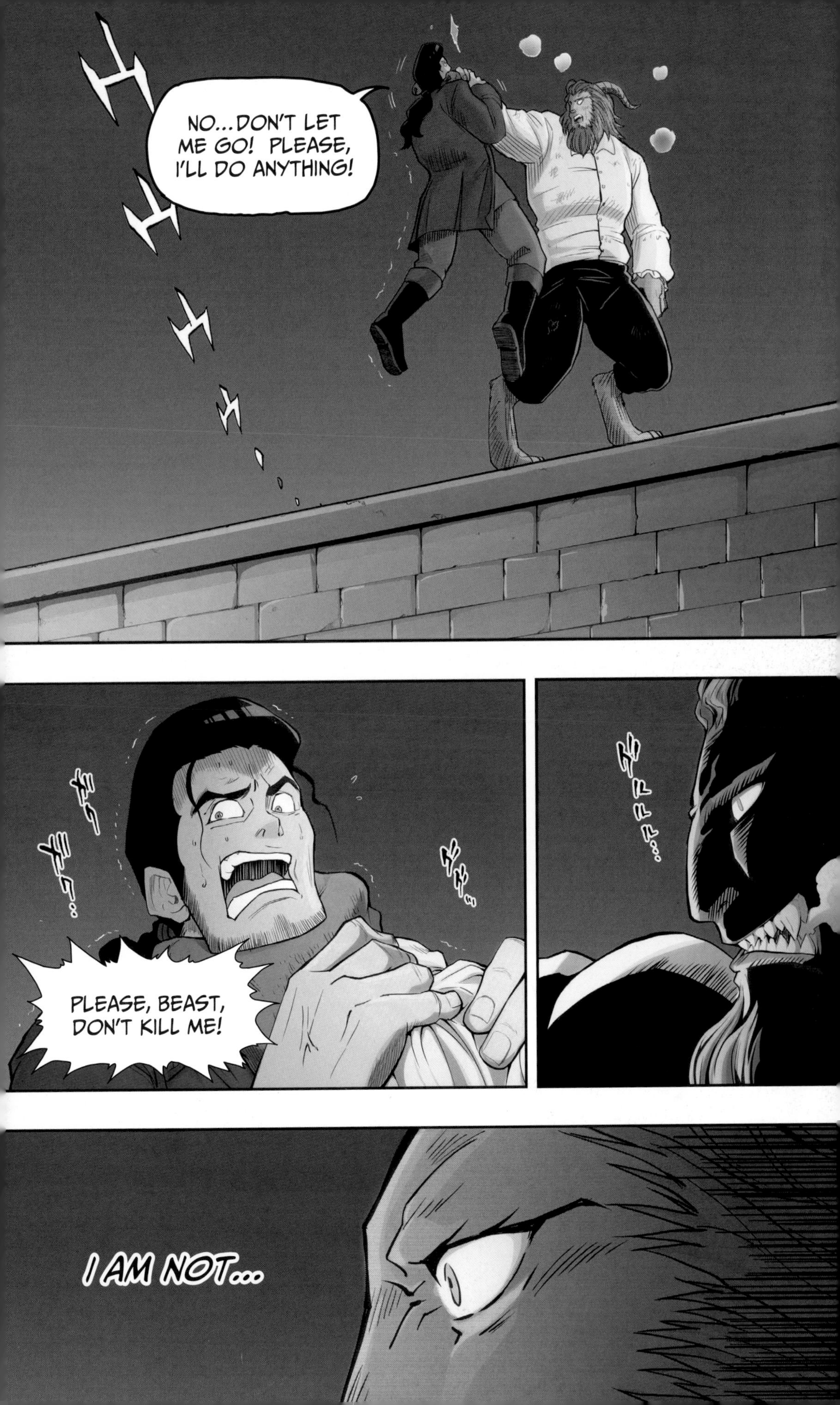
NO...DON'T LET ME GO! PLEASE, I'LL DO ANYTHING!
PLEASE, BEAST, DON'T KILL ME!
I AM NOT...

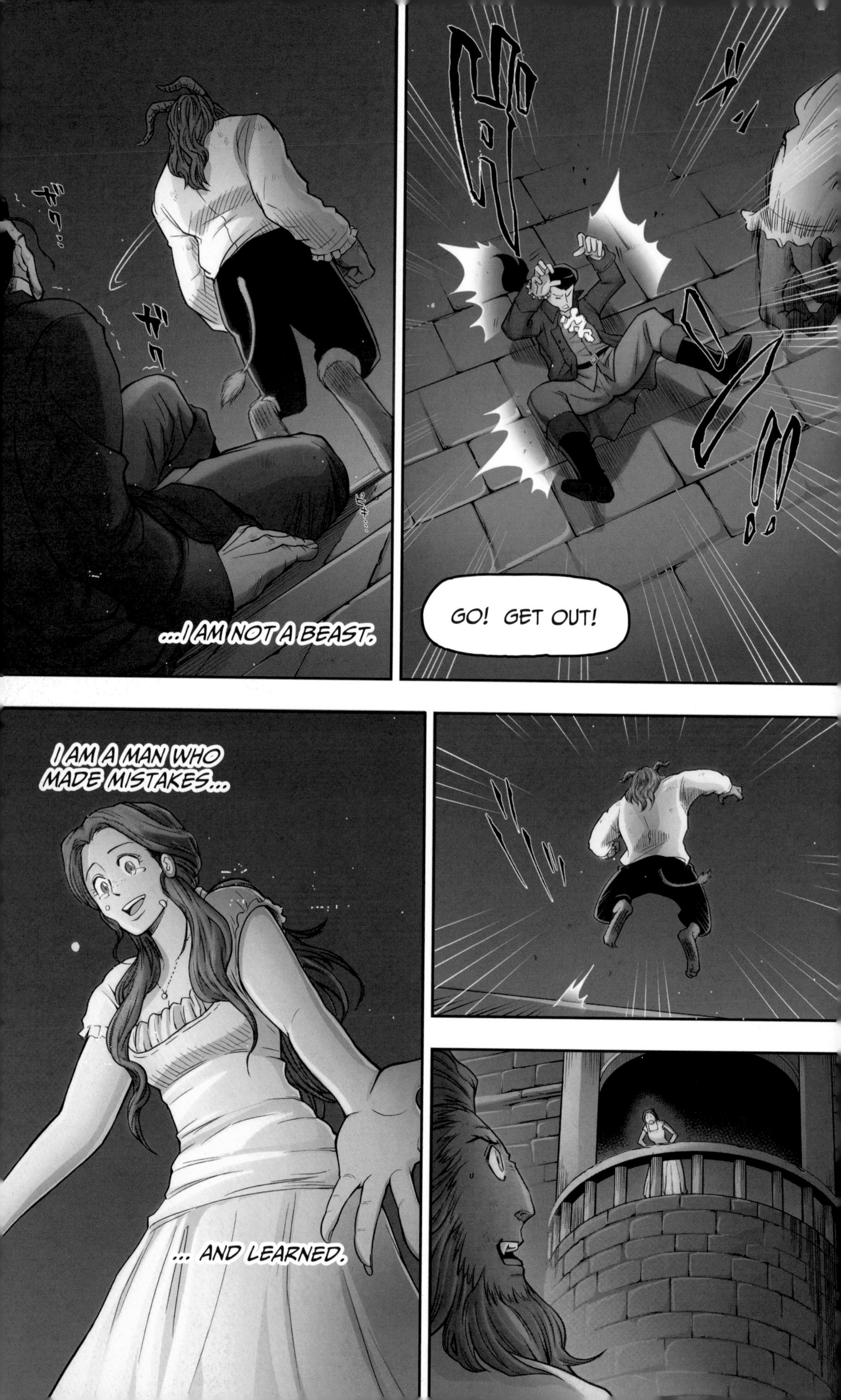
GO! GET OUT!
...I AM NOT A BEAST.
I AM A MAN WHO MADE MISTAKES...
... AND LEARNED.

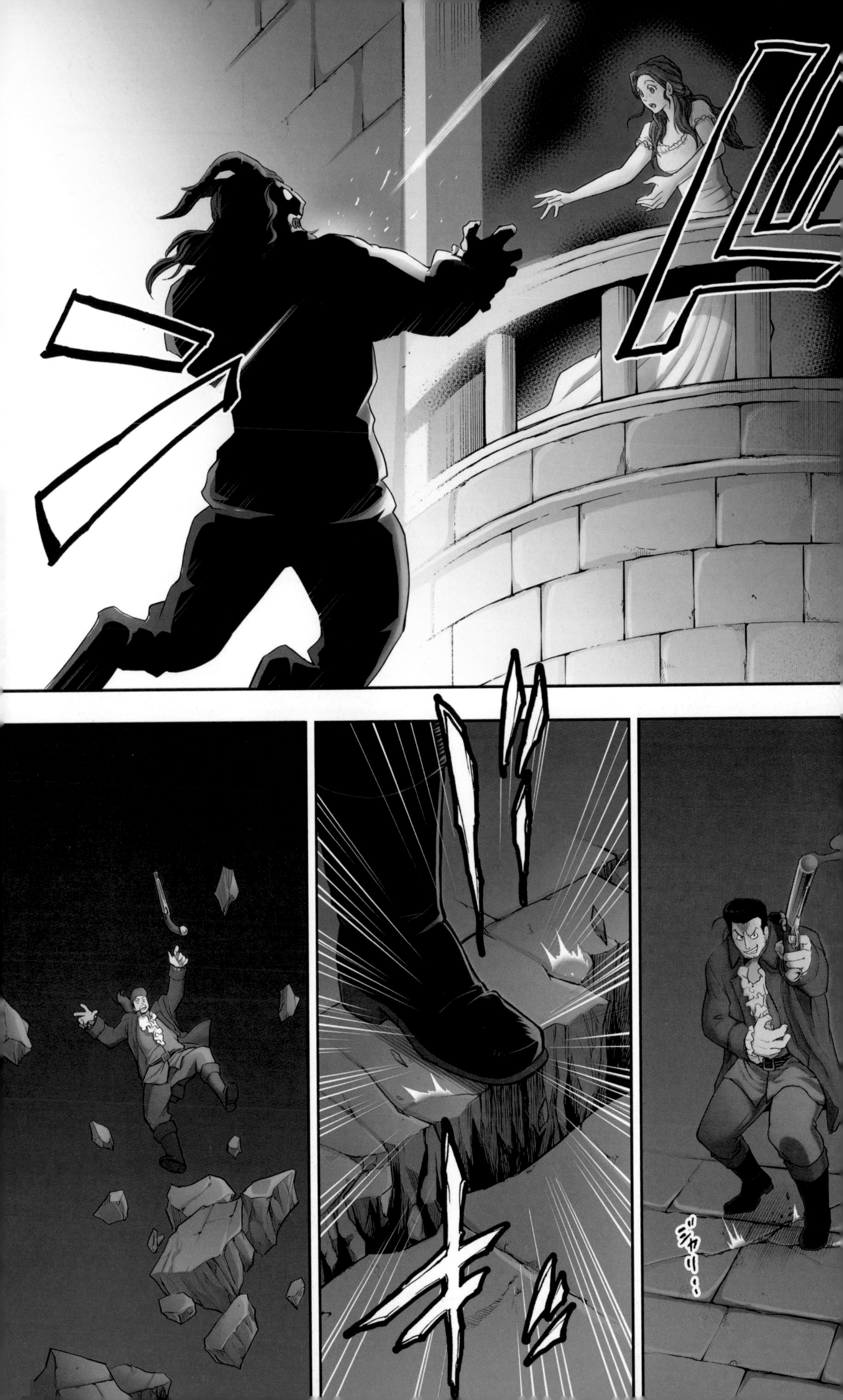
ジャリ‥

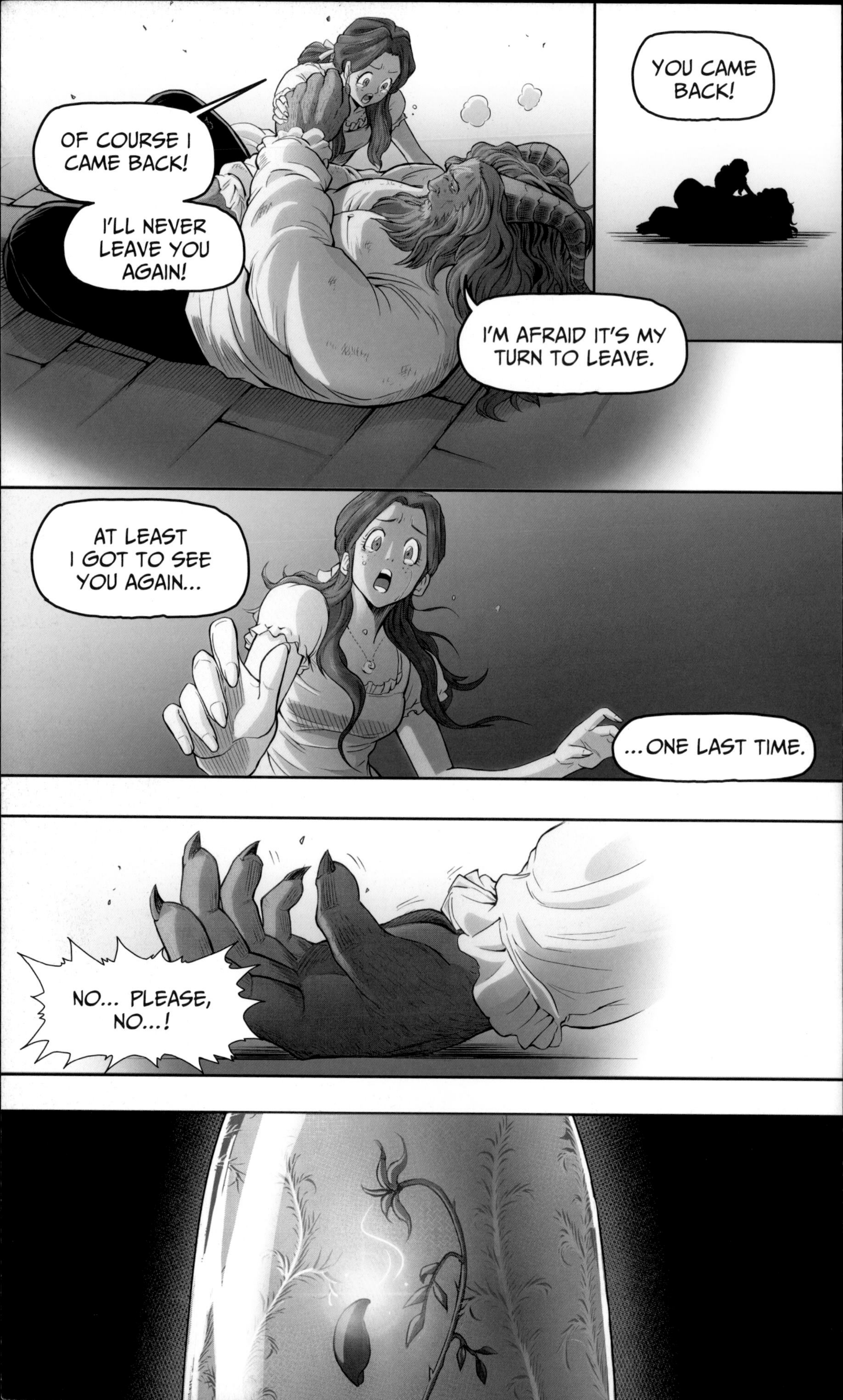
YOU CAME BACK!
OF COURSE I CAME BACK!
I'LL NEVER LEAVE YOU AGAIN!
I'M AFRAID IT'S MY TURN TO LEAVE.
AT LEAST I GOT TO SEE YOU AGAIN...
...ONE LAST TIME.
NO... PLEASE, NO...!

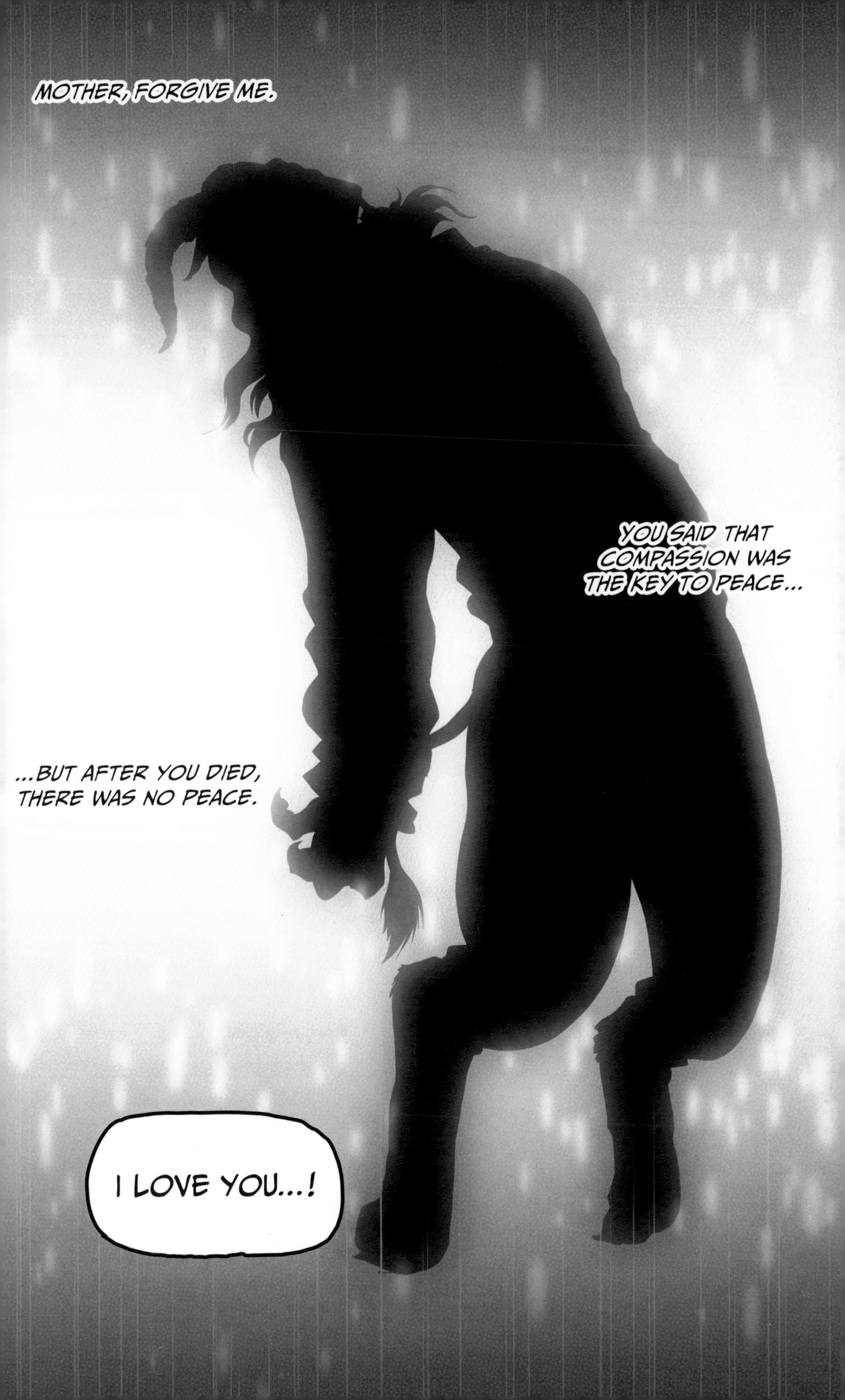
MOTHER, FORGIVE ME.
YOU SAID THAT COMPASSION WAS THE KEY TO PEACE...
...BUT AFTER YOU DIED, THERE WAS NO PEACE.
I LOVE YOU...!

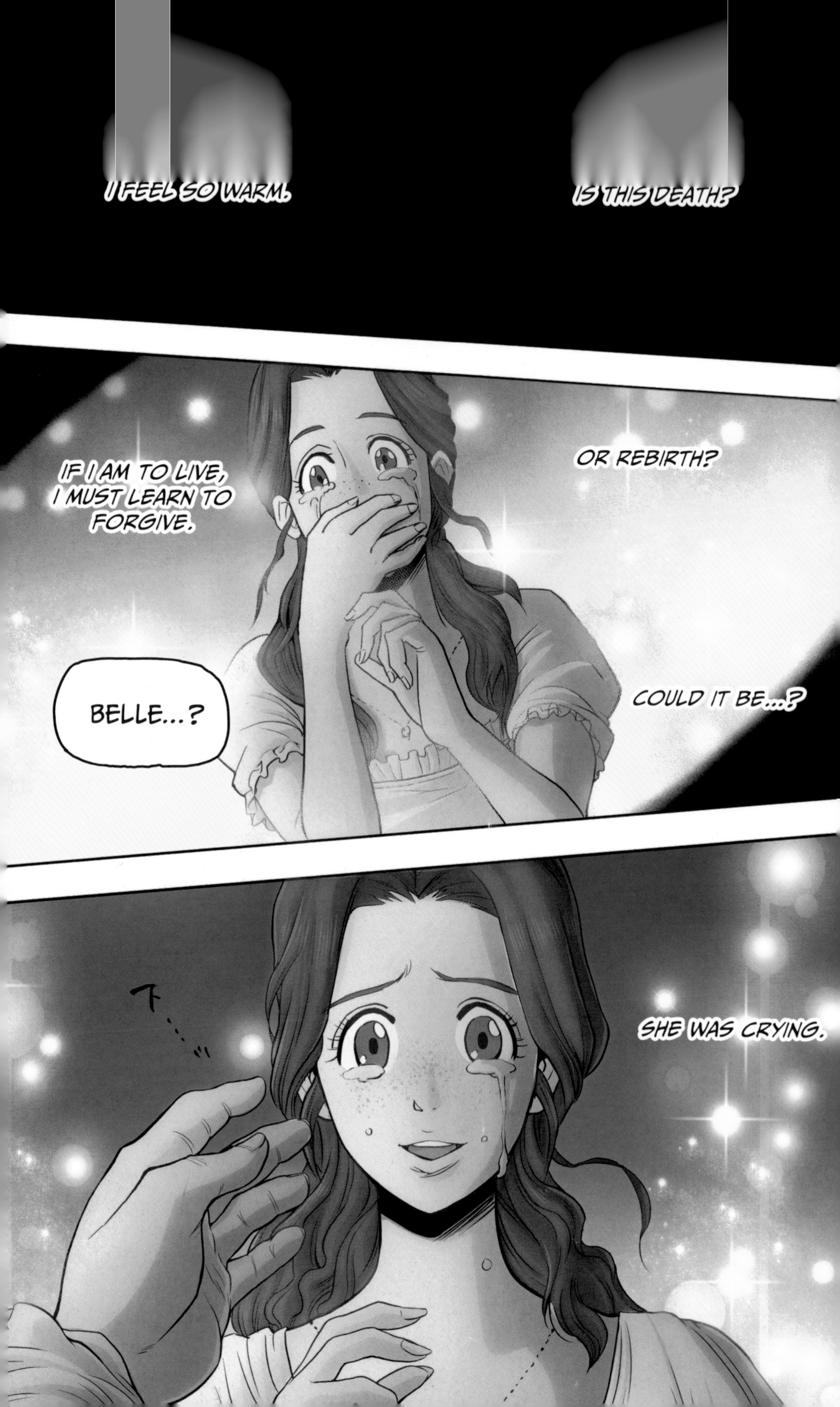
IS THIS DEATH?
I FEEL SO WARM.
OR REBIRTH?
IF I AM TO LIVE, I MUST LEARN TO FORGIVE.
COULD IT BE...?
BELLE...?
SHE WAS CRYING.

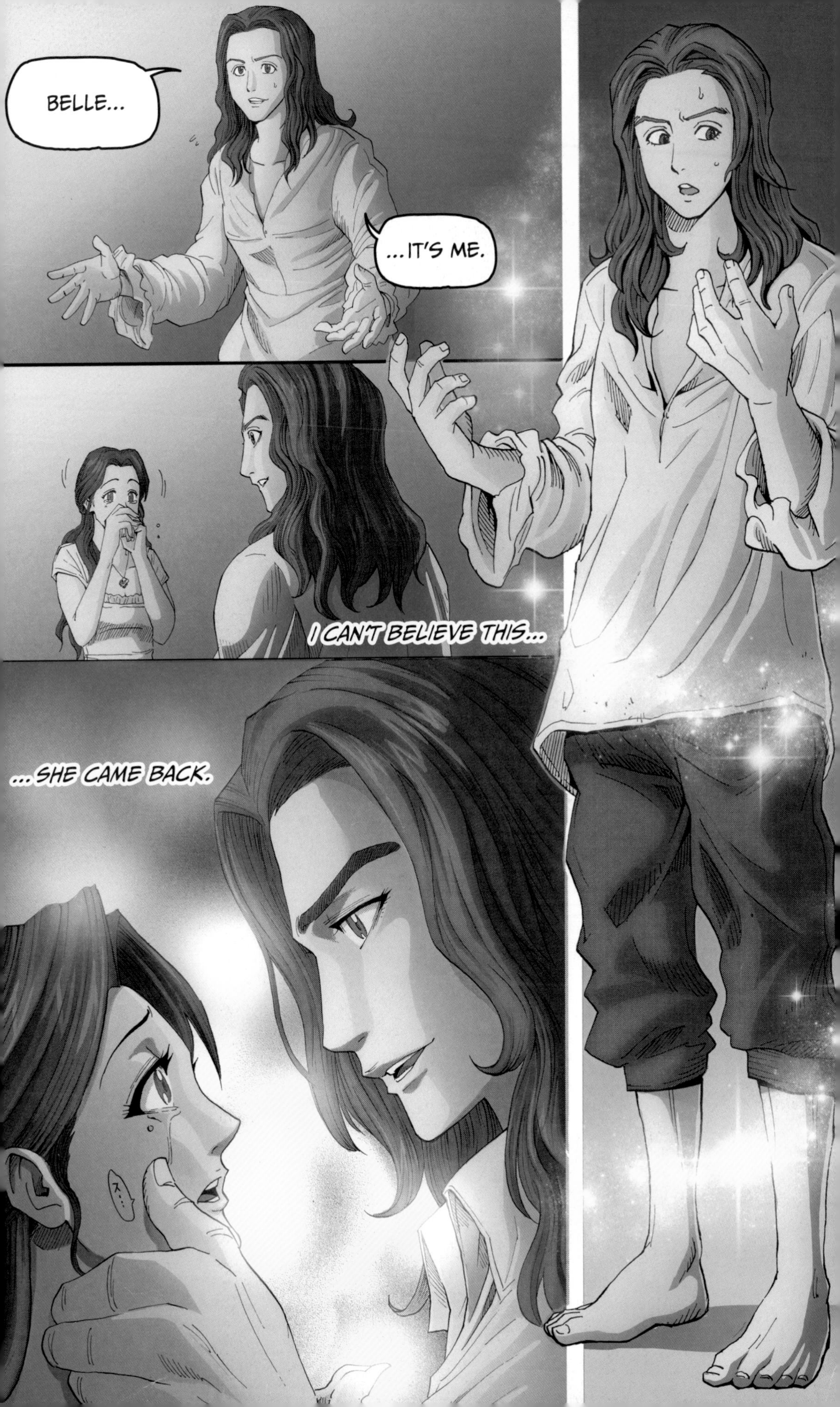
BELLE...
...IT'S ME.
I CAN'T BELIEVE THIS...
...SHE CAME BACK.
ス…

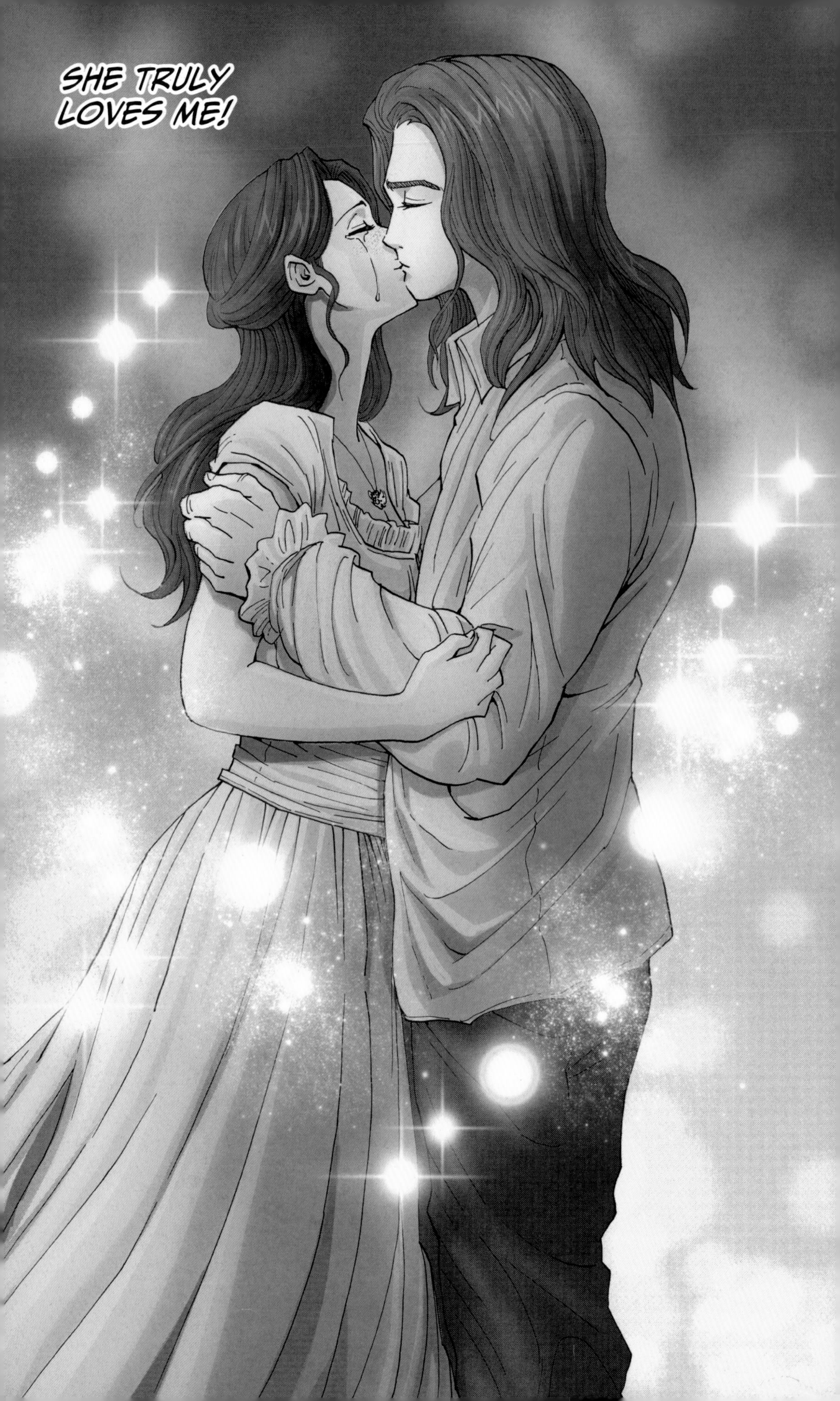
SHE TRULY LOVES ME!

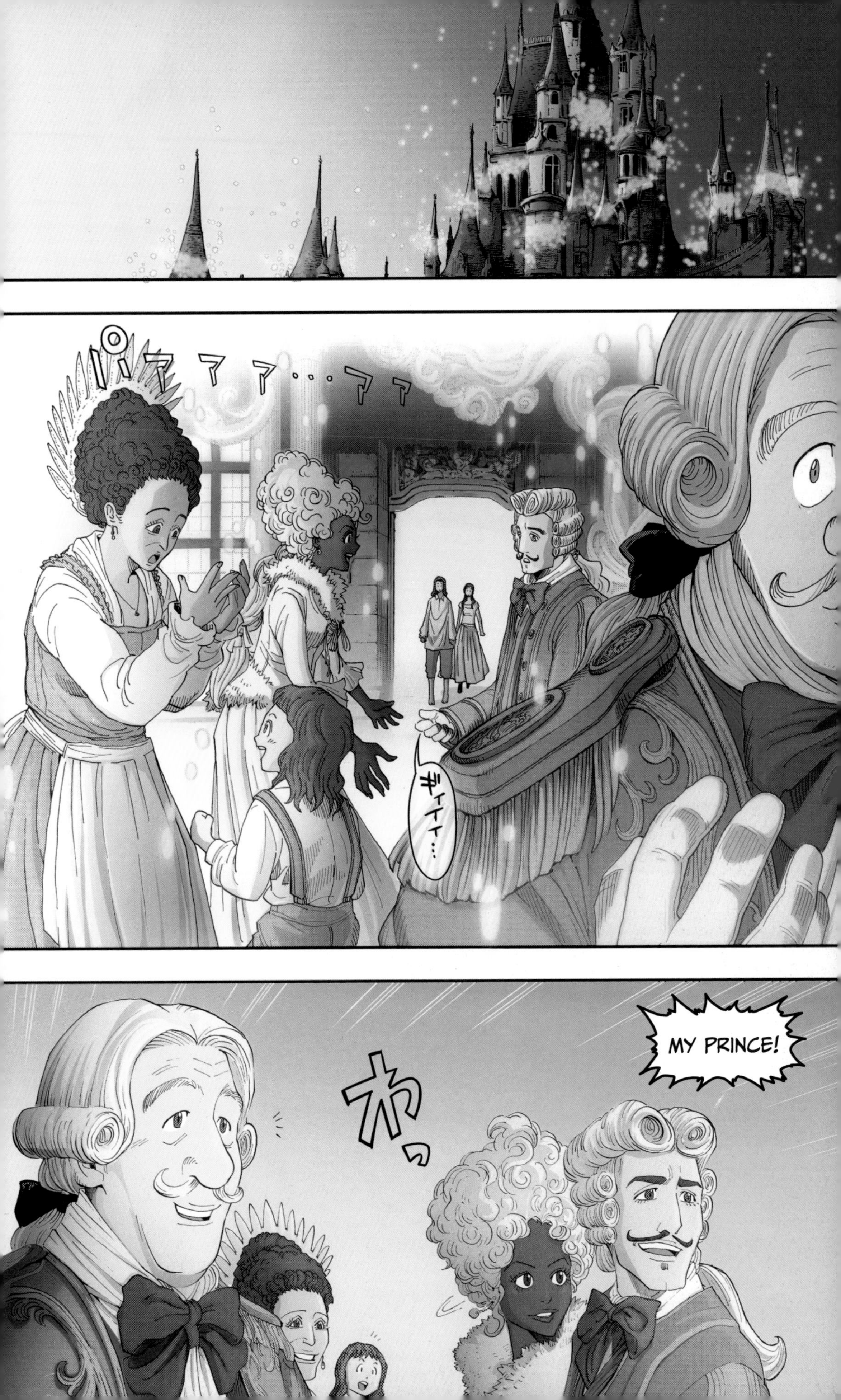
パァァァ…ァァ
ギィイイ…
MY PRINCE!
わっ

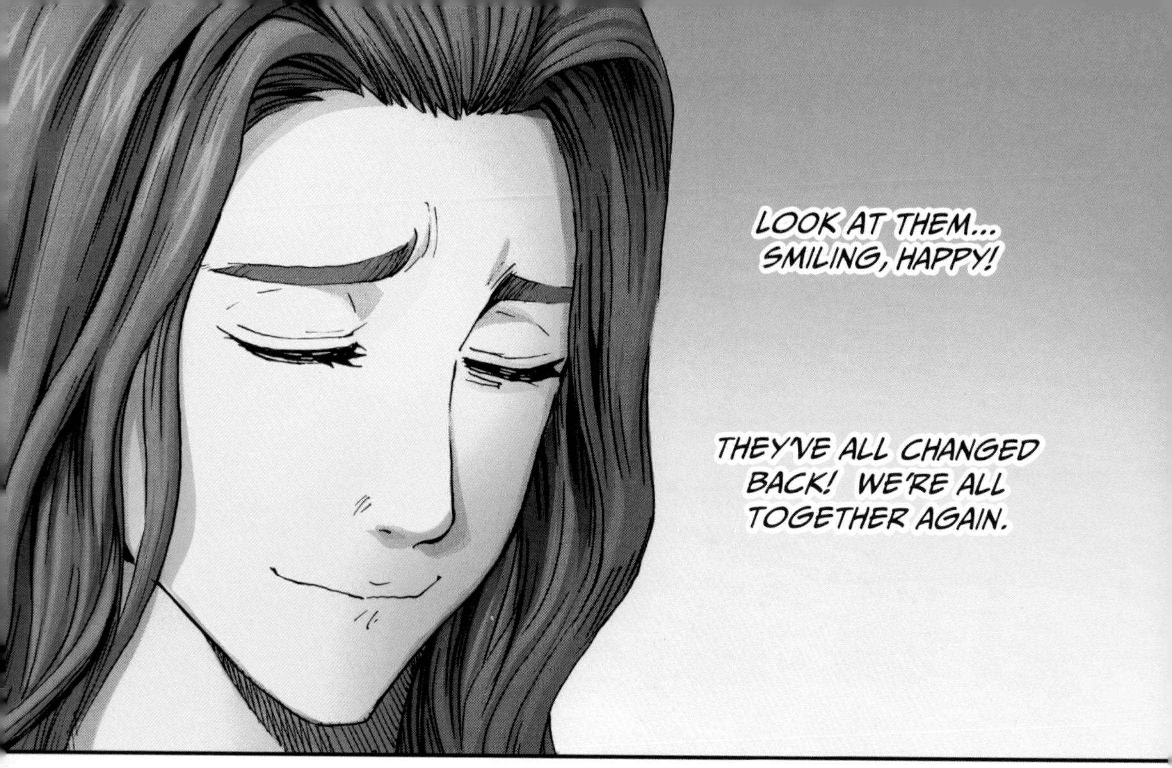
LOOK AT THEM... SMILING, HAPPY!
THEY'VE ALL CHANGED BACK! WE'RE ALL TOGETHER AGAIN.

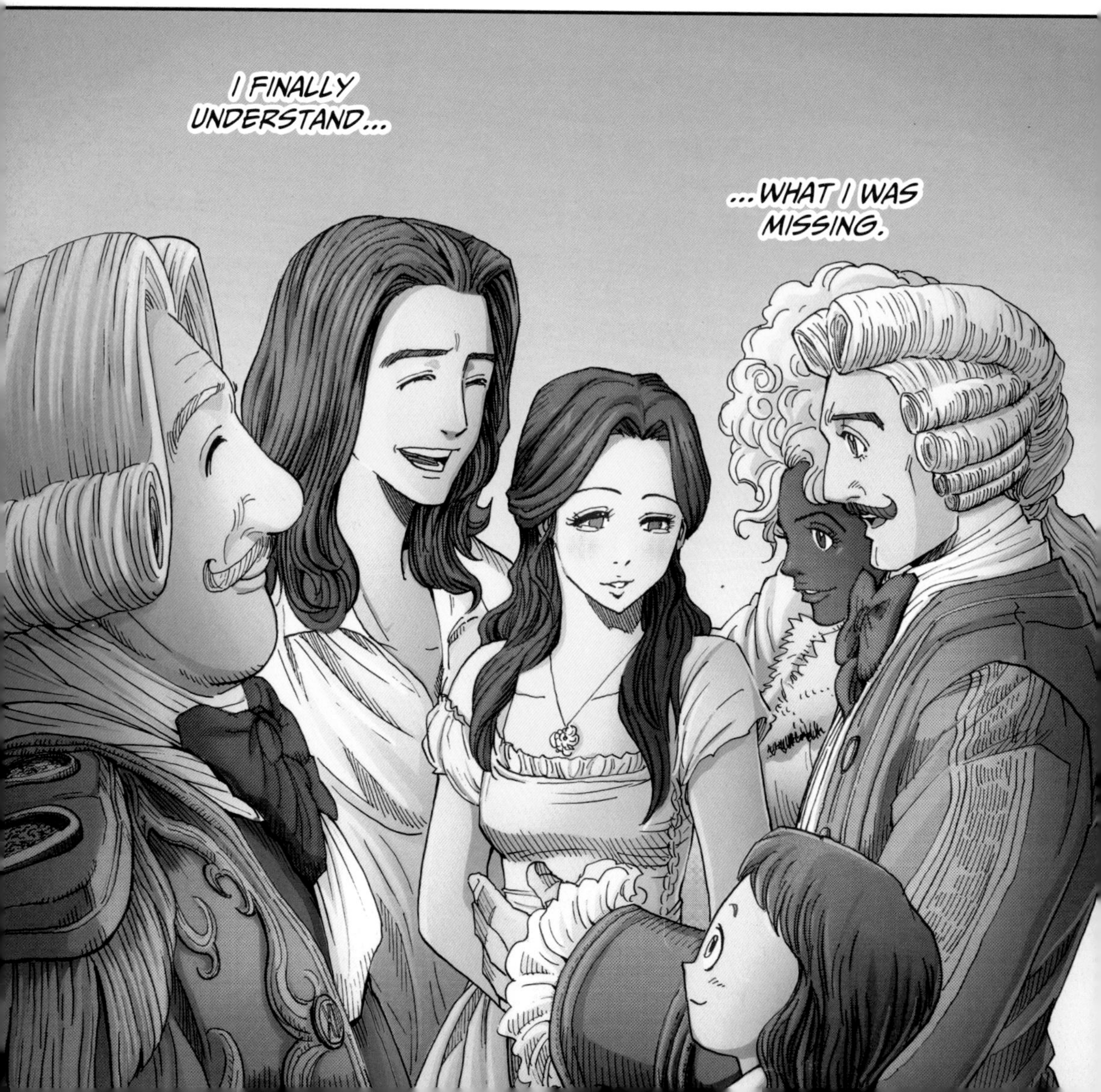
I FINALLY UNDERSTAND...
...WHAT I WAS MISSING.

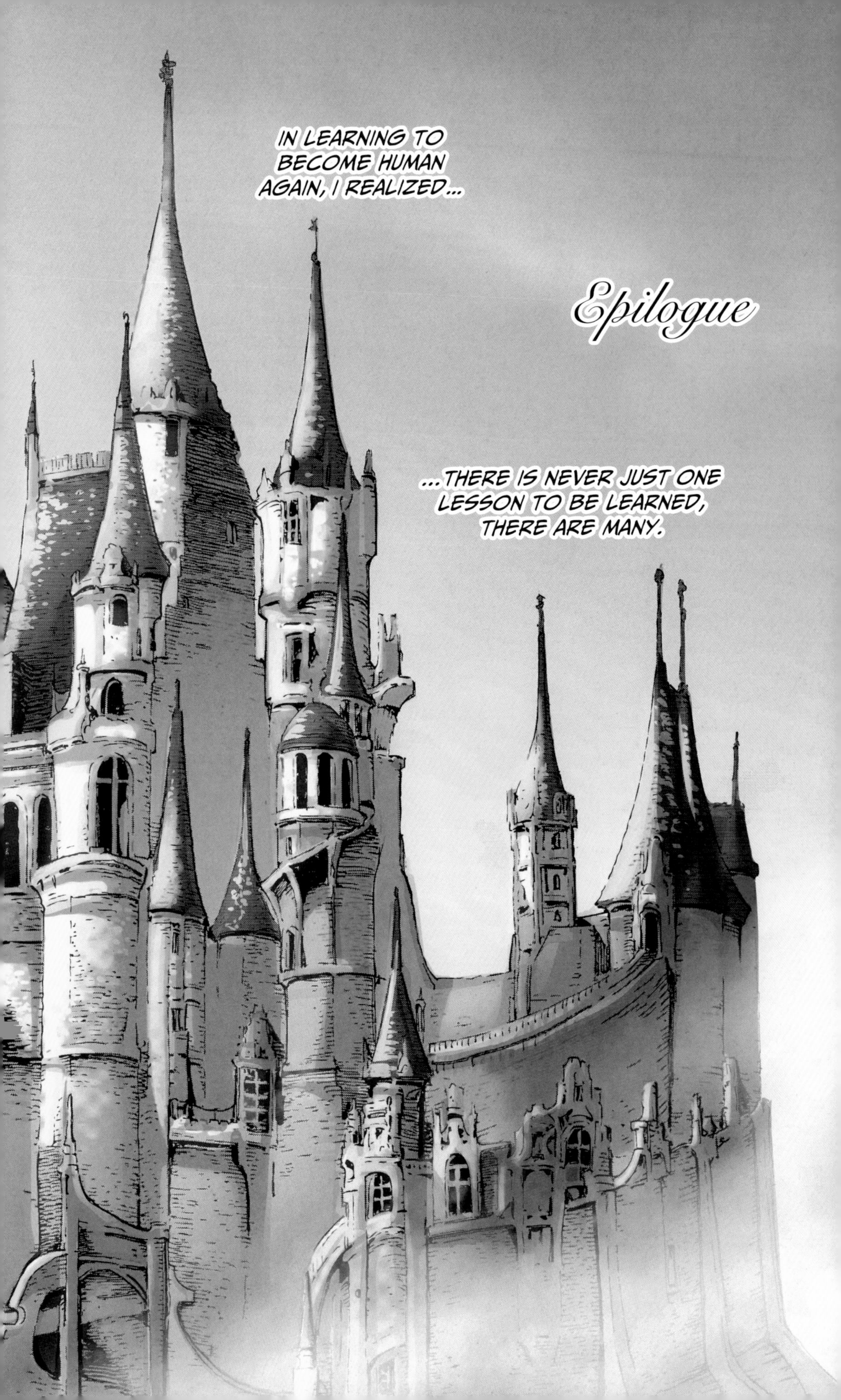
IN LEARNING TO BECOME HUMAN AGAIN, I REALIZED...
Epilogue
...THERE IS NEVER JUST ONE LESSON TO BE LEARNED, THERE ARE MANY.

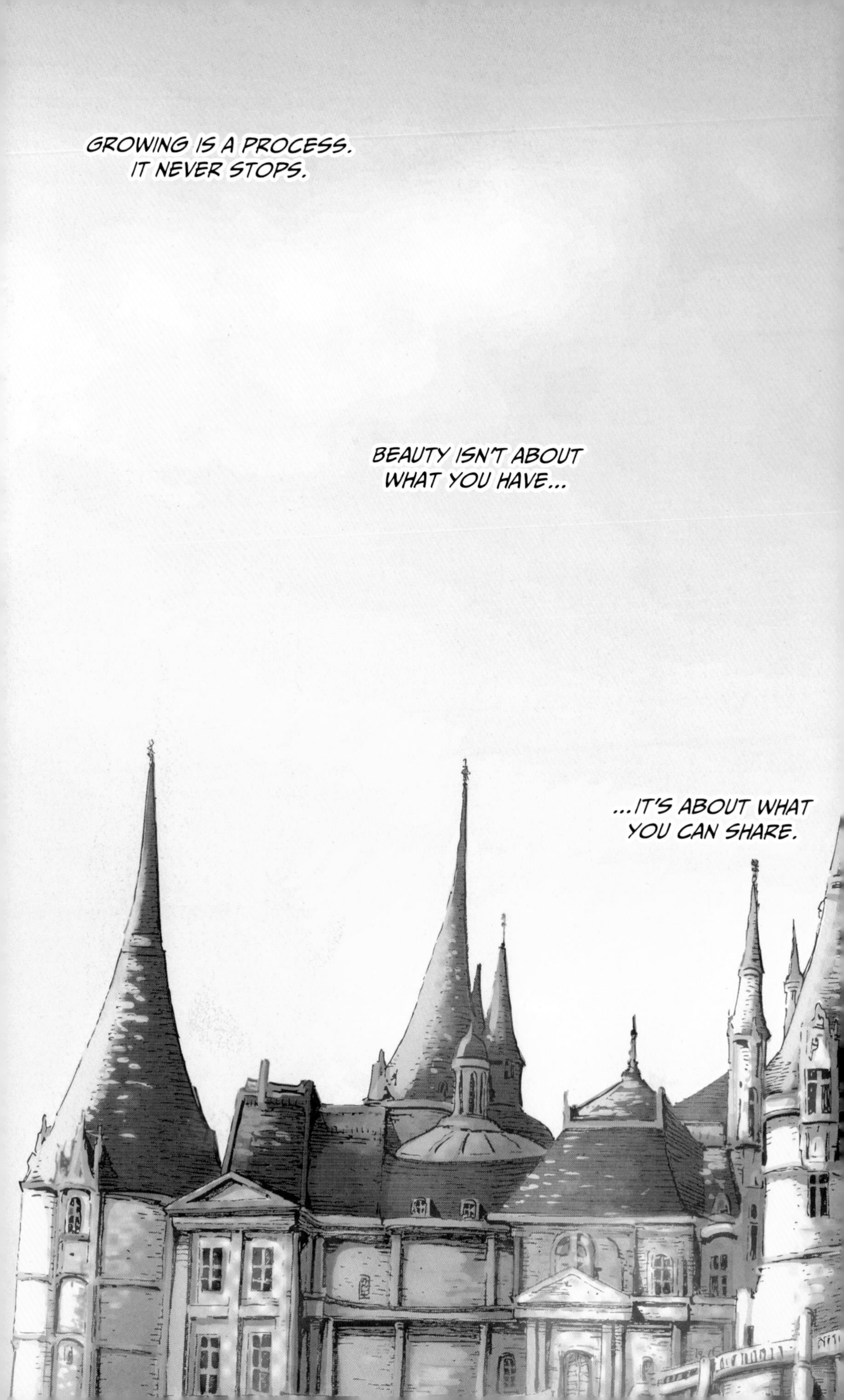
GROWING IS A PROCESS. IT NEVER STOPS.
BEAUTY ISN'T ABOUT WHAT YOU HAVE...
...IT'S ABOUT WHAT YOU CAN SHARE.

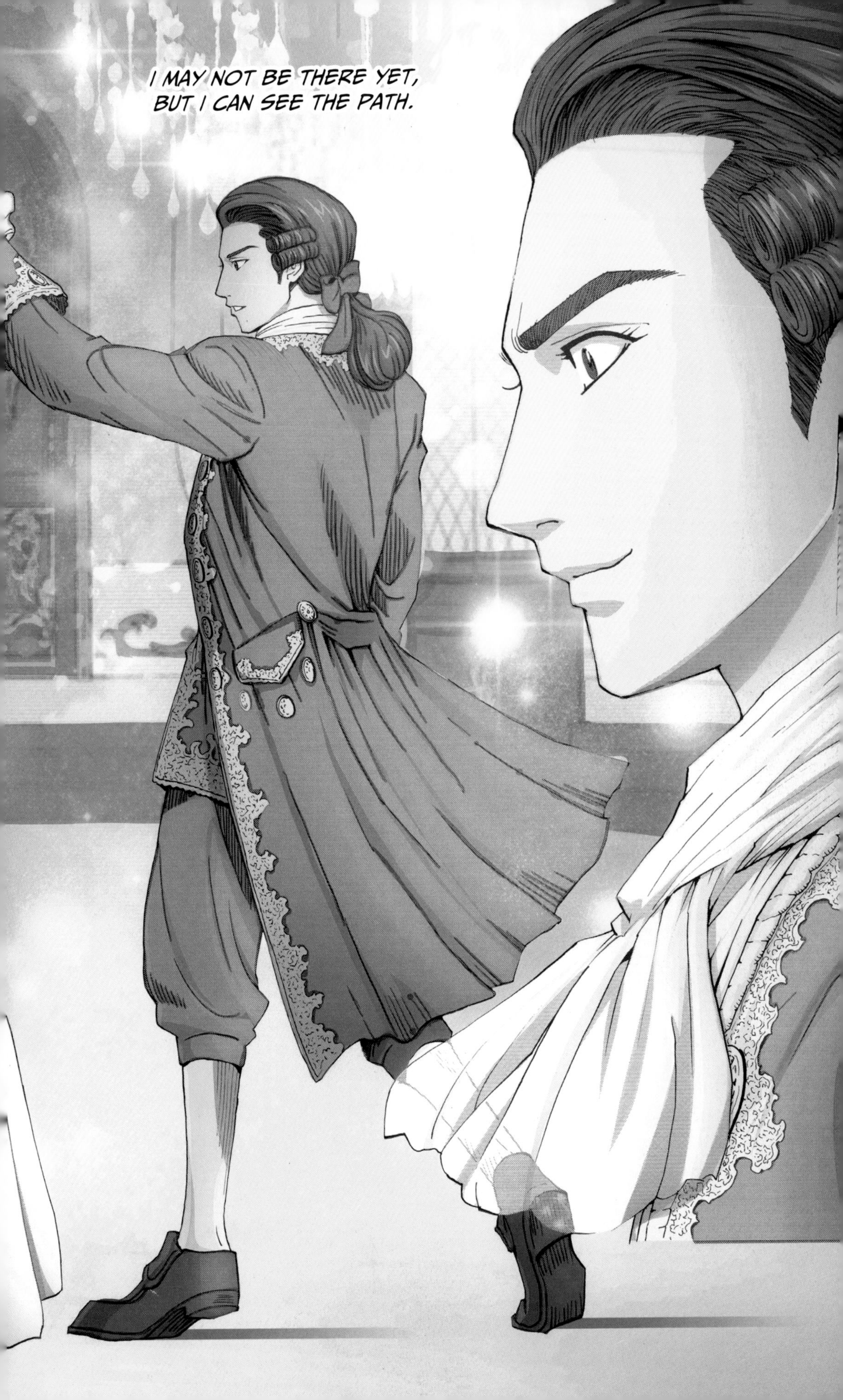
I MAY NOT BE THERE YET, BUT I CAN SEE THE PATH.

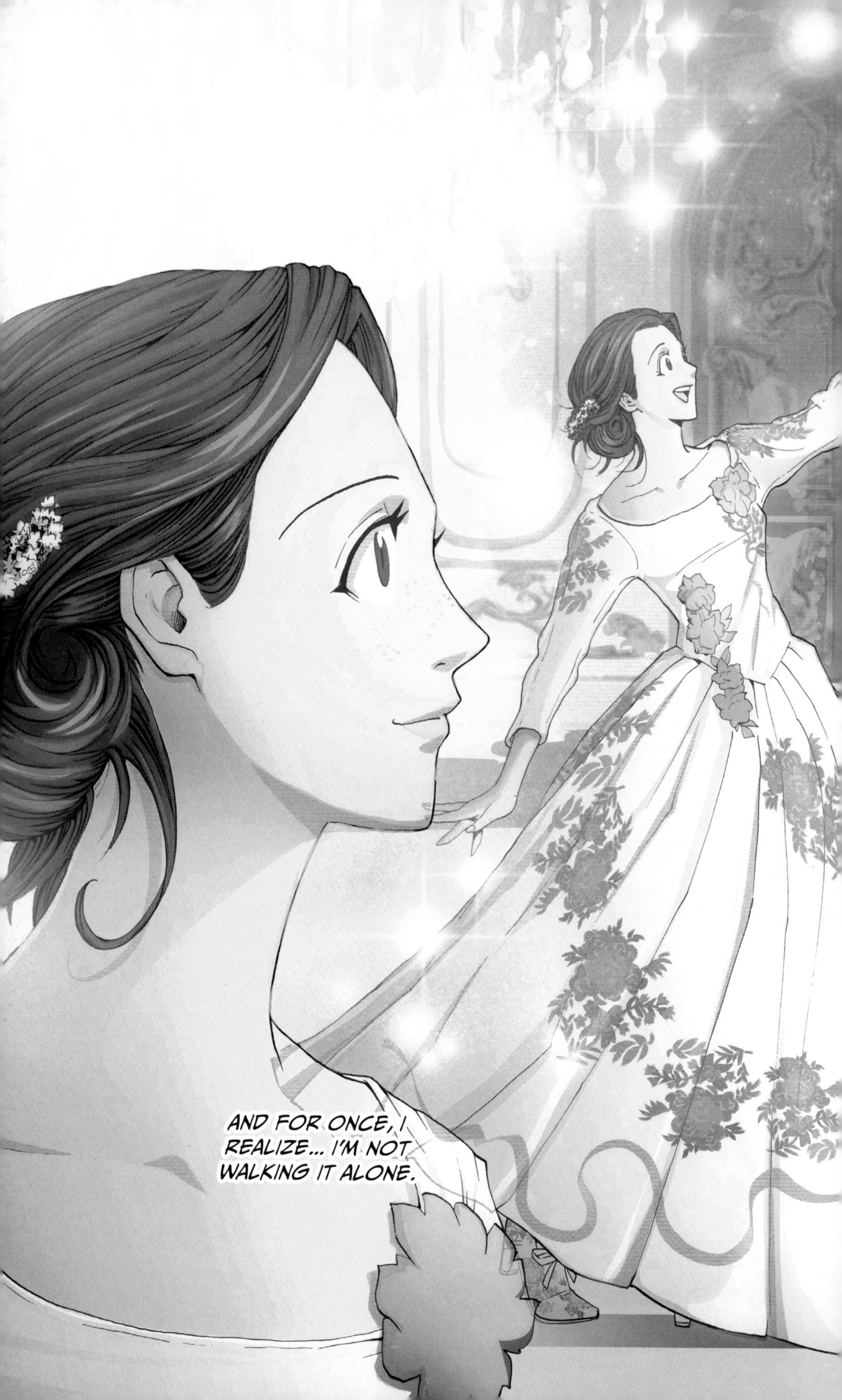
AND FOR ONCE, I REALIZE... I'M NOT WALKING IT ALONE.

Disney

BEAUTY
AND THE
BEAST

COVER ROUGH CONCEPTS

It took many variations of rough concepts
to find the version that best captured
the essence of the film character while
maintaining a manga look and feel. Take
a look at a few designs from the original
release black-and-white manga version!

Final Cover Inks

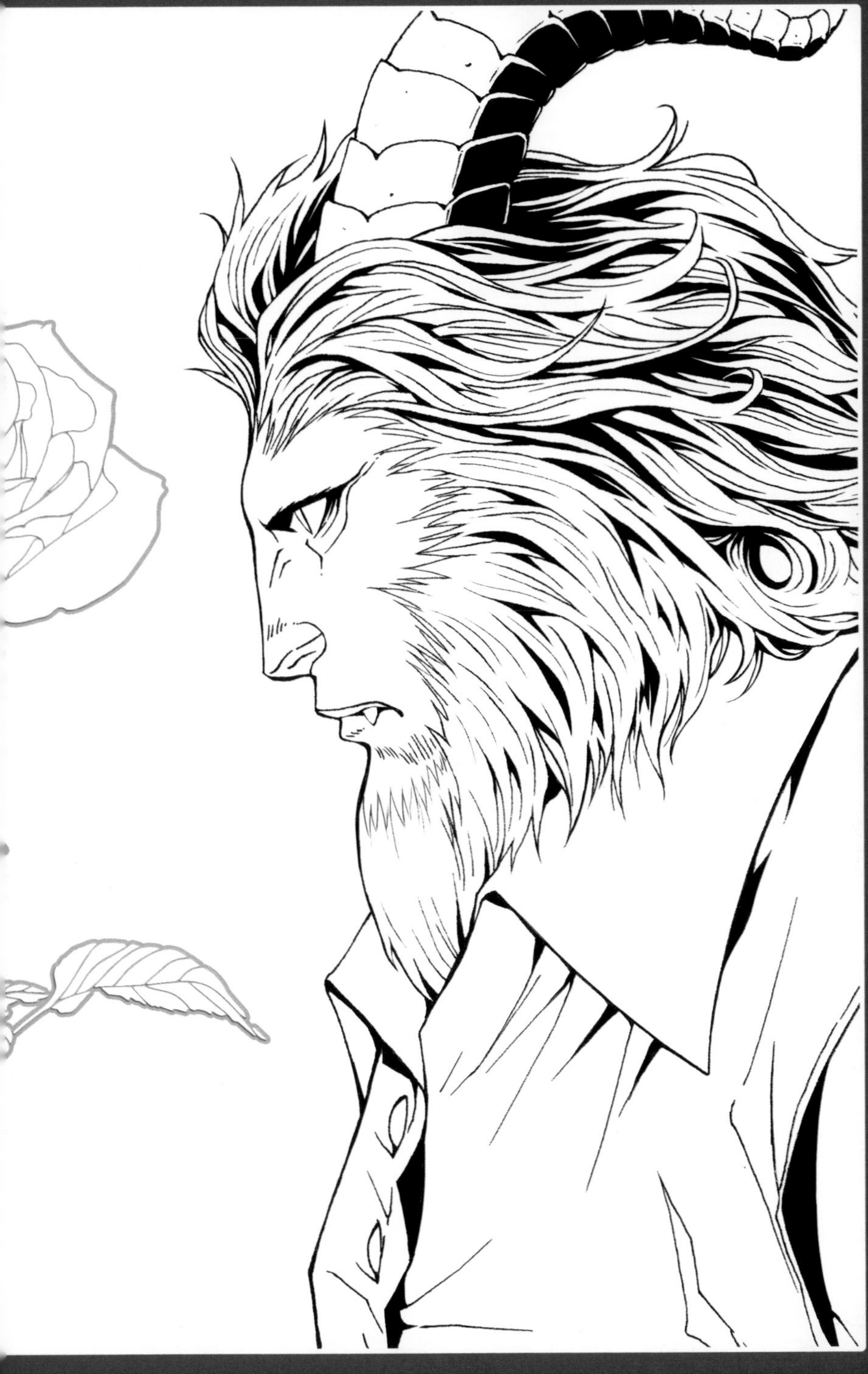

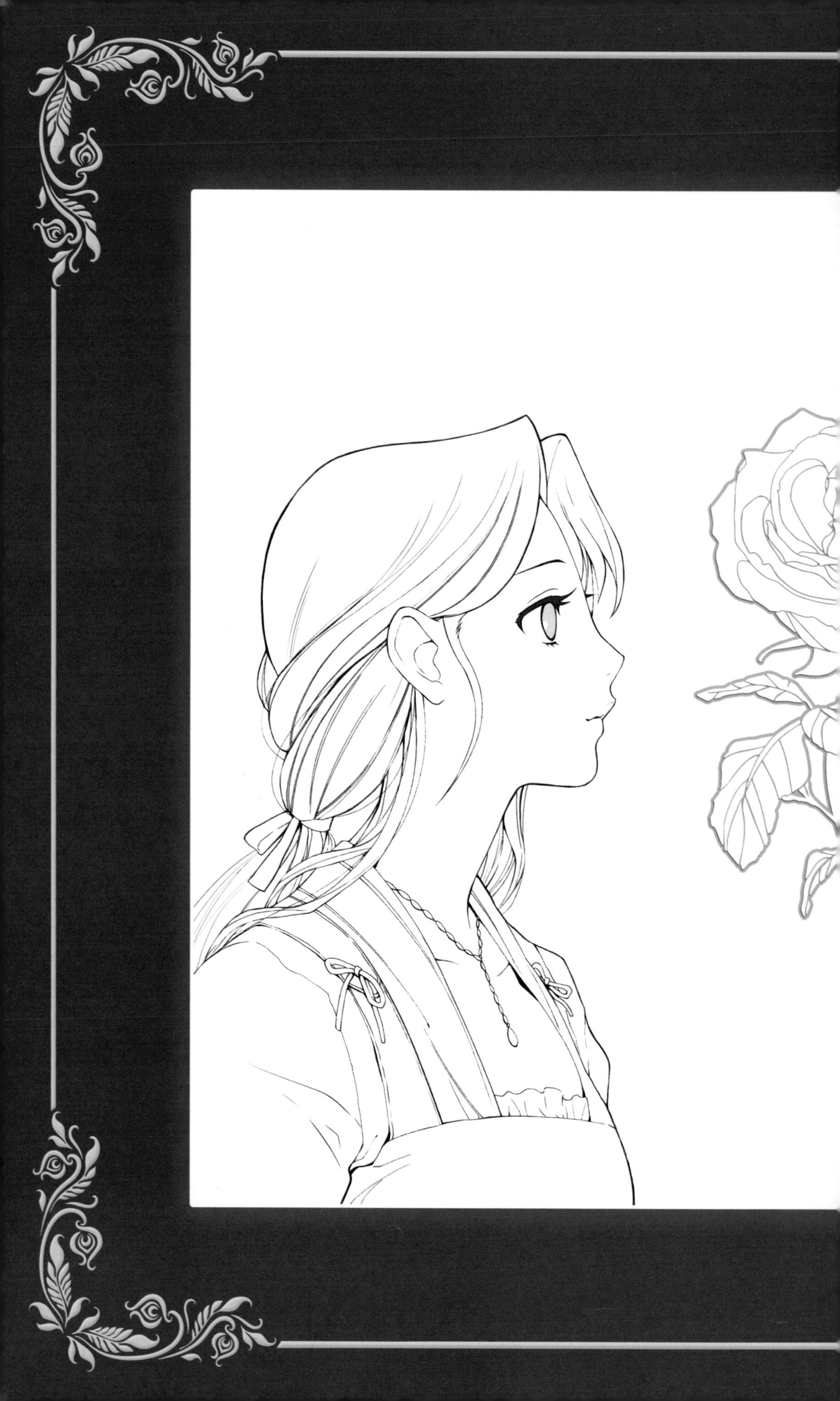

Cover Concept Art #1

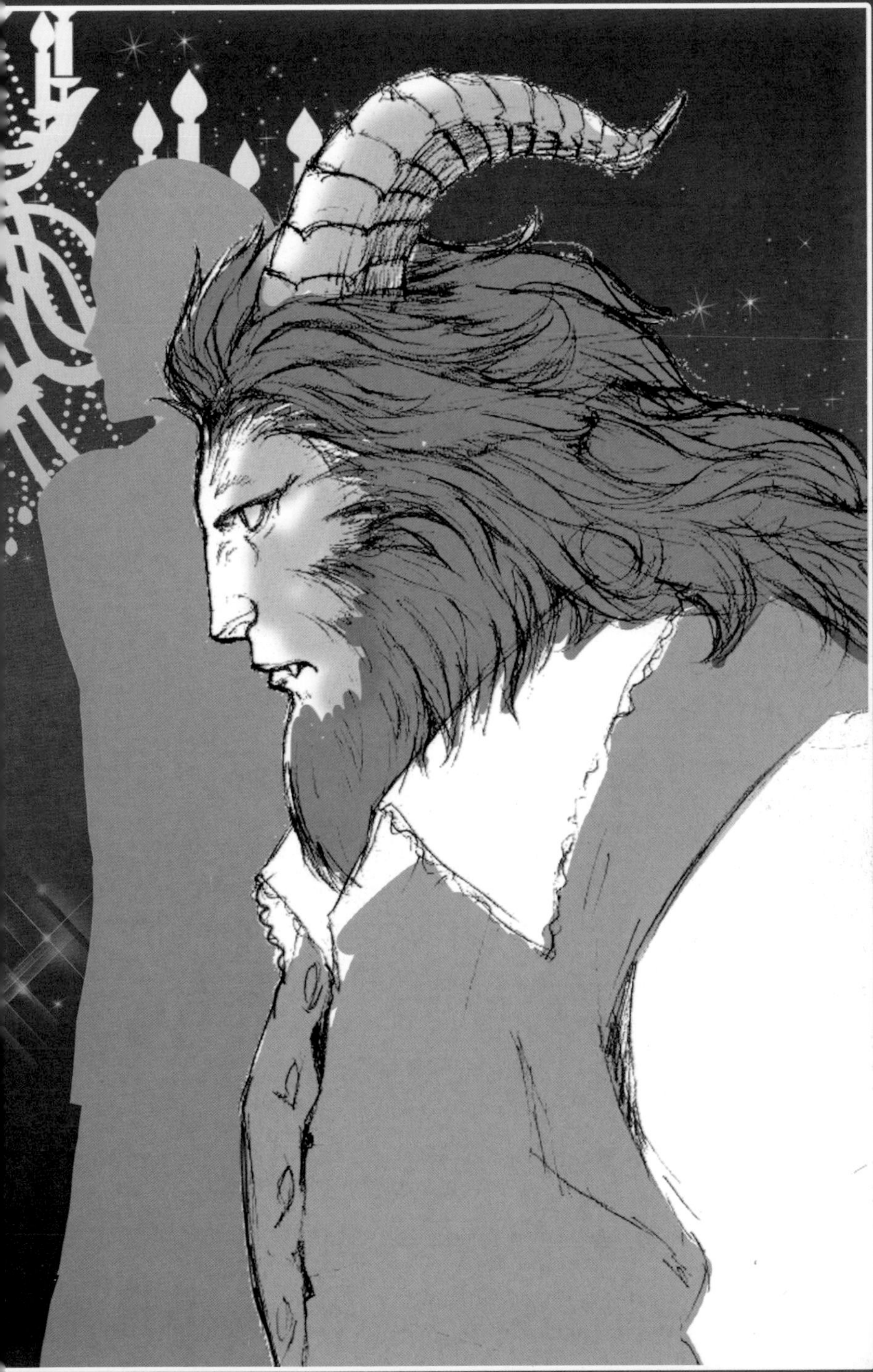

Ultimately, none of the following concepts ever made it to print.

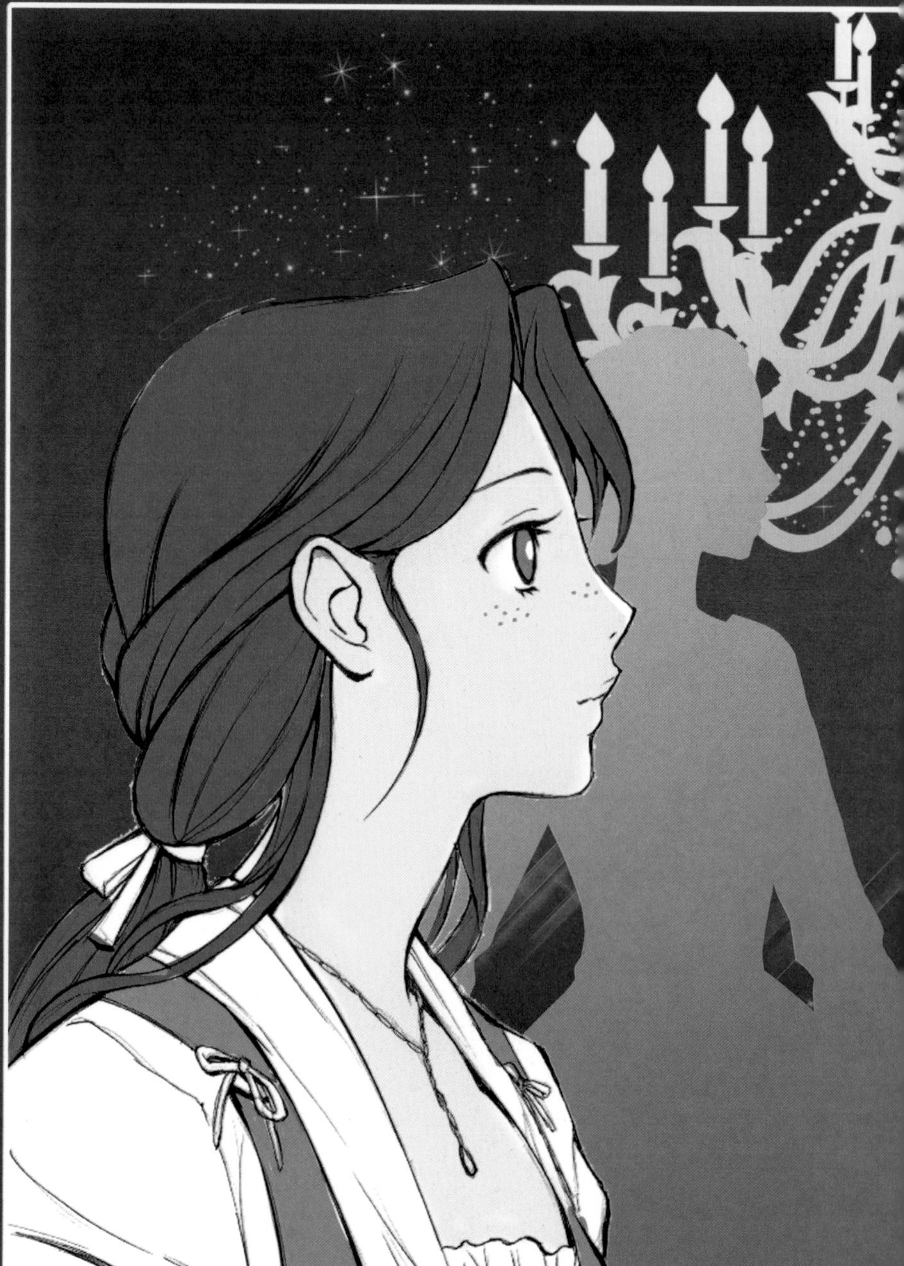

However, concepts are an important
step towards developing a final look!

Cover Concept Art #2

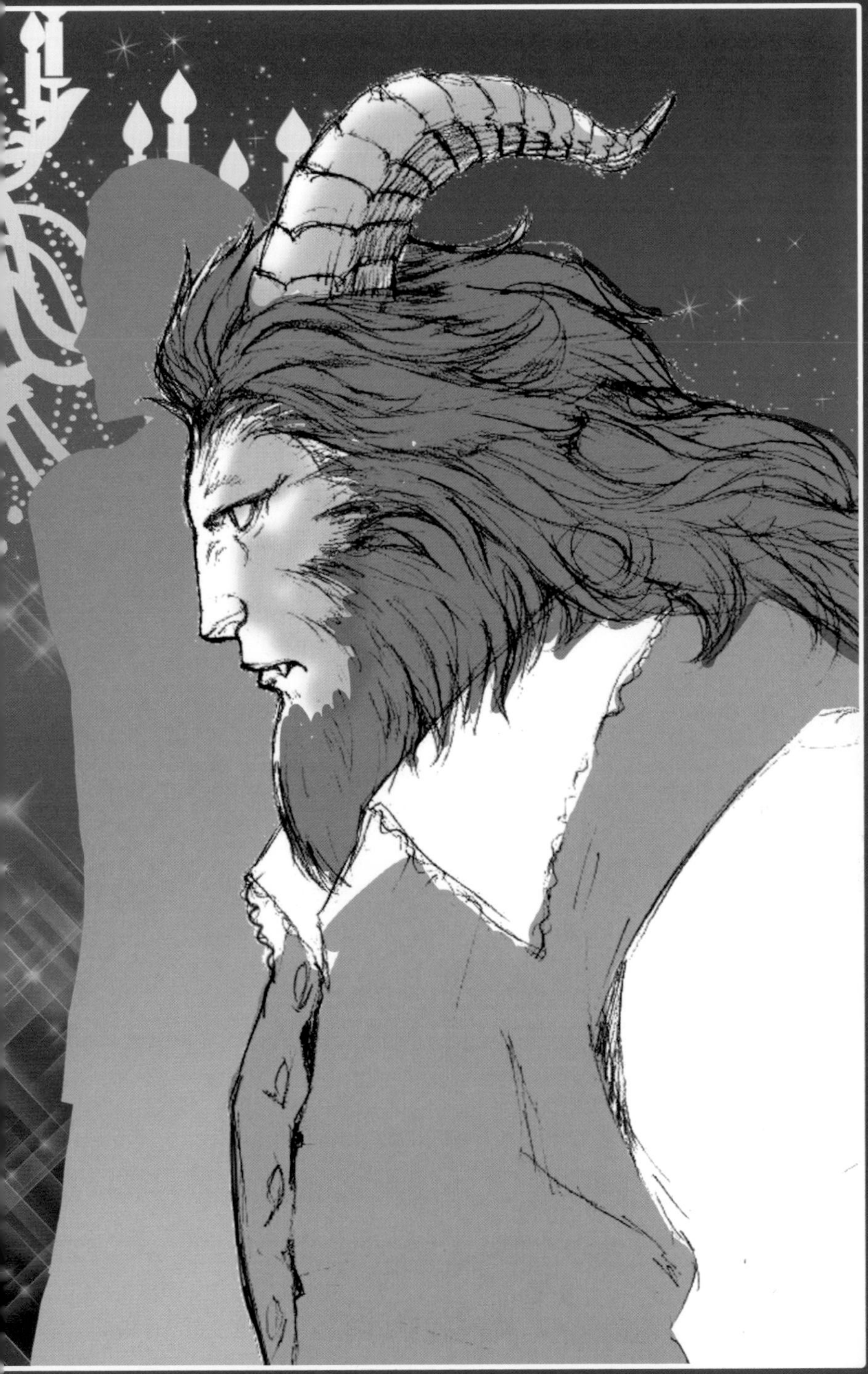

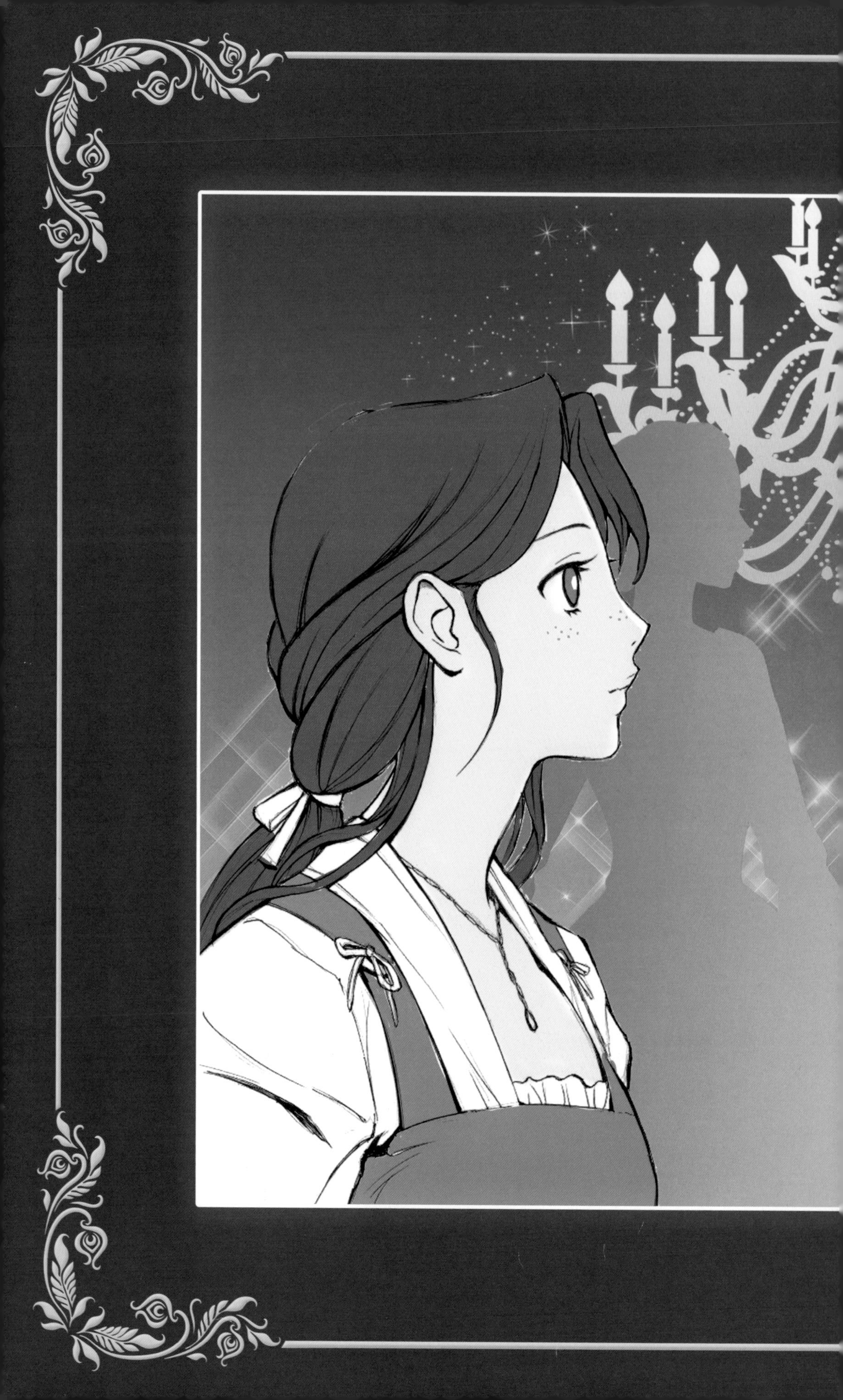

Cover Concept Art #3

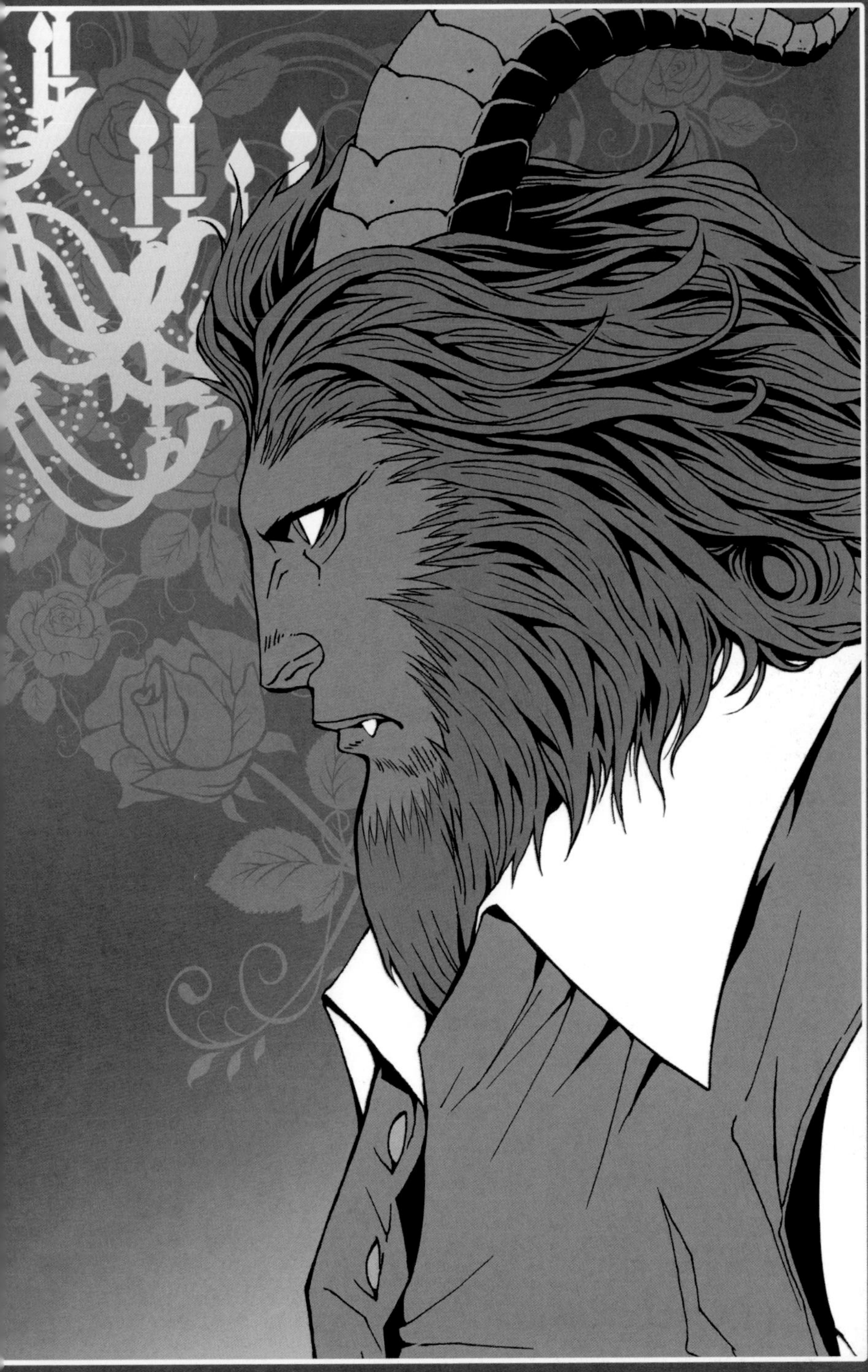

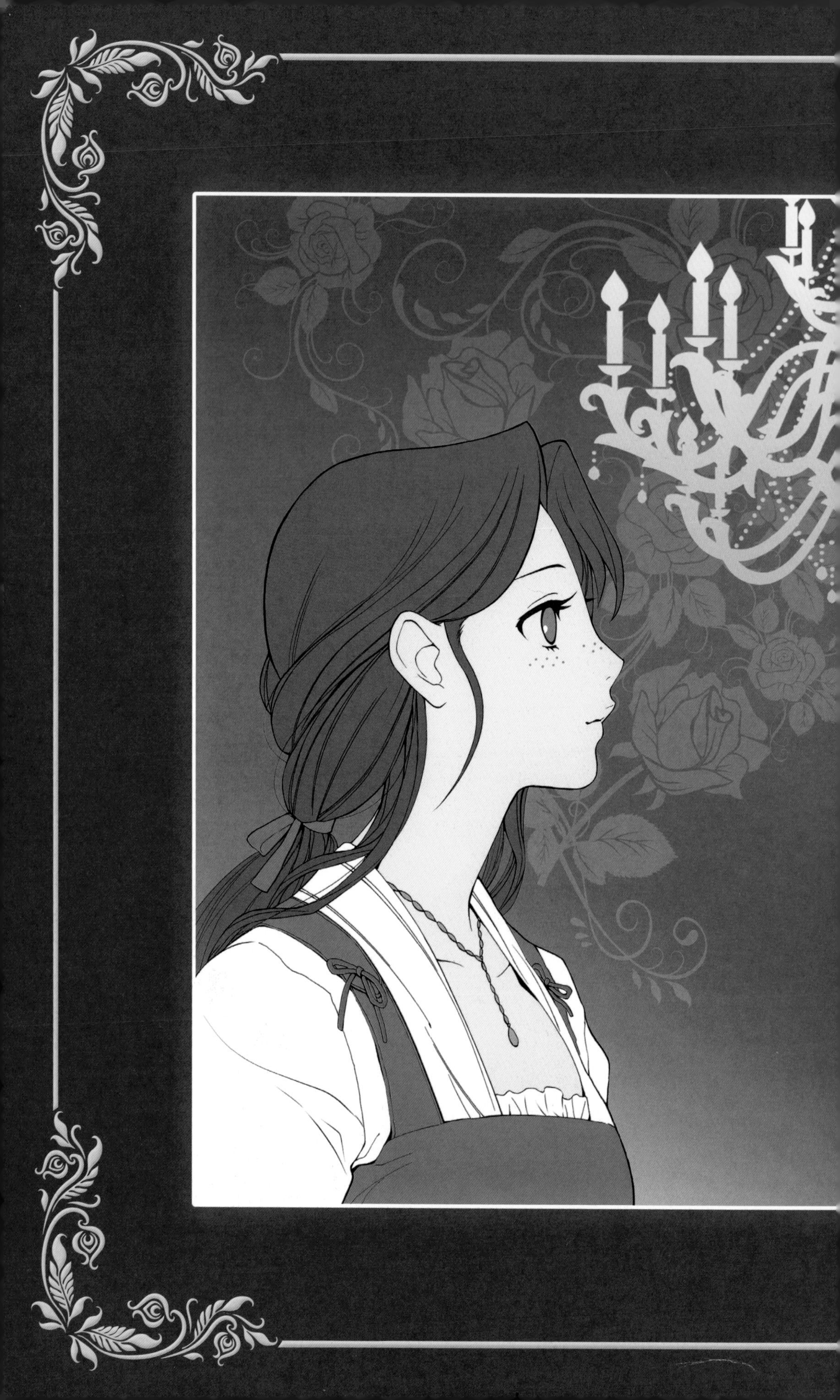

Cover Concept Art #4

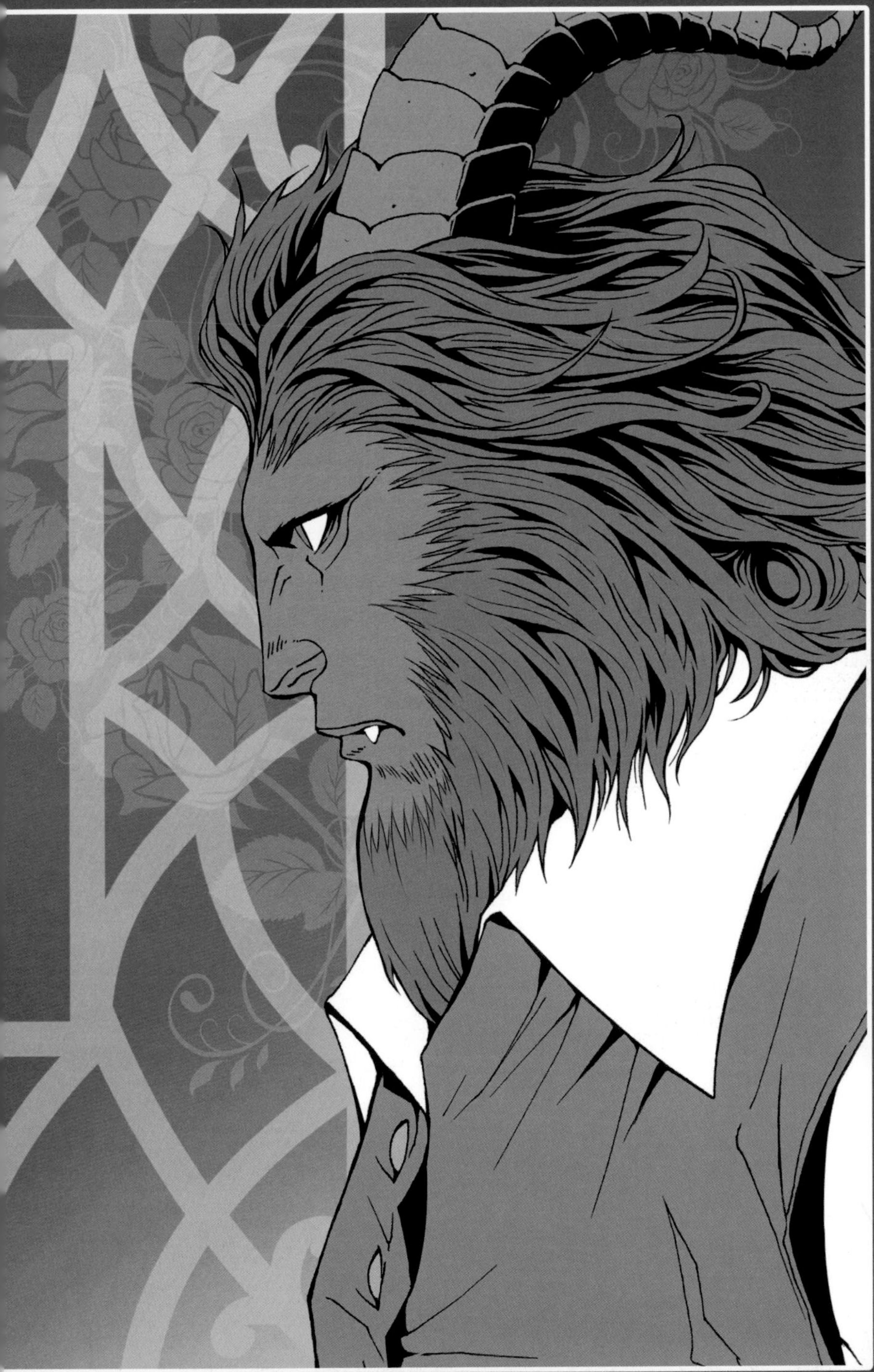

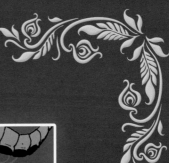

Disney Beauty and the Beast: Beast's Tale (Full-Color Edition)
Art by: Studio Dice
Story Adapted by: Mallory Reaves
Colors by: Gianluca Papi

Editorial Associate - Janae Young
Marketing Associate - Kae Winters
Retouching and Lettering - Vibrraant Publishing Studio
Project Manager - Antonio Solinas
Editor - Janae Young
Graphic Designer - Sol DeLeo
Editor-in-Chief & Publisher - Stu Levy

Studio DICE

Hachi Mizuno	Rie Osanai	Tatsuyuki Maeda
Kousuke Takezawa	Masashi Kuju	Sachika Aoyama
Pon Tachibana	Eriko Terao	Aya Nakamura
	Hisashi Nosaka	

Concept Art by Hachi Mizuno
Cover Art by Hisashi Nosaka
Cover Art Colors by Gianluca Papi

Coordination by MITCHELL PRODUCTION, LLC
http://mitchellprod.com/en

A  Manga

TOKYOPOP and 🐌 are trademarks or registered trademarks of TOKYOPOP Inc.

TOKYOPOP Inc.
5200 W. Century Blvd. Suite 705
Los Angeles, 90045

E-mail: info@TOKYOPOP.com
Come visit us online at www.TOKYOPOP.com

f www.facebook.com/TOKYOPOP
🐦 www.twitter.com/TOKYOPOP
📷 www.instagram.com/TOKYOPOP

ISBN: 978-1-4278-6809-1
First TOKYOPOP Printing: February 2022
Printed in Canada

STOP

THIS IS THE BACK OF THE BOOK!

How do you read manga-style? It's simple!
Let's practice -- just start in the top right
panel and follow the numbers below!

READ RIGHT TO LEFT

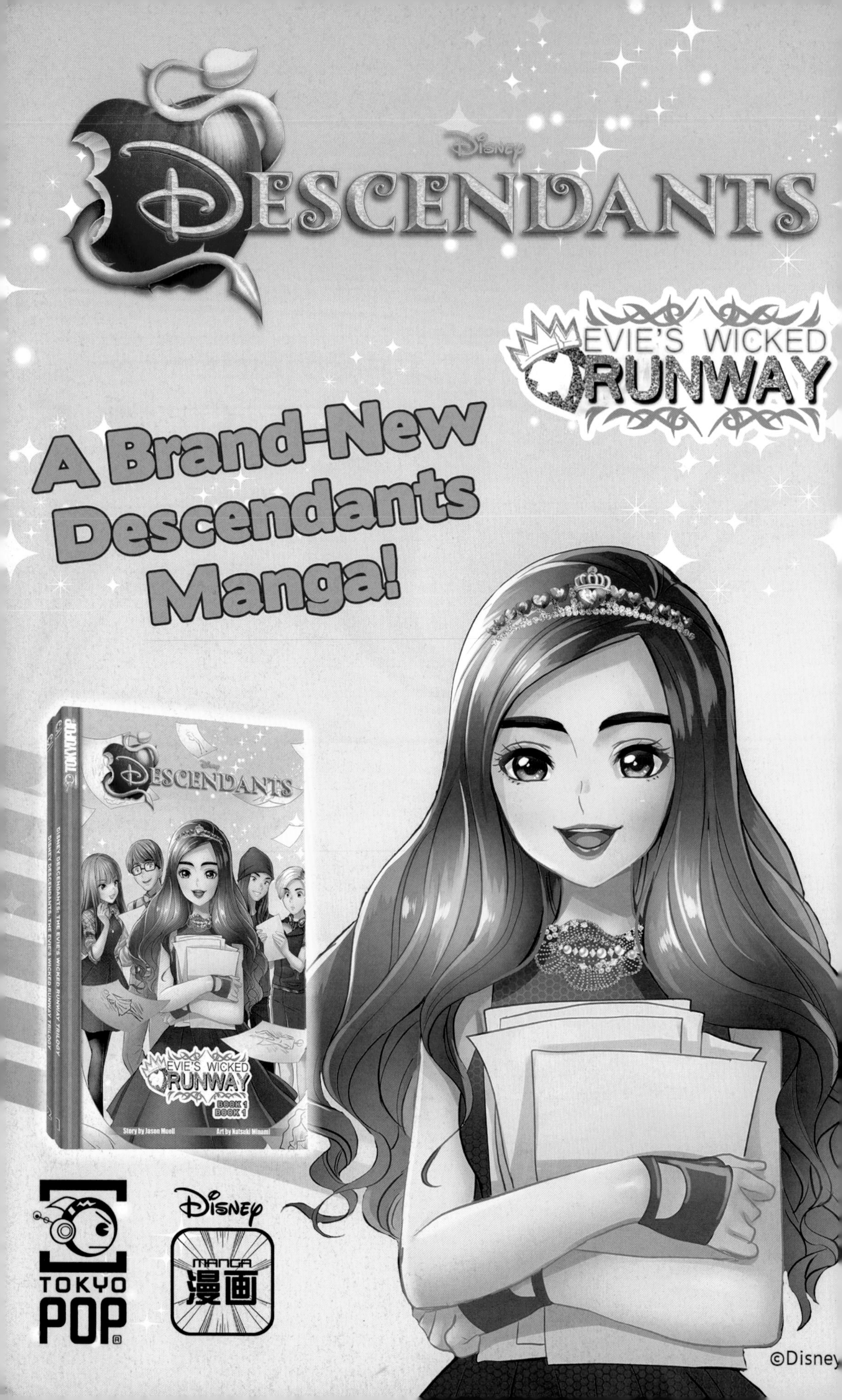

Disney
DESCENDANTS
EVIE'S WICKED RUNWAY
A Brand-New Descendants Manga!
DESCENDANTS
EVIE'S WICKED RUNWAY
BOOK 1
Story by Jason Muell
Art by Natsuki Minami
TOKYOPOP
Disney
MANGA
漫画
©Disney

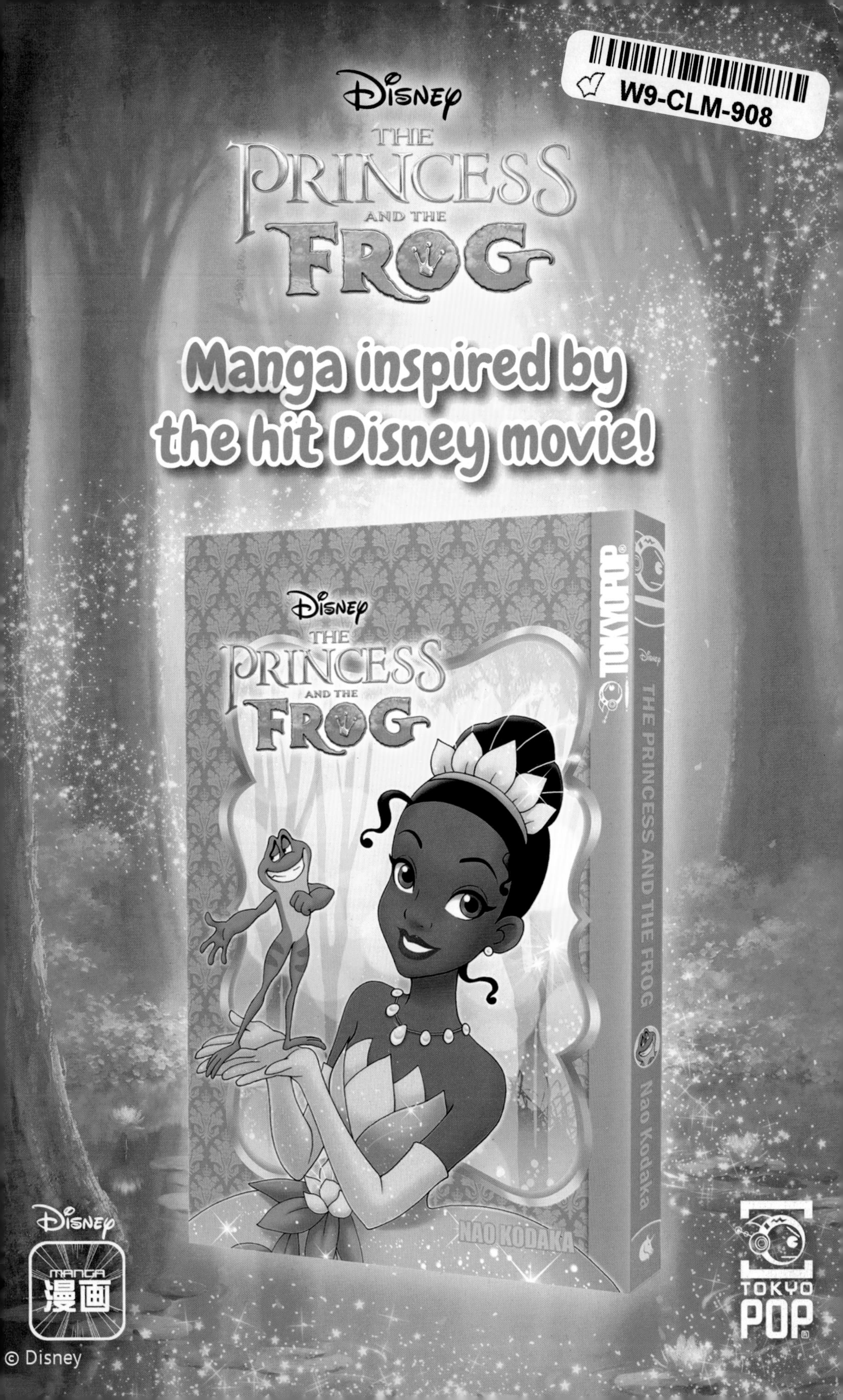
Disney
THE PRINCESS AND THE FROG
Manga inspired by the hit Disney movie!
Disney
THE PRINCESS AND THE FROG
NAO KODAKA
TOKYOPOP
THE PRINCESS AND THE FROG
Nao Kodaka
Disney
MANGA 漫画
© Disney
TOKYO POP